# ROLL CALL

## Book #1 in the Roll Call Trilogy

Joni —
Loyal? Add your
name to the List —
Gwen Mansfield

# G W E N   M A N S F I E L D

www.rollcalltrilogy.wordpress.com

ISBN: 1508400180
ISBN 13: 9781508400189

To

Colleen McInnis, Joseph Morris
and Katie Shaw

Thanks for sticking with me from "DeTornada"
to "mother."

# PROLOGUE

DeTornada. That name and the legacy of leadership has been on my back, haunted me and tracked me down for most of my life. It sets me apart from others left on earth, and I hate it. Twenty-two is too young and too inexperienced to be thrust toward the front of the pack. The asteroid *Jurbay* fell and sliced us in half. Those of us who remained, The 28 United, now oppose The Third—the rulership in power. But disaster doesn't care about enemies, and it doesn't discriminate against foes. It rips who it wants from comfort, from family, from purpose— from life. Looking back on our shared catastrophe I realize, even with an enemy, disaster offers us something in common.

———

Somewhere around mid-century the two parties of polar opposites within The United, our political world, forgot to watch their backs. Subtly, and with much charisma, The Third slithered in while the fighting wolves tore themselves apart in the government arenas of the Senate, the House and the Oval Office. And pretty soon there wasn't any Senate or House or Oval Office because Commander Dorsey slipped in the back door of power and assumed the front seat of command. The Third rotated out the senators by proclamation and floated in their officers by decree, shredding democracy and revamping a republic into an unrecognizable rulership with unquestionable power that, at first, seemed so appealing. In the midst of it all, a decade and a half ago when the galaxy let loose one of its rogue asteroids, The United took a hit like it hadn't taken in 4 billion years. We named the asteroid *Jurbay*, christening devastation with a personal endearment. *Jurbay* took us by surprise, hiding up there in the earth's orbit on the far side of the sun, its centuries of weight-gain finally flinging it toward earth, causing a planetary collision. The force of its impact severed our continent, amputating 22 western states and submerging them into the Pacific Ocean in the course of a day. Horrific. Altering our future in ways we couldn't imagine. Most of us thought what was left—The 28 United—would find a way to patch up the holes in a government sliced in half by a natural disaster. However, we the citizens were all so consumed with grief, re-routing infrastructure and a new coastline, that there was no awareness of The Third's tyranny until we finally began functioning again—and by then it was too late. Disasters soften the soil for new crops, and all of us godly humanitarian workers, trying to rebuild a lost and weeping nation, didn't realize what had been planted until the seeds sprouted up and the weeds of The Third were choking us to death.

# Chapter I
# GEB IN THE HOUSE
# THE CITY OF
# REICHEL, 2083

It doesn't seem like two years ago since McGinty, Shaw and I finished our compulsory service and discharged from The Third's Elite Special Forces. We had a few beers at Geraldine's to celebrate then secured an indefinable housing unit identical to hundreds of others that lined countless city streets, and began the process of melting into the armpit of The Third. As subterraneans, we are passionately committed to placing The 28 United in power, to rule with compassion and justice, so we willingly work undercover inside The Third. There are only five of us. McGinty, Shaw and I are common workers in the Plethora Plant, and Pasha, the fourth subterranean, would have roomed with us, but The Third snapped her up to work underneath the plant with the top neurosurgeons in the city. And while we never see her at the job (after all she works in a lab that is supposed to be a secret), we see her almost daily at our housing unit due to the rogue zip cable that she connected from her roof (where she keeps her homing pigeons) to the window of our unit. Now, the fifth subterranean? I'd rather not think about.

It's evening and McGinty unseals his dinner peps and pops a few in his mouth, as he reads one of his treasured dance history books by the light of the single window in our housing unit. Three years ago The Third took out the stoves and refrigerators from every unit after the Plethora Plant perfected the combo of capsules that would keep each citizen reasonably healthy, hydrated and regulated. We, the people, call them *peps,* and they are delivered on a zip to our window once a month in a package with our housing unit number pasted on the front.

Pasha splats against the outside of the window with a noise only a diminutive person going full force on a zip could create. Startled, McGinty leaps up, spilling his coffee (coffee, homemade wine and eggs are stored in a secret closet behind a false wall in what used to be our kitchen).

Pasha hangs from the zip in front our window, placing her hands on the glass, pleading with McGinty to allow her entrance. He tries to stare her down. Impossible. We both laugh at her hair, covered with homing pigeon feathers.

Zip cords have replaced taxis, limos, cars and motorcycles in the City of Reichel. Since the government failed on its most recent attempt to provide transportation, Pasha stepped in. Four foot eleven with ebony skin, she presents herself as six ten and her dynamics border on crazy.

She figured with a little careful planning that a brain surgeon should be able to lay out a spider web of cable routes for city transport. Within a month Commander Dorsey, the top officer inside The Third, eliminated motorized vehicles, implemented the free transportation and plagiarized the idea of zips as his own. Most of us carry registered hook-ups on the backs of our uniforms that allow us zip transport through the laser scanning of an invisible number on our right knuckles.

Of course zips are for the workers, not the justices and commanders. The privileged travel by float cars. McGinty, Shaw and I never wanted a float car and we're glad for zips. There are no VATs, visual-audio trails, tracking conversations or actions when we ride the web of cords all over the city. It is far too difficult to bug a zip.

Coffee is rare in Reichel, and since Pasha just caused McGinty to spill his, I don't think he's going to let her in even if she is hanging outside our window. So I run across the unit and slam my hand on the alcove button, causing the window to open. Pasha steps in and raises her fist to the scan pad, unhooking her from the zip.

"Don't do that again," McGinty says as he polishes the coffee drips off his Rumba book.

Pasha throws me the package she carries. "Peps for the month," she says, walking directly to the hidden closet behind the wall, pulling out a bottle opener from the pocket of her coverall and prying open the façade. I wonder how such a tiny person can bark with such a husky voice. Not only did she create the zip cord design and zip routes for Reichel, but she invented the brilliant still that provides a bottomless supply of homemade wine from the fruits and vegetables of children's garden just outside the city.

"Making another social call to the children that belong to Reichel's justices?" I ask.

"Daily. The justices think I'm concerned for their kids' mental development, but I just want their squash." She opens her pack, gingerly lifting out three small squash and beginning their dissection for the wine-making process. All the while, the pigeons inside her pack coo.

"We've never had squash wine before," says McGinty as he glares at Pasha's pack. "Can you shut those pigeons up?" He holds his Rumba book in one hand, copying the seductive hip action from the pages as he reads the book. He uses his free hand to paint the "picture of the dance" as only he can do.

I grab the book, holding it high. "No gyrating in mixed company, Romeo." If we hadn't gone through two years of Elite service together in The Third and worked inside the plant as subterraneans for another two years, I might have found him attractive. Everyone else does and everyday somebody stops to look at him. 'Course each time that happens he says, "Avery, they're looking at you again." But I know better. I'm in Elite shape, but I have black hair like all the female workers are required to have, and I can't think of one thing about me that would turn a head, unlike McGinty's sharp jaw, olive Catalonia skin and piercing brown eyes.

"Teach me to dance," Pasha says, wrapping her minute form around his muscular body. He laughs and sets her on a chair slat that extends from the wall. But Pasha doesn't sit and she bolts back to the still, catching her foot on the strap of her pack and releasing a pigeon.

"You'd better get those birds out of here before Shaw gets home, or he'll put you out the window without a zip," McGinty says.

"He'll get over it once he gets to know Herman and Orbit."

"He's had plenty of time to get to know them, and he's not over it. He hates those birds." Orbit flies to the ceiling, roosting on the light tube and dropping an assortment of feathers in operative shades of gray.

"All right, Pasha," I say, "Get it down." Orbit flies to the top of the still. "Come on, grab that bird!"

Pasha stealthily approaches the pigeon. "If you wouldn't call her an 'it' she'd do exactly what I want her to do." The pigeon is not to be caught and flies at angles from one perch to another. Pasha continues her gentle steps to try to calm Orbit down, and McGinty and I chase the piece of poultry around until the door to unit 791 busts open and in steps Shaw. We all freeze, staring at him. He stares back, and then his eyes trace the projectile of a floating feather.

"Cute," he says. The three of us exchange a quick glance. We expect anger from Shaw, not sarcasm.

———

As of a week and a half ago, I think we got our own GEB, a genetically engineered being, living right in our housing unit. Call it a sixth sense, but if I'm right, it's Shaw's replacement. Of course it's supposed to *be* Shaw, but I call him Trader Bob from a historical reference half a century ago when the West was still intact—a very popular food store that specialized in inexpensive snacks and deals on wine. Our Trader Bob is a cheap imitation of the original, and he might fool Shaw's mother, his sister and the justices at roll call, but if he's a GEB, he won't fool McGinty and me. We've been trained by The Third's military Elite. And they should know better than to put a GEB in with us, 'cause if I'm right and Trader Bob is a GEB, our mission in life will be to find out what this GEB is programmed to discover about McGinty and me, and what The Third did with our Shaw.

———

Trader Bob crosses to the still, throwing his jacket over one of the three sleeping tubes that stand upright in the corner and pulling out a tin cup he found in an archeological dig on a northwest beach of the New Coastline. He holds the cup below the funnel spout. Whether Trader Bob or Shaw, he always acts like he owns the day.

Pasha clasps her hands around Orbit who keeps its beady eyes on Shaw and allows Pasha to return it to the inside of the pack. McGinty presses the window button, retracting the glass and exposing the night. Pasha, her pack and pair of cooing buddies hook up to the zip and shoot down the cord. They are swallowed by the mouth of darkness. "What about all these feathers?" I yell after her.

"Vacuum suck," she shouts. *How appropriate,* I think. *She could care less about the pigeon feathers left in our unit 'cause she lives with a flock of birds shedding hundreds of feathers a day.* I picture her zipping across the expanse from our unit to the roof of hers.

McGinty pulls two small glass bowls from the closet and pours enough wine to fill them. "Cucumber," McGinty says as he passes me the wine. "But we'll have squash wine in about a week. The Third would probably consider this part of our vegetable allotment."

"But they'll never know," I say and take the bowl he offers. I stand in front of Shaw, not moving my eyes off of him. As McGinty sits on the chair slat the metal groans, and I wonder how it holds his bulk—his muscle. I don't have to turn around and face him to know he too fixates on Shaw who sits on the stained loveseat the three of us salvaged from a dump outside the city. Old, rotting furniture remains banned from Reichel, like most other things from our past, but Pasha found it sentimental and a reminder of our hidden individuality and our loyalty to The 28 United.

"Where have you been?" I demand, to which Shaw opens one eye and looks at me. I say, "You can't just be gone for a night without letting us know."

Shaw closes his open eye, talking a gulp of the cucumber wine. His arrogance pushes my buttons the way an older brother might.

"What's with the pigeons?" He finally breaks the silence.

"Where were you?" I try again to elicit an answer, crossing to the button alcove and selecting the vacuum suck button, pressing it harder than necessary. The little whir lasts about fifteen seconds while the wall opens up a mouth-like hole and an octopus of small hoses appears to do their duty, sending the feathers in a momentary spin and then they disappear along with the sucks.

"The Commander wanted overtime. Couldn't exactly say no." Another gulp.

"It's cucumber wine. You might try to sip it."

"I don't sip anything."

McGinty crosses to the closet for a refill. He doesn't sip either. "We thought you were dead, you know," says McGinty.

"I thought you were drinking cucumber wine in 791, you know," Shaw retorts, and he finally sits up and stares back at us. "It's all part of their plan. The Demoralize plan. Demoralizes me 'cause I have to work twenty four hours instead of ten and demoralizes you 'cause you think I'm dead. Not a surprising plan—it's The Third's plan."

Someone knocks at the front door. Immediate tension fills the room. The screen to the left of the door registers Annalynn's picture, our eight year old neighbor. She's adopted us, and we're a strange trio to adopt. Like so many of Reichel's residents she is what we call "homebound." She knows something's missing—all her family memories have been removed. There's a hole in her life that she can't fill or plug or cover up, and she's searching. And that's what *locasa* has done to the residents of The 28 United.

———

My father, Carles, was Catalonian. He and my mother Quinn were visiting relatives on vacation in Catalonia and were present when The Third invaded with the Elite "peacekeeping" force. There was no war in Catalonia, but there was a device, *locasa,* that the Catalan's top scientists had been experimenting on, and The Third wanted it. With the intent of healing the minds of those broken by war and its trauma and providing relief for those victims of heinous crimes, the Catalonian neurosurgeons and scientists developed this device for the benefit of humanity. After decades of failures they had finally hit upon the elements that focused on the withdrawal of memory, so specific it could target certain events, people—even a detailed moment in time. The Catalans knew *locasa* was sought after by The Third. Carles DeTornada, my father, unofficial leader of The 28 United, and my mother, Quinn, were taken into confidence by the Catalonian leaders in an effort to protect their experiment from the threat it posed if placed in the hands of the enemy. As subterraneans undercover and posing as Elite soldiers for The Third, McGinty, Shaw and I needed to seize *locasa* for The Third as our official duty, while our secret status as subterraneans demanded we protect it. That's what brought the three of us to Catalonia—and that's what got my father killed.

———

Annalynn's picture beside the door receptor flashes intensely, and McGinty finally punches in the code on the alcove wall that allows her entrance. She struts in like a commander of The Third, her pitch black skin glowing, and I have to remind myself she is only eight, precocious and at times irritating. However, she is always a welcomed respite from the stress of constantly looking over my shoulder for a guard who might find the one dreaded slipup that would land us smack in the middle of The Third's headquarters with no escape route.

Annalynn raises her palm flat in front of her and it is met—an inch from touching—by McGinty's palm, held in the same fashion. This palms-up replaces the greetings from the past that our grandparents shared. The fist-bump, the high-five and the hand shake. She greets me in the same fashion, "Peace, Avery. Hippies rule."

"Peace, Annalynn. Pigeons rule. Eggs in the cupboard," I remind her.

"Zoom. We're friends forever." Her voice is lyrical like a melody and joking like a child, providing stand-up comedy for a kindergarten class. Shaw is now looking out the window, acting like he can't stand to be around Annalynn. I guess that's what happens to a man who works twenty-four hours straight. However, when she pulls on the arm of his coverall and he doesn't respond or even turn around, I find it odd.

Annalynn looks hurt. "Hey, Uncle Shaw, wanna play 'Dance with McGinty'?" McGinty winces. We tease him without mercy about his love for dance, but lodged in the back of my mind is the memory of him taking the stage with a group of flamenco dancers in a dark, hot underground club in the recesses of Catalonia where we did part of our training. Unforgettable.

Annalynn tries again to gain Shaw's attention. "How 'bout 'Clichés'? Wanna play 'Clichés'?" She holds the record for the most clichés used from a past decade in one continuous conversation.

"Not tonight," he says and brushes past her hand, held in the palms-up position, without acknowledging it. He fills his cup and plops on the sofa again.

Annalynn doesn't move and stares at Shaw. "Zoom. You are so lucky I don't nail you to the wall and report you to The Third for your secret closet with the hidden still." We all continue to focus on Shaw. McGinty scoops Annalynn up in one quick movement and heads for the alcove.

"Come back tomorrow for game night—except none of that 'guess the dance junk,'" McGinty says.

She protests, kicking her legs and flailing her arms. "But who will teach me to dance if you don't?"

"Shaw."

"No way. He hates dancing and pigeons and, I guess—I guess he hates me."

After McGinty presses the button by the door and sets Annalynn outside, he squats to her level and says, "Thanks for keeping our secret about the still." He holds his palm-up, but she throws her arms around his neck, holding tight. He pulls her gently away. "Now, in exchange, what can *we* do for you?"

She holds high her two pigeon eggs, one in each hand. "I've got my eggs. It's good enough. Zoom." McGinty tries to straighten her wild hair, steps back and closes the door.

He turns to me and we both glance at Shaw. Then my eyes jet in the direction of the window. With a punch of the button the window releases, and McGinty's fisted knuckles cue the hookup. I see one of Shaw's eyes pop open, looking at us. I remain casual and say, "Going to take a run to the dump, see if there's anything good for salvage."

He closes his eye. "Yeah, well don't wake me up when you get back. Eight hours from now I got another 24 shift."

We zip out the window, secure in the fact that no VATs from The Third invade the zips. We've tested the hook ups and the cables many times for bugs. It's just too complicated and time consuming to try to bring surveillance to the zips. While McGinty and I zip to Pasha's roof—not the dump—I'm the first to mention the subtle differences I saw in Shaw.

"So, we're sure he's a GEB?" I ask.

"You're the one with the sixth sense—you confirm it."

"It has nothing to do with a 'sixth sense,'" I say. "Look at the facts."

"You mean how he never got mad at Pasha about the feathers?"

"Exactly. He always gets furious."

"What about how he doesn't even turn around to see or acknowledge Annalynn?"

"Yeah, just keeps his back to her."

"And when she calls him Uncle Shaw—"

"He always answers, 'Yes, Uncle Annalynn?' It's weird, and we've got to keep an eye on him."

"Yeah, but if I'd just worked 24 hours straight I wouldn't want to play with Annalynn either."

"So you think there's a chance he isn't a GEB?"

"You're the one with the sixth sense." Then he zips away. I hate it how he forces me to make a choice.

We continue on the zips, and I think of what I've learned from my sage called "mother." Of course those gems of knowledge have been reaped mostly through observations on my part, for long ago Quinn DeTornada chose commitment to her floundering country over time with her floundering daughter. We both have this *sixth sense* McGinty speaks of, when it comes to strategy, but even that doesn't allow for the detection of a GEB. I would hope that our sixth sense coupled with the fact that we are Chipsters might be the magic bullet of detection, but Pasha hasn't perfected the chipster implants enough for them to recognize a GEB.

Most everyone still loyal to The 28 United found a way to have a chipster implanted somewhere in their bodies before we were scattered over what's left of earth. My mother's is on the smooth inside of her left middle finger. No evidence on the epidermis—the thin-skin that disguises the implant looks eerily organic. All she has to do is gently rub her left thumb down to the tip of her middle finger and a translucent film appears for less than two seconds. Its message, located below the picture of the person she's encountering: lie or truth. That's it. May not seem like the perfect weapon unless you're surrounded by lies on a daily basis and your life depends on you remaining a subterranean undercover. My mother's good at all that.

And then there's my chipster. Right eye. Tap the temple and infrared capabilities kick in for thirty seconds, maybe longer, depending on my adrenaline surge which, if infrared is needed, is intense. No demand for it recently though. McGinty, Shaw and I have been subterraneans for two years at the plant, waiting for the moment urgency demands our action. It's coming.

———

Later that night when McGinty and I return from Pasha's roof, after discussing Shaw's behavior, our unit is dark. We open the window, step in and see Shaw asleep. Neither of us say a word, but at that point we both know we have a GEB in the house, sixth sense or not. Trader Bob lives up to his expectations. In the housing unit we sleep standing in our sleep tubes. On the ready. We learned it in the Elite. We hook our wrists through the straps in the upright tube and our feet attach the same way. Never lay to sleep. It welcomes vulnerability. Just a quick yank on the restraints, and they disengage and we are off and running. Our Shaw sleeps like us—on the ready. Trader Bob is asleep lying down. He has moved his sleep tube to a horizontal position and is sleeping like a baby—except he's never been a baby or a child or adolescent. Trader Bob is a GEB— McGinty knows it. I know it. Trader Bob tried to steal Shaw's childhood and his life with us, and that was a mistake.

In the morning I snap up my dark gray coverall with a vengeance, making sure my Z-Colt is loaded and securely strapped to just below my left collar bone, my place of preference. McGinty, Trader Bob and I zip to the Plethora Plant and quickly stand at attention for roll call.

Gray. The sky. The factory. The conveyor belt. The little pills that feed us, heal us, alter us—stabilize us. Gray. Our coveralls, our boots, our lunch peps and our transports. The ground cover, the color of steel and smooth like metal, glints in the sun. It's antiseptic and easily cleaned. A thousand of us stand at attention below the reviewing window as pop-up screens reveal our silver-toned photos for the Reichel justices on morning duty. They match our voice recognition to our photos. Can voices sound gray?

I look across the rows at Trader Bob who, as near as I can figure out, has been with us for a week and a half now. The Third developed the GEBs for two reasons. First, a genetic replication of a human may still be considered morally compromising, but to The Third these GEBs are technologically achievable, even in the experimental stage. Just harvest the original's DNA from the inside of his gloves that were assimilated in the laundry warp at the end of his shift or locate a hair follicle from an employee's storage conduit where her uniform cap is kept—and you've got yourself the makings of a GEB. And second, GEBs (even though we believe there's just a few that have infiltrated) more than earn their keep in The Third, slipping into daily life as replacements for their human counterparts, undetected by loved ones and friends because of a complete memory dump done at the time of their creation, as well as the GEBs' impeccable physical replications. At least that's the way they're supposed to work.

My eyes shift to McGinty, standing in a row of workers thirty feet from me. As I stare at him, I give nothing away. The position of my head does not flinch. My eyes return to the straight ahead point. We know how to remain targeted and on task while strategizing alternatives. I wonder. *When someone is replaced by a GEB what happens to the original?* I guess now would be the time to find out because not only has Shaw been gone over a week, but as of this morning, Pasha's missing too. It's time to stop standing at attention in a row. My name comes before McGinty's in the roll call, so I guess I'll be the one going inside the building we wanted to avoid at all costs.

"Avery DeTornada." The justices call my name. I must get inside the bowels of the Plethora Plant and see if Shaw and Pasha can be found. In our routine work lives, behind the plant walls, we mix the formulas for various food capsules, and in other rooms workers replicate a multitude of medicinal pills. But on the levels below the factory we know there are labs where intelligence teams experiment. Is Pasha still operating as an integral part of those neurologists perfecting *locasa* and creating GEBs, or has her refuse—the hair from her cap or her laundry in the vacuum suck—become the makings of the next GEB, rendering her extinct?

Again they call, "Avery DeTornada." They wait for my "yes." I've proven myself as a loyal worker, so this will obviously surprise them.

"Here, but wish I wasn't," I say. All eight justices look up from the roll call screens in unison then raise their heads to the viewing room, like a team of hired assassins. Within eight seconds (I count) The Third's guards surround me. One guard steps forward, placing my hands in front of my waist and my thumbs together. He positions his master-punch on my right thumb. Firing the trigger he connects the left thumb to the right with a slim pellet that hurts like crazy, and he proves why the archaic handcuffs of a half century ago have been retired to the Smithsonian.

———

It is my first time in the viewing room, and I glance out the forty foot windows to see that roll call is still in process. The commander stands tall and majestic on the viewing platform, protected by the colt-proof glass. Flawless complexion and silver hair, as is the custom for those in command, she moves toward me like a glacier, deliberate and confident of her goal: me. I am her goal. Suddenly I think proving myself as a loyal worker to The Third means nothing and I imagine an ice cold wind blowing by me as she passes. I counter her with a turn of my own, my eyes following her steady pace. As of yet, the master-punch hasn't bound my feet.

I stare her down, but no one wins. The Z-Colt burns hot against my shoulder, begging me to release it from the holster, pull the trigger and take this commander to the ground. But after all, she is my mother and a subterranean so my training wins out, as it should. I know the ultimate goal has nothing to do with one dead commander or one ineffective mother. It has to do with gathering The 28 United and building an army of more than five to stand against The Third, but first I have to find Shaw and Pasha.

"So where is it you want to be, Avery?" I don't answer, but I match her stare and hate her freezer voice turned down below zero. "You don't want to be here...so where?" We both know everything we do and say is being monitored by The Third.

"Here, of course, Commander. What happen out there in roll call—just a momentary slip-up," I say, but the sarcasm I try to bury rises to the top. "Can't wait each day to be in this plant, stuffing peps with some unknown formula."

"We all work together to make a powerful, smooth running United—"

"That's the old name. United. Before *Jurbay*."

"That's right. We're The Third, now. And even more united."

"I do what I'm told to do. I have a solid record." A man enters with silver hair braided down his back. He seems familiar with the Commander, like they share some secret.

"Borden," she says.

"Commander DeTornada?" he honors her authority.

"It's her first offense, Borden."

"Still, we should make a significant withdrawal." They exchange a look, and I am very aware that I just might get exactly what I want. To get to the underground *locasa* lab and the GEB nursery, in search of Pasha and Shaw. I hope I'm right. Yet, I hope not.

"Borden?"

"Commander DeTornada?"

"No special treatment."

This time the guards master-punch my left ankle to my right. The pain from this punch turns out the lights.

# Chapter 2

# THE CAGE

I awake to the rattle of a centripetal whirl. The room is spinning, and I sit on a chair slat, sensing right away that the master-punch has been removed from my thumbs and ankles. Yet the pain still pulsates, reminding me that The Third sees me as a disruption to their roll call. Or am I a threat of something more? Am I still a subterranean securely embedded in their ranks as just another irritating plant worker, or have I been discovered as one in alliance with The 28 United? The clatter of the turning lab unnerves me, like a twister sucking bathtubs, furniture and roofs from houses. I focus on breathing. Try to clear my head. Attempt to regain control. I should know how to do this. The Elite taught me, but in my groggy state, siting in the midst of a GEB lab as the next *locasa* experiment, the sound of this circulating whirr triggers a memory from my past and slashes through my barrier to fear, wrenching my defenses right out of my gut. And the memory taunts.

———

McGinty, Shaw, Pasha and I had finished basic training with The Third. Pasha had been assigned to the technology assimilation division, and the rest of us had been designated for The Elite Special Forces to prepare for The Third's assault on Catalonia.

The first day of training the captain strapped us, with 35 other trainees, to an enormous metal centrifuge with gears that snaked their way around and through the crisscrossed trellis that we lay on. The contraption started spinning quickly. McGinty, Shaw and I held on instinctively to the bars around us to avoid being hurled to the center of the training apparatus, unlike many who had let their guard down for a fraction of a second. I was suddenly grateful for Pasha's eccentricity in her approach to all aspects of her work. She had created a glove that slipped on the hand with elastic strands that strapped to each fingertip causing resistance with repetitive stretching, building muscles in fingers, palms, wrists and elbows—muscles that were not easily observed when looking for the brute strength of an enemy, but muscles that Pasha was convinced might balance out the assets needed for survival in extreme circumstances. This was extreme.

When the rattle started around me I thought gears were malfunctioning, but the sound of simultaneous screams forced me to squeeze the slits of my eyes open in spite of the wind from the whirling of our spin. I could see each gear was fitted with a saw-tooth that sliced to pieces those that failed to hold on. And the rattle? The rattle was the stirring of their bones through the spiraling creation of the Third's Elite training machine. Vicious. They would make sure the only survivors were the ones who could hold on. We did.

———

I curl myself into a ball to force the rotation of this lab to deal with me as a tight, round sphere instead of an elongated noodle spread out for dissection. The moment my feet leave the floor the spinning stops. A quick evaluation reveals no corners to this lab, only curvatures that begin at the baseboard and ascend thirty feet upward to the rounded ceiling with a kaleidoscope of Plexiglas panes. The walls—smooth, shiny metal—remind me of the old-fashioned salad spinner my great-grandmother kept in polished condition to wash and dry her lettuce, and I feel (even though the movement has stopped) like there's someone outside here spinning me around.

I focus on one spot, the back of a head without hair. The being sits with its face away from me, motionless. Next to it two others sit, stone still and identical to the first. The end one leaps up and faces me, neither male nor female and looking like a naked newborn without the wrinkles. The eyes of the being, devoid of lashes or brows, lock on mine. The spinning has stopped. I force regular breathing, control my terror and feel the throbbing of the master-punch's damage on my ankles and thumbs. This bald form approaches me alternating a ghostly gliding step with the stomp of a monster targeting its prey. *It is learning to walk*, I think. If it is learning, I will treat it like a sponge, and I conjure a raging, brawny voice and command it. "Stop now!" It halts.

I am alone with Baldy and his friends. Where are the guards that dragged me to the scientists in this lab? I test the floor, placing the tip of my toe to the cold steel. The spin begins again, and I quickly lift my foot, realizing no guards are necessary when a salad spinner is on constant alert. I remember leaving my mother in the reviewing room, guards dragging me away, me fading in and out, but retaining some cognizance and miming complete unconsciousness, for the benefit of my captors. During one of those "fade-ins" where I faked continued unconsciousness, I heard Commander DeTornada's voice and imagined it as a mama's lullaby. Then realized that was only what *I* wanted to hear. She was actually conversing with Officer Borden and a small assembly of scientists.

"What should we withdraw from her, Commander?" asked Borden.

My mother, Quinn, said, "Take her Elite training." I could tell immediately what she was doing, protecting my family, saving my memories that connected me to my father—to her.

"Hardly significant if we leave her with an attitude of strength that throws sarcastic barbs at the justices," Officer Borden argued.

"Without her Elite training her power's gone."

Borden recanted. "And without the power, the attitude is gone? That's significant."

"Yes, significant." My mother smiled, having the last word without speaking.

After that, a scientist approached me, *locasa* in hand, and pain from somewhere in my body roused me from my half-conscious state, forcing me to recall the Tibetan language Pasha had been drilling into the minds of McGinty, Shaw and I on the roof of her housing unit amongst the coos of the roosting pigeons. I would do all I could to intercept the power of *locasa* with the confusion of foreign language. *Locasa* only received memories in English.

————

About twelve years into their reign, unbeknownst to the populous, *locasa* had been an instrumental contribution to The Third's magnetic appeal. Holding out the hand of CMS (Comprehensive Medical Satisfaction) to each and every citizen, it did not take the four of us long to figure out that The Third's generous invitation for complete medical care, beginning with an inoculation series against the 14 Deadlies, was a ruse. Though the little ink scar on the back of the right wrist in the figure of a 14 promised immunization, it actually meant The Third's doctors had used *locasa* to extract memories connected to family and home. Mothers departed the clinic without thought or concern for their children. Children stared blankly as their parents walked away. Husbands had no memory of their wives and wives recalled no passionate feelings for the men they had loved. But The Third prepared for those details and had an employee pool of guardians by the hundreds retained to feed and clothe the abandoned children. We called the caretakers "pocket-watches," for the guardians only emerged from the pockets of their housing units to *watch* that the children received the basic necessities of life: water, food peps and shelter. Home had been taken out of the equation. Having no ties to home, adults had a yearning for something to fill the void *locasa* had created, and it was quickly satiated with an opportunity to aid The Third. Without questions or probing, people eagerly signed into service, thinking allegiance would fill the ache, and for a time it did.

———

I rubbed the ink-imprinted 14 on the back of my wrist with the thumb of my left hand, remembering Pasha teaching McGinty and Shaw the imprint process, using the unique paint flecked with silver, developed exclusively for The Third's medical centers. Pasha had liberated a container of the paint during an early morning shift when guards directed their attention to the outside of the plant, and ignored a tiny doctor working on *locasa* and filling paint canisters to prepare for the morning influx of patients, receiving their inoculations. For Pasha, securing the paint to create an artificial inoculation number posed little challenge.

When those loyal to The 28 United started visiting Pasha's roof roost with its secret clinic (we called it "pigeon square"), my assigned job was to track those who received the simulated #14. My father taught me to journal by hand, without technology, and I never expected that this would be a skill a subterranean would need on a rooftop in Reichel. At first when just a few came seeking the artificial number, it was easy to keep records, but soon the list of loyals grew and several others besides Pasha were sketching the #14 to the back of wrists. In order to process many through the procedure, I'm sure names were missed and never entered in the book. Were there hundreds artificially imprinted? Or was it thousands? The days when I worked at the Plethora Plant I needed sleep at night, and I didn't come to the rooftop, but Pasha kept the process going all though the night. Maybe someone wrote down all the names and maybe, like me, they missed some. How valuable it would be to have those records now, to know how many loyal ones live and work in Reichel or scrap for existence outside of the city. These rebels, who visited pigeon square had quietly raised a fist against The Third by seeking out an artificial immunization and avoiding the withdrawal of *locasa*. They'd found out about the threat of *locasa* in the quietest of ways: a neighbor heard a rumor, a mother had an instinct or a worker slipped a note in the pocket of a friend.

They came in small groups to pigeon square, and they entered the center of the roof through a vacuum suck, large enough for an average sized person. Suck walls appeared to have no openings until the suck button was selected and pushed, according to the size of the refuse. In Pasha's unit, the largest suck had no incineration device on the inside, so push the correct button and the wall opened its mouth to the visitor, sucking him up the tube and spitting him out the vent on the inside of Pasha's secret clinic room. She had designed the roosting pens in a large rectangular shape. Pens were stacked five high on all sides of the rectangle and pigeon pens covered the top as well, like a roof. These pens encased a small room 8 feet by 6 feet with three stools, a cot, Pasha's imprint supplies and the instruments she needed to get the job done. When the visitors were imprinted they returned through the unit vacuum suck and then zipped off in various directions through Pasha's unit window.

The artificial imprint of #14 was displayed on my wrist too, and I had never experienced *locasa*. So when that scientist approached me in the salad spinner, after I'd left my mother in the reviewing room, I thought only in Tibetan, anticipating the pain ratcheting up when he began the withdrawal. But instead I felt the slightest of pressure on my skull and then, like the massages of the past when strangers still touched, the *locasa* effect began at the top of my head. A light vibration in the beginning, releasing all apprehension and working what seemed like soothing hands down my body, releasing muscle tension until the effect had passed down my back, legs and feet, and all I wanted was more. When something feels this good, the Tibetan language may not be the weapon Pasha imagined it might be. Not hard to understand why thousands had come willingly to Comprehensive Medical Satisfaction,

CMS, and left with no suspicions, departing only with a number on the back of their wrists and a newly created submission to The Third. Yet, cemented in their souls lay a hunger for the missing withdrawal *locasa* had secretly taken. Home.

———

I hate Baldy staring at me. "Sit down," I tell it, thinking it will return to its buddies and leave me alone. But it sits right where it is, glaring at me, and I suddenly have an urge to decorate it like my mother before its creators compile the details that will give it gender, personality and identity. I will return Quinn DeTornada's hair to the russet color it once was before she attainted the silver command of The Third. Decorate this GEB to look like her when she climbed the trees of the forest with me—when she and daddy and I sailed boats through the islands of the West before *Jurbay* destroyed it—and when we had camp circles with relatives before they were buried in the sea when I was seven years old. I will paint a smile on this GEB's face that never fades and build a voice that welcomes love instead of executing commands like the subterranean leader Quinn DeTornada needs to be. I will place a heart in this GEB that prioritizes family above the demise of The Third.

*Get a grip.* I tell myself. *Acting like a vulnerable child will not get you out of this salad spinner.* Of course there are no guards. The second I place pressure on the floor beneath my feet the spiraling begins again. Suddenly Baldy becomes my hero. Its feet do not start the spinning, only mine. "Baldy, come here." This time its steps are all monster stomps, and it rams into my chair slat. I realize two commands are necessary for this newborn, so I issue the second. "Stop." It stops. It's a quick learner.

"Baldy, pick me up." It grabs my feet and holds me upside down like a prize catfish in a fishing contest from past decades. I'd seen pictures of those fish in the culture section of the History Labyrinth. Strange. Just fifty years ago we ate that which no longer exists.

"Hold me upright." It flings me in the air and catches me just before my feet touch down. "Button alcove," I command. Now the ghostly glide is back and we sail across the salad spinner to the wall. How can I have this much control over Baldy? Is Officer Borden peering at me through the visual-audio trails of The Third? *Worry about it later.* I push the button marked "hallway." A metal door slides open.

Baldy carries me into the corridor. "Down," I say. He drops me head first, but I break the fall with my forearms. At least the room isn't spinning. There are no doors lining the hallway, merely open entrances. Translucent pictures of people I recognize from roll call pulse above all entrances, and beside each picture a flashing update reads: transition or terminate. I snap into alert mode. Not that I haven't been aware that at any moment Borden, or a guard or my mother might come in and set the room spinning again or seal me in one of these rooms with an update that might say "terminate." But I now lock into a place McGinty would call "sixth sense."

A place that involves more than an acute awareness or a sensitive strategy. A brain level that as humans we are not taught to use. It is a gift beyond instinct, and I must use it to survive.

At the end of the corridor a picture of Shaw and Pasha flashes with the word "transition" next to it. *They're in transition all right,* I think. *We're on our way to being terminated. Our death is imminent, and we need an escape.* An eerie awareness overtakes me as I realize Baldy is following me into the room without receiving my command.

The first thing I see after entering the room is a huge sphere-like cage configured in a circular steel grid. The cage looks like a framework where pigeons might roost. Perched in one of those grid-like sections is Pasha. She seems to be asleep, but after I yell her name, she glances up, looking at Baldy and says, "See you found him."

"Actually, he found me. You have something to do with it?"

She pats the chipster in her left forearm and says, "Gave him a little poke in the neurons—kick in the butt. He's not supposed to be active for another month." Her fingers move so rapidly across the chipster they are blurred—not fingers at all but a small wave of movement, hopefully hitting the right inputs.

Several inches out from the grid, an encasement of electrical current rotates around the cage, prohibiting Pasha and Shaw from escaping out of the lattice of steel. Shaw stretches between two bars on the grid in push-up position, sweat pouring from every part of his body.

"Where have you been?" He asks.

"Missed you too, buddy. Never mind that I have a sexless, hairless naked 'it' hanging out at my elbow," I say.

"*It* saved your life." Pasha reminds me.

"Why are you limping?" Shaw asks.

"Master-punch."

"Ouch."

"Tell me about it."

"We can't put our feet down inside the cage," he says.

"No? Really?" I ask. "Let me guess—it spins. I've been spinning in the other room for I don't know how long." Shaw ignores me and starts counting his push-ups at 273. "Shaw! Stop it with the push-ups. You figure out what the vulnerable part of this structure is yet?" Shaw has pilot training and is an engineer whose chipster is on his right thigh. Through it he is capable of testing flaws in any structure. He stops the push-ups and starts jamming both his feet against one of the rods that forms his section of the grid. His strength often seems beyond human as Pasha has taught him how to maximize every muscle in his body, but she has also been slipping him her own version of peps over the past year. I wonder if she just wants to perfect a specimen that cannot be defeated. The bar in the grid breaks loose. I guess Shaw found the structural weakness. The dislodged rod has a ragged edge that I know Shaw will use as a weapon, if needed.

Baldy climbs the cage grid and roosts upside down staring at Pasha. The electrical current does not affect him. I reach my hand toward the edge where the current begins.

"Hey, Pasha," I say. "What happens if I touch this?"

"Fry," she answers.

"Me or you?"

"Both." I pull my hand away.

"Go away," Pasha shouts at Baldy. He doesn't move. "See. These GEBs aren't near ready to be placed anywhere. First it follows your commands. Then it doesn't. Now it's defying mine. Got its own mind and that could be bad news for The Third." Baldy holds its hand up in the palms-up greeting. Pasha scoots away, staring at him, breathing hard, and I can tell Baldy has scared her. "How'd he know to do that?" She asks in a whisper.

"And how come he gets through the electrical wrap and we don't?" I ask.

Pasha rubs the top of her head very quickly the way she does when she can't handle the world's ignorance. "Avery! Track with me here. IT'S NOT HUMAN." Baldy takes its pointer finger and jabs Pasha's cheek. She stares it down. "Stop," she tells it, and it reaches out to take another poke, but she catches its hand before it reaches her cheek. "No." Baldy leaves Pasha alone and scrambles around the grid to stare at Shaw.

Like an atomic blast, my mother's voice smashes through the cage, resonating off the metal walls and bouncing from bar to bar in the grid-like sphere. "Secure the three of them. Secure them now."

Officer Borden's voice rages, "Guards open the lab. Get the lab open."

"They're coming for us, Pasha." I want to climb the grid in the direction of the circular skylight forty feet above but can't get past the electrical wrap. Pasha's fingers fly across the chipster in her arm.

"Holding them off, but not for long. Going head to head with their tech assimilator right now," she says.

I scream, "Use the other chipster. Pasha!" She's the only person I know that's got a double chipster, and she opens the second chipster in her right calf and simultaneously works them both.

"Get rid of Baldy," she says without looking at me.

"What do you mean?

"You know what I mean—get rid of Baldy."

I hear the start of a cry that never has the breath to finish and a thud. I turn and see Shaw has bashed Baldy's head in with the rod. And now I know that GEBs have blood 'cause it's all over the antiseptic floor and nothing's antiseptic anymore. Shaw is using the raw, jagged end of a metal splice from the cage's sphere like a shovel on Baldy's chest, digging. "Pasha," he yells, "What am I digging for?"

"Right ventricle. It's where the information he collected is stored. Take it with us. We'll destroy it later. We got to go." She closes the chipster on her forearm.

"Get to the top of the cage—by the window." says Shaw. Pasha finally interrupts the electrical current with the chipster on her calf and pulls my arm, yanking me up the sphere, her on the inside and me on the outside. I stop part way up, jerking off my boots and stuffing one of the boots inside the other, and as Pasha scurries to the top of the cage, I scramble down, picking up Shaw's bloody pipe below the sphere and ramming it into my boots.

Pasha, furiously working the chipster in her leg shouts, "Can't keep them out."

I run down the hallway reaching the edge of the salad spinner just as Officer Borden and the guards burst through the entrance. I throw my boot toward the center of the room and the spinning starts. Whirling, pulling them into the clanging rotations with a force that yanks at their arms and shakes the skin on their faces like an unhooked zip blowing in the wind. Across the room I see Commander DeTornada outside the spin, staring straight across at me, and for the briefest of moments I want to stop the spin and run to her, but instead I dash back down the corridor and up the side of the cage.

Shaw spikes at the chipster on his thigh. "I got the weak spot in the window at the top," And he moves his hand away from the chipster, releasing a miniature star-blade toward its mark. "Duck," Shaw yells, but all we can duck are our heads, and the exploding shards from the Plexiglas ceiling slice my uncovered portions of skin. Then all three of us extend our knuckles in the air, and we are yanked by the zip chords straight through the hole of the shattered ceiling and off into the night. And as I sail away I glance over my shoulder one last time at Baldy. His eyes pop open, and I try to tell myself he is an "it." Still, tonight, he is my hero.

———

We meet in the middle of pigeon square, Pasha and me. Pasha's eyes are wide shooting glances around the perimeter of the secret room inside the roosts. Ten or twelve pigeons flock to her, roost on her and coo with her. "Not going to leave them, Avery," she says.

"Listen. You can't hook up and zip hundreds of pigeons out of the city." I try to help her up from her fetal position on the roof, but she glues herself down with determination. "Just let them go, Pasha."

I start picking the feathers out of her hair, like a mama bird preening her baby. The blonde of her roots has started to grow back, and it's time for her to dye black. Hardly necessary now. We are all exposed. All those months positioning ourselves as the perfect crew of subterraneans, dynamically prepared to confront The Third when the timing was right, and now it means nothing. The only one left is Quinn. She stands solo inside The Third.

I say, "Take Herman and Orbit. They're a male and female. You can breed more pigeons." Pasha doesn't move. Doesn't talk.

I think of the place we call Red Grove, so far from here. McGinty says it will be our headquarters one day. That was Quinn's intention when she had it built years ago. "Pasha, how far away are you from using your chipster to get in touch with all the other Chipsters—calling them to Red Grove?"

Pasha sits up, her head drooping, cupping Herman in her hands, stroking his back. "Close," she says. "Maybe a lot closer since none of us have to show up at roll call anymore.

I'll have lots of extra time." Then she hops up, disrupting the settled pigeons and causing a tornado of flapping wings, and she pulls scraps of paper from her pack and a small charcoal pencil. She lies down on her stomach and looks my way. "What message should we send?

And suddenly all eyes are on me. Hundreds of sets of pigeon eyes. I wonder if they are staring at the areas on my hands and neck that were unprotected by my coverall, now cut and bleeding. I long to pluck the shards of window from my skin, but instead kneel close to Pasha, trying not to disturb the cloud of pigeons that peer from her scraps of paper to me and back again, as if gathered around their teacher in a reading group, waiting for the climax of a book to unfold. She repeats, "What message should we send?"

I stare at the pigeon eyes and say, "Let's have a roll call of our own." I grab Pasha's arm, rushing with the cooing pigeons to the edge of the unit roof. I sketch the letters on the paper. *Roll call.* It is a code that most Chipsters will know, if they find a note. They will assemble at Red Grove.

We write the words over and over on the scraps, and Pasha teaches me how to roll each paper in a tight scroll and attach it to the wire on every pigeon's leg. She picks a pigeon up and holds it close. "Let them do their job, Avery."

"Where will they go?" I ask

She throws one into the air, "Home to Red Grove," she says. Taking another she thrusts it off the edge of the building, "Home to the children's garden." Then one by one she tosses pigeons to their destiny, "Home to the minstrel tree—home to the dump." I should have known Pasha would never train all her pigeons to fly home to the same place. Home is different for each group she's trained. I realize that on their way to "home" these pigeons might meet some Chipsters, and maybe they will make their way to Red Grove.

I pick a pigeon up and stroke the top of its head, whispering in its ear—imagining my words might direct it. "Go home," I say and give it a shove into the night air.

When all the pigeons (except Herman and Orbit who are securely in Pasha's pack) are released, we hook up to the zips. Pasha asks, "What about Shaw and McGinty?"

I answer. "Shaw will go right to our unit and pick up McGinty, and if I know Shaw, his introduction to Trader Bob the GEB will be Trader Bob's last introduction ever."

# Chapter 3
# UNDER-AGE WARRIORS

Our final zip drops us at the edge of Reichel. It is a city that just expires, like a period on an obnoxious run-on sentence that desperately needs to be ended. No gradual melding into a suburb like when I was a child, but only an abrupt stoppage of buildings, units, plants and zips. With no threats, rebellions or symptomatic protests anywhere, The Third is only concerned with their city, their technology and their experiments. Yes, they know there are subterraneans out there, but they are also aware that the number is small maybe because, as of yet, Shaw, McGinty, Pasha and I have done little damage to impede The Third's tyranny.

"Ouch." My only comment unhooking from the zip, bare feet are miserable. Pasha assures me that we can get a pair of boots at the children's garden. I trust her because my feet hurt. She'd better deliver.

"How far to the children's garden?" I ask.

"Close," Pasha says as she squats by some sort of green bush with leaves several inches wide. Working quickly, she begins to pick and stack them in two piles.

"What's close?" I ask and catch on immediately to what she's doing. Together we create a pair of shoes that might get me by until we secure the boots. From the pack I assembled before we left Pasha's unit, I grab a spool of twine and unwind a length, using the knife tucked in my coverall side pocket to cut two sections, binding each stack of leaves together.

"'Close' means twelve zip trips end to end," she says, and I would love to remember how long a mile is, but we haven't measured anything in miles since several years after *Jurbay*. Life in Reichel produces measurements of zip lengths and how far it is from one end of a roll call line to the next. I add more leaves to the stacks and tie them to my feet.

"We better hurry," I say and begin a steady jog, feeling the rocks and branches through my newly crafted shoes.

"Short legs!" Pasha yells at me from behind, and I realize her gait is half what mine is. At this rate, if I don't slow down, she'll disappear quickly into the thickening shrubbery. I turn to face her and wait for her to catch up when a pigeon lands, cooing on her shoulder.

"Great," I say. "Pigeon returned home all right—right to you. Worthless bird." The moment I say it I regret it. Pigeons are family to Pasha.

Pasha's face clouds and she gets defensive. "The message on his foot is gone, Avery. That was his job, and he did it." She charges past me.

"Okay," I say as she runs ahead of me. "Okay—I'm sorry. Good bird. Good bird." I follow her as the shrubs turn into trees, scrawny but tall. "I think we have maybe twenty or thirty minutes before they can ready their float cars to search for us. They're not used to being challenged and…" Pasha dives at the ground the same moment I hear float cars above. I recognize immediately this is a fleet that needs repair. They have a distinct whine like a goat caught in a cougar snare in the mountains where I grew up. It's a bleating plea that increases in volume as the cars float closer. The sound amps up to screeching, like the chorus of sinking humanity that I imagine *Jurbay* brought on the day it surprised us. The day people were eating dinner and food suddenly became unnecessary, or they were weeding gardens when both weeds and gardens became irrelevant. The day they were studying for Monday's school exam when in a heartbeat school, exams, students and teachers were snuffed from the earth by a collision with the largest falling rock in four billion years.

I dive to the ground, following Pasha, and we dig as deep as possible under piles of decaying leaves, their smell familiar and evoking childhood memories of forest times with my father. Still I am repulsed by the dirt. My life has been sanitized for quite some time, living in Reichel.

The float cars send a pod of star-blades to the area we hide in. "Don't move. Pasha, don't move," I recite in hopes of convincing her any movement will be deadly. These little five inch lines of stars come attached to a paper thin blade that can cut through metal easily and bone without effort. Once hitting the ground the stars separate from the blade and light up the area for fifteen seconds or so while the blade shimmies like a pepped-up worm seeking flesh as a target.

"Can't hold still. Want to run," Pasha whispers in a panic, but her body stays motionless even when the pigeon on her shoulder flies away and is caught mid-flight by a star-blade that decapitates the bird before Pasha can call it back. She sobs.

"Pasha," I talk calm and as much like a mother as I can imagine, "Herman and Orbit are in your pack. Lie very still and they will follow your stillness." No more sobs. I hear the float cars tortured screams diminish until the night is still. The only sound left is a pair of hidden pigeons, cooing comfort to their master. "They're gone. Didn't see us," I say. "Let's go."

I ease out of the covering, brushing the musty blanket of leaves from my coverall, and I watch Pasha bury the dead bird with a clump of leaves. "You did your job," she says, allowing her hand to hover above the bird for a moment. Then, we run.

———

By the time the children's garden is in sight a thin forest emerges around us. A few clustered trees at first, not enough to hide or screen anything, but I know by the time we reach Red Grove the forest will be lush and so thick our only option for passage will be hiking, unthreatened by low flying float cars with little maneuvering capabilities. My lungs burn and we suck peps for hydration. The leaves on my feet have worn away, and I wonder how long it will take the bleeding blisters to turn to hardened calluses. Dawn is on the rise and all night long we have heard the patrols passing over our area and then dispersing to the next gridded section.

From the forest a mist creeps through the morning air. My father called the mist the "crying of trees," and assured me that tears always pass within the early hours of the dawn. I remember the sound of his voice. As the vapors arrive with the dawning, a breeze swings in through the trees catching the haze and dancing it in circles over the children's garden. With just a hint of light the garden looks enormous, the size of the space they use for roll call at the plant, but instead of men, women and GEBs standing at attention there are corn stalks, sunflowers and hedges of fragrant lavender much taller than a man or a woman.

The sun finally breaks above the horizon, causing colors to flood the garden. My eyes pop wide as the corn stalks display green wrappings around their treasured rows of kernels. Sunflowers wave their golden circles, each petal, bowing to the dark brown caps at their centers. And the lavender hedges, rolling their scents toward me, begging me to take note of their purple jackets standing tall above their legs of sage green. I am starved for color.

Stepping out from behind the corn stalks is a creature I might call a boy. Maybe he is nine or ten with brown hair curled in so many long ringlets the breeze catches it from the nape of his neck and pulls it high above his head making him look another foot taller, otherworldly. He's petting a pigeon, and as we move closer I see the tiny message around the pigeon's leg has been unrolled. For a moment we stare at each other and then his eyes brighten with mischief, and he pops the message in his mouth, swallowing it and running toward the stairs of an incredibly old four story building with crumbling letters, chiseled in stone where the roof meets the top of the outside wall. *Foxglove Library.*

"That's Raghill. He's a possum," Pasha says. "The Third thinks kids are sleeping, but they are wide awake." The screech of float cars approaches. "Like to read, Avery?" Pasha grabs my hand, dashing for the library doors. Even though my feet throb I outrun her, yanking open the front door to the building without an invitation.

We stand in a grand entryway that I know hasn't served as a public library for at least a decade when paper production was officially stopped and electronic readers were embedded on our retinas.

Pasha thrusts her nose in the air and sniffs. "I love this smell." In all the years I've known Pasha, she's never "loved" anything.

"Smells like dust and I'm not used to it," I say and skate across the accumulated film on the floor, noticing right away that mine are not the first footsteps here. Many others have skidded their way in and out of the library. The entrance to the library, guarded by a monolith herd of marble elephants, welcomes us to a desolate cavern of a room. A forty foot long counter of aging wood stands before us and hanging behind it a broken mirror framed in brass, its reflective area shattered into hundreds of fragments, making Pasha and me look like a unit of warriors instead of two tired girls on the run. The wallpaper seems in a battle with the walls, paper attempting to escape in giant peeling shreds while the walls boldly try to hang on to the last remnants of decor. I want the walls to win and return to a regal, compelling place, communing with those who visit. I glance at the grand staircases on both sides of the entry, ascending to additional floors. I am anxious to explore. There is something about this place. The sound of float cars fades.

I reach out to touch a cabinet with scores of little drawers and stifle a scream from the shock of the loudest snore I have ever heard. My father's military comrades snored like this, but since peps became our source of nutrition many biological sounds have been eliminated. I search for the source of the sound and find a man at the end of the counter, propped up against a full coat of armor which has its own covering of dust. The man is sleeping.

Pasha stands nose to nose with the specimen and blows one big breath at his face, sending particles of accumulated time flying. "Heeeeello, Guardian Degnan. You wretched pocket-watch," she barks. Draped on his body, a cover-all two sizes too big and faded long past gray that makes it impossible to tell if he is thin or heavy, old or young. Degnan's pale face is covered with freckles and red dots that scream *step back for your own safety*. I do step back and recognize that while he is fully alive he is also fully unaware of us. Pasha leaps on the counter. "Give me your foot," she says, and I hold up my foot while she takes a quick measurement. She disappears from sight for a moment, and he doesn't move, other than the rhythmic rising of his chest. "Hey, Avery," her head pops up. "He's sleeping 'on the ready.'"

"Was that a joke?" I ask, but she doesn't answer. I recognize her personality is different here. Jokes in the middle of a life-threatening moment are hardly part of Pasha's scenario.

She squats behind the counter again, all the while singing, "When the saints come marching in," and I am certain I hear a sporadic chorus of children's voices singing with her from somewhere up the staircase.

"No time for jokes or saints," I say. "And I didn't know you were religious."

"I'm not. Song's just stuck in my head. Every time I come in this library all sorts of weird cultural phenomena overwhelm me. You'll be singing too."

"I doubt it."

Pasha holds up Degnan's boots and says, "He won't miss them." I start to pull the boots on my feet. "His feet were kind of small and your feet"—she peers over my shoulder as I secure the boots in place—"your feet are... well not small."

"Thanks."

She salutes the pocket-watch, "Guardian Degnan. Lucky for us, you're *not* doing your job."

Then she bounds from staircase to hallway yelling, "Morris—Raghill? Prospero—Lear?" And they begin to arrive—a colorful assortment of children who look like they've just raided a circus costume cupboard. No coveralls for them. Clothes too big and some too small in every pattern imaginable, the colors rich and bright, and the one called "Lear" wearing a ridiculous Polka-dot golf hat. I envy them, after dressing in the same gray coverall for years. I want to sit in a pile of dust and just watch them, but I can't.

I grab Pasha's arm, urging, "We got the boots. Let's get out of here."

Her face close to mine, she mimes the word: weapons. Feeling exposed without my Z-Colt I stick with her. If she knows something, we might score a weapon or two.

I count children. Raghill's hair appears before he does, rising up from behind the library counter. Slowly, he eases himself onto the wooden bar, sitting cross legged, with a green onion sticking out the side of his mouth. His face, dirty—his hands dirtier. Raghill's cut off pants are leopard print and his shirt a plaid made with the soft flannel fabric like my father used to wear when not dressed in military attire.

"Raghill," he introduces himself.

"Avery," I reply.

Sliding down the bannister of the staircase, come three boys, broadcasting their names as they land on the dusty floor, "Morris," says the first. "Prospero," the second says. "Lear," proclaims the last.

Other boys, cluster on the stairs, filthy hands propped against grubby chins. I count eleven. Nothing they wear matches. Every piece of clothing has a different fabric and print, shouting their freedom of choice. I am jealous and want to wear a ball gown of satin and chiffon like my mother wore on her anniversary when I was a child—me waist high to her and daddy, twirling in my dress-up skirt, the three of us dancing.

Morris seems to be the leader of the circus librarians. He approaches me, bowing gracefully from the waist like a gentleman sent forward from Queen Victoria, beckoning me to her kingdom. I want to accept such an invitation, but there's no time. His bright green satin vest still shines through years of dust, and the striped orange shirt displays a variety of holes, frays and attempts at mending.

"Follow me, my lady," says Morris. And how can I not follow these colorful, gentle children, the ones that have no #14 on the back of their wrists? I notice Morris has eyes twice the size of a normal child.

Raghill rapidly approaches my side, guiding me by the elbow and ushering me up the stairway, speaking confidentially in my ear regarding Morris. "So you ask: why does he have such big eyes?" He pauses for dramatic effect. "Borden's experiments, they say." At first I think he's joking, but then I wonder.

Morris stops abruptly and turns to face Raghill and me on the stairs, defending himself. "Why does he have such big eyes, you wonder? Because *he* reads twenty-four hours a day at least three times a week with very little light, while his lessers are content with comic books. That's no experiment, Avery. It's brilliance." Morris sends a glare of superiority in Raghill's direction. He leans close to my face and says in unison with all the boys, "Intellect, my dear, is clearly seen through the discipline of the eyes." They laugh uproariously and Pasha joins them in a chorus of *When the saints go marching in*. I marvel at the familiarity they share with each other and Pasha, and it seems to me her time at the children's garden and Foxglove Library was spent doing more than collecting cucumbers and squash.

We reach the top of the staircase on the fourth floor and enter the room. Chickens wandered freely, clucking and pecking at the dust and years of dried crumbs. In his Elizabethan manner, complete with a practiced English accent, Morris faces me, bows and says, "Perhaps you'd like to look in the fiction section, under 'B'—if you need any extra."

"Extra of what?" I ask.

"You'll see, under 'B'. I'd go with you, but we're off"— and they all say together—"to the races!" The whole group of them explodes like a detonated dynamite stick, cackling with excitement and running to an aisle a few feet away. Pasha starts to join them, and I hold her back. Then together we peer around the corner where the children disappeared—the "M" aisle.

The library shelves are lined with books from the floor to two feet below the ceiling. The shelves run ten feet high, impossible to reach a book from the ground, so wooden ladders with wheels are attached on tracks to each side of the aisle. On the top of one ladder stands Morris waving a sunflower above his head, holding on with his other hand. Facing him in fierce competition is Raghill, displaying a corn husk between his teeth and clasping the ladder with both hands. Prospero and Lear stand below the ladders, each in control of pushing the racers to the goal line— the end of the aisle. "Go," all the boys yell, chanting and rooting the racers on. Pasha is fully engaged as one of the crowd.

From behind I feel a small hand clasp mine. I turn to face the tiniest of the boys, gazing up at me. "Look under 'B,'" he says. He leads me to the aisle. His mass of tangled red hair bounces down the back of his football jersey that says *Manning* in big letters, and it must be at least half a century old. I remember the day The Third ended all athletic events and took with it our city pride and unity. *Competition leads to rebellion. Let us focus on a united Third.* If there were objections to that radical decision, they weren't made public. Blind trust by the people. But here at the children's garden and the library it appears the justices' kids do pretty much whatever they want. No gray coveralls here, just circus-like clothing, a football jersey and not a single #14 marring the back of any wrist.

"What about Degnan?" I ask the small guide.

"He won't wake up until exactly 4:00." He turns to me, beaming with pride. "We have a clock."

"Exactly 4:00?"

"Pasha's peps guarantee it." He leads me on, and I think of how often Pasha visits the children's garden on behalf of The Third to attend to the justices' children's "mental development." And how many times she brought back vegetables for the still and claimed that was her only interest. Come to find out Pasha was in the business of making friends. I can see how she'd be drawn to these boys. She fits in here with a bunch of children whose father is a library and whose mother is a shelf of books.

The littlest librarian squats down and pulls out a book from the "B" section. It appears to be a leather-bound copy by an author with the last name of Boswell, but when he opens the book it has no pages inside the binding, rather it is a container, box-like, hiding a treasure. And the treasure is several packets of bean seeds. The boy passes them to me, and I make room for them in a deep pocket of my coverall.

Then the young librarian begins to point at different books, which I quickly examine, finding: a bottle opener, a binky, a beer bottle, and bullets. I shout at Pasha who remains several aisles over, "We got bullets over here and where there are bullets there are"—I find her in the "R" section—"Where there are bullets there are weapons." I finish my sentence and hold my hand out to her, showing her the bullets, but she ignores me, standing on the top of the ladder with her chipsters open in both her leg and arm, scanning documents from something she's found in a book-box of her own. "What are you doing?" I ask.

A band of children have followed me to the aisle, now draping themselves over the ladders, while the littlest librarian lies on his stomach looking at me.

"'R' is a good place to look, Avery," he says.

I squat next to him. "Why?"

"'R' is for things we need to remember."

The children chant in unison, "'R' is for 'remember.'"

As usual Pasha focuses on her task, uninterested in interaction or eye contact. She says, "Cyber-pirates cut all the undersea cables five years ago. Pretty much everything. All the records of how to do anything were in cyberspace, and so we don't have much left to tell us how to create the things we lost. She holds up a document with printed instructions. "But here, Avery, someone collected the data—the 'how'—and now we have it. Lear says there are 78 book-boxes with instructions. Someone back in time planned this so all of the knowledge wouldn't be lost." Pasha continues working. "I have internet from the ground up—electricity—wind power—and a recipe for Edna's pumpkin bread." She looks with scientific wonder at the recipe card similar to the one my great-grandmother used when cooking was a daily routine and not a forbidden activity considered unhealthy and detrimental to the populace.

Morris asks, "Did you find gene based therapies?"

Pasha holds up the file, "Right here."

"Good. We don't wanna lose that, 'cause in my short life I've been cured of autism, type I diabetes and bipolar disorder."

Raghill and the other boys say, "But they couldn't cure him of—abandonment." Then the team of circus characters giggle and hop off to other aisles chanting together, *My papa is a library, my mama is a book, I know that I'm dysfunctional—but no one ever looks.*

"Pasha," I watch her scan pictures of the instructions through the chipster in her leg. "After Shaw cut out the GEB's ventricle, Baldy's eyes opened, and he looked at me." Pasha places the book with the hidden contents back on the shelf and pulls out each consecutive book looking for another that has a box full of guts and no pages. I shake the ladder back and forth from below to make sure she listens to me. "He opened his eyes and looked at me."

"Residual energy, Avery. 'It' wasn't alive. "

"But you said they were just beginning to figure out the defaults in the GEBs. What if there was enough residual energy to tell The Third something about us before Baldy died?"

She waves her hand forward, commanding that I move her down the aisle by pushing her to another spot, so I shove the ladder three feet forward.

"What's to tell? They know we escaped; there are three of us and they're going to hunt us until they find us."

"They won't find us."

Raghill skids around the corner of our aisle and Morris follows, frantic and gesturing to the top shelf of the "R" section. I hear heavy footsteps racing up the stairs. Morris whispers over and over, "Get up! Get up!" Pasha jets the rest of the way up the ladder and places herself on her stomach in the space between the top shelf and ceiling. I am right behind her, racing to the hiding spot, positioning myself flat in a line with Pasha, my head behind her feet, nose buried in the thick dust, trying not to breathe it in, but my breath is urgent, quick—full of fear.

The ladder, directed by Raghill, clanks back to the end of the row where a second ladder waits on the other side of the aisle. Several children scream and yell, cheering for Raghill and Morris to begin the race of ladders once again, and trying to use their normal activities as a cover-up for Pasha and me. I hope my breathing is not as loud as the pounding in my chest.

Prospero and Lear push the rolling race cars from below. I realize we have more than one possum in the children's garden. They are all possums, seemingly harmless children, but out to do some harm to The Third. Above the distraction I hear a man's voice yelling for Morris and the sound of collective boots moving closer.

The voice, threatening and distinct, says, "Morris. Come on, front and center here, boy. I need to see you." It is Borden.

The rhythm of my breath—staccato and intense—fills my nostrils with the dust from the decades of negligence. I look forward to Pasha's feet right in front of me and see that they are shaking. I know I hid my pack in a corner under the front counter, and hope she concealed hers in a place where pigeons' coos cannot be heard.

The sound of the boots stops at the end of the aisle. I cease breathing all together. A long pause. Then I hear someone scramble down from the ladder and Borden says, "Get up, son."

I picture Morris, kneeling at his father's feet. This possum will do anything to keep the con going. Flashes from far back in my memories appear in quick succession. Me on my father's lap reading. Me in my father's arms, saying goodbye. My father lying on the floor with me—both on our stomachs—working military puzzles that he'd brought home from work.

"It's good to see you, Father." Morris sounds confident and calm, an expert at this game. It's not fair that Morris has Borden for a father, but I guess it's not fair that Pasha and I are lying face down in a film of dirt, hoping to keep our lives.

"Where's Degnan?"

"He's been sick, Father. But he's on the mend. We put him to sleep for a few hours to make sure he recovers well." I notice the English accent is gone. No play around Borden, that's for sure.

"He's been hired to take care of you—not the other way around." The ladder begins to roll slowly. I think Borden's hand must be on it, sending it in my direction. The paces of Borden are crisp and powerful, like an executioner's footsteps on the platform of a guillotine. I am unnerved, but I force myself to lie still. The ladder stops directly below Pasha's prone position, and I see bits of dust floating off our shelf to the floor below. *No. Please—no discovery. There's so much to do. We're not a mighty force, but without us The Third stays entrenched in power.*

"Degnan needs to request cleaners for this place," Borden continues. "Dust is disgusting and breeds disease. You'll tell him?"

"Yes, sir." A long pause. "How's your health, sir?"

"Well. And yours?"

"Excellent, sir."

"And Raghill?"

Raghill answers, "I'm full of corn, squash, berries and an occasional pep, sir."

Borden laughs, and it sounds like a broken zip cord, raking against the outside of a brick building. "Well, you're probably the only children left in the entire Third that still eat food. I'm surprised you look so healthy. Healthy, but dirty. I'll make a note to have a float car pick you up for a trip to the baths at the compound next week."

"Thank you, sir." Morris and Raghill answer in unison.

Now Borden is pacing. "Morris, you and Raghill and the other children must be on alert—intense alert—for absentees. We need you on the lookout. Have you seen any?" When he asks that question he uses the same tone as when he spoke to my mother in the viewing room. I recognize it, and believe he wants to derail someone—maybe Morris—maybe all of these possums. But Morris is quick with his answer, and I see this boy knows how to be on the ready.

"Absentees, sir?" Morris asks.

"Only three. Shouldn't be that hard to capture, but we haven't had any in years. So we could use your help. One unkempt girl, a miniature and quite helpless." I see Pasha's leg jerk back and forth in front of me. "One hulk of a man, but stupid—and a tall skinny girl who poses no threat. Not like her mother at all." My whole body stiffens, and I think: *Thank God you see the differences. But no threat, Borden? Just wait.*

A single pair of boots moves away as Borden continues to talk. "So, children—you send immediate word through Degnan if you see or hear anything awry?"

"Yes, sir," all the children answer. Then the collection of boots marches away.

"Sir?" I hear Raghill call and all the boots stop.

"Raghill?" Borden responds, and I imagine he has turned to face the boy.

"Sir, could you tell my father I send my greetings?"

A long pause. "Yes, Raghill. I will tell Commander Dorsey you send greetings." My stomach turns at the thought of the commander of a nation abandoning his child to a deteriorating library. I think of Quinn. The boots begin again, and Pasha and I stay stick-still for minutes after the sound of their marching has faded, and we hear the float car whining away in the distance.

I jump, startled, when I see Raghill's mop of curls peering over the top of the shelf at me in my hiding place. His eyes are wide open, and he is unable to hide his fear. "Do you need a pep or two, Avery?"

He scoots down the rungs of the ladder to make room for my decent. As I negotiate the ladder step by step, I wonder how I am descending with my knees shaking this badly. "No, I don't need a pep, Raghill. I need to get out of here." I roll the ladder to below Pasha. "Pasha, get down here." No movement above me. "Pasha, let's go."

She scuttles down with a fury, yelling, "He called me an unkempt, helpless miniature." She steps from the ladder to the floor. "Did you hear him? He called me an unkempt, helpless—"

"I heard him." I grab her arm and direct her down the aisle.

"Doesn't he know *I'm* the one that designed the zips. *I'm* the one that created the chipster?"

"He wouldn't know that. They don't even know what chipsters are." I guide her steps at a rapid pace.

"I'm the one that's gonna end those dysfunctional GEBs before they end us all, and I'm the one—"

"I know, I know—let's just get going to the forest." I grab Morris by the shoulders and ask, "Where are the weapons?"

"Under "Z,"" he says.

We are running to the "Z" aisle, Pasha saying, "Z-Colt. Makes perfect sense."

At the "Z" aisle I begin to pull the books off the shelf, trying to find the Z-Colts. Raghill gently places his hand on mine, stopping my frantic search. "Just ask," he says. And goes to where he knows I need to look. Pulling out the first book that has a Z-Colt inside, I kneel down, unzip my coverall and buckle the holster over my shoulder. Pasha mimes my actions, moving quicker than me. Neurosurgeons have incomparable dexterity, and along with that, I apparently lost more than my weapon when I was in the salad spinner. *Locasa?*

She runs a few feet down the aisle and pulls out another book, following the direction of Raghill's pointed finger. From inside the book Pasha yanks out a SE454, loads it and slings it on her shoulder. Morris pulls out a book and loads a similar weapon, placing it around my arm. "Snake-eye 454. Ought to be under 'S,'" I say as I adjust its strap across on my back.

"Too predictable," says Morris as he opens the next book.

"No time," I say. "Got to go." Pasha and I jet toward the staircase with Raghill and Morris following close behind, Morris carrying a small leather bag tied with twine.

"Avery, you have to take these with you." Morris says, dangling the bag in front of my face.

Raghill adds, "All you have to do is get one of these in someone's mouth—"

Pasha finishes Raghill's sentence. "And instantly paralysis takes over for eight hours."

Morris continues, "These peps are blue. Don't use them for anything else by mistake."

"How'd you know that?" I ask

"Pasha told me."

"My invention," Pasha says, "a year ago." She takes the bag from Morris.

Skipping the last three stairs we leap to the bottom of the staircase just as Degnan steps in the way while we're mid-air. We collapse on top of him. I try to get my face away from those wretched red spots and notice a small patch of white hair that remains on the left side of his head, but other than that he is bald. "Morris," I yell, "it's not 4:00 yet. He shouldn't be awake."

"Who are you?" Degnan asks, and Raghill pops a pep into Degnan's mouth. The pocket-watch's eyelids close.

"Blue. Told you, Avery." Morris and Raghill remind in unison.

Raghill helps us up and Morris says, "He won't remember a thing, believe me. We know."

Pasha and I rush to retrieve our bags then run out the front of the building.

We are half way through the garden when Morris calls, "Avery." I stop and turn to look at him. "Will you come back?" He waits a moment and continues. "I mean—you know, for more of what's in the books." He offers me a sunflower broken off at the stem.

I quickly go to him, retrieving the flower. "We *will* come back for what's in the books." Holding my palm-up, I offer friendship, and he responds with his hand mirroring mine. Our eyes lock—his huge oversized eyes looking at mine. For a moment I am very aware that the battle I've been waiting to fight with The Third is already underway. And I realize how arrogant I've been to think that the five of us subterraneans, Elite trained to the max, are the only ones involved in taking a stand for The 28 United, taking a risk to bring down The Third. Many of the under-age warriors in this inevitable war are children who have not been innocent for quite some time.

Time presses. Pasha and I sprint to the thickening forest, and I wonder how many zip cord lengths are we away from Red Grove?

## Chapter 4

# A ROSE BY ANY OTHER NAME

Pasha and I pick our way through the dump. Pitch dark might have been better than starlit night. I'm still working out the quirks in this chipster Pasha installed in my eye, and beams radiating from the sky have occasionally caused it some confusion. I maybe get twenty seconds tops of infrared when I tap my temple, realistically only fifteen. This is what I would consider a flaw.

"Flaw? Did you say flaw?" Pasha asks, trying to whisper, and following so close I feel the toes of her boots lapping at my heels. Irritating.

"Every chipster you create is a prototype. Of course there's going to be bugs to work out."

"Fine. Just tell me what you want me to fix, and I'll fix it."

"I can't tell you unless I use it enough to find out." Instantly instinct kicks in, and I freeze, sensing Pasha has halted behind me. My heart rate elevates, and I imagine the sound of my breathing is amplified. *Tap you're right temple.* I tell myself. *Now.* The infrared activates, and I scan the area. The device works fine this time. Pasha will be pacified to know when I tell her later—if there is a later. I have a bad feeling about this. All my senses are in overdrive, and I need to sort them out to gage the threat. *Locasa* has marched through my brain, and I'm unsure of my response time.

There is a slow-motion, rolling movement beneath these mounds of garbage that I can't explain. Ominous. Like these heaps of refuse are inhaling, staring at unwelcome visitors, and exhaling with a menacing evaluation of intruders, like we are hazardous material. Is it my imagination or is there no stationary ground in this garbage dump?

My infrared pops off, out of time, and the sucking sound that faded, after tracking us for the last fifteen minutes, is back and moves from the rear of our miniscule caravan to the front. *Right* in front. Slothful breathing comes from under the oozing decades of waste. Tap again and infrared detects an area of ground three feet in front of us and maybe six feet wide, crawling with some sort of underground activity and an odor so repellant it seeps through the protective sealings in our nostrils that were designed to replace gas masks. I'd return these defective sealings to The Third if I could, the devices leak, but it's a little late for that, and the smell begins to permeate my taste buds. I fight nausea, knowing my life depends on stopping the gag reflex. I'd go *beyond* this smell, like my Elite training taught me to do, but *beyond* doesn't quite cut it now, 'cause *beyond* isn't quite here. How much of Elite is gone? Gaps. Too many gaps.

I hear Pasha vomit behind me. Pasha's skills were always applauded from the neurological realm, not Special Forces.

With almost imperceptible movement, I reach behind my ear and tap the troop-to-troop com embedded behind my earlobe. If Pasha does the same, we will communicate without speaking, words detected between us through neural energy. I give credit to The Third for this invention, but more credit to Pasha for stealing it. She'll be ready to make it available to The 28 United when needed.

"Pasha," I communicate. "The SE-454." I mirror the slow-motion movement of the garbage mounds, unhooking the 454 from my back and adjusting it to firing position in front of my chest. Pasha, I know, mimics my movement in a synchronized dance of assault preparation. "Are you ready?" I communicate to her, but even as I do I find the 454 foreign to my touch. I've had enough hunting experience with my father to know where the trigger is and how to stabilize a weapon but truthfully, I have no idea what will happen when I pull the trigger. More gaps.

"Ready? I don't know what to be ready for," she sends her thoughts.

"Anything. Calm down." There is no response from Pasha, but I know she can fire a weapon, and she's had my back before. She'll follow my lead. I rapidly slide the release toggle to the SE454. Pasha steps up beside me and does the same. That very moment a horrific creature bursts through the surface of the sludge. Its massive head is seven feet wide and as soon as its mouth opens it becomes *all* mouth—all seven feet of it. It releases scores of miniatures, looking just like it. They are shining like phosphorous, vicious cat-heads with fish like bodies. Their mouths open and close, exhibiting four inch teeth, and sending out an ungodly shriek straight from their innards. We fire, and the barrels of our steel weapons open to a ten inch diameter hole, spewing snake-like combat sensors in a barrage in front of us. They go after the hostile creatures with microwave bursts of light targeting the open mouths of our attackers and boiling them from the inside out.

We don't have to fire a second time. Upon impact with our 454's combat sensors the imp's shrieks dwindle to a desperate gurgling noise as the enemies fall to the ground, leaving a mere shell of their exteriors, melting into the toxic mounds of the dump. The big mouth withdraws, and we watch its round head retreat underground, its form rippling just under the surface, heading up the refuse hill and over to the other side of the garbage mound.

I reach behind my ear deactivating the com. Pasha does the same. *It could be a long ways to Red Grove*, I think.

"Coo," she says, sounding like her pigeons. "Unscientific. I don't even know what that was." Digging through her pack, she gently removes Herman and hands him to me. "Here, hold him for me."

"You probably forgot. I don't like birds," I say and step away, slinging my 454 back over my shoulder.

"Perhaps you forgot. This is my only connection to my former life which *you* made sure I'd never see again."

"Better to die on the run than in a salad spinner or on a rooftop with a hundred pigeons. I would think you'd be grateful." I take Herman for Pasha but hold him at an arm's length.

Pasha carefully extracts Orbit from her pack, whispering in its ear. "And in the quiet night we find the peace of pigeons."

"Oh, please," I say and start to scout of the area.

"I'm a romantic," she says, trying to defend herself.

"You're a cynic. Neurologists are never romantic."

Pasha kisses Orbit's head and takes Herman from me, holding one pigeon in each hand. She could never defend herself in this position. Pasha has always struggled with being "on the ready," but I guess, now, maybe I do too.

A series of ominous snorts radiates up from somewhere in the vicinity of our feet. Pasha jumps, looking under her boots for the source of the sound, while Herman and Orbit fly to the tree branches. I unholster my Z-Colt. The light on the barrel triggers, and I point it straight-armed in front of me, circling the area, assessing.

Lyrical laughter joins the snorts and a chorus of sounds seems to be mocking us from below. Pasha picks up some sort of tube, an inch or so in diameter, that extends up from the ground. Holding her eye directly to the hole at the end of the tube, she peers inside. The laughter stops, and a gravelly voice speaks. "You've killed the little biters. Good work, lady heroes." Pasha drops the hose, stepping backwards, petrified. I keep my weapon in position.

A second tube, appearing from the camouflage of night and the garbage sop, snakes its way from beneath the earth. I pick this one up and look inside. A new voice says, "Hey, leader, I could do with one of those 'coms.'" This voice is smooth with a sensual, disarming rhythm.

"One com won't do you any good. You'd need two. Don't call me leader." I say.

"Then I'll buy two," he quips, waiting for an answer.

"With what? The sludge of the hillside?" I ask. My defenses are disintegrating, but my Z-Colt remains in position. I like his voice.

"I can trade."

"I'm listening."

Two other tubes begin meandering around the ground, and voices rise from them as well, younger voices, childlike. "Lady Hero, you got the biters," says one as the other says, "They won't bother us again for a long time, 'till Big Mouth can fill up with more of the same."

A rustling noise comes from the tree where Herman and Orbit roost. They coo urgently, and I shine the light from my Z-Colt in the direction of the sound. A man ascends from the below the ground. Maybe he climbs up an underground ladder, but with all the forest slash, it's hard to tell. His hair's a rat's nest of stringy gray, and his clothing, mostly rags, displays random items like a walking general store. While repulsed by him in some ways, I hunger to look closer at the assorted goods that I haven't seen since I've been inside Reichel. A small coffee pot hangs from his elbow, and winding around his arm to his shoulder is a length of rope. Tied on it, securely in place, are a screw driver, hairbrush, razor, flashlight and a garden claw.

"Tea?" he asks.

"We don't have any," Pasha answers.

He laughs again, the sound gritty. "I'm not asking. I'm offering. Do you want tea?"

My Z-Colt is aiming right at his head. "Let me see your wrist." He offers up the back of his hand. No #14. "Who else is down there?"

"Just three more," he says. "Does this mean you don't want tea?"

"Get them up here," I jerk the barrel of my Z-Colt, indicating their presence is required.

He yells down below, "You heard her. Up with the garbage." Groans waft from beneath the earth, and then two young children, maybe five or six, appear, arm in arm. Staring at me, they seem curious, but unafraid.

The boy turns his back on me without speaking, showing me his wares. He sports a cowboy hat, tattered on the brim, and from underneath his hair cascades the collection of items up for trade. They swing down his vertebrae connected by pieces of twine. A stapler, chewed-on slipper, bracelets—some woven, some rusted metal—a spatula, a photo frame and a broken clothespin soldier.

The girl's hair is mostly covered with an upside down bandana that may have been blue at one time. Swinging from the twine on her shoulder hangs a tiny baby doll, some filthy ribbons, a broken tea cup, a collection of mismatched pens and a battered notebook. She squeaks, "He's El, and I'm La."

The owner of the smooth voice appears from below. "Old Soul," he says pointing at the gray-haired man, "was studying Spanish, when he named them." Now that he's standing above ground, I see his tall frame towers above the children and Old Soul. When it comes to this "smooth voice" it is easy to overlook the thin coat of dirt that completely covers him. There's a lot worth looking at. Toned arms are evident under his set of rags which hang, exposing muscles here and there, indicating his whole body has adjusted well to the rigors of surviving in the dump.

I force focus and do my job. "Come on. Show us the back of your hands," I say and thrust the Z-Colt with a threat. All three display their wrists, and they are numberless like the gray-haired man.

"Tea?" Old Soul insists once more.

"Can I bring them?" Pasha asks and points to the tree.

El and La jump up and down, "You have birds," La says.

"Can we hold them?" asks El.

"How about you?" I ask smooth voice, placing the Z-Colt in its holster. "Were you named during a Spanish lesson?"

He smiles a smile as smooth as his voice. "Wasn't around for the lessons. It's Raben."

"Raben, then," I say and without taking my eyes off him I answer Old Soul. "Yes, tea."

The descent to the underground room is by way of seven mud-caked stairs etched into the earth below the dump. I wonder why, with all the dampness of the dump, these stairs aren't slick. Then I realize it's because there's so much light in the hovel, sucking up the moisture and the darkness. I feel warm for the first time since we broke out of the Plethora Plant a day ago. *Has it only been a day since we escaped and claimed rogue status, inviting the entire Third on an all-out manhunt for subterraneans?*

Fragments of broken mirrors, dozens of them in all shapes and sizes, hang from the ceiling by ropes, strings and fabric scraps, amplifying the light hundreds of times so that this dingy, underground hut shines like a king's palace.

El and La each carry a pigeon and rush across the circular room to settle on big round pillows that conform to their bodies when they sit. Whatever stuffing is inside the pillows makes a rustling sound as the children move. Raben's beside me, like a teacher about to begin a history lesson. He says, "Beanbags—from the '70s." His shoulder length hair, matted in dirt, reminds me not everyone has been groomed in unison by the justices. That thought disarms me, or maybe Raben disarms me. In any case, I feel a curious burn inside my soul for individuality. That concept of uniqueness, supposedly obliterated by The Third and put on hold in subterranean service, still fights for recognition.

"You have a name other than 'leader'?" asks Raben.

"Avery DeTornada," I answer as my eyes peruse the steam coming from a kettle across the room. Old Soul prepares tea on an aged hot plate that sits on a counter carved into earthen clay.

"It's wind driven," says Old Soul, noting my interest.

Pasha teaches "pigeon grooming" to El and La, and as they study the birds Raben studies me. At least I imagine he does.

I move to the light source of the room—five elongated cylinders filled with primary colored liquid in which huge bubbles chase each other in vicious circles. Pasha and I both squat in front of the ensemble of lights, fascinated with the colors, the process.

"Lava lamps," Pasha says. "A hundred year old relic. Annalynn told me about them." She looks at Old Soul. "How'd you get these? Were you born in the '70s?"

"Not quite," he says. "I've been trading at the Junk Heap since *Jurbay* came down. Finds like these come up sometimes when you don't expect them, and I like the seventies." Something about him reminds me of my father's history lessons on hippies and social revolution.

While the tea leaves seep in a pot of water covered with a broken plate, Old Soul sits on a faded denim beanbag chair, takes a leather pouch from his pocket and flicks a cigarette paper out from the depths of the bag. Then after sprinkling a small amount of tobacco on the paper, he masterfully rolls a cigarette with one hand. This amazes me and I say, "I haven't even seen a cigarette in ten years." Old Soul offers it to me. "No, I'm good. Been living 'antiseptic' for way too long,"

Raben rolls one for himself in the same fashion while the pigeons play chase on the beams of the low mud ceiling. The smoke, lack of ventilation and pigeon feathers are too much. I can't breathe.

Raben notices I've gone pale and grabs one of the tubes from the ceiling, saying, "Here, breathe through this." I put the tube in my mouth and breathe, taking a hit of air from the outside. I don't know if the air filled with these rolled cigarettes is worse than a hit of air from the dump, but it seems to help me recover.

"DeTornada?" asks Old Soul. "Your family name?"

"Yeah," I say, surprised he'd care.

"Means 'homeward' in Catalonian."

"How'd you know that?" I stand, curious enough to tear my attention from Raben, lava lamps, and breathing tubes.

"Know all about your father and his Catalonian background. Carles DeTornada. My commanding officer for a short time right before *Jurbay* fell."

I can only stare. Part of me wants to ask every question I can about my father, but I don't know if I can trust this man. He's a stranger, but a stranger without a #14 on his wrist, and that's a good thing. "DeTornada," he says again. "'O, be some other name! What's in a name? That which we call a rose by any other name would smell as sweet.'"

"An English lesson in a high alert crisis?" I ask.

"I just wondered if you agree with her?

"Agree with who?"

"Juliet. That a name—a heritage—it doesn't matter?"

"I'm not the leader my father was, if that's what you're trying to ask."

"The DeTornada name's been connected to leaders—to generals—to those who've made a difference for generations. Carles, Quinn."

"Look, if the name DeTornada means something to you, good. Maybe 'cause you're called Old Soul you think you're some sort of seer or prophet, that you know something about me. But me? I'm just trying to survive here and bring a few others with me."

Old Soul blows a series of rings formed from the smoke curling out his mouth. "Quinn still living?"

"Oh she's living all right. Tucked away nice and comfy inside The Third."

"Subterranean?"

"Take a guess. I don't know." I protect the information I hold about Quinn. She is the only remaining subterranean inside The Third.

"So then you *don't* agree with Juliet?

"Quit it with the Shakespeare lesson." I check the workings on my weapon and notice Pasha stroking Orbit's head, keeping a cautious eye on El and La who examine Herman at close range. She rubs the top of her head, and I can see her mind racing.

"Did you know pigeons are monogamous?" Pasha asks El and La, finally finding an audience that's interested in all she has to say about pigeons.

"What's mon-o-ga . . .?" asks La.

"Monogamous," says Pasha. "Creatures that live their whole lives with only one mate."

"Sounds like a good idea," says Raben. He makes me nervous, and I'm not sure why. I take another hit from the air tube.

"Like marriage?" El pronounces.

"What's marriage?" asks La.

"Ancient custom with pros and cons," says Old Soul and takes another drag off his cigarette, holding the smoke in his lungs then puffing out more of the strange looking rings. I wonder why it doesn't burn his lungs, and how a person could make a circle out of nothing. I guess he's had the time to practice. Herman hops on Raben's shoulder and he scoops him off, gently kissing its head without a second thought. Pasha kissing her birds revolts me, but somehow I find this charming.

Pasha asks Raben, "What was that up there in the dump tonight?"

"Biters," he says. "They'll tear your arm off, and if two latch on together—you got—at the most fifteen minutes."

Old Soul adds to the story. "Biters. Who knows what they were before. Rats, cougars—maybe a coyote. You can mutate into anything if you hang around a garbage dump long enough." I look at Raben pretty sure he's not a mutation. I wonder if the tea is ready and go to take a look.

El marches over to me and pulls his tattered shirt sleeve away from his upper arm, showing off his bite marks and a hole with a large section of skin missing. "Got me a biter scar. They don't kill everyone they bite."

I lean over to look closer. "Nasty," I confirm.

"Only come out at night, though," says Raben.

La reassures herself. "And we're in here at night. So it's okay."

Old Soul rolls a second cigarette, occasionally glancing at me from below his bushed-out eyebrows. "So what's your strategy?" he asks.

I don't answer.

"Oh, that's right—you're having a roll call." Raben says. *Now how did he know that,* I wonder? He nods in the direction of El who twirls one of Pasha's homemade notes from a pigeon's leg.

Raben joins me by the single burner, removing my hand from the stewing pot of tea and motioning me to sit. I want to stay right by him, but I suddenly forget how to pour tea. So I perch myself on the bottom of the stairs, watching the steam from the kettle and Old Soul's smoking ritual. Raben hands me a blue chipped mug, then passes his cigarette to Old Soul who puts it end to end with his freshly rolled one. The glowing ash from Raben's cigarette ignites Old Soul's when he takes a puff, then returns Raben's to him.

While Raben continues to smoke, simultaneously assembling the tea for the others, I speculate about what happened when Shaw met Trader Bob. *Was McGinty surprised to see Shaw and his twin standing side by side? Which one—Shaw or McGinty—delivered the lethal blow to Trader Bob and Shaw's stolen identity? Have Shaw and McGinty reached Red Grove before us? And if they have are they assembling a plan for the future of The 28 United?*

"And Quinn?" Old Soul prods. "Maybe she'll be there for the roll call—to lead the assault?"

"There is no assault," I say. There is a long pause.

"Okay. So then, Pasha, maybe *you'll* be putting a plan together?" I sense Old Soul moving the marionette strings of my existence, and I want him to stop.

"Quinn's sneaky," says Pasha. "I'm not." She hands off Orbit to El and La and takes back Herman. She puts her face to his beak and asks, "Like children, do you?" Then she answers Old Soul. "Avery's the best one at plans. I never finished Elite training. They hustled me away early to experiment on destroying human dignity."

I move out of the way as a boy of about seventeen noisily rushes down the stairs, coming to an abrupt stop at the bottom. He is not expecting visitors. "This is Trellis," Raben says. "Our brother." Raben asks him, "What'd you see?" Seeming hesitant to comment, Trellis remains silent.

Raben nods our way. "They're okay. Working for The 28 United. Go ahead."

Trellis collapses on the stairs under the weight of El and La who abandon Orbit and climb on Trellis' legs, chattering like blackbirds. Wrestling the kids to a seated position, he quiets them and gives us his report. "Float cars hovered about half a mile from the dump where the others couldn't hear them. I was waiting up in the trees on the edge, just like you told me to." Pasha secures Herman and Orbit, holding them close. I stand, on the ready. I relearned that right away.

Trellis continues. "They sent a squad down on cables from the float cars above. Maybe thirty in all. They hit the ground and fanned out. Weapons on alert, quiet. I didn't have any way to warn the pickers on the hills. I followed the troops at a distance from behind, but I couldn't do anything to help. The Third just mowed them down and kept going. So many bodies, and I knew them all."

"How many dead?" asks Old Soul.

"Maybe fifteen. Maybe more. Old Soul, there's only about 50 of us left now." And suddenly this very fit young man looks like the children he holds, fragile and sobbing.

Raben reaches out his hand to Trellis, clasping his forearm then embraces him. Old Soul loads up his satchel, saying, "We'll do 'words' for the fallen before we leave. Trellis, Raben, El, La—everybody—pack it up. Now."

El comes to me, holding his pack in front of his chest. "Are you the one taking the roll call?" he asks.

"Yes. And you're the one that found the message?"

He runs over to what looks like a cellar door and flings it open. A rush of cooing and flapping ensues as seven pigeons flock to a ceiling beam, roosting and observing the scene below. "We read *all* their messages."

The room quiets except for the gentle coos, and for just one moment I imagine these dirty pigeons to be dove-like saviors, delivering hope to their chance encounters. La marches over to me and says, "I *heard* the message." Holding up her left palm for me to see, she crosses her thumb and taps the center of her hand. Slim skin slides away revealing a tiny chipster.

Pasha runs to La, yanking her by the arm and staring at the chipster. "I make chipsters! I'm the one. Ask Avery. Ask anyone. How did you get this chipster? I sent a message to all Chipsters. Roll call. No one responded. That function doesn't work yet. We can't communicate chipster to chipster." She shakes La by the shoulders and the little girl, whose eyes are huge by now, begins to cry.

I tear Pasha away from La. "Stop, it, Pasha!" I yell. "Stop it."

Pasha continues to grill the child while I hold her back from harming La. "Did you hear my roll call through your chipster?" She whispers her question, jerking away from me, rubbing the top of her head, desperate for an answer. Pasha's eyes are so intent on La that the kid can barely nod her head in agreement.

"Yes," says La. "I heard the roll call through this." Very carefully she holds the hand with the chipster out to us.

Old Soul grabs Pasha by the shoulders and turns her around to face him. "Someone had to start making chipsters besides you, Pasha. There's a man on the other side of the dump. He's had medical training, and he's a mechanic now. He's perfectly capable."

Eyes flashing, Pasha wrenches away from Old Soul, grabbing me, and for once looking me directly in the eyes. "Avery, it worked. It worked!" She jumps up on a reclaimed sofa, and a spring catapults out of the middle cushion. "Do you know what this means? Now we can get our roll call to all the chipsters—no matter who made them. We can call all Chipsters. We can assemble an army. Train an army."

"Easy, Pasha," I say. "It's just *one* chipster—*one* response. We haven't had any others."

"To prove a hypotheses you start with *one* result," says Raben. Pasha leaps off the sofa dashing to Raben, wrapping her legs around his waist, kissing him full on the mouth.

"Thank you," she screams.

"Thank you," he says.

I couldn't have been more embarrassed—more jealous. Pasha dashes up the stairs to the exit, and I start to charge after her. But before either of us can reach the door a tremor ripples through the sod room, and the hanging mirror fragments, like an ember's slow journey to flame, begin a cautious dance. The walls of the underground sanctuary quiver, and the movement expands into an all-out unearthly vibration. "It's them," says Trellis and he steps back into bravery, his strong hands wrapping around the tiny palms of El and La.

Old Soul places his hand on the earthen wall, testing the intensity of the tremors. He says, "There have never been troops here before."

"*We've* never been here before," I say.

Raben yanks the tube hooked up to the outside wind generator, and the lights go out. Total darkness. He stands so close to me I feel his whisper on my cheek, "Old Soul said you were valuable. He didn't say you were hunted."

Pasha speaks. Urgent. "The birds. If the troops stop above, the pigeons will coo and give us away. Just give me one light for twenty seconds." I unholster my Z-Colt and activate its beam, placing Pasha in the spotlight and illuminating the room that's about to become our tomb. The pigeons, all nine of them counting Herman and Orbit, roost on the ceiling beam cooing with the innocence of babies, unaware of the huntsmen. Pasha stands staring at their beady little eyes with beady eyes of her own and raises her arms like a conductor in anticipation of the orchestra's first notes. She snaps her wrists and all the pigeons twitch their heads toward her. Gradually, she lowers her arms to her sides, and as she does, the birds become silent. With her arms still, she commands, "Lights." I snap off the ray of my Z-Colt.

The marching is right above us now, and it's impossible to tell how many there are. It seems like hundreds when the ground is shaking this hard. And in the dark, I imagine the hovel beams heaving up and down. Is it worse to go above and face a foe that far outnumbers us, or to be buried alive in a collapsing hideout? For the sake of The 28 United we need to live, and that is my answer. We ride it out in hopes that the ceiling beams don't give out and in hopes that we, the hidden, remain unseen.

It doesn't take the troops long to pass and the vibrations to fade. We wait until early dawn, planning to exit the underground room with our packs loaded and supplies ready for the trek to Red Grove. Trellis and Raben have been scouting all morning for any traces of The Third's squad and found none. Pasha has talked everyone into carrying a pigeon or two with them in their packs. She carts the final bird with her up to the outside, and I'm wary she will ask me to be its host on our journey. No way.

I follow her up the stairs, my Z-Colt un-holstered, ready to scout the area before I beckon the others to join me.

From fifty feet away I see him, crouching in attack mode, facing Pasha, who does not notice him. He wears the uniform of The Third. He comes at Pasha from the rear with full power. Nimble, his six foot three frame crashes the butt of his SE454 on the base of her head. Her helmet's on and the force of the blow slices it in two and then slices further into Pasha's skull. Blood gushes.

The Elite does a one-eighty to face me. I discharge my Z-Colt precisely into his gullet. I try to tell myself this is no different than the elk my father and I shot when I was eleven, but this is not the same. He falls straight backward, hitting the ground hard. I know he is dead, but I catch a glimpse of Raben making sure.

Kneeling by Pasha's side, I pull the rolled blanket attached to the underside of my pack and place it below her head to stop the bleeding. Her eyes are closed. She is breathing but not conscious. Old Soul rotates her head to the side to evaluate the wound. "She won't heal by herself. She's going to need surgery. I don't know how complicated it is."

"Degnan. At the children's garden. At the library," says Trellis.

"He's just a guardian," I say.

Trellis continues, "I've heard the pickers talk when they come back from the children's garden. He was a surgeon for The Third, until he screwed up big time and ended up as a guardian." He confronts Raben. "I can go get him. There's no one out there but some pickers. No one suspects that Avery and Pasha are here."

"No," I say tightening the straps on my pack. "Raben and I will go. I'm used to running that far, and I know the children there. They'll do whatever I need, and Raben can handle Degnan on the way back." I grab Pasha's weapon from her side and hand it to Trellis. "You're needed here to keep watch. And don't assume there aren't any more of them."

By now, Old Soul has fashioned a secure bandage around Pasha's head from a piece of my blanket. "Avery—" says Old Soul.

I hold up my hand, stopping him. "Don't tell me not to go. This is what I do."

The gravel sound in his voice grates and he says, "I was just going to say: Go. Go now."

Zipping down the front of Pasha's coverall, I un-holster her Z-Colt and pass it to Old Soul. "She's in your hands. We'll be back as soon as we can. Get her downstairs. Try to make a sterile area. And keep those cooing pigeons out of your underground."

Raben and I run into the gray of the morning in hopes that Degnan, that pocket-watch of a guardian, hasn't been fed any blue peps for the last few hours by the children of the library. This renegade doctor of The Third is going to have to be fit for travel, if Pasha's ever to travel again.

# Chapter 5

# THE STRENGTH OF ASHES

I can run four zip lengths in 9:52, but I'm sure since Raben and I left the dump I've cut some time off my record. In my mind, I am constantly refiguring how long we will take to get to the children's garden, locate Degnan, rig up some sort of pallet to put him on and cart him back to the dump. The reoccurring image of the raised weapon and the Elite soldier splitting apart Pasha's skull flashes in my mind, replaying with every step I take. I can't make the memories of the blood red blanket around her head disappear.

Raben runs in front of me. We alternate taking the lead, so that one of us is always scouting for danger. Maybe it's the pounding rhythm of his worn combat boots, probably "picked" on a good day of foraging at the dump, that sends my soul back to Catalonia and the last days I spent there as an Elite.

———

The Catalonian President halted in front of the vacuum suck I hid in. Installed in this late 1800's church it seemed a contemporary invasion of the hallowed stone structure. I could see the grill of the suck reflected in the back of his spit-shined shoes. And right behind the grill I waited with McGinty. We lay on our stomachs, extended in a stick-straight line, followed by Shaw and two other Elites. These two others were not subterraneans and had no idea they were working with those of us loyal to The 28 United. We all controlled our breathing to avoid setting off the vacuum sensors that would slice, dice and disintegrate us into ineffective mincemeat unable to succeed at the assigned mission.

The President paced past the vent, and my vision was no longer obscured. I saw, standing by the polished wooden pews beneath the 30 foot stained glass windows, my mother and father, Quinn and Carles DeTornada. There was an exchange about to take place, one I knew would change the lives of every citizen in what's left of our nation back at home. Orchestrated by The Third, *locasa*, a neurological invention, would be stolen to control and minimize any rebellious threats to The Third's domination.

The President stepped forward, *locasa* in hand, and passed it to Carles who handed it to Quinn, and she slipped it in her bag. I noted that the bag was an exclusive name brand made of expensive russet leather. *Always one for style*, I thought with cynicism, but yanked my roving mind back to business.

I recited The Third's orders: *Minimize damage of historical structures. Evaluate necessity of eliminating the President. Contain* locasa *at all costs, without damage. Terminate both DeTornadas.* Carles and Quinn, friends with the President and self-appointed protectors of *locasa,* had come specifically to Catalonia to protect this device. DeTornadas had dark brown eyes, but my mother Quinn's shone white-blue and stood out in a crowd. *Keep your mind here, Avery. Right here.*

I was the Elite hiding in the front of the line inside this dormant vacuum suck, and I was the one who would bust through its grate and come in with my Z-Colt firing. I was the subterranean who must save these DeTornada's lives while trying to convince the Elite: we had minimized damage, salvaged the President, contained *locasa* and left the DeTornadas dead on the stone cold cathedral floor. I tried to focus on the mission, but even my Elite training didn't eliminate the mental snapshots: his penetrating brown eyes and hers of shocking white-blue. They screamed at me: parents.

One word, communicated in my com through the neurological settings in my ear, put our plan into action. My commander said: *Now.* A single punch of my Z-Colt on the grill, and I burst forward into the room followed by my squad and accompanied by continual sprays from the barrels of our weapons. I saw my father push my mother under a pew and draw his weapon. During that instant McGinty tackled the President and hovered over him, shielding his body. Shaw scooped up *locasa,* placing it in a protective metal box and dashing back to the suck entrance. McGinty, Shaw and I intended to find a way to keep *locasa* with the Catalonians, but the second our commander assigned two additional Elites to the mission, we knew we would have to bring it back to The Third or our cover would be blown. As subterraneans there was only so much we could do and saving Carles and Quinn would have to be sufficient.

I dove under the pews a few feet from Quinn, and used my arms to scuttle forward to the pew she hid under. I came face to face with her Z-Colt, honed in on me. Her finger was on the trigger, but recognition was in her eyes. "Avery," she whispered.

"*Locasa* is gone," I said.

"We'll worry about that later," said Quinn. "For now, make it look good." I squirmed up to a standing position in clear sight of the visual-audio trails The Third was using to scan our activity, and I shot a single bullet an inch away from Quinn's head and one just missing Carles. But my theatrically placed shot was unnecessary for him because someone else's Elite bullet found its intended mark. The hole in my father's forehead was clean, direct and the perfect handiwork of a trained Elite. The haunting hole crippled my heart, but my Elite trained mind won out and directed me to process it all later, but later often meant never.

———

I feel the drag of my boots weighing down my feet as we conclude the run to Foxglove Library. It's the golden petals of the sunflowers I notice first, so tall, like they are watchtowers protecting the garden, the library, the children and—I hope—us. Looming behind the vegetable garden the library waits, holding Pasha's salvation within its walls. Up the stairs I run, anxious to find Degnan and begin the trek back to Pasha before it is too late.

"Avery," Raben calls from behind me and grabs my arm, twisting me to him, "Avery, there are all sorts of kids in there, and once we go through those doors it'll be chaos. Let's make some sort of a plan before we go in."

"We have a plan. Get Degnan and get him back to Pasha."

"Let's do it this way: I'll get Degnan, bind his hands and feet—"

"Okay, I'll work with Morris and the other kids," I add. "We'll find some sort of cot to pull him on. We'll make one if we have to." We sprint up the stairs together. "I'll have Raghill package the peps that can revive Degnan once we get him to Pasha."

I pull the Foxglove Library door open and standing on the top of counter is Degnan pointing his version of the SE454 right at my head.

"And you want—what?" he asks.

"I need to talk to Morris," I answer.

"The only one you need to talk to is Borden. I've been warned about absentees. Leastwise you, DeTornada. Not him." He nods his weapon toward Raben. "Haven't heard a thing about a dirty traveler from—I'm guessing—the dump?"

"Morris," I yell. "Morris!"

"Now you can yell all you want, but the kiddies have gone to bed." He twirls a package of peps in his hand, and I note how sloppy he is with his weapon. *He'll probably shoot us by accident before he manages to do it intentionally,* I think. I see a cluster of boys on the stairs above. All of them have their fingers pressed to their lips in a command of silence. I stall Degnan. "You don't have to let Borden know we're here."

"Oh, I'm not going to let him know. He'll find out himself in about twenty minutes when his float cars arrive to pick up the library boys for their baths at the compound."

Screaming down the staircase, eleven boys scurry, creating ungodly noises and catching Degnan off guard. He pivots in their direction as the boys scuttle over the banister, onto the counter and toward Degnan. Raben and I dart across the marble floor, me grabbing Degnan's weapon and Raben pushing him off his feet so he hits the top of the counter hard with his backside. I see that Raben is already at work using straps from his pack to tie Degnan's hands.

I yell at the boys while leading the way up the stairs. "Do you have anything like a cot to haul Degnan on? We've got to get him to Pasha. She's hurt bad, and he's got to be her surgeon."

The littlest librarian shouts from the back of the group, "Look under 'L.' Look under 'L.'"

I yell back at him, "What's under 'L'?"

Right behind me Raghill, breathing hard, says, "Lashings—ropes, cords, ribbons." Then to Morris he says, "You know what the little one is thinking, Morris?"

"Yeah," Morris says. "He's thinking: lash a travois together to pull Degnan on. Native style."

"What about poles?" I ask.

"There's a pile of poles on the other side of the garden, by the edge of the forest. We use them all the time for staking up vegetables and sunflowers."

I protest, "We've only got twenty minutes."

"Well, we don't have a cot, Avery."

"Okay," I say. "You get the box with the lashings, and I'll go with the boys to the pole pile by the garden." Everyone but Morris turns abruptly with me, and we descend the staircase.

We meet Raben half way through the garden. He has Degnan thrown over his shoulder. Degnan twists and turns, but can't escape Raben's grip. I say, "Get him to the pole pile. They're going to build a travois. It's a native—"

"I know what it is." Raben interrupts me. We use them in the dump for hauling junk." Degnan's attempts to break his bindings gain intensity, and Raben pops a blue pep in Degnan's mouth.

"I hope you have the antidote for that," I say.

"Got it covered," he answers and holds up a vial of peps. "He'll be dead weight for the next three miles back to the dump. Then, we give him one of these, and he'll be a master surgeon, *if* you can convince him to do the work." He slips the vial in his pocket.

Morris passes us in a flat out run, holding on to a book-box marked "L." He positions himself on a mound of dirt shouting directions to the other eight boys. They collect the poles, form a triangular shape by lapping one stick over the other diagonally and then lash the two poles together. Arranging a crossbar for stability, they span the inside of the triangle with a limb for Raben to hold onto as he runs. The last three crossbars are knotted at the widest part of the triangle. That is where Degnan will be tied.

It occurs to me that these eight sets of children's hands work together in exquisite synchronization, and I wonder if they've been practicing for this very task. That's impossible, but still, they anticipate each other's movements. They integrate their efforts like a technologically perfected machine. A memory fights to stand center stage in my mind, and it shimmers between past and present. *I am young in the Sequoia Forest with mother and father. The trees loom hundreds of feet above our three man tent that lies limp on the needled floor. The three of us work in unison to erect the canvas structure— one handling the poles, another receiving them and the other wielding the hammer that pounds the stakes to secure the shelter.* Like we once were, these boys are a family.

The boys chant their melancholy song as they complete the travois with twelve minutes to go before the float cars arrive: *My papa is a library. My mama is a book. We know that we're dysfunctional, but no one ever looks.* I think about writing them new lyrics. Raben lifts Degnan onto the travois and steps inside the pole triangle, positioning himself for the pull.

"Go," I yell at him. I start to follow, but realize I can't leave these boys here. Borden will know something's wrong when he discovers Degnan is gone. I shout to Morris, "Let's go. You all have to come with us." He grabs my arm.

"No! There's still three boys inside."

"Okay, I'll go get them." I turn to Raben. "I'll catch up as soon as I get the rest of the boys, and I'll get as many more weapons as I can." I'm not sure he hears. He is already running through the forest at top speed, as if someone's life depended on him. It does.

I expect the boys to follow Raben, but hear their feet rustling behind me. Glancing over my shoulder, I find all eight in tow. Time chases the boys and me through the garden, up the library stairs and to the fourth floor where the boys pull the weapons from their dummy books on the shelves. I am determined to load as many as possible on every part of my body in the remaining minutes.

From an assortment of shelves, the children cart the armaments to me in a frantic procession. These weapons have been concealed for I don't know how long. I pack the arsenal all over my body and the boys do the same. For a brief moment it flashes through my mind that there are others out there loyal to The 28 United, loyal enough to make a plan to hide weapons and save instructions to recreate needed parts of an infrastructure that they anticipated might be destroyed. How can we find these loyalists? It was Pasha who was working on a way to call the Chipsters so we might develop an inkling of our true numbers. I haven't prayed since long before my father died, but I pray now. *Please, let Degnan remember his surgical training. Please, let Pasha live.*

Just as the heaviness of my newly outfitted gear sinks in, I sense a quiet. The boys are still, no more urgent scurrying. I turn around to see what's occupied their attention and there stands Borden with a dozen soldiers behind him, weapons trained on us.

I stare at him, and the injustice of two decades consumes me. "So, Borden, you must have finally lined up a good mechanic to fix the screech of those float cars. I didn't hear a thing." I look back at the closed doors to the fourth floor. "Couldn't take the stairs?"

"It's an easy climb on the outside of the building," he says. Even though his façade is calm, I sense the volatile nature of his arrival. An Elite soldier removes the weapons from my body, piling them together. This unnerves me. They are not making any attempt to take these weapons with them.

"Never underestimate the power of evil," I say, without taking my eyes from his.

Borden's squad of armor-clad Elite stands at attention their climbing gear still hanging from their uniforms. They remain on the ready. Borden crosses to one of the overstuffed chairs in the reading area and sits, making himself comfortable. He lifts a small flame thrower from his belt, pulls a cigar from his coat pocket and lights it, using a ridiculously long flame. Out of the corner of my eye I see Morris pull the littlest librarian close, holding his hand.

Still, I look at Borden, considering my options which are nonexistent. I say, "Thought smoking was banned in The Third."

He puffs the cigar to get the tip burning and answers, "There's always an exception." I hear a roaring from outside the fourth floor library door. "But you know what there are no exceptions for?" I see smoke seeping under the crack at the bottom of the door. "Traitors." Now all the children see the smoke.

Morris goes dashing to his father. "You can't burn this place! You can't burn us! We're children!" He pauses then says, "I'm your son."

Borden rises up out of the chair, and I don't see a single glimmer of concern for his own child. I've been standing face to face like this before with my own parent—in the Plethora Plant before the master punch bound my ankles and wrists, but Quinn was doing what she needed to do to keep our subterranean status undercover. Borden only needs me, not eleven children. He says, "There are no exceptions for traitors." He looks at us individually, enacting a death sentence with his eyes. He strides back toward the balcony, tossing a command over his shoulder. "I'll take the lead float car and a pilot. The rest of you make sure the place is engulfed before you follow. Burn it to the ground."

I rush toward him, but am restrained by two Elite soldiers before I even get ten feet. I watch Borden rappel over the side of the balcony with his pilot. The eleven boys attack the soldier who shakes accelerant from a can, dousing the furniture, the floors—the books. There are plenty of men to contain a desperate group of boys.

"Come on," one soldier says to the Elite holding the can. "That's enough. Let's go." They begin to repel over the edge.

And for one second, before the remaining soldier knocks me to the ground with his fist, I see that he too is desperate. He doesn't want to burn children, but he has even fewer choices than I do.

I'm out for a second, and then the foul air and the littlest librarian slapping my face revive me. I see the children trying to stamp out a growing fire.

The flames arrive with a fiendish flash, ignited by the devil himself. With a deliberate sneer they meander through the books, licking as they browse. At first, tasting delicately, planning their meal with measured design. Strolling through the J's, the F's and the P's, they decide their strategy, contemplating when the point of no return should arrive.

But we have a strategy of our own and organize our battle plan during the seconds it takes to run to the veranda-like balcony of the fourth floor. If statistics say a twenty-four foot fall can kill a man, what would a forty foot plunge do to these eleven frail bodies? "Get that sofa out here and push it over the balcony," I shout, and immediately eleven pairs of hands shove, pull and thrust the sofa over the edge of the marble barrister that hedges the balcony. The crumbled sofa leaves a bed of pillows as a base and flop point for dropping children. As the fire consumes more oxygen and vies for our attention, pungent odors invade our nostrils. The children compete for their lives as they rush all the pillows from the overstuffed chairs in the reading area to the balcony and fling them below, building a pile on top of the sofa.

I rush to the weapons pile, throwing the 454 over my shoulder, lifting my Z-Colt and shooting round after round into the hinges on the top of the ladder on the "M" aisle, and finally the ladder falls to the ground. The children do not have to be told to pick it up and cart it to the balcony. Morris takes the lashings left over from the travois from his belt and hands them to Prospero and Lear who lash each side of the ladder to the slatted banister of marble.

Soaring through the sky directly in front of me are the two float cars carrying the troops who lit the torch to burn the children and the only home they'd ever known. I sling my 454 into firing position, depending on instinct to send my fingers into action, but there is no instinct. So I waste valuable seconds remembering my earlier use of the 454 in the dump. I release the trigger, and the weapon discharges with a violent kick against my shoulder. A dozen sensors shoot out the mouth of the weapon and clamp onto the first float car, taking it down. I fire again. Both cars are ablaze in the sky and descending at an unstoppable speed, but I don't watch their landing.

I glance at the ladder lashed to the edge of the balcony. It only extends down a story. We are going to have to drop the rest of the way down. I rush to the window and yank the heavy drapes from their rods. Unsheathing my knife, I slit the top of the curtain into two parts, disconnecting it from the rod. Now the fire decides this is the point of no return and stops its nibbling on the book-hors d'oeuvres, taking huge bites of walls and floors, devouring its way up and down the staircase, eating the banisters for dessert.

From the balcony I start to climb down the ladder. While hanging on the last rung, I tie the drape to it. Trying to descend the curtain with my hands, I half-cling, half-fall down the awkward escape route onto the sofa and the pillows. Nothing is broken.

Morris is coming down the ladder with the littlest librarian on his back. Somehow Morris keeps himself and the child on the ladder, falling onto the sofa's pile when he reaches the end of the curtain. "Step out of the way," I yell.

None of these children cry. They do not scream or whine or become hysterical. They are calm, methodical, and I desperately want the cowards of The Third to know that courage is in the hearts of these children Borden seeks to destroy.

Raghill, Prospero and Lear slam to the ground simultaneously, as the ladder and the drape burst into an inferno making any other escape futile. Now we scream. All of us below, separated by four stories with six children left standing on the library balcony, looking down at us with a sinking sense of hopelessness. There are no more staircases to offer a saving grace, no float cars to hover and drop a rope to extract the victims and no Pasha to concoct some sort of formula to miraculously squelch the flames.

The children move to the right side of the balcony as the left side is consumed in fire, collapsing as we watch. The flame's strides become longer and are on a direct collision course with the children. An eerie quiet settles over those of us standing on the ground looking up. We are like ancient Egyptians peering in on a tomb about to be sealed, forced to watch a slow motion demise.

One child on the balcony holds up a vial of peps. They are blue. The eight-hour-paralysis-blue. Powerful peps that should not ever be in the hands of a child. The flames lap at the children's hair and they all look to Morris who nods his head. Quickly the blue vial is opened and passed through the cluster of children, each taking one. And then together, like a line of troops trained with military precision, they take their peps in unison. I spread my arms wide enough to grasp all the five children on the ground and hide their faces against my chest. But I do not turn away, I watch the children lie down on the balcony in peaceful sleep as the flames eat one more bite. Then, I can look no longer.

———

At the end of the day two demolished float cars lie splattered on the library grounds, their parts strewn the length of the garden. The remains of the library stand like a charred forest. The garden is a plot of ashes. It takes us an hour working together to fashion six crosses to mark the lives of children who should be camping with their families, attending normal days of school and making forts in their backyards. The remaining children—Morris, Raghill, Prospero, Lear and the littlest librarian—kneel by the crosses. I stand behind them wondering how, in just one generation, life has become so cruel that children are burying children and a twenty-two year old girl, trying to save the world, has suddenly become the mother of five.

It was Morris who insisted on the crosses. Each of these surviving children had thrown two or three books (the secret storage kind) down from the burning ladder to the ground, and in one of those book-boxes there was a Bible. Morris clasped it to his chest, sobbing, trying to explain to me the significance of the cross. I finally said, "Morris, you don't need to explain. Let's just make the crosses." And we did.

The hand of the littlest librarian slips into mine. He says, "Don't worry, Avery, fire makes ashes, and ashes make a garden grow." I forget my need to act like a leader and scoop this boy up in my arms, promising myself that I will never let The Third take another one of our children. He whispers in my ear, "You'll see, Avery—next year. Next year when we come back."

I know we should start for Red Grove. Eventually, Borden will figure out the men he left to do his burning are long past returning. He will send trackers to find us. "Come on, boys. Got to get out of here."

The littlest librarian salutes me and says, "Don't worry, Commander DeTornada, we can keep up."

"I'm sure," I say. "But I'll feel better if you call me Avery." I squat to face the littlest librarian. "And what should I call you?" He remains silent, kicking his combat boot into the ashes.

Morris whispers in my ear, "He doesn't even know which justice is his father."

Raghill adds, "He never got a name."

"Well, what do you call him?" I ask.

"Never had to call him anything. We just look at him and talk. You know, like, 'Go water the vegetables.' Or 'Time to go to bed.' Or 'Do you want more squash'?"

The littlest librarian looks up at me unexpectedly. He asks, "Do you have a name for me, Avery?"

I nod my head without hesitation. "I do." I wipe the ashes from his face. "Carles. My father used that name for a very long time. He doesn't need it anymore, so I'm giving it to you." I stand and point the way. "So, Carles, boys, let's get to the dump quickly." Raghill picks up Carles and places him on Morris' back, and our rag tag caravan begins. I run backwards a few steps taking a count, like a chaperone at a grade school picnic, and when I'm sure we number six, I face the front again.

Our steps find the rhythm of running, even though we are an unusual combo. I start to wonder if Degnan will save Pasha, and what an unlikely savior he would be. And if she does recover, will she ever get to the point where she can call all the Chipsters? How many more are out there who are loyal to The 28 United? Whoever they are they will assemble at Red Grove *if* they've had a chance meeting with a pigeon, carrying a crude message wrapped with wire around its scrawny little leg. I wonder. *When we've finished with this roll call and decide what to do with those we've collected, and when they realize their commander is only a twenty-two year old girl, will they follow me?* Suddenly, I am very aware of how much slower I run with a squad of children.

97

# Chapter 6
# CLEAN AGAIN

The distance between what was left of the children's garden to the underground residence at the dump, where Pasha waited unconscious for a savior, was the length of a twelve zips. However, we have no zips and must maneuver through treed terrain. Raben and I had run the distance to the library in just under thirty minutes, the forest posing no obstacle for us as we slipped easily between the trees. I have no idea how long it took him to return to the dump carrying a drugged-out pocket-watch on a travois, but for me, there had been nothing in my life to prepare me for the challenge of returning with a crew of five children. Their longest hike ever had been up a library staircase to the fourth floor. I don't know much about children. I never had any brothers or sisters and my mother and father always kept me close with them and their military friends. In my life there had been no neighborhood hoops, block parties or cul-de-sac barbeques. So today, just making it back to the dump with this entourage seems a successful feat.

We hobble from the tree line of the forest to the open area, and this time, as I approach these uninviting mounds, it is the pickers that catch my eye. Our arrival here the first time, less than twenty-four hours ago, came at night. Now, with the late afternoon sun burning hot, I see these pickers crawling all over the dump with their homemade claws roped to the bottom of waist high sticks, sorting and sifting the slopes to allow discovery of usable discards and, perhaps, some sort of buried treasure. By night the slippery oozing earth, the toxic smell and the heightened danger of unknown threats had consumed all my senses. Now, in the light, I grasp the vastness of this region, and I understand that this is more than a dump. It's a livelihood for many. The loveseat in our unit was picked from this dump, but that was two years ago when larger items could still be rummaged, before a population of pickers staked out this refuse collection as their territory.

The Third was never challenged by its citizens, so the patrols spent no time outside the city rooting out pickers who chose to reject city life. However, since we've come along, these pickers will now have to watch their backs because of us. While they may not have had units where they could sleep in comfort, or peps delivered to their window sill, they have made their way here, and they have done it without the eyes and ears of The Third watching and listening to their dreams and fancies. That is, until now. And I realize that everyone I come in contact with from this point on has my stamp—subterranean—and will be hunted just like me. Old Soul, Raben and his family, and all the other dump pickers that are left cannot stay here and continue life as normal. Even Degnan cannot go back. He's failed The Third and is no use to them. And just like the pickers finding their own brand of treasure buried in the sludge, I have uncovered a rag-tag army incapable of using weapons, untrained in military strategy and confused as to what battle actually is. But I have found them to be very good at following and that puts the job of "leader" solely on me.

I feel a dribble of spit from Carles' open mouth trickle down the back of my neck. He slumbers with his mouth open, and I wonder how a kid can sleep on my back in the midst of a steady jog or how his hands stay clasped around my neck in spite of the jostling. We were barely a few zip lengths from the library when Morris transferred Carles to me. I didn't mind.

We pause, and a moment of rest allows Raghill to flick his toe at the garbage of the hills and uncover a broken rake. He reaches down to retrieve the shattered wooden handle, cling-ing to some rusted tines, and right away, coming down from the mounds, racing toward Raghill and wielding crude weap-ons in their upraised hands, charges every picker in the area, maybe seven or eight.

I reach for my Z-Colt, knocking Carles latched hands apart and causing him to tumble to the ground. I step in front of Raghill and train my weapon on the closest picker. "Stop. Don't come any closer," I say.

A woman, whose clutched weapon looks like a stripped tree branch, forces out a guttural response, "Belongs to us," she says and points at the defunct rake.

Raghill throws the rake to the woman. "Take it," he says. I hear fear in his voice. "I was just looking at it."

The hoarse voice of the woman loses its venom as she grunts softly, maybe expecting us to interpret her sounds as a diplomatic apology. Creeping forward, she dips to the ground in a crouched position, grabbing the rake and backing away so she is out of reach of Raghill, but not out of range from my Z-Colt. The pickers converge on the woman who holds the prize. They surround her with a circle formation, plucking at her rag garments. She turns slowly in the center of the ring, appraising her confronters. Then she bursts toward the edge of the circle in an attempt to escape, falling on her stomach the rake underneath her, protected. A man reaches out to her, and I tighten my grip on the Z-Colt. I expect him to push her aside and try to gain access to the broken rake, but instead he gently helps her up, puts the rake back in her hand and says to the group, "Together." An awkward formation assembles so that each one lays a hand on the rake, and as a group they climb the mound, carrying the find of the day. When the man turns from watching the pickers climb to the crest of the garbage hill, I see that it is Old Soul. His eyes search the area, and he spots us, transforming from tranquil mediator to urgent guide in a matter of seconds.

He is jogging, even as he beckons us to follow him, and we are right behind.

Leading the way to the underground hut, he says, "She's still alive."

"The surgery?" I ask.

"Just started."

"You couldn't do it sooner?

"Had to get Degnan to agree to it first."

"He didn't have a choice."

"That's right, but *he* had to know that, and once he got the right pep I think he did."

"Think?" I ask as we arrive at the stairs to the underground.

"Well, he's in there now giving the directions."

"Directions?"

"His hands aren't what you'd call stable."

"But Degnan's the surgeon. Who's operating on Pasha?"

"Well, it's not El or La."

I charge through the entrance, chanting "no" with each stair I descend. In the short time I have known Raben I have found him to be courageous, a fixer and someone who can build or repair anything with an abstract mish-mash of a supply list, but not a surgeon. How I hope it isn't him holding a knife to Pasha's head.

The last step into the circular room rapidly brings back memories. I lived and breathed sanitation in Reichel. Everything from peps to coveralls to work quarters were sanitized and programmed for a cleansed environment. What did I expect a surgical set up to be like in the center of a room located in a dump and etched from mud? Not this. I note a pot of boiling water on the wind generated hot plate at the edge of the room. In that pot rags boil. Dry, clean rags cover the mud floor. A hundred miniature reflections of Raben standing above Paha's skull swing on pieces of the hanging mirrors, reflecting the tension in the room.

Raben does not turn to look at me but says, "Don't talk. Don't."

I sit on the bottom stair and hear the children tiptoe in behind me. "Get them out. No noise," he says with carefully controlled breathing and no agitation in his voice. I gesture the children away, and they obey.

"Make that cut diagonal and small, an inch long." It is only as he speaks that I become aware of Degnan sitting on a stump just out of the light and chained to a metal pipe in the wall. The closer I look the more my eyes adjust to the light. I notice he speaks to Raben, but his ferocious stare penetrates me. I am thankful he is secured.

The pigeons coo on the beam above. Lying on a rudimentary table are the instruments of surgery that have been pulled from Pasha's medical pack. This table too is fashioned from the stump of a tree, with a stack of salvaged bricks propping it up on one side. Now these instruments, in the hands of an untrained picker, will save her life—or so I hope.

"Is there blood? Any gush or a spurt or a flow?" Degnan asks.

"Blood, but very little," answers Raben.

"Then look for a clot. A hardened—"

"I know what a clot is, and I am looking. There's more than one." Raben's voice, focused and confident, barely registers above a whisper, and yet our collective breathing sends a puff of air to the ceiling, causing the mirror fragments to collide and send a delicate chime-like ringing through this room of rags. And I can't help myself from praying to the image in Morris' Bible, in hopes that there is someone bigger than Raben, Old Soul and me who cares if this woman lives or dies. Somewhere in the midst of these desperate unfamiliar thoughts is a small center of thanksgiving, regardless of the outcome, for this man with the scalpel who willingly stepped into the role of Pasha's redeemer. Maybe it is more than thanksgiving I feel for him, but there is no time to sort that feeling out. We chose to run from Reichel, to defy The Third. An inkling of fear races around my heart, and I wonder if that time of "figuring out" will ever come, or if our feelings will remain jumbled, twirling through eternity.

———

The smell of the caked mud wall rouses me to attention, and I lift my head from its resting point, trying to sort out how much time has passed. How could I have dozed during a life and death moment? And at this very second I recall *locasa* and the salad spinner, and how I haven't had a chance to weigh and consider what the scientists took from me. I handle my Z-Colt well, run a steady pace without fatigue, but before my run-in with *locasa* at the Plethora Plant I would never have fallen asleep, even if I was sleep deprived for forty-eight hours.

I try to focus my eyes, and I see that Raben no longer stands in the position of surgeon. Instead, Old Soul sits by Pasha, taking vitals in an antiquated fashion, his fingers to her wrist. I stand up from the bottom stair, stretching as I walk to Pasha's side.

Degnan growls from his confinement on the perimeter of the room, "Unfortunately, the prognosis is good. She'll live. Couple days of rest—"

"We don't have a couple days," I say, and look at Degnan, not wanting him to be the one who has the medical answers, but knowing he's right. It means I must depend on him for the criteria regarding Pasha's health and when to pack this dump up for traveling.

"It's a brain injury. There's always a risk if you move a patient." His sarcasm makes me angry.

"How much of a risk?" I ask.

"Count the numbers. All of you get out now, at her expense, or keep her here a couple more days, at your expense. You calculate."

I am frozen. Numb. How many seconds go by before my calculations add up to the futures of Pasha, myself and all of these people? Thought process over. Now, only the plan matters.

I need air and am desperate to be somewhere besides in Degnan's presence. I say, "Old Soul—upstairs." We leave Degnan tied to the wall and Pasha lying unconscious but breathing on a tree-stump-table covered with rags. I say to him, "Collect the children and head north." Suddenly I am aware that all five of the library boys plus Trellis, La, El and Raben are staring at me, listening to my instructions. "You'll be followed by Raben." I lock eyes with Raben. "You and Trellis alternate on the travois, pulling Pasha, and I'll follow up with the prisoner." I give these commands and everyone follows orders, except Morris who bounds to my side.

He says, "I'll stay with you and guard the prisoner."

I hear Degnan yelling from below. "Yeah, let the little snot stay with me. We haven't been apart for almost a decade." Now I remember clearly why we called the guardians "pock-et- watches," never watching the boys except when absolutely necessary and always retreating to the private pockets of their lives, ignoring the kids whenever possible. I would love to put Degnan in a coat pocket and forget about him forever, and if it weren't for Pasha I would.

To Morris I say, "El, La and Carles are younger than you. You're needed up in the front with them. Keep them calm." He salutes, and I notice Raben watching me as Trellis readies the travois and Old Soul helps El and La collect their things and bundle them on their backs.

I check my weapon and say to Raben, "I wish he wouldn't do that."

"Salute?" he asks.

"Yeah, salute." Suddenly I can't seem to give my weapon my full attention. "Thank you," I say, noting that his hazel eyes continue to focus on mine. "Thank you, for Pasha."

"Always wanted to be a surgeon." With the corner of a rag attached to his belt, Raben wipes off a small piece of junk he's been holding in his hands. He passes it to me. "I picked it," he says. "A reminder."

"Of what?"

"Of biters—of an old soul—hanging mirrors—me." I laugh, and he responds with a sincere smile, not the sarcastic smile of McGinty and Shaw, but a smile I remember seeing somewhere before. I think maybe it is a smile not unlike my father's.

"What else?" I ask. "What else should I remember?"

"New friends." His eyes, still steady on mine, make me wish The Third would forget about us all and consider us worthless and nonthreatening. How I wish conversations like this might continue and develop, instead of constantly being terminated in order to give escape the top priority. Raben adjusts the 454 on my back, his hand brushing my cheek as it passes, and I don't feel "on the ready at all." And for the first time in a very long while, I'm okay with that.

Raben helps Trellis prepare the travois, and I look briefly at the piece of junk in my hand, presented as a gift. It is a small metal box—scratched, marred and crushed on the bottom, but still able to open. It is empty, and I realize it is the box that is the gift, not that I expected contents. I tuck the remembrance in the front of my pack.

Trellis, Old Soul and Raghill carefully carry Pasha, with as little movement as possible to the travois, gently tying her to the supports. The children have surrounded her traveling bed with a half circle of concerned observers. Morris and Raghill are deep in discussion and beckon the other children to accompany them to the underground stairs. "Forgot something," Raghill calls to us over his shoulder as they run to the hidden room.

Moments later they march back to our caravan, each carrying one of Pasha's pigeons. Morris and Raghill hold two birds apiece one under each arm. Morris clutches one of them, offering it to me. "Will you put Orbit in your pack, Avery, just to get her to Red Grove? Then we can build a new roost."

I walk away, "No way. I'm not carting poultry all the way to Red Grove."

"I'll take one," says Raben, scooping up one of the pigeons from Raghill, but Old Soul stops Raben from putting it in his pack.

"I've got it," says Old Soul, securing the cooing bird in his bundle. "You and Trellis focus on Pasha," Old Soul helps El and La pack the pigeons in their bundles, and Raghill does the same for the library boys, but Morris continues holding Orbit out to me, immoveable like a statue watching traffic from the park.

"Please," he says.

Then Raghill begs too, "They'll fly back to the roof of the unit if we don't take them and retrain them."

Prospero says, "You know what will happen to them there?"

Morris continues the appeal. "Either they starve death or The Third uses them for target practice. We can't just—"

"Okay, okay. I'll put it in my pack," I say.

"Her," says Raghill. "Put *her* in your pack."

"Okay just for a short while, then someone else can make room." I turn my back on Morris, while he and Raghill open my pack and convert it into traveling quarters for Orbit. Part of me would be ashamed to have an Elite training officer observe my actions, but part of me envisions Pasha waking up and us placing Herman and Orbit on her chest like nurses uniting mother and child in a delivery room. Which part of me is stronger? Of course, it is a question for another day.

I move to the head of the line. From the convoy behind I hear the voices of Morris and Raghill warbling the song I heard them sing at the children's garden by the library. But this time the song turns from an ironic chant by orphans claiming their parents to be books and a library, into a prophetic lullaby, comforting El and La as they leave the oozing dump and its biters by night and pickers by day, as they leave the only home they've ever known. *My papa is an old soul. My mama leads the pack. Together we're dysfunctional, but we ain't goin' back.* The words are awkward, but the melody gentle. They try to keep their voices at a whisper. None of us knows how long it will be until we hear the sound of float cars approaching, or don't hear them, as was the case just hours before the library burned. When the garden was still tilled and nurtured by a quirky group of abandon boys. I begin the journey to Red Grove with a steady jog, and everyone matches my gait.

———

There is no end to this forest and the further we trek the more intense the web of low branches, underbrush and closely grown evergreens becomes. If I wasn't on a mission to get to Red Grove, if life wasn't so urgent, so threatening, I would pause, meditate and soak up the power of this breathing forest. I can hear the voice of my father keeping pace with my steps, telling me the story of the trees. "A root system connects all the trees. Together they can withstand draught, lightning, fire and windstorm. They are dependent on one another. To continue this constant life, a cone from a giant branch must drop a seed directly in a nurture tree, a seemingly dead hollowed out log that welcomes the seed and cultivates it to sprout and grow." Over two thousand years old these trees will never stop living unless another *Jurbay* brings unwelcomed surprises. I can't quite put those thoughts behind me.

A tangled mesh of evergreen and deciduous trees prompts us to draw machetes and slash out a path. I hope this will only be necessary for several hundred feet, and that we will not still be cutting hours from now. I cannot stop thinking of Pasha at the back of the caravan, every bump or jerk threatening to yank her out of life. We need her. I need her. Did I consider friendship in the Elite Special Forces? Doubtful.

One slice through the snarled underbrush slashes a hole for me to observe nature's surprises. Two pools of dark blue-green water loom in front of me. One pool sits five feet above the other, fed by a spring, perpetually filling then spilling its contents in the form of a waterfall into the second pool. The pools, framed by a ring of ferns and white trilliums, seem to invite me to join the tranquil setting. I face a choice to delay the caravan or press on. Am I crazy to even consider a bath?

The Third's idea of baths comes in two varieties. The boys of the children's garden, who belong to the commanders and officers, are taken to the underground artisan wells, given a towel, bar of soap, and a twenty minute time limit to scrub, scour and emerge with skin squeaking. For the rest of us, what used to be a shower, before The Third demanded water efficiency, is now offered in the form of a vacuum suck, perfected to suck off any dirt, sweat or excrement in a series of calculated seconds. No muss, no fuss and the amount of water saved is enormous.

For a brief moment I ponder our collective morale. They are scared, confused and following a girl most have known less than a day. We could use a quick boost to our spirits. Do El and La have any memory of baths? Born after *Jurbay* and the occurrence of the 14 Deadlies, they would be expert scavengers trained to find a water source, but for drinking only. High school science and my mother's basic cleanliness lectures remind me of the connection between filth and disease. I consider the young librarians and the dump pickers to be extremely fortunate so far. I hack into the vegetation again, increasing the size of the hole so it looks like an open door, welcoming our human caravan to a secret immersion. I weigh the interruption in our journey. *Tie Degnan to a tree. Raben and I will fill the water flasks and place the iodized purification peps in each vessel while the others bathe. Place Pasha by the water. Cool her feet. Be back on the trail in five to seven minutes.* Decision made.

"Seven minutes, max," I say. "Get clean. Then we're headed off again."

Trellis leads the kids to the water. The boys from the children's garden dash to the pools and dive in clothes and all. Standing on the edge of the lower pool, El and La stare at the water, watching Trellis strip off his shirt and ease into the pool. He splashes a small amount of liquid onto El's face, and El reaches his hand to his cheek, rubbing the water unsure of what to expect. He scoops a small amount in his hand, letting it escape through his fingers. By this time Trellis is waist deep, leaning over and dunking his entire head underwater, washing his hair.

Unable to enjoy the water, Degnan taunts from the tree where he is tied. "Water's probably poison. Watch yourself. There's snakes swimming around in there." Old Soul sticks a rag in Degnan's mouth and the taunting turns to unintelligible grunts.

Raben and I ease Pasha's travois through the hole in the entangled brushwood and settle her by the lower pool. Old Soul collects the drinking containers, handing them to Raben for filling and purification tablets.

This leaves me free to attend to Pasha. While slipping off her boots, I remember the sterile surroundings of the medical compound where I had my appendix out when I was six. Nothing but a pristine hospital gown covered my body, certainly not filthy clothing and dirty feet. The dust has sifted through the boots, covering her feet. Mixed with sweat, they are dirt-caked. Pasha's feet are tiny, matching every other part of her petite frame, and I marvel how one so small has stood up to the rigors of planetary disaster, a secret invasion of Catalonia, emersion in the neurological ranks of The Third and separation from anyone she might have loved. We got out of touch from the time she was in her late teens until we reunited in Elite training. I always wondered if she'd had a family during that time. There are parts of Pasha that are so mother-like. The way she treats her pigeons. Her patience with El and La scrutinizing Herman. If she had a family, Elite training prevented her from mentioning it, and later, once she was selected by The Third, they wanted nothing to interfere with the use of Pasha's intelligence. Has she, like me, had a run in with *locasa*? Considering where we've all come to, it's better she remembers nothing, but if there was a family would they remember her?

I ladle the cool water from the pool onto her feet, massaging away the dirt until I eventually see clean skin. She does not respond to my touch. I long to see her flinch from the sensory overload, but she remains still, unmoved by the shock of the cold on her feet.

"The canteens are full," says Raben to me. "Your turn." He points at the pool.

"No time," I respond, and as I move away to tie the water containers to the packs, he scoops me up from behind and throws me in the water. I burst through the surface and everyone is frozen, looking at me. There have been times when

113

anger was my first response. Calculated anger. The kind I knew would illicit action and serve as a much better motivator than a gentle approach. It doesn't take me long to survey the many pairs of eyes in the group and realize this response should be calculated too, but not anger. I focus my gaze directly on Raben, making it clear to the others that they have my permission to retaliate on my behalf. Everyone charges him, dragging him under the water. The waterfall trickles into the pool and harmonizes with the children's squeals and Raben's protests, but the sound of Degnan's muffled complaints have ceased. I face the tree and see that he has wriggled his right arm out of the rope. I am just in time to observe him uncap a vile with his teeth and throw it toward the pool.

"Out of the pool!" I scream and the entire group, except for Prospero, scramble up the banks. I realize he cannot hear me from the top of the waterfall. In a slow motion roll we all face the water and see Prospero jump into the lower pool just as the open vial hits, dispersing its deadly effects.

"Deadly #12," sneers Degnan. "Water soluble. Results immediate. Residual life only forty-eighty hours, but time enough to do its job." When I met him, he was an impotent old man following orders from The Third, pepped down or up depending on the whims of gardeners and librarians too young to be at war. Now he is the devil himself, and I won't let him call the shots.

Prospero surfaces with screams, ungodly patches of skin peeling from his body. Old Soul, Raben and Trellis hold the other children back from surging into the water for an attempted rescue. *Please, not more than one casualty,* I beg the printed-paper Jesus in Morris' book, hoping he is more than history, but Deadly #12 makes quick work of Prospero's small form.

I bash my body hard against Degnan and feel his chest concave when he slams against the tree bark. "You devil," I yell. His eyes bulge, and I sense the increase in his heart rate. I take my knife from my coverall pocket and hold it to his neck.

He spits words in my face. "You murder me, and it will follow you the rest of your life. Not that you'll have a 'rest of your life.' They're tracking you." He holds up a tracker device in his untied hand, and I grab it, throwing it into the water where it momentarily rests then descends after Prospero into an impromptu tomb, following a thin line of bubbles to the depths below.

"This isn't murder," I say. "You're a casualty of war." I press the knife deeper into the skin folds of his neck, making him sweat before I kill him.

He sneers at me. "You have to have an army to have a war. You've got a few dump pickers and even fewer undersized children."

Raben pulls me off Degnan, his urgent voice barely above a whisper. "Right now, you need him for Pasha. I'll put eyes on Degnan for the rest of the trip. Trellis will pull the travois."

The screech of the float cars wails a warning above us. They hover mid-air, and I am glad The Third's mechanics didn't fix the entire fleet. Raben slashes the rope tying Degnan to the tree and throws him over his shoulder, heading for the forest on the far side of the pool.

I race to the forest edge, beckoning the children and counting each one as they run with Old Soul toward me. Trellis stumbles under the weight of travois, and I hope there is a quick way to pull Pasha through the forest underbrush.

I am the last one to leave the slashed doorway through the trees, coming face to face with McGinty in full combat gear, his FE-297 mounted on his shoulder and holding his finger to his lips for silence. No problem there. He lifts up a four inch sleek bullet, which I recognize as a brainy, developed fifty years ago as a smart bullet. The improvements have been dynamic. This bullet will follow a target around a tree, into a hole or if necessary reverse direction to hit its mark. McGinty stands ready, on the offensive, to face The Third's soldiers. I understand his intent and nod at him in agreement. He points to my right, and I see Shaw is there, also on the ready, holding his well-used knife in his teeth. I expect The Third will have a brainy, left over from stockpiled weapons, but I am certain they don't have the anti-brainy. That little invention belongs to McGinty, forged in the confines of our former unit 791. That's where McGinty's expertise came into play. His Elite training had focused on the study of weaponry, but his inventions remained a mystery to The Third. *Was Trader Bob able to get that information to The Third?* I think not. It seems the storage of GEB information must be extracted by removing the right ventricle where the fact-collection takes place. Shaw saw to that, putting Trader Bob to rest and carving out the ventricle, making sure his information never reached The Third.

Glancing at McGinty's FE-297, I see the two barrels for delivery, mounted one on top of the other, and two triggers. Why have two separate weapons if brainy and anti-brainy can ride in tandem?

I watch the enemy arrive and hold up my hand in the ready position, McGinty and Shaw watching for my command to fire.

Examining the tracker in his hand, one of The Third's Elite troopers points silently to the pool, and his sergeant's eyes follow in that direction. I think of Prospero, dead and resting now at the bottom of the pool infected with the Deadly #12. The other five troopers join the soldier who holds the tracker by the pool, and their sergeant says, "She's Elite trained and can stay underwater for minutes. Degnan had the tracker, and his command was to place it on DeTornada." There is silence as the troops wait for a command. The sergeant speaks quietly, distinctly. "If the tracker's under water—so is she. Get her out." He motions to the water with his weapon and four of the six troopers turn on their underwater head lights and descend into the depths of the pool, abandoning their weapons on the bank. It does not take long for them to shoot up out of the water with ghastly screams, ripping their clothing from their body as the #12 erodes their flesh with the vehemence its creators intended.

The sergeant again points his weapon toward the water, and the other two Elites fire shots, putting the writhing soldiers out of their misery and plunging them to their final rest. I cringe, thinking about Prospero sharing the watery tomb with four strangers from The Third.

I motion the command, and without delay McGinty and Shaw fire three shots apiece, and as the enemy troops run for cover behind the forest trees the brainy bullets have no trouble hitting their marks before The Third's Elite can fire off a shot.

A bit disappointed that I will not see the anti-brainy in action, I turn to McGinty and Shaw and say, "You're late."

# Chapter 7
# BLACK, SEARING HOLE

"McGinty. Shut up," I say, setting a quick pace, weaving in and out of the trees on our journey to Red Grove. "It's too early to declare a leader." In my soul, I know I spearhead our small group that searches for Red Grove, but public declarations terrify me.

"You're the logical choice," he says.

"Not likely. I'm the youngest."

"DeTornada. You've got the name."

"I can never tell if you're kidding me or serious."

"I'm not going to kid about something like this. Shaw might, but not me."

Shaw jogs up to the front of our serpentine line and is so close and in my face I'm claustrophobic. "Shaw might what?" he asks, but I don't answer. With cynicism he says, "I have no interest in the job at the top." He pats the knife strapped to the front of his vest like it is his first born. "My only interest is in ventricle surgery."

I don't find this funny, remembering how I'd witnessed Shaw's brutal extraction of Baldy's right ventricle before we left the cage. I try to shut the conversation down and say, "You don't need a leader if you don't have an army. No troops, minimal weapons, and last I checked not even The Third was conscripting children into battle."

"They might, once they find out they're *in* a battle," says McGinty. "Right now they think they're after four subterraneans, some pickers and a few kids."

"And they're not?" I respond. "Let's talk about it later when there's a reason to talk." I reverse direction, heading for the rear of the caravan. "I got the rear," I yell over my shoulder. "Shaw, you lead the way."

"Yes, sir," he says. No response necessary from me on that one.

First in line behind McGinty and Shaw is Morris, carrying Carles on his shoulders and holding La's hand, showing her the best way to maneuver through the trees. Next, Raghill and Lear follow. They have crisscrossed their wrists to create a makeshift chair for El to ride on. Little El, his form so tiny compared to the ten year old boys carrying him, looks at me passing by and tip-taps his pointer finger on the left side of his upper chest. I abandon my efforts to reach the end of the convoy and ask him, "What hurts?" I think of the bacteria that thrived in the dump and imagine some sort of terminal pericardial infection raging inside his waif-like body. Momentarily, Pasha comes to mind, and I think how diligent she would be, if she were able, to check these little ones out, determining the condition of their bodies and what kind of treatment they would need to be healthy, to be gaining weight, to be strong and whole. I ask again, "Is it your heart that hurts?"

Looking at me with vacant eyes, he wonders out loud. "Home?" And I am painfully aware that, no matter what age or what level of understanding, we all have this traveler's remorse: On the road, with no choice for a return trip, wanting a reunion, yet aware that death might surprise us at any impromptu gathering. These travelers hope Red Grove will provide the answers. I know it won't. Red Grove offers only a temporary safe haven, a place to rest until strategy grows the legs to march into a battle still to be defined.

I tap the spot on El's chest, synchronizing my tap with his. "Home's in here," I say. I know for some this is true, and I want it to be true for me.

I continue my jog toward the back of the caravan. *Ironic*, I think. *McGinty, Shaw, Raben, Pasha and I should have been the generation next in line for the hand-off of a reasonably stable universe. At our age, we should be anticipating the fulfillment of our destiny, taking our turn at fixing humankind and all its errors. Instead, we got handed half a continent, a reduced population and more problems than ten generations could solve.*

I imagine I hear El's finger pounding on his chest like death drums, beating in a jungle. The ones born after *Jurbay*, the Raghills, the Els and the Annalyns of this world, what will we hand them? A wandering existence that eventually must take a violent stand in hopes of a future that holds integrity as sacred? I say a quiet prayer, asking that we all might be up for the challenge, asking that we all might live long enough to try. I hear no answers, and I wonder if I can train myself to listen to that silence.

Continuing down the line, I find Trellis pulling Pasha in the travois, and as I pass I can't help but take a glance at her face, wanting to see her eyes open or hear her barking voice spitting cynicism as easily as The Third spits lies. Nothing seems alive on Pasha, only a barely discernible rise and fall of her frail chest. I'll take that as encouragement for now. Degnan trails thirty paces behind the travois with his wrists tied behind him, and Old Soul hanging onto the tail of the rope connected to Degnan, like he's walking a dog.

I insist Trellis and Raben take turns checking on Pasha. There is no way I will allow Pasha within Degnan's reach. He just murdered an innocent child. Poor Prospero. We all came so close to sinking in the pool and out of life with the Deadly #12 as the victor. We were lucky this time, not like before when *Jurbay* gobbled half our nation and much of the continents to the north and south of us. The Third saw its chance, as the continents attempted recovery, to gain world domination. They developed a long line of communicable horrors in an attempt to take all international threats away. The designer deadlies marched into one country, spinning the display of their strains, then moving across the borders and striking again. By the time the parade had dwindled to an end it had succeeded in accomplishing its purpose: reducing the world's population and eliminating any threat to our nation. However, as usual, The Third viewed the future with limited vision. The 14 Deadlies had also stomped though *our* populous, decreasing our numbers again, after *Jurbay* had taken its toll. Infrastructure erodes when there's no one to run it. Scientists forget their hypothesis, writers misplace their words and government seizes the opportunity to grow into a manipulative monster in solid control of a catatonic nation.

I try to bring my mind back to the business of escape and notice Raben, trailing at the end of the line, meticulously concealing any signs of our travel. Using the needled end of a tree branch, he camouflages the travois tracks and any sign of footprints. *Impressive,* I think, *Making an intuitive decision without my prompting. Maybe he should lead The 28 United.*

"Good idea," I say and grab a tree branch to join him in the cover up. I notice him salvage a small piece of twisted metal and pocket it, and within a few seconds he collects a handful of seed cones and loads them into his pack. "I like that about you." The look on his face is quizzical. "The way you save what I'd pass by. The way you see value in what others might dub 'worthless.'"

"Everything's waiting for collection," he says, and his smile seems out of place in the current scenario, yet like a welcome sign on a stranger's door. As the caravan advances forward, so do Raben and I, sweeping ground, moving in short steps toward each other until we are no longer sweeping, just staring at one another. For long moments we face each other, me feeling his gentle breath on my cheek. Him, I'm sure, feeling nothing, for I have stopped breathing, mesmerized by close proximity. It is Raben who breaks away and speeds up his trail maintenance, trying to regain the pace of the travelers, maybe even regain composure. He is on one side of the trail, and I am on the other.

Lear races through the trees, stopping abruptly when he reaches me, staring up into my face. "Shaw needs you in the front." He still wears the polka dot golf hat, and I think about asking him to remove it. It sticks out in a forest, and we need to blend in. Then I think of how much he's lost in such a short time and somehow the golf hat seems irrelevant. It would be a selfish request on my part.

"Tell him I'm on my way," I say and watch Lear continue past us, heading in the wrong direction. "Hey, you're going the wrong way."

"Lost my copy of *Macbeth*. Know right where it is."

"You're kidding, right?" I can tell from his furrowed brow he isn't kidding. "You need to stay with us."

"It's close. Over there."

"Be back in under a minute," I caution him.

"Register that," he says. Of all the boys from the library, Lear seems to know the most about the forest. I had asked him earlier if he had ever been camping like I had as a kid. "No," he said. "Just spent a lot of time in the 'T' aisle."

"T?" I asked.

"Trees. Deciduous, evergreen, oak and fir." I like the way he applies his book learning to the here and now. To the forest.

"Been having some strange dreams recently," says Raben to me. "Terrifying. You ever get those?" he asks.

"I've had too many real nightmares. Can't let my dreams haunt me."

"So how do you do that?"

"Block them out."

"But how?"

"I speak Tibetan. Pasha taught me." I smile just a little when I say her name. "If I wake up with any remembrance or fear, I just divert it by thinking in Tibetan. Dreams are easily confused."

"Well, maybe I'll have to take lessons from her."

"Don't get too excited. I'm finding it doesn't work in all the situations she thought it might." His face is troubled. "That bad?" I ask.

"It starts with a star exploding in my head." He continues working to eliminate the trail.

"A star?"

"Like a stimulus—a trigger—calling me to something I should remember."

"I've had a few of those."

"But then it turns violent. The star starts to poke at my brain, prickly at first—then gnarly, hard, pressing, pounding, screaming to get out, and it does. It rolls down my wind pipe, cutting holes as it goes. Then bouncing against every organ, severing them from their purpose until the star spikes at my feet, needling the bottoms of my soles, my blood running out." He stops. The caravan has moved through the trees, out of sight. We stand alone, facing each other. "I've never talk-ed about the dreams," he says, moving toward me. Now, he seems unconcerned about leaving his footprints on the forest floor. He takes my hand.

I say, "By speaking we confront the meanings of our—" But there is no finish to my sentence, only the beginning of what we have both felt, both feel. He kisses me. I kiss him back. It seems like I am home.

A twig snaps in the thicket, I raise my hand for silence before Raben can speak. Another snap followed by a swishing noise, sounding similar to Raben sweeping the ground with the needles of the tree branch, but louder, more dramatic. I ready my SE454, but the magazine needs replacing. *Why would I carry a weapon not loaded and on the ready?* Then I realize I don't know how to load it or even where I carry the extra magazines. I search the pockets of my coverall vest. Right beyond our tree line at the back of our makeshift trail I hear a cracking sound and a rustling, this time closer and ac-companied by a low hiss. Then, a brain-swapper slithers out toward us.

I whisper, "Brain-swapper. Looks like they've mixed wolf genes with a python."

"The Third loves experiments," says Raben, barely au-dible. We inch our way backwards, slowly. "You thinking we need to be a diversion for the rest of the caravan?"

"Yeah." The brain-swapper winds its way toward us, belly on the ground. Its wolf-like head cocked to the side, mouth in a vicious snarl and tongue lapping like a thirsty dog. Suddenly its head snaps to attention and its eyes, hungry for prey, appear almost contemplative, sizing us up. Maybe deciding which of us it will eat first. I see a rolling movement down its serpent back. Something as big as a medium-size animal undulates around the inside of the beast, like digestion from a recent lunch. "I don't remember how to load the magazine for this weapon," I whisper.

"Where's the ammo?"

"I don't know that either. Maybe my pack."

"Hand the weapon to me. Go slow." I pass it over to Raben, and he takes it with one hand. His other hand reaches to the pocket on the leg of my coverall, lifting the ammunition from its storage. He didn't even try my pack.

Sweat pours into my eyes, and my heart races like it's trying to leave my body. Its rhythm chants and pounds: *You used to be steady. Nerves like steel.* There is no time to settle up with my insecurities. The brain-swapper raises its wolf head, three times the size of a normal wolf, opening its snarl and revealing a cavern-like black hole. It is then I see Lear's polka dot golf hat, tattered and covered with blood and slime, clinging to the tooth of the brain-swapper. The monster continues to raise its scaly, cylindrical body upward, maybe twelve feet in the air, in what I believe is a strike pose. I smell urine, as the swapper lets loose spraying the ground before him. I feel drops splatter my skin and the reek stinks with an unforgettable order. "You climb trees?" I ask Raben.

"Best place for a picker to spot unclaimed treasure." He glances behind his shoulder. "Tree—ten feet to your left. Get behind the trunk where it can't get at us without passing the tree and turning around."

"Yeah, it's too big to do a quick turn."

"But eventually it will turn." I hear Raben breathing heavy, but not as heavy as the swapper that smacks its lips, emitting a raspy howl. "Now," yells Raben, and we sprint behind the tree. I scramble up the branches and feel the scales from the back of the beast rake across my calf, slicing through my coverall and into my skin as it begins the process of turning its mammoth body around.

"Faster," yells Raben, his body right behind me. As soon as my hands vacate a branch, his hands take over the branches. We advance up the trunk. The smell is closer. The howl pierces the air, and I know the swapper is headed up behind us, using its snake-like belly to slither up the tree. Then silence. The swapper drops from the tree and the ground vibrates with the force of its fall.

"Come on, swapper. Come for us," chants a choir of voices. Looking down, I see the pickers from the dump, ones that have not been traveling with our caravan. How long have these pickers been following us? They wave their walking sticks and broken shovel handles at the beast, daring it to chase them. The swapper chooses to follow the gang of taunting pickers, and twenty or so of them rush the beast with the tools of their trade transformed into weapons. They slam their homemade picker claws into the back of the brain-swapper, some breaking the surface of its scales causing a greenish-yellow river of liquid to spurt from the monster's wounds. Others, not able to penetrate the beast's skin, fight a losing battle as the swapper swings its tail, tossing them like feathers against the trees. Three pickers hold on, claws entrenched in the beast's neck. It turns its wolf head toward them, teeth snapping.

Raben tries for the third time to load the magazine in the 454 with no results. I'm thinking maybe I could remember the process, but just as the brain-swapper opens its jaws, a round from the magazine zings through its open mouth, lodging somewhere in its body, exploding the thing into hundreds of pieces.

Raben and I climb down from the tree, slipping on the swapper guts as we descend and running to the injured pickers sprawled on the ground from the blast of the explosion. The old woman from the dump, that had earlier claimed the rake from Raghill, lies stomach down on the forest floor. I turn her over, and she opens her eyes. Looking skyward she asks, "Did we get him?"

"Yeah," I answer overcome with gratitude for her courage to charge a brain-swapper and for Raben's persistence to figure out how to load the magazine. I turn to thank him, but am met by a shove on my shoulder that sends me to the ground.

Shaw stands, confronting me, yelling, "You didn't run the zig-zag!"

I shout back, "I wasn't trained to run from a brain-swapper!"

"And you didn't plan to have anyone cover your back."

"Raben covered my back."

"Yeah, I can see that. With *your* weapon."

I see McGinty standing behind Shaw. He grabs Shaw away from me to calm him down. The veins in the temples of McGinty's head pulse, and he comes face to face with me as I regain my footing. "It's the first rule, Avery. Protect self and cover team," says McGinty. I can't bear to tell them why Raben had my 454. What kind of leader can't load a weapon? I don't have the answer to that—or maybe I do.

It's only now I see the entire caravan standing just beyond our conversation. Shaw turns in a sulk leaving me behind, then stops, looking back to stare at me, an assault on his lips. "You better find out what you lost, Avery—what *locasa* took— or we'll all be lost."

Raben hands me back my weapon and follows Shaw to the front of the caravan. The pickers help one another up and follow in the same direction, expanding our convoy by another thirty or so.

Degnan looks on from his leash, still held securely in tow by Old Soul. A smirk expands over Degnan's mouth. "Maybe we ought to ask those scientists to swap your brain with something else, DeTornada. Your mother's, perhaps?" Old Soul is pulling Degnan away out of ear shot, but I hear him continue to hurl his sarcasm, even as the forest closes in on him. "What about a swap with Carles? Oh, no, wait—he's dead. I've got it—Officer Borden." It is only as I glance back one more time to make sure he's gone that I see the boys, making their way through the trees.

Morris leads the way, stepping into the clearing, his eyes glued on the remains of the brain-swapper splattered across the forest floor. Raghill follows behind, holding Carles' hand. With my eyes I track them. Then I see it. Lear's polka-dot golf hat lying in the mess. Morris and the boys surround the hat, staring. Morris flicks a chunk of swapper guts with the toe of his boot. Then he kicks another pile and another. Raghill and Carles do the same—angry kicks over and over again until all three are exhausted and breathing heavily, hardly able to stand. Only then does Morris pick up Lear's hat and start to make the trip back to the caravan.

Following close behind, Raghill and Carles keep pace with Morris until Carles sprints ahead and stops Morris. Carles takes Lear's hat, slimy and spackled with blood and puts it on his own head. The boys march together to join the group, leaving McGinty and me alone.

McGinty gives me time to speak. Maybe he thinks I will defend myself, but I don't. I am silent. Finally, he says, "You want to talk about it? Figure it out?"

"What's to figure out?" I ask him. "With *locasa* you can't figure out what's gone until things turn up missing."

"Your training?"

"Yeah. I still know how to use my Z-Colt, but when I went to load the 454…"

"Yeah. Yeah, I know." We are both still for a time. "You know, Avery, it wasn't the training that tied us all together." I nod. I know what he means. McGinty places his hands on my arms just below my shoulders and draws me closer to him. His touch is electric, yanking me up from my stew of self-pity. "We got you covered, Avery. We can protect you, keep you safe. We got your back. But the rest of it—the person in charge—the decision maker—"

"The fall guy?"

"Yeah, the fall guy. That's you. Can you cover us on that?" He looks at the caravan. "Can you cover *them* on that?"

I continue to nod my head steady, sure, but my insides cramp from contact with the truth. The grief from this black, searing hole within me surpasses reason and drags me to the mirror, taunting. *Look! You are not who you used to be.* And I realize that Avery DeTornada left, cleaving to her competent weapon skills and her stealth so honed that the most brilliant of enemies failed to detect her. She carted away her martial arts repertoire, her Elite training and now that she is MIA, the searing hole gets bigger by the hour. I am left to wonder: *Who am I?* McGinty seems sure. I am not.

Loss pounds beneath my skin, searching for an exit, and for the first time since I was very young, I cry. My body shakes, rebelling against the sobs. McGinty pulls me close, holding tight, and the little girl inside me swims to the surface. The injustice of The Third's corruption fires darts at my spirit and, for a moment, McGinty's arms repel them. The fear of what I can't do fights for control of what I can do, what I'm called to do. What I must do. That's all it takes, a moment. Then I pull away from McGinty, take a restorative breath, check the line of travelers, move to the front of the group and start the progress of the caravan. Barring the unforeseen, we will reach Red Grove by nightfall, settle in for some rest and strategize our future. Unfortunately, the unforeseen always has a plan.

# Chapter 8
# THE TIGHTER GRIP

The discovery of the four float cars must be credited solely to Morris. His indomitable curiosity, mixed with a bit of a chip on his shoulder, led him on a search west of the convoy. Of course he did the unthinkable, separating himself and going alone, but how could I be angry when his incorrigible bravery provided us with the means to lift out of the tangle of the forest and reach the heights of Red Grove? I'd never thought of having children of my own until I met this boy. If motherhood ever visits, let her bring me a gift like Morris. His inquisitiveness can be simultaneously exhausting and therapeutic. I think his curiosity might spring from a familiarity with books, but there is instinct within him too. In spite of our psychological fatigue from the recent tragedies, he continues to divert us, prompting us to contemplate and prodding us to argue and debate. When I remind myself who his father is I am struck by Morris' resiliency. Borden deserted

Morris, his own son, to Degnan a pocket-watch. Morris, child of abandonment, who never abandons us.

Though only together a matter of days, grief is the bond linking our travelers, each experiencing his own loss, and yet joined together as a community through the death of Prospero and Lear. We share rebellion too, quiet as it is. These fresh, raw wounds make us desperate for rest. Is fatigue the reason I scoff at myself for the tender thoughts I have for this new family. Thoughts that have nothing to do with the tactic of survival, but everything to do with the necessity of life. An Elite mind negates the humanity of the universe in favor of the objective. Maybe *locasa* did me a favor. In some ways it is good to have my humanity back.

Dawn, peeking through the canopy of three hundred foot trees, might be easily missed in the Red Grove forest. Light filters slowly from that far up, dropping a limited number of sunbeams. Had I been sleeping, I would have missed the moment when dark was sucked away by the breath of day. But I don't sleep. There is no option to camp along the way, especially since our group, with the addition of the new pickers, is much larger and cannot be hidden anymore. We are forging on, determined, no matter how dead-tired we are, to arrive at the safe haven as soon as possible. I still refuse to call Red Grove "headquarters," as Shaw and McGinty do. Maybe someday I'll feel comfortable with the name when it actually becomes a command center and a strategic hub for operations.

"That's thirty-two new ones," says Raben as he stares into the faces of his comrades from the dump. "Adding all of us, that's forty-five, and there might be a few more out there, lagging. So, say fifty, tops."

I ask McGinty, "How far to Red Grove now?" He and Shaw just made the journey to find us, and they know the terrain, the challenges.

"Just under thirty-six zip lengths," he replies. I know that is no different than one hundred or five hundred without supplies and proper boots. Most of these pickers are barefoot or have fashioned wraps of rags around their feet, simulating shoes. So Morris' discovery of the float cars left by The Third placed opportunity before us to reach Red Grove by late morning.

"So how is Red Grove? Fit for command?" I ask.

"We've only been there three days," says McGinty. "We came straight over after Shaw met Trader Bob. The whole time we trained in Elite and worked in the plant, Quinn had her people busy in Red Grove. I think you'll be pleased."

The travelers forage for food, while McGinty and Shaw stand at the ready with their weapons. Raben and Trellis keep watch over Pasha while Old Soul continues on Degnan-duty a couple hundred feet away, out of ear shot. Morris and I lash swags from small branches together, making handholds to be tied around the metal structure of the float cars. Four of them must carry us all to the top branches of Red Grove without crashing. A sudden movement might shake a passenger from the frame. These planes are maybe thirty feet long with an open scaffolding framework. Morris tells me these float cars have no artificial intelligence. Rather, intuitive controls using three bars at knee-level. The mechanical system depends on pilot instinct and rotors started by hand—the wind they stir fuels the float car.

As we prep the planes for flight, Morris and Raghill embrace the art of recitation. After all, they had salvaged as many book-boxes as they could from the burning shelves of the library and aren't about to leave the guarding of information to another storage facility, another fire. With paper and computers limited, the human mind seems like the perfect spot to build a retrievable library. I hope Morris and Raghill will never again meet with the fire of Borden, or confront the torture of the deadlies or ever have to face the one we call Commander Dorsey. However, while the information stored in the boys' brains may be our salvation, if The Third ever gets hold of Morris and Raghill the regime will retrieve and use the information, and it won't matter if the boys choose not to give it up.

While Raghill and Morris recite, I finish the handholds and begin the process of arranging the travelers according to weight, placing each one strategically in a position to balance the plane. Of course these planes were never designed to hold more than eight trained soldiers and supplies, so fifty dump pickers, kids and subterraneans do not offer hope for stability or speed.

The shape of the scaffolding on the vehicle is more elongated than what a painter might use on the side of a building, a bit egg-shaped.

"They look like a fleet of metal rainbows," Raghill says, standing fifty feet from the float cars, observing.

"Might be a sign," says Morris. "Like when the great flood covered and destroyed earth and a rainbow—actually, the first rainbow—was sent to promise that the earth would never be destroyed again by a flood."

"Great," I say. "At least we don't have to worry about rain."

And I wonder what I would have to do to obtain that kind of a promise? A promise that there would never again be a *Jurbay,* or a Third or designer deadlies that gobble the world's population.

———

The under-sea cables were cut by several angry nations in retaliation for the 14 Deadlies that The Third had sent to invade these overseas countries. This damaged the world-wide web, already limping along due to satellite destruction by *Jurbay.* And once the deadlies had reduced our population and the world's as well The Third had some choices to make. They could not pursue the reclamation of everything. Infrastructures do not run without millions of people firmly in place to operate them. So the world-wide web, technologically advanced strategic air systems, food provisions, distributions of goods, trade and anything else requiring collections of people simply stopped, and The Third ended up putting their efforts into concocting genetic recipes that had no place in the scientific laboratories of a world leader. Discarding morality like a toxic, unsuccessful formula, their only motivation became the protection of what they had left: a small, efficient city in their complete control. GEBs became the weapon of choice, in an experimental stage of course, leaving the nuclear, chemical and bacterial warfare for re-creation at a later time. GEBs, when perfected, would be sent by The Third to distressed countries, offering assistance to rebuild what The Third had destroyed in the first place. By that time GEBs would be disease resistant, highly trained for the evaluation of hostile settings and an efficient fighting force able to root out any remaining national loyalties. We don't know how many GEBs have moved from the lab to trial infiltration, but we know for sure Trader Bob was out there and was eliminated, and Baldy never made it out of the lab. So for now, The Third remains content and focused on the power of deadly disease, laboratory birthed duplicates and, of course, *locasa*.

*Locasa*, while brilliant in its conception, belonged to the scientific minds of the Catalonian people. When stolen it was not complete in its design. Its projected vision: remove traumatic memory. The hope was that those memories might be returned to the victims when they gained the tools necessary to handle the trauma. *Locasa* was to allow a psychological sabbatical, giving the psyche time to heal and learn to employ techniques of coping and restoration. But The Third only concerned itself with the removal of information that might stand between them and their complete power over Reichel, and once the GEBs passed out of the experimental stage, The Third would seek total control over the devastated world. Arrogant, they never imagined Quinn and Carles DeTornada were silently declaring resistance.

———

Just finishing his recitation on electrical power grids, Morris' hands are calloused and bleeding from wrapping the lashings to the float plane structure. He says, "I feel seventy."

"Are you an old soul too, Morris?" I ask, realizing if it wasn't for my memory of Morris and Raghill racing on the library ladders, I might forget that he's only ten and exhibits far more wisdom than most adults I know.

"I never cried for Prospero," he says and bends the thin, supple branch he holds around the five inch diameter piece of steel on the structure on the plane. "I never cried for Lear."

"Understandable, Morris. You can't really take the time to cry when you're hunted and on the run."

"I think I have that old people disease from a long time ago where tears dry up and disappear. Am I happier without tears, Avery?"

"I think you and I are a lot alike. I almost never cry."

"Are you happy?" I don't answer him. "Are you happier without tears?"

"Maybe we'll find out together," I say and let my eyes follow Raben who climbs the structure of the float car to the top bar, then lies on his stomach and reaches across the spider web of framework to test the stability of the lashed branches. He looks like both a kindergarten child from the old days, reaching the heights of the monkey bars and at the same time fills the role of itinerant warrior. His muscles, well-toned from the constant physical activity of picking, do not go unnoticed.

I lie on my back on the forest floor, arms pointed upwards to the cross bar of the float car frame, making final adjustments before loading our remnant of loyal ones. Raben, facing downward from the top bar by the pilot's seat, accomplishes the same task as me.

"Marriage," says Morris and begins another recitation of seemingly random information. In the past two hours he and Raghill have covered the options of reclaiming the undersea cables, the benefits of expanding zip lines (Pasha would be proud), the history of what used to be called Congress and commerce on the Mississippi River pre-*Jurbay*. Now they are onto what The Third calls: antiquated institutions.

"Marriage," he says again, though everyone continues to work and no one appears to listen. "A perpetuation of species, declaration of property rights, protection of the bloodline," he recites, like he's reading from a leather-bound book. "I think it's more than that," says Morris, and I knew he'd have an opinion.

"Arranged fates of strangers," says Raghill. Raben stops tightening the lashes, staring down at me.

"Arranged fates of strangers?" questions Morris. "Hardly. Pope Nicholas declared in 866, 'If consent be lacking in a marriage all other celebrations are rendered void.'"

I break eye contact with Raben, working steadily on securing the handholds. I say, "The Third voided marriage, Morris, and I don't think there's anything a Pope ever said that will bring it back."

Morris argues. "The Third didn't give you permission to leave the cage, but you left." He jumps off the plane and kneels at my side, giving me a prime view of his moon-like eyes. "Did they say the pickers could leave the dump and join a caravan of rebels? They voided marriage. We let them take our family unit away."

"*Locasa* did that. *We* didn't let them," I remind him.

"Maybe not, but we can put it back. The family. The marriage."

"We can start family units without marriage."

"Your parents were married, Avery. It's the commitment The Third hates." Morris climbs back up the framework of the plane like a spider examining his newly formed web. "Marriage becomes a weapon. With every marriage we tell The Third: 'We don't yield. You don't rule. You can't take our history, our beliefs—our family.'" Now he stands in the open cockpit on top of the plane like a historic union organizer, except we have no unions and our history is slipping away.

"How old are you, Morris?" I ask. "Thirty?"

"Hey, Morris," Raben interrupts Morris' rant. "Come show me how to fly this thing. We're gonna need four pilots."

Morris climbs the bars to the open cockpit, calling over his shoulder. "*Locasa* grabbed our families. We'll redefine marriage and defy The Third with every vow."

"Are you always so opinionated on everything you memorize?" I ask.

"Always. My father taught me."

"Borden?"

"Not Borden, the Library." He and Raghill sing a robust chorus of *My Papa was Library, My Mama was a Book. We know that we're dysfunctional, but no one ever looks,* all the while showing Raben and Shaw the basics of flying a float car.

I cringe, thinking about the new family the boys had built within the confines of the garden and the library, and how they must long for that unit now that it's gone. Nausea twists through my stomach as I glance over at Carles, still wearing Lear's hat. Only three are left of all their garden comrades, their fellow librarians, and if Pasha were conscious she would know how to talk to these kids about loss. Maybe the best therapy I can give is to try to let some sort of normalcy rise up, and if that's Morris reciting and debating every topic on his agenda, then let it be.

Orbit squawks a holy ruckus from the interior of my backpack. I can't imagine what it will do when the rotors fire up. Unsure why I ever agreed to allow children to pilot two of the float cars, I watch Morris and Raghill finish up the training for the pilot recruit, Raben. Shaw will fly the final car. He has been a pilot in the past.

The pickers are now evenly balanced on the framework of the float car, and I explain to them that their hands must be secured under the lashings even if the branches cut their skin. They parrot back the instructions to me. "That means never moving. No matter what we stay still." Their chorus strikes me as funny 'cause they stream the words back to me in one voice, copying my every intonation. Elite trained subterraneans do not laugh in the middle of a mission, but I can't help it.

All four planes are loaded, and I make sure Degnan is not on my float car. Of course he missed the lesson about balance and hand holds, so with any luck he might fall off. I slip into position beside Pasha who is now lashed onto the plane in her travois, like a body in an open casket waiting for viewing. My fingers from one hand dig into a hold position, and I balance my other hand on Pasha's leg, hoping nothing will shake her out of the carrier. All four pilots engage their rotor buttons and three appointed pickers join McGinty in giving the rotors a manual start. Then they leap to their positions on the framework. The noise from the rotors, whirling in circles, is deafening and causes continual gusts of wind whipping our hair and clothing. The gusts shake us all, and we flinch in unison from the force. Then, we all settle, determined not to upset our pilot's intuitive balance. Even above the rotor whir Orbit screeches to the heavens.

Here, in the turmoil of eight rotors working tirelessly to advance us upward to the height of the grove, in the epicenter of this attempted escape, I feel her hand take mine, and I look into Pasha's face. With open eyes her ghostly countenance recognizes me. I mime the words, "Stay still."

I lean my ear to her lips in hopes of hearing her first comment as she returns from what we feared was an untimely death. Barely audible she says, "I can fly this plane better than them." Pasha's back. She closes her eyes, but her lips continue to move. "Give me my pigeons," she says. I think *Oh, lady, first step inside Red Grove they're all yours.* I try to count the rotor whirls, estimating how long it will take before we climb to the tallest branches of the forest. Any estimate I make is not soon enough. I am tired of running, of escape. I want to rock in the arms of Red Grove, the sanctuary my parents created.

———

As a kid, I did not recognize Quinn's sixth sense that gave her an advantage when making decisions in a way other mothers might not make them. She exercised these abilities in a manner so subtly crafted that as a child I thought all mothers operated with the kind of insight that yanked their children from a car moments before a traffic collision occurred.

One day Quinn and I traveled in the outdoor corridors of a street market in the middle of an exhausting search for the perfect bike. She suddenly grabbed my arm and held it firmly. "Let's just wander up the street and find some shaved ice in your favorite flavor."

"I want to keep looking for the right bike," I argued.

"Tangerine Ice?" She turned us in the opposite direction. Reflecting back, I could feel her urgency in that firm hold on my arm. Walking swiftly away from the market, I felt a jarring vibration. Swiveling around, I saw a semi-truck smashing the market booths and sliding the piles of venders' goods in our direction, like the water of garden hose, its power unleashed on a leaf strewn driveway. The speed it traveled was terrifying and left no options for the victims in its path. They were jumbled into the mix, gaining momentum as everything swirled into a speeding ball.

Quinn grabbed me in her arms and ran to the end of the block, abruptly turning the corner, letting the twenty foot high clump of twisted metal, bike parts, tent covers and assorted flower shops come to a final resting spot right beyond us. The pedestrians we had walked with moments before had been crumpled in the pile.

As I look back now, Quinn's premonitions, insights and discernments seem an extraordinary gift. Now I recognize that my father, Carles, acknowledged this gift in Quinn and facilitated her using it. Their joint venture included his military brilliance and her supernatural perceptions. Together they planned to do whatever necessary to stop The Third from creeping into a power like a hooded, faceless being bearing a death sentence for a once united nation. This union between my mother and father, between two different but very powerful warriors, each qualified in their own right, led to the conception of Red Grove.

It was four years before *Jurbay* claimed half our world, while The Third pretended to be the righteous guardian of the government, that Quinn's sixth sense identified The Third's disguise and unmasked their true identity. This truth, shared with Carles, led to the conception and embryonic stages of The 28 United. Guarded in secrecy, two warriors gave birth to a command center to protect the emerging group of loyal followers in a hideaway called Red Grove.

Even before The Third provided Comprehensive Medical Care, using *locasa* to retrieve the memories of families, Quinn said, "There must be a place where they cannot reach us.

Where we can reassemble, if it becomes necessary. A strategic sanctuary. An invisible asylum. A haven where they could not imagine we would be because no place like it exists. We must create it from our imaginations."

From that moment on I never played with other children. My parent's suspicions wrapped around the households of previous schoolmates, so I was taken out of school and began to learn at home. Carles taught me in the beginning while Quinn pored over electronic libraries of scientific architecture, historical nature preserves and hacked the university records of the most brilliant medical students. She briefly reviewed their academic credentials and then dissected their doctoral theses with the skill of a university department head. She knew what she wanted, and eight years after she began her search, I started to see the name Dr. Pasha Lutnik appearing on the screen of Quinn's transmitter, scratched innumerable times in the margins of her research materials and printed at the bottom of diagrams she sketched, drawings that made no sense to me.

My mother Quinn knew how to spot a treasure. Be it the discovery of a descending eagle in quest of her midday meal or the unearthing of a delicate four leaf clover camouflaged in the twisted arms of crabgrass. Quinn valued the moments never to be repeated and encouraged my curious search for the wonder of the ordinary.

Nonetheless, I found it odd when I was eleven years old and came home one day, opened the door to our bathroom and found Pasha, sitting fully clothed, in our bathtub. She was another treasure recently acquired by my mother. The water was a little brown, having flowed through rusted pipes unused since the vacuum sucks took over our hygiene. A small pigeon roosted on her right shoulder then, seconds later, carefully side-stepped its way into her matted hair, dusted with feathers. She seemed not to notice me, and counted, in a muffled voice, as she worked on an outdated Rubik's Cube, her hands underwater. Her demeanor, so small, made the bathtub seem enormous. Surrounded by many Rubik's Cubes lined up along the tub edge, she was counting the ones she had completed. "Eleven, twelve, thirteen," she said, and then she set the one currently in her hand with the others on the tub-rim, declaring, "Fourteen. Done."

She cocked her head the way most birds do, looking at me and jutting her chin in and out with a poultry-like movement. "You like pigeons?" she inquired.

"They're dirty," I said, wrinkling my nose.

"They're friendly." She waited for me to take my turn, selecting an adjective, and when I didn't, she said, "And smart."

"Suppose it solved all those stupid cubes for you?" I pointed at the lineup of square, multi-colored blocks.

"She's smart. But not as smart as me." The pigeon flew from Pasha's shoulder toward me causing me to step backwards and utter a ridiculous squawk. "You sound like a crow," she said.

"And you look like an idiot sitting in brown water with your clothes on working games with a dirty piece of poultry on your head."

"Name's 'Reuther.'"

"That's an absurd name for a girl."

"It's her name, not mine." She reached up and stroked the pigeon's back.

I yelled out the door in a voice that could easily reach downstairs, "Mom. Mother! Have you been in the bathroom lately?" But I knew she had. I knew Quinn had been making plans for Pasha long before Pasha even knew who Quinn was. And so began the nurturing of Pasha Lutnik by Quinn DeTornada. Quinn, the discoverer of treasures.

Pasha stood up, dripping wet. "I'm Dr. Pasha Lutnik. I'm fourteen years old, and if the Rubik's Cube hadn't been invented, I would have invented it myself. I'm proficient."

I scrutinized her strange attire—a long tattered skirt, a jacket too big for her tiny frame, an umbrella tied onto her belt and military boots that looked like they'd belonged on someone twice her size. "Are you playing dress-up or what?" I asked her.

She stepped out of the bathtub, holding up her right hand and allowing Reuther to land. "I'm inspired by the clothes I wear, and the water electrifies my imagination." She reached her left hand to me. "Hand me a towel."

I grabbed for the vacuum suck button, and she shrieked at me with an unearthly voice that didn't fit such a tiny person. "Don't touch that button. Vacuum sucks can strip the feathers and skin right off a pigeon's back."

"Dinner for two tonight?" Wrong thing to say. She pushed me backwards, and I landed on my backside as she stepped over me, yanking a small towel from a hook, exiting the bathroom and squishing down the hall in her sopping military boots. I yelled after her, "How'd you get to be a doctor at fourteen?"

She mumbled her answer, "Ask your mother. She's been hunting the most brilliant minds left in Reichel. Guess you know what that makes me." Pasha Lutnik was positively the most irritating person I had ever met. I watched her walk down the hall away from the bathroom, holding her right arm up in the L position, with the hand hooked outward like a dancing Egyptian princess on the hieroglyphics of a tomb, all the while Reuther riding calmly on that hooked hand. Was it my imagination or did that dirty pigeon turn around and glare at me?

———

Which is tighter? The grip of my right hand, holding the lashings on the float car, or Pasha clinging to my other hand, like I might keep her from slipping back into the grip of death. I know the tighter grip is my hand on the lashings, for it is the only thing keeping me and Pasha from tumbling to the forest floor, and I am determined not to lose her again.

# Chapter 9
# BEYOND THE GROVE

Monster trees, some with a circumference of 30 feet, formed centuries ago on the Pacific coast long before *Jurbay*. The majestic forest was my father's favorite. And I am ever thankful for the technological advancements of a company called F9 Transplants. Their ability to transplant parts of the most dynamic forest in the world from the Pacific Coast to a state barren and without trees has created infinite opportunities for oxygen production. It also rooted down my father's favorite forest in an unlikely location in a place that *Jurbay* didn't gobble away. I look back now and wonder about destiny, for in the arms of these branches may lie our salvation. Do I believe, like Morris, that some divine god of the universe allowed this grove to be transplanted for this very moment, like a centurion on assignment protecting our safe haven? Hardly, but that's an appealing legend. Am I convinced, like Raben, that living creatures and trees bind together when evil is rampant, defending one another? I want to be persuaded. Can I advocate, as Pasha does, that her design and construction of Red Grove are infallible and offer us a significant refuge to build a strategic command center? It's hard not to believe Pasha, nonetheless I irritate her by calling Red Grove a hypothesis while she calls it legitimate fact. Regardless of what I think or hope about the grove, my senses awaken as we approach.

The air changes. Moisture, mist-like and faint, alerts me that we are entering the heart of the forest where the most majestic trees grow, tightly entwined like the arms of a Red Rover team bent on winning the prize. My skin shares a drink of the wetness that surrounds the environment. Red Grove needs a constant sip and soaks up the fog, weaving its droplets up and around the trees.

Pasha raises her head a couple inches from her pallet, sensing we are on the approach. She doesn't open her eyes, but I watch her nose twitch as together we smell the musty odor, rising from the forest carpet, calling us to shelter. I taste that scent as well. Our float cars climb, precariously easing through branches, and at times are almost still while our pilots plot a path of inches and feet, maneuvering between trees both vertically and horizontally. Collectively we hold our breath, anticipating potential collisions.

Pasha lets go of me, clenching both her hands into fists and then quickly releasing them. She alternates this pattern over and over and begins to chant "span bridge, span bridge, span bridge." I can't hear her over the sound of the rotors, but

I read her lips, and in spite of myself, I smirk at the memories stirring in my repertoire of Pasha-tales.

———

Quinn had learned quickly, after employing Dr. Pasha Lutnik, that she was most productive and successful when working in environments that stimulated her scientific thinking. Several months after I had first met Pasha and her collection of Rubik's Cubes, I found her sitting in a forlorn sandbox in our backyard. Together with Quinn they'd built a bridge spanning one side of the sandbox to the other out of a crude collection of sticks and pebbles. It had failed in the center, its structure crumpled, mixed with the sand. Quinn whispered an explanation to me, "Suspension bridge model—possible basis for a safe haven someday. Pasha got as much information about it as she could off what's left of the web. Now she's making it up as she goes." We both looked at Pasha, weaving grasses in long lengths. "She's making cables for the model."

"With grass?" I asked.

"Hey!" Pasha squawked at Quinn and sneered at me. "Your kid doesn't need to know that." As always her attitude stunk, and I stepped forward ready to smash the rest of her bridge, but Quinn put a hand on my arm. Pasha rubbed the top of her head, her eyes locked on her project. "The bridge is mine," she said.

Quinn pushed her way between Pasha and me. "Avery's not going to take the idea, Pasha. Stay focused."

Pasha took a clump of moldy sand that had been in the box for long over a decade and threw it at me. I was going to bow out of this ridiculous argument that she initiated, and my mouth was agape, poised to say so, when the sand landed right inside my open mouth. Enough. I threw myself on top of her and held her face down in the sand. "Like the taste?" I asked.

Quinn, always stronger than she looked, pushed us out of the box onto the ground. "Fight as much as you want, but don't wreck the progress of that model." She pointed at the fallen bridge. "Go at it girls, but I need a suspension plan by morning." We put the pause button on the scuffle, watching Quinn walk away, Pasha spitting out a much larger mouthful of sand than me. The next thing I knew she was the one laughing, and there were three or four pigeons pecking at my hair. The smell of pigeon doo running down my forehead ended the fight. I got out of there quick.

———

When Shaw steadies our float car at the top of the trees, I see no sign of the span bridge that Pasha created as the basic structure for Red Grove. I'm not surprised. She had already birthed the thin-skin that covered the chipsters implanted in our arms, legs and eyes, and I expected she would just magnify the thin-skin concept to cover the entire safe haven and the supporting cables at each end of the structure. Pasha once told me her invention would be half a mile long and three stories high. This I believe.

McGinty carries Pasha over his shoulder and as gently as possible hands her up the camouflaged ladder through the entrance to Red Grove and into the arms of those waiting to receive us. I imagine a small welcoming committee, anticipating our tiny band of escaped subterraneans, surprised to see that we are accompanied by The Third's abandoned children and the dump pickers. Instead, as I ascend the ladder I hear the distinguishable voice of one I know well.

"Hey, Baby, what's slammin'? Are you thinkin' you're all that and a bag of chips? Boo-ya, get yourself up here and give me some love. Cha-ching, Cha-ching, girl!" Annalynn. This eight year old has apparently found a repository of nineties clichés. Red Grove might not be big enough for both of us.

Annalynn wraps her arms around Pasha's neck in a death grip, crying, "Cha-ching, sista'. Welcome home!"

"Coo," Pasha answers. "You gonna help me take care of my pigeons? Might name one after you."

Annalynn, digs into the pack lying on Pasha's chest. "Orbit!" She pulls the pigeon from its shelter, stroking its head, then peeking inside the pack. "And Herman too. Give mama some love." She nuzzles both their heads at once. I cringe. Filthy.

"We're gonna to have to breed a new flock, Annalynn," says Pasha.

"Just remember pigeons are monogamous. Might take some time."

"Don't need to remember. I taught you that," Pasha says, and for the first time in a week I don't worry about her. I know Pasha is just fine.

Everyone we brought to Red Grove, except the pilots, is finally within the structure, and the entrance to our fortress is, at last, secure and hidden. Shaw and the other pilots fly to the far side of the grove where a landing dock awaits their hook up.

I step forward and Annalynn and I exchange the palms up greeting. Then, she pulls back, slaps her thigh and bellows, "Zoom! Got myself adopted, Avery. Just like them." She points at the ones we've collected along the way. "What do you think about that?"

"I think this is a really big family to take care of," I say. "Do you have enough room for them? Can the slim skin hold us all? There may be more on the way."

"I'm not the one you should be asking that question. Pasha knows better than me. She designed it."

Pasha begins the repetitious flexing of her fists, and she forces her eyes open to look at me. "Don't question me. Of course it'll hold—lots more." After Shaw secures the planes, he runs diagnostic tests on the structure of Red Grove, processing data through the chipster in his thigh. All the while Pasha taunts him, "Hey! No need to test it. I built it." His test comes up clean.

McGinty says, "I'm thinking you don't need any more medical care, Pasha. You're ornery as ever." Everyone laughs, but before the humor dies out most are already busy, working at the tasks of Red Grove. McGinty hauls Degnan off to the Room of Constraints, promising to search him before he is left alone to think about his crimes. We don't want any more deadly surprises. Old Soul organizes a feeding schedule for Degnan and a sleep schedule for the children. I wish him luck, as he will be dealing with Annalynn and Morris. Morris and the library boys sort through what is left of the insides of the book bindings, while the dump pickers take tallies of their findings from earlier in the day. Somehow our exhaustion has subsided and been replaced with the challenge of settling in. I am sure we will sleep well tonight.

"Tour in progress," Annalynn yells as she zips in on what appears to be a duplicate of Pasha's zip cords in Reichel. The zip disengages ten feet from the ground crashing Annalynn in a heap on her back. "My bad," she says, looking up at the swinging zip. "That's da'bomb, yeah? Needs a little Pasha-touch to perfect it." Wrapping her wild hair under a scarf, turban style and with the usual Annalynn panache, she calls, "Come on. We're kickin' it on this tour." I follow her, recognizing my need to memorize the layout of this place before I form some sort of ruling council who can work together at job distribution, strategizing our next step and our future plans. I beckon all the children to join Annalynn and me.

We step through an archway and enter a long oblong room with a corridor of doors circling the perimeter. "We're livin' large in the grove," Annalynn announces as we follow her joke trail like a line of mountain goats fixed on Billy Goat Gruff at the front of the herd. I offer an occasional snicker as she practices her 90's banter, but my heart mourns for the librarians, for Prospero, for Lear, maybe even a little for the soldiers who sunk in the pool with the Deadly #12 clinging to their backs. In spite of the validity of Pasha's design here, I still feel I'm on a cliff, suspended over the edge.

Annalynn moves quickly at the urgency of my request. "Weapons Cave," she announces and points at the labeled door. "McGinty's mega stock pile." At the word "weapon" Carles reaches his hand up to Raghill, nervously, and Raghill holds it. "We got it all: brainies, anti-brainies, your Z-Colts, your SE454s—got to blast those little biters in the dump." Just inches from Carles face, Annalynn spews off her list of the dangers confronting us, including the brain-swappers. He buries his head on Raghill's shoulder.

"Enough of that, Annalynn," I say.

"Just trying to be realistic."

"You can be realistic without scaring the kid. He's been through a lot."

"It's all good. And we're just gettin'started, girlfriend."

"Great."

"Anyway. Weapons Cave. McGinty's workin' on some-thing much bigger than a 454. More bang for your buck, if ya' know what I mean."

"They don't need to know."

Morris stops, turns to face me, indignant, his hands balled in fists by his side. "Avery, stop treating us like children."

"You *are* children," I say.

"I just saw my brothers swallowed by flames, eaten by a Deadly #12 and devoured by a brain-swapper. My father condemned me to death and"—he stops, caught in a mid-sentence thought then begins again—"and I just flew a float car up through the branches to Red Grove, landing it safely. I am not a child."

I step away holding my hands in the stop position, urging him to back off. "Okay, *Not-a-Child*, I'll try to remember that. What's next, Annalynn?"

We stop in front of another door. A smile on Annalynn's face always comes with an attitude. This one creeps to the corners of her mouth like a slow and treacherous exploration of the New Coastline. I can see her mischief forming maybe even before she has identified it. When the boys and La collect around her in a half-circle she adjusts her voice to a lower register, speaking with a ghoulish sound and pointing at the sign on the door. "The Room of Constraints," she whispers. Poor little El hides behind Morris.

Morris asks Annalynn, "A veritable torture chamber of silence and anticipation?" I can't tell if he's adding to her story or trying to one-up her horror. And the English accent is back.

"That's exactly what it is, my man," she answers and pushes a button in the alcove. The stucco wall recedes, like a large piece of thin-skin peeling away, to reveal a floor to ceiling viewing window. On the other side of the window is Degnan, sitting in a niche, his hands resting on his knees. "Behold the puppet." Annalynn's sinister laugh sets the scene. We all take a step back, remembering the tracking device and the destructive vial of deadlies that he used against us. "No big. He can't see us unless I push this button here." She readies her finger. "And when I do, I want all tongues stickin' out and fists raised at the Deg-man. Got it?" And once again, I see the child in them all. I step off to the side, out of Degnan's line of vision, and watch them open their mouths, twisting their tongues and preparing the meanest fists they can muster. After a moment of posing, up goes the barrier between Degnan and the children. He sees them and runs for the window, and as he does his arms are jerked upwards and seem to be attached to some invisible track. Just before he reaches the window Annalynn closes the barrier, and he cannot see us. Annalynn thrives in the role of puppet master. It appears she and the others think vengeance is reasonable justice. Maybe I agree.

"This time we're gonna laugh and point at the Deg-man. Got it?" Annalynn asks.

The choir responds, "Got it," prepping themselves for the next round of torment. Barrier up. Laugh and point. Degnan tries to get at the window but can't due to the restraints on his arms that hold them upwards above his head. Yes, he is a puppet. Annalynn could do this all day long. I can't get to the alcove fast enough.

I push the button that returns the covering to the viewing window and closes off the Room of Constraints. I say, "Annalynn, we're going." We leave Degnan behind and as a group we approach the next room along the oblong corridor.

"Sweet. We're gonna chill in the finest room of the grove. Pasha's Roost." Annalynn palms the button and the door is whisked into its cubby, allowing us to enter a lab fit for the best scientist in the world. That would be Pasha. Three stories high, there are stations built in many locations around the room. Some hang from the sides of the walls, two stories up. Others are firmly established on the ground floor and a few are suspended from the ceiling. In eight or so places around the room there are spiral staircases following the wall up all three stories. At the top there are a series of cat-walks crisscrossing the ceiling horizontally, allowing the workers that are buzzing above to travel from the wall to the center of room by means of these cat-walks which enable access to the roosting pens. They are empty, but nonetheless Pasha thought of everything, designing a room for Herman, Orbit and their soon to be growing nest of eggs.

While I survey the scope of the lab, Annalynn hangs herself upside down by her heels in a contraption I've seen Pasha use to stimulate concentration and keep her back aligned. Morris is already hanging beside her in a device of his own, and Raghill is helping Carles turn upside down while El and La wait patiently in line for his assistance. It seems, through this community of heel-holds, Pasha has allowed for collaborative discussions. Raghill calls to me, "There's room for you, Avery."

"Pass," I say climbing the stairs to a station perched on the wall of the second story. "But that would be a great place for all of you to hang out for the rest of the evening." The chatter of Annalynn and Morris trading tales fades into white noise, and my attention turns to the sign on this station. "*Locasa* Reversal." Instantly I know my suspicions of Pasha's research are right. She had always intended to complete the step in the development of *locasa* that the Catalonians had been unable to finish because it was stolen by The Third. Pasha would work on the replacement stage and the reinsertion of the withdrawn memories until she succeeded. Then, those having met *locasa* in the past would face their greatest challenge: the return of their stolen memories and integrating them back into their lives, hopefully as stronger people, whole, able to cope. Pasha wanted to bring the families back together. A reuniting of father and son, husband and wife, grandmother and grandchild and, of course, mothers with their children.

The conversation from below strikes me as such a contrast to those conversations I had as a child before the severing of our land and our lives by *Jurbay*. Back then we talked of bikes and of camping and swimming at the beach. Not these kids. "Pasha said she'd teach me slang in Tibetan," says Annalynn.

"You ought to be thinking about revolution, not historical lingo," Morris quips.

"I'm a kid, not a revolutionary," she shouts at him. The five of them hang upside down like a cluster of bats resting before a nightly flight.

Morris swings down from his heel-hold, righting himself and pacing in his senatorial style, hurling words in his English accent. "Even now, Raghill and I are drafting the 'Marriage Revolt.'"

Raghill answers, "He uses that accent when he knows he's right. Too much Shakespeare at the library day in, day out." Raghill unhooks himself then assists Carles, El and La back to a standing position.

"Marriage was banned before I was born," says Annalynn.

161

"Exactly. It was thrown out by The Third." Raghill says, "It's a battle without weapons."

Carles chimes in, "They took our families."

Morris continues, "There is nothing that's going to get The Third's attention more than defying what they forbid. They forbid us to be loyal to any person. Only allegiance to The Third. Marriage is a perfect way to stand against them."

I lean over the station on the second floor, looking down at the children and groaning. "Morris, you're going to have to run anything like that by the council first. You can't just go out on your own preaching revolt."

"Who's the council?" he demands.

"Ask me tomorrow."

"You know there's been marriages already, don't you?" Annalynn asks, and we all stop as she commands attention. "Yeah, baby. Had some marriages right here in Red Grove. Our artists are into it."

"Artists?" Morris asks.

"Yeah, they came from all over, unannounced. Didn't even know one another. Came to paint the thin-skin. Camouflage it," Annalynn loves relaying information no one else knows. "Just showed up. Most of them with pigeon notes in their hands. Said: 'Count us in on the roll call.'"

"Where are they now?" I ask.

"All over. Some working here in the lab, some in the garden."

La calls from below, "I'm hungry, Avery."

"Say what, music note?" Annalynn swings off her upside down perch, scooping La up and placing her piggy-back. "Got the answer for hunger. Come on."

"Cha-ching, girl," Morris calls, his accent gone. Annalynn stops abruptly, part way to the door.

"Say, what?"

"Our marriage revolt doesn't work with a few artists buying in. Everyone needs to buy in. You know, follow the leader." All five of them look up at me, and I point directly at them.

I say "Not me. *You* marry. After all, you're *not* children."

They all say in unison, "We're too young," and point back at me.

"*I'm* too young," I say.

The group chases after Annalynn to the lab exit, and just as I step off the final stair to return to the ground level, I note a huge painting covering the three story wall at the far end of the room. The space is draped with a canvas map. It doesn't need a label. I recognize the severed coastline with only part of our country intact. Someone has drawn a circle surrounding the entire map and inside the circle is the huge number 28. Painted above the number is the word "the" and below it "united." Leave it to the artists to conjure up the image that says it all. *This is what we have left. The Third thinks they've taken it from us. They think they've renamed our home. Yet here, boldly hanging on the wall is what still belongs to us. The 28 United.*

"Come on, Avery," La waits by the door riding on Annalynn's back. Carles too rides piggy-back on Raghill. I catch up just in time to see the thin-skin of the next corridor door open. It's marked *G.G.*

"Growing garden," says Annalynn. "Help yourself." El and La chase after Annalynn through the entrance, and she shows them how to pull a carrot from a vegetable pot. Yet moments after we enter the room Morris, Raghill and Carles are all still standing, staring at the garden.

"Aren't you hungry?" I ask.

"Never thought I'd ever see a garden again," whispers Carles.

Morris steps near a plot of watermelon, lays on his stomach, putting his nose right up next to the fruit. He scratches the melon with his thumbnail. "Smell," he says. I lay down next to him, my nose an inch away from the plant.

"It does smell good."

"Look," Raghill says as he maneuvers his way to a sunflower, towering above him. "Just like at home." Then the giggling begins. Laughter from the tickle of the carrot's feather-like topnotch against La's cheek. Chuckles from the boys cutting melons open, all three lying side by side on their stomachs, eating from the same piece. Hysterics from El and La after Annalynn unearths a potato shaped like an old man's head.

"I'll be back after your dinner," I call over my shoulder, finding my way to the thin-skin exit.

"Girlfriend! Check out the landing dock two doors down. Then in the morning I'll take you to the minstrel tree. People living up there in trees."

"Like us?" Morris asks.

"Not exactly. Different kind of tree. Different kind of people. They've got more music there than you've heard your whole life."

———

I search for the landing dock door. *Leave it to Annalynn to discover a new community hidden in a minstrel tree. And here I thought dump pickers were the only ones that had carved out a place to live other than Reichel. And what about these artists, coming with their buckets of paint and pallets of color? They used their brushes, sponges and an assortment of tools to create a camouflage so detailed that I can't tell where the safe haven ends and the horizon begins. There really is a world beyond Reichel, and we are part of it.*

After pushing the button controlling the entrance to the landing dock, I watch the cover disappear in a two second suck from somewhere above me. I step out onto an expansive platform covering most of the width of Red Grove. Half of it serves as what I would describe as a launch pad, and half as a landing dock. The entrance to the dock and pad is open. How careless of someone to leave this entrance vulnerable without its camouflage.

The night sky is radiant, breathtaking, its beauty so compelling that I must sit to watch the splendor displayed for me alone. Well, almost alone. I know it is McGinty approaching from behind me before he speaks, his smell, like the needles of the firs from the forest. "You've lost the element of surprise," I say.

"Wasn't planning on slitting your throat," he responds and sits beside me.

"Thanks for that."

He points to the float cars. "Shaw calls it a fleet."

"It's four stolen float cars and a flyer-9," I say, "and if you don't count the float cars it's *one* aircraft."

"Takes two to be a fleet. He's half way there." The silence between us is a bit awkward, and I don't know why. Finally, McGinty tries to ease the tension. "So. You here checking out this pet project of Shaw's?"

"I'm checking out one better than that." I point to the sky.

He joins me, star gazing. "Spectacular galaxy. But don't let Shaw hear me say that. He's got eyes for nothing but the "Silver Flyer." I glance at the name painted on the aft of the plane and wonder how many flyer-9s Shaw has planned for his fleet. Moments pass while McGinty and I sit, our silence turning to comfort.

"That beauty up there. It's constant, dependable, you know?" I muse. McGinty looks at me, then back at the heavens.

"Yeah," he says. "I do know."

"Regardless of the crumbling world below it. Regardless of the chaos. We have that."

My eyes move from the heavens to a sideways glance at McGinty. I ask, "What's your pet project? Stockpiles of anti-brainies?"

"Hardly," he says, taking my hand and pulling me to my feet. "My pet project? Dance floors." I feel the night breeze lift the wisps of escaping hair around my face. The touch of his palm on my waist prompts memories. We have danced before. "There needs to be a dance floor in Red Grove," he continues, and I raise my right hand to the dance position, meeting his.

"No dancing in The Third," I say.

"We're not in The Third anymore. So, let's dance." He moves me around the launch pad with skill and, as usual, I feel awkward, untrained—not natural. Very subtly, ever so slowly, he brings me closer. I wonder if *his* scent to me is like the needles of a fir, what is *my* scent to him?

I say, "I was about to ask you where the music is coming from, but then I remembered: the music's in your arm."

"Chipster. Hear it?"

"I hear it."

———

McGinty and I showed up at Esperanza's Bar before Pasha, Shaw and the others. Ironic we would choose a Catalonian bar that named itself "hope" when we dared not hope for anything in the midst of Elite training. The training facility, hidden away several stories underground in a remote area of the country, was the location of our last drill earlier in the afternoon. Now graduated from our training and free for one evening, we'd catch a few pitchers of beer before our first mission was laid out for us in the morning. Maybe the Third had eliminated alcohol from the menu and replaced it with hydrating peps, but in Catalonia cantinas abound.

We were two pitchers into the evening, still waiting for Shaw and Pasha, when McGinty took to the dance floor, motioning me to join him, "Rumba is the dance of love," he said, laughing and holding his arms out to me.

"That's your way of asking me to dance?" He started dancing by himself. "There's no music," I said.

"Music's in here." He points to the chipster in his right bicep.

"I don't hear it." He danced his way toward me. His moves, dramatic and lyrical. His hips, captivating and seductive. He put his hand on the back of my waist, and then I heard the music. Pasha would explode if she knew McGinty was using her chipster invention for entertainment. And this was entertaining.

————

Forcing my mind to return from the memories, I pat the bicep where his chipster is installed and ask McGinty, "How'd you get it to play music?"

"Picked up some rewiring skills in training. I'm supposed to use it for translation of foreign languages should I encounter someone not speaking English."

"I speak English." We dance without talking for a minute until I say, "You know this has absolutely no practical value?"

"Pleasure only." McGinty rotates us around the launch pad, leaning me backwards for a final dramatic dip. I smell another scent on his skin, the unfamiliar odor of soap. I guess Pasha's design includes shower facilities. It's been so long since anything but a vacuum suck has cleaned and scanned my body. The odor's luxurious. I can't decide if it's my fixation with the smell that mesmerizes me or McGinty himself.

"Avery," Raben calls, rushing onto the launch pad and interrupting the climatic finish to our intimate dance. McGinty and I quickly break our pose, giving Raben our awkward attention.

McGinty speeds past Raben and out the exit. "I'll be in the weapons cave when the council meets."

"That'd be now," says Raben. Then staring at me he says, "They're looking for you."

————

The calling of the council must hold a record for the quickest government ever formed. I think that's the kind of decision-making you get when most everyone's a novice. It was simple, really. McGinty, Shaw, Pasha and me. We brought in Old Soul. We all trust him. And he suggested creating five more positions that we would put on hold for now, but fill at a later date as loyal ones step forward and The 28 United grows. Of course they were all waiting for me to suggest Raben. I didn't. In my own mind I have evaluated: Conflict of interest. I care about Raben in a way a leader should not care. If he's to be part of the council, the others will nominate him and agree on his potential contributions.

Now that the council has met for the first time, I remain alone in the hollow leaders room. Today our only agenda was the establishment of a governing body. This we had accomplished. A circular table at the center of the room is maybe five feet across, a table where government will be hammered out for the citizens loyal to The 28 United. I climb to the center of the table, sitting cross-legged, picking at a tear in the knee of my drab coverall. *If the 28 United ever raises an army we will not be dressed in gray.* I focus on the wall niches lining the circumference of the council room and imagine that someday a full circle of rulers will sit here, not just five of us forging out the beginnings of a formal stand against The Third.

My body shivers as someone from behind gently gathers my hair into a ponytail at the crown of my head. I turn to look. It is Raben, holding a grubby red ribbon from his portfolio of dump pickings. He wraps the ribbon around my ponytail, securing it in place with a knot, then strokes my hair the way my father used to do when I was a child exhausted from mountain hiking, whining to be put to bed. But I am not a child, and this is not my father. I shiver again. Then I hear the minstrels beyond the grove. Distant. Raben guides me to my feet and says, "Let's follow the music."

## Chapter 10
# FOR THE SAKE OF A SONG

The moon, double-sized and golden, spins its lunar lights across a small meadow that is overgrown and thick with waist high daisies. Annalynn leads the way. She's been here a week and she walks through this maze of flowers like a landowner of prominence.

I say, "I don't know why you just left a whole group of people out here in the forest when we have a safe haven waiting to protect them in Red Grove."

"Zoom, girl. They like their trees. And we've been a little busy, in case you haven't noticed, just trying to figure out what to do with Red Grove."

"Do you hear the music?" Raben asks. We all freeze.

At first, I'm sure there's nothing to hear. My breath is shallow and alternates with the breaths of Raben and

Annalynn. Then, like a dandelion wisp riding on the back of a hazy smoke trail, the music drifts, lassoing me in with its mystique.

"Eerie, huh?" Annalynn says like she holds the keys to the universe, and I hate it when this eight year old seems smarter than me.

"It's unfamiliar," I say, and the three of us continue walking through the waist high overgrowth, Raben's fingers weaving through the tall daisies to intertwine with mine.

"'Course it's unfamiliar. They had to find new ways to play their instruments, keep the song alive." Before I can ask her what she means Annalynn lopes back toward Red Grove exclaiming, "I got you here. Now you're on your own, baby. I'm needed at the lab." The music vanishes mid-note, leaving Raben and me silent and alone.

I let go of Raben's hand, but his fingers still brush mine. I ask, "What direction was the music coming from?"

"Maybe east, but it darted around. Sprang from here," he points at a tree limb, "to there." He indicates the meadow. "Your choice. Which way?"

"Be still. Wait. The minstrels may show up," I answer. The daisy stem he's picked bounces in his hand then traces up and down my forearm looking for a destination. A vase. A flower pot. My neck. I'm drawn again to his eyes. Hazel. Haunting. Staring. We wait, together.

Raben chooses five or six sticks from the ground, fashioning them together with some scraps of string he carries on his belt, building something that looks very much like a small raft Tom Sawyer might have used in the old tales of literature when fiction was still valued.

"Sometimes waiting takes too long," he says, picking up a loose stick and rolling it against his creation held in the palm of his hand. The sound it produces is light, percussive. Raben's crafted an instrument. *The man's unable to waste a thing, not even a moment of waiting. I love that.*

By now the moon has disappeared and dawn marches through the meadow. It doesn't take long for Raben's music to draw a response. A hand reaches down from the branches of a massive white oak, at the center of a grove, growing at the edge of the meadow. As we draw closer, I see it is a small right hand, made smaller by the absence of three fingers, the pointer, the ring finger and the pinky. It is impossible to see who is on the other end of the hand as the body is hidden by leaves. Raben sees the hand as a road sign, pointing the way, an invitation. Climbing the tree, he disappears through the limbs. I see the hand as a greeting and hold my palm in front of it in the palms-up position, but the hand grabs mine, and I too work my way up to the mystery beyond the branches.

*When you're invited in you always wait for the host to speak first.* My father taught me that in Catalonia after we'd visited a diplomat's home, and I'd barged in asking all sorts of questions about the gold filigreed sideboard in the entryway. After the visit, I argued the value of curiosity, and my father took the opposing side, debating the propriety of customs and culture. I won, of course. Surely my father would understand the necessity of me extending safeguards to these vulnerable people. So, I speak first, addressing the waif-like teenage girl connected to the hand.

"We're here to offer you our protection. How many of you are there?" I ask. She holds the delicate pointer finger from her left hand to her lips in a gesture that halts my speech, but not my curiosity. I notice that this hand is missing fingers too: a thumb and the middle one. The girl's eyes direct us to seats fitting into the joints of tree limbs made from odds and ends of wood scraps. We sit and face a wooden platform suspended limb to limb constructed of the same materials.

A rustle in the leaves above our heads alerts us to the entrance of the minstrels. Like lines of snakes slithering together down the branches, the minstrels descend with efficiency and grace. Their toes bruised from clinging and their legs muscular from climbing, they swing down to the tree platform. I want to applaud, paying homage to their precision. This time I wait to speak, knowing my father would be proud. I count thirteen minstrels, including the girl whose hand we followed. Hers is not the only one with missing fingers. The tally is not a pretty one. Many severed digits, with skin healed in the shapes of nubs and knots at the end of amputations. Several hands are unaccounted for, and a skin flap grows over a hole where an ear used to be. One old man with the letter M etched scar-deep into his cheek glares cautiously at us through clouded retinas.

A powerful man, with skin so dark he would disappear at midnight, speaks as he offers a palms-up greeting. "I'm Clef." He has no eyes, just sockets.

I do not hesitate to place my palm in front of his, even though I know he can see nothing, and Clef responds. Raben does the same. I look momentarily into the carved out caverns that used to be his eyes, knowing that a commander who burns children is very capable of this kind of work too. Clef says, "Pasha wants you to have a discussion about marriage."

"So, you have a chipster?" I ask, trying to avoid the marriage topic and livid at Pasha for intruding into my life. The idea of those at Red Grove discussing Morris' historical ideas about marriage—my marriage—flips my stomach back and forth. My parents married for love, but that was long before The Third stripped memories of family, and before *locasa* excommunicated passion from the human equation. Today when new citizens are needed in the Third's gene pool, logical choices are selected by the government. Of course time is provided for the matched couple to produce the child. When the delivery is finalized the child is raised by pocket-watches who will supply its needs until it has reached the age to serve The Third in a position preordained for it. Male and female creators never see each other again and are never allowed to see their child. I am suddenly very thankful for the memories of my mother and father's love for each other.

Clef lifts his shirtsleeve, revealing a chipster in his arm. I say, "Pasha might have served you better to install something for your eyes." The pressure on my hand exerted by Raben makes it obvious that my father would have questioned my tact, and Raben would like me to shut up. "Sorry," I say.

"Pasha can be a bit irritating sometimes. Didn't mean to take it out on you."

"I haven't missed my eyes as much as you might think. And the chipster? I don't know Pasha. Got this chipster from a doctor operating in the caves up on the New Coastline."

"How many others did he install?" Raben asks before I have a chance to voice the same question.

"Maybe a couple a day while I was there."

Raben and I exchange a glance. "That's two other doctors besides Pasha that have learned the surgical installation process," I say.

"That's just the ones we know about. There could be more." I hear the excitement in Raben's voice, and I feel the tension rise in my chest. I'm unable to sidestep the hope of tracking those loyal to The 28 United through the chipsters. If only we knew how many people we are dealing with. Is it a hundred? A thousand? Ten thousand? With a hundred we are only trying to hide, avoid The Third and maybe convince them that we are no threat. With a thousand we might attempt planting a few more subterraneans in the Plethora Plant or in their GEB lab down amongst the salad spinners and Baldy's buddies. But with ten thousand we form an army. With ten thousand we go to war. The thought of war repulses me, yet the thought of ridding this nation of The Third stirs my adrenaline with a paradox of joy.

The other minstrels arrange themselves among the branches, listening as I continue talking quietly to Raben. I make no attempt to be secretive. The minstrels are with us and to be trusted. "With Clef's chipster Pasha communicated one on one, but she's got to figure out a way to reach all the chipsters at once, to decipher how many are really out there. That's her priority right now."

Raben says, "We've got to nail down how many there are to work with, or chipsters are no better than pigeons."

"Agreed."

"How many do we need before we consider training an army?" Raben asks.

"Army?" Clef asks.

I address Clef and the minstrels. "The Third knows there are a few of us out here who oppose them. Eventually, they'll organize and try to root us out. Could be tomorrow. Could be a month from now. We need to be ready. If you come with us to Red Grove, we'll all be together, and we'll have the best opportunity to organize and resist." The minstrels seem nervous unable to sit still and their movement causes the leaves to rustle, like electricity igniting sparks in the air. The man with the scar etched in his cheek plucks a single string of his lute. He captivates us with a haunting one note tune. The other minstrels join and soon the reeds are bleating, stomping on the beats of the djembe drums. With twelve minstrels playing impromptu, the ghostly single note transforms into a raging dissonance, like a battle cry hunting for a target.

Clef speaks for them all. "We offer you our instruments. We will go before your armies in battle."

*Before us? In front of?* I find that almost laughable, but press my lips together, commanding myself to silence for now.

177

Yet, in my mind I commit to never letting these gentle ones set foot in any combat situation. No, they will be used to lull whatever troops we assemble to sleep at night with peaceful lullabies.

Clef continues. "Allegra," he calls the girl who greeted us earlier. She seems to understand his meaning, letting her reed fall behind her back on its leather string. She scurries up through the limbs and returns carrying a leather-bound book with its cover tattered and its pages torn. Turning the folio gingerly, Clef allows his fingertips to be his eyes, guiding him to a bent corner of a page. "It's not the first time minstrels have been used in battle. We found the story here."

"Do you want me to read it?" I ask.

"You can't read it. It's torn and words are worn away. But we have pieced together the tale." In unison they recite with a cadence. If I believed in a chorus of angels, this would be it.

"From the ancient book of Chronicles: King Jehoshaphat believed in a powerful God. Three kingdoms rose in alliance against him. Land. They wanted land." A minstrel without hands uses his forearms to beat a rhythm on a two-headed drum. Others join him, forming a trio despite their missing fingers. "The king, outnumbered, looked to the heavens for a word of hope. His word? Let the minstrels play." A quartet of strings blends with the percussion, and I am transported back to centuries past, imagining a kingdom facing a war they are unprepared to fight. "Jehoshaphat believed righteousness would be victorious. So the king sent minstrels to lead his troops into battle." Their music is beautiful, laying a backdrop for their story, enriching every word with a note, a chord, a harmony.

"Did they win?" I ask. The music ends abruptly, and once again I feel Raben's warning in the squeeze of my hand. "Whose side won? Righteousness or the alliance against it?

"Not all the pages are here." We stare at one another, Raben and I facing a band of thirteen minstrels who are willing to lead armies to war with a song. After moments of silence, Clef says, "Minstrels are the voice of faith."

"But we don't know if minstrels leading the way into battle was a good thing or a bad thing," I say. "The pages are ruined."

"That's the definition of faith. We don't know for sure. But we *believe* for sure."

I bring this conversation back to realism. "Clef, we're probably not going to put you in front of an SE454 or a brainy. Are you coming with us anyway?"

"Yes, but I think there's something you need to discuss first." He points to his chipster, reminding me of Pasha's impertinent message. "Framing marriage for one of us is a proud stand against The Third, but very inconsequential to them. However, let one who's escaped from The Third's grasp, one who's destroyed their float cars—their troops—let *that* one frame a marriage, and it becomes an implement of war that sheds no blood." The minstrels ascend back up through the branches, causing me to wonder what life looks like up there for a dozen minstrels and their leader.

I rush to grab Clef's leg before he disappears up the tree. "The Third took your fingers, your hands, your eyes. That's why you left Reichel? So they couldn't take anything more?"

Clef pauses, looking down, finding my eyes with his empty sockets. "We left for the sake of the song." He gently touches the side of my cheek then follows the others up through the leaves.

Raben and I are alone, and the silence between us is broken only by the chattering of gray squirrels and the cooing of the morning doves. Again, he wastes no time. Raben draws me close, his hands on my shoulders, and his eyes capturing my attention. "Listen, this is not such a strange topic to discuss—framing a marriage. The day you broke Pasha and Shaw out of the cage the speed of your life changed. And everyone you've met since then has accelerated with you."

*Part of me analyzes Raben's words. Wise and discerning. And the other part of me wants to reach out and brush the hair from his forehead.*

Raben continues, "In just over a week we've lived unthinkable horrors and built lasting friendships."

*Us. I think. He's talking about us building a friendship.*

"We're not going to stay a hundred people for long, Avery. Within days we could be thousands strong."

*Can he read my mind? Does he know I am simultaneously thinking strategy while trying to sort out my attraction to him?*

He gives my shoulders a slight shake. "They're following *you*, Avery."

I step back from him. "I'm not a pawn to frame a marriage," I say. "I'm not going to be manipulated by a bunch of minstrels or a ten year old kid."

"But they're all following *you*. The minstrels, the pickers, the librarians, the subterraneans. They're all—"

"I *know*. I know they're following *me*." I listen to my voice. It is the first time I have said this out loud. I have pondered it, doubted it, embraced it, rejected it, played with it, tossed it into the sky to see where it might land and caught it right before it crashed to the ground. I turn away from Raben and look through the green leaves at the sun coaxing a scarlet orange horizon. My view is interrupted by a cluster of acorns attached to a spray of oak leaves. I push them aside and see the constancy of the coming morning. Dawn was here before *Jurbay*, before my parents, before my Catalonian heritage, and it will be here when I'm gone. If we ever call another place home, that same dawn will rise above us. *That's* worth fighting for, and we fight in behalf of every missing finger, hand, ear and cruelly carved cheek. We fight for every child orphaned by *locasa* and each man and woman who have no recollection of what it means to be a parent. For every librarian buried in a tomb of fire, every boy who's left his golf hat on the tooth of a monster and for every child dashed to a chilly underworld by a deadly vial. It is worth the fight for Pasha's brilliance, quirks and friendship and for Shaw's "Silver Flyer" and McGinty's rumba dance. Worth the fight for the Chipsters here and those yet to come, and for the pigeons that soared in hopes of adding to the roll call. Worth the fight for the friends that made it out of Reichel, and for Quinn who stayed behind. It is worth the fight for the sake of a song and for the sake of The 28 United. Suddenly, my mind seems curiously sharp and my muscles strangely bulked, and it has nothing to do with Elite training. I hear Raben behind me and realize what he's saying.

"I care for you, Avery."

"As much as a person can care in a week's time?" I ask.

"Yes. In the same way we've all lived a couple lifetimes in the last few days. I've grown to care a couple lifetimes for you."

"Then I guess there's been enough time." I take his hand. "Let's frame a marriage." I reach up to the branches and begin to shake them as hard as I can. Raben joins me, and we are like travelers pounding on a door for entrance. Clef descends first, followed by the others. They stare at us.

"You've considered Pasha's proposal?" he asks.

I'm still angry with Pasha for butting into my life, so I give credit elsewhere. "We think Morris has a point about the power of marriage and resisting The Third." The musicians pluck their chords and play their notes in a loud applause. And they erupt in a joyful, lyrical, wild celebration.

Clef quiets them by raising a hand and says, "To frame a wedding: two rings, two vows and a holy celebration."

Allegra, in her timid way, reaches in her pocket and withdraws a slender twine strung through the interiors of a dozen or so rings. She extends them to us and says, "The ones we no longer use." Raben receives the gold and silver circles hanging from the string. *Never waste a thing*, I think, and notice

Allegra rubs the end of the nub where her ring finger used to be.

My fingers stroll through the choices and come to rest on a braided bronze band, coated with patina, the story of age. Raben unties the twine connecting the rings, sliding off my choice. "Which finger?" he asks.

Holding out the first finger of my right hand, I whisper, "We point the way." Raben slips the ring on my finger. Then I hold the string in front of him while he chooses a ring of a golden tone, plain and dulled from wear. I place the ring on his finger, the same finger I chose for my ring. He hands Allegra back the string and its collection.

"Now," I ask of Clef, "what vows?"

"You decide," says Clef.

I take Raben's hand. "I guess we can make it up as we go."

"You may want to think about it," says Clef.

"No need," I say. And for the first time in this framing-of-a-marriage discussion I am aware of the place at the center of my heart that I have protected all my life. Entrance is exclusive. It's a place where celebration occurred when my father told me my poems were brilliant, and when my mother, Quinn, explained no other child had wisdom like mine. My soul feels full of a limitless friendship with Raben and a joy that begs for eternity. I open this protected place in my heart and willingly invite him to enter.

"I'll go first," he says, beginning his vow. "I frame this marriage with a kiss." He lifts my chin, his lips meeting mine, slow and purposeful. "I frame this marriage with a ring." He draws my hand, adorned with the braided ring, to him and kisses the circle on my finger. "I frame this marriage with a vow: Avery DeTornada, you were born to face The Third, and I will face it with you. You were given an identity many will follow. I will walk by your side. I will care for you always, hope with you at all times and honor the framing of this marriage." He is stunning. Hazel eyes fixed on me in unshakeable sincerity. How can any vow I compose come close to these perfect words? I want to speak with earnestness as well. I want to speak what I feel and feel what I speak.

"I'll go—second," I say and feel—ridiculous. Who else would go second but me? I wait for what seems like forever, hoping I can be articulate, but knowing I may not be able to make the words come out at all, let alone beautiful. Taking a deep breath, I know there is only one way to begin and that is to open my mouth and speak. "The Third has told us family has disappeared, marriage has disintegrated and human passion is no longer tolerated. We reject this." I start to sweat. This is not a marriage vow. It is a manifesto against the current government. I try again. "Together we frame a marriage because we care for one another. We frame a marriage to state our faith in humanity, in family and in the continuation of The 28 United." That's it, I think. I take Raben's hand and with my thumb rub the ring he has selected and add. "Every moment worth celebrating needs a symbol and this is ours." Now, I kiss him, and I am not so mad at Pasha anymore.

Allegra motions us over to a large branch several feet above where we are standing. Clef says, "Follow Allegra. Climb up there with her." I shadow Allegra up a couple branches and Raben moves behind me. She reaches into the leaves and pulls out a zip cord.

"Pasha's been here?" I ask.

Allegra answers. "No, Annalynn brought it. A way for us to get from tree to tree." She hands the cord to me, and I take it, remembering how Annalynn collapsed on her back due to faulty installation. "It's not perfect, but it works most of the time. Take the zip to the next tree over. You can make it. It's only about a hundred feet."

We hear Clef call from below. "Pasha and Old Soul know you won't be home until tomorrow morning."

I look at Raben who takes my hands placing them on the zip and covering them with his. "Oh no," I say. "Only one of us goes at a time until Pasha checks this zip out."

"Okay, you go first." He steps back a bit, and I place myself in the take-off position. He places his hand on my forearm, halting my progress. "Just don't forget to send it back." The smile we exchange is ours alone.

I zip off, sailing through the air and landing easily on the platform of the other tree. Winding the zip around a primitive pulley system, I send it back to Raben. I look in amazement at what the minstrels have created on very short notice for Raben and me. The platform, like the other tree, is built with odds and ends of wood and probably measures ten by ten, its perimeter outlined by candle holders fashioned from carved-out tree limbs, hollow rocks and collections of acorns cemented by tree sap. Each holder contains a candle uniquely crafted, different sizes and a variety of sunset colors: magenta, garnet, orange, golden. None are lit. It is still early morning.

In the center of a platform is a bed made of fir needles, covered with a worn, but clean quilt and a second quilt topping the first and folded neatly back at the head of the bed. Two fir needle pillows are positioned side by side. Chords woven together in net-like fashion hold a collection of instrument suspended eight feet above my head. How foolish The Third appears for trying to cut away the music from the minstrels of Reichel.

To one side of the bed, sitting on the flat top of a small stump there is a pitcher with two tin cups, a loaf of bread and a bowl of apples. On the other side of the bed a basin of water and a small pile of clean cloths, resting on a pyramid of rocks. Hanging on the crook of a branch are two blue gowns, boxy style, long. I cross the small area and touch the fabric of the gowns. They feel silky, and I am incredibly grateful for the kindness of these strangers who chose to lavish us with gifts of comfort and rest.

I hear a thud behind me and turn to find Raben standing there. "They did all this for us," I say.

He pushes my hair behind my ear, "It's a gift to have a night without Z-Colts and knives," he whispers. He unhooks and removes both the holster and the Z-Colt from my collarbone where it is secured. Setting it and the knife from his belt to the side of the platform, Raben looks at me, takes my hand and leads me to the bed. We sit on the side of the fir cushion, and I feel a few sharp needles poking at my legs and smell the sweet scent of the freshly broken fir boughs. He takes a cloth and dips it in the basin wiping the dirt of travel from my face.

During the hours between noon and dusk we lead each other on a journey of discovery, and we exchange much more than vows. I know him well now. His family, his dreams, his sorrows and losses. He knows the private parts of my heart that have been revealed to no one else. The abandonment I felt from Quinn when she chose country over daughter. The grief that still punches my spirit at the sound of my father's name. I uncover, willingly to him, qualities in me that declare: *I am not fit to be a warrior; I am not worthy to be a leader; I can never be a savior.*

At dusk we light the candles, and by dark they flicker as the night turns black and their flames wave blessings on the marriage we have framed. The music from the neighboring tree weaves through the branches of our hideaway, wrapping us in the harmony of notes meant to be together. Raben whispers words I do not hear but only feel at the nape of my neck, and I think I will like sleeping under quilts sewn by those who lived before a country was severed, when our world was whole. He kisses me.

————

I am the first to wake. The sound of doves, finding morning peace amongst the racket of the hungry jays, stirs me. A silky garment caresses my back. I lay my hand on Raben's shoulder smoothing his untied hair to one side. "I care for you,"

I whisper, but he sleeps beyond the sound of my voice. Too soon my thoughts are elsewhere.

*How many more pockets of humanity are hidden away in minstrel trees, among library shelves and in the obscure underground hovels of dumps? Left alone and undetected they will eventually die out without the resources that community provides. It is my job now to find them, collect them and turn them into some sort of fighting force that will face The Third. But, I want to stay in this tree forever. I never want to leave this moment, this bed, this man.*

My infrared chipster flips on without my command. I know I have not touched the temple on my forehead to activate it. Directly in front of me, instead of an activated infrared function are words that I read: **Calling all chipsters. Report to the northwest edge of the last forest outside of Reichel. We will meet you there. The 28 United.** Then the words are gone.

I scramble, yanking on my clothes and boots, rousing Raben and saying, "She's done it. Pasha's got the word out to anyone with a chipster. It's on!" Now he too is working to tie his boots, grabbing his jacket as we race for the zips.

He says, "I'll get the minstrels."

"I'll meet you at Red Grove," I say and grab the zip, but Raben holds my arm. Our eyes lock. We know what this means. Our lives will change. We will no longer be escaping. We will engage in some sort of warfare. He kisses me, quickly. I zip into the morning, hitting the ground running, so very glad we framed a marriage last night. 'Cause this morning— there's gonna be a roll call.

# Chapter 11

# ENOUGH FOR A LIFETIME

No float cars lift me to the entrance of Red Grove. I climb the branches, connecting to the camouflage ladder, entering the thin-skin door. The place is deserted and eerily quiet. The glowing lights, recessed into the smooth corridor walls, provide plenty of light, and there is no mistaking the emptiness. I work my way to the lab, pressing the button in the alcove, allowing the door to open. Stepping through the threshold, I'm able to see the void, the absence of workers. My suspicions grow as I jog to the landing dock, finding the door open and discovering every artist, every picker, every kid, Pasha, Shaw and McGinty lined up on the edge of dock staring off into the forest. I join them, standing by McGinty and ask, "Where's Degnan? Locked up tight?"

He doesn't break his gaze, but says in a low controlled voice, almost a whisper, "Yeah. He's locked up." He pauses only for a moment and continues. "Didn't expect you back so soon."

I feel a flush on my face, and stare at my boots. "Work to do," I say. Then he turns ever so slightly, just enough to see my face and waits for my eyes to wander up to his.

"You mean like framing a marriage?"

"That's already done." Only now do my eyes travel with the stares of the others on the edge of the landing dock, and I cannot stop a gasp from escaping. I do not expect what I see. Several hundred people, maybe a thousand, stand on the forest floor, facing Old Soul who is addressing the crowd from below. Trellis is positioned by Old Soul's side, holding an antiquated revolver, a relic from the dump, maybe thinking he's a peace keeping force. I rush to where Pasha stands with Morris. He holds both Herman and Orbit, and it occurs to me how much we onlookers must appear, to the crowd below, like roosting pigeons, waiting for our next assignment.

"Pasha, how could this many come so quickly?" I ask.

She enters data into the chipster on her forearm, not looking up at me. "Knew they would, Avery. Just had to link all the chipsters to mine, even the ones made by someone else. Eventually, we're gonna know how many of The 28 United there really are."

"I'll call a council meeting. We need to decide what to do with them. They can't all come up here."

"Not tonight, girl." It is Annalynn. Then she and Pasha say together, "Cha-ching, baby. We're having a party."

Pasha hugs me and whispers in my ear, "Got to celebrate this marriage, you know." I've known Pasha eleven years, and she's never hugged me. 'Course, I've never hugged her either. I note that blood still seeps through the bandage on her head.

Shaw slings his arm over Morris' shoulder and says, "Me and my little buddy here had a party of our own today, scouting."

"Looking for float cars and all," says Morris. "No sign of The Third anywhere." He stares at me through his enormous lenses.

"Course we started a raging fire on the far side of Reichel," Shaw smirks.

"They'll be headed in the wrong direction all night long," Morris mimics Shaw's smirk, but on him it looks ridiculous, like Degnan with a smile.

I pitch and toss the idea of a party back and forth in my mind. I don't know what a celebration entails, but the fact that I am the center of it makes me off kilter. I leave the loading dock, wanting to be alone for just a few minutes to try to process the last twenty four hours. I should be filled with brainstorm strategies for the hundreds of followers who will be spending the night in the forest. Instead, I am consumed with Raben, the beginning of our marriage and the memories of the best night of my life, the first night of many.

The corridor is quickly filled with the children surrounding me from behind. Raghill says, "You need to come with us, Commander."

"Avery," I say.

"Avery, come on. We have a surprise for you. "

They run in front of me, grabbing my arms and guiding me toward the surprise they wish to reveal. In the chaos of the hallway I fail to see McGinty approaching from behind. He says to the kids, "Give us a minute." They scurry down the hallway where they cannot hear our conversation, whispering in a huddle, waiting for me.

McGinty says, "We've been friends for four years." His eyes are intense, and I try to figure out if they are filled with anger or hurt or both. "We've been to hell and back in our training. We've lived together with Shaw in unit 791 and worked side by side as subterraneans in the plant."

"Your point?"

"My point is that you could have told me—told us—Shaw, Pasha, me. Asked for my input. Our opinions."

"*Your* opinion on whether or not I should frame a marriage? How is that supposed to factor into my decision?"

"You married him to take a stand against The Third. That affects our council, our future."

"That's not the only reason." There is a vast chasm spreading between us, filled with nothing but silence. Moments pass until I reverse directions and head toward the kids, but McGinty grabs my arm, way too hard.

"What's the reason?"

I shake my arm away from him. "I don't owe you any explanation."

"You do owe us!" I stop as he continues to fling words against my back, but I do not face him. "You can't just walk out one day in the middle of a crisis and 'frame a marriage.'"

Now I turn to him. "Yes, I can." This face off is uncomfortable, full of history. History that is all good. Why does he have to ruin that now? "I had every reason to frame a marriage, many reasons. Did I make a mistake? No. I made my own choices for me and for The 28 United. For Raben. I did not make a mistake."

"Well, then. I guess most of us will be celebrating tonight." He pushes past me so hard I lose my balance and slam against the corridor wall.

I call after him. "McGinty!" He stops, confronting me. "Be happy for me. That's what our four years are about." I cannot see a muscle in his body move, or twitch. He is still, frozen.

Finally, he raises his hand in a mock toast. "To the last four years, Avery. And to your happiness." Then, he continues down the hallway as quickly as he arrived. There is a fragment of my heart that hurts, but there is an even bigger chunk that is captured by caring for Raben, a man I intend to be with forever.

Anxious to reunite with me and guide me to their surprise, the children grab my hands and skip me down to the lab. I really don't have time for games, but they're giggling and carefree, and for them there have been so few of these moments. They palm the button and the lab entrance peels. They lead me past the stations and up the staircase to the third level, stopping on the catwalk by the door of an unmarked room. El and La pull me down to their level, where I squat and El whispers, "There's someone here to see you." Raghill presses the button and I step into the room, the door closing behind me.

Pasha sits at a counter with some experimental technology in front of her that I have never seen. There is someone lying on an exam table in front of Pasha's station, but I can't tell who it is. I move closer to Pasha and see a screen in front of her, monitoring the patient on the table. I cover my mouth, stifling a scream and stepping back several feet. Massive silver ringlets frame the face of the woman lying on the table. It is Quinn.

Irritation fills Pasha's voice as she whispers, "Don't talk. Shut up. Sit down." A needle is hooked to a vein in Quinn's arm and Pasha's replica of *locasa* waits, lying dormant next to Quinn's head.

"Pasha, what are you doing to her?"

"Little experiment."

"Not so little when *locasa*'s involved."

"Let's just say I think the Catalonians will be very proud today."

I grab her arm, forcing her to look at me, aware of how fragile her wrist bones feel. "You're not trying to put the memories back, are you?" She looks at me but doesn't answer. "You're not trying this for the first time on my mother?"

"I'm on a schedule, Avery. Quinn's lightly sedated. If you want to watch, sit down." I continue to stand. She glances sideways at Herman and Orbit perched on the top of her equipment. "You want to hold a pigeon, Avery? Might calm you down."

"Shut up." I sit down. "Don't hurt her, Pasha."

"I wouldn't be doing this if it wasn't ready." She leaves her chair and crosses to the table where my mother lies. Picking up *locasa,* Pasha turns Quinn's head to the side, placing the device on the back of her skull. Quinn's entire body shivers, then jerks several times in succession.

The screen beside me pops to life with a picture of Quinn's face, eyes closed but rapid movement under the lids. A small dot emerges at the center of my mother's face. At first it looks like a tear, but it begins to expand, and I see my father's image emerge. It grows quickly, consuming the screen and overtaking Quinn's face. He is smiling, and I want to cry. Then, like being kicked with incredible force in the gut, my breath is gone, escaped in a moment of realization. *She has no memory of him. Quinn lost my father to* locasa. *No wonder she can function with such detachment as a subterranean inside The Third.*

Through the next hour, while the memories are returning, I feel embarrassed to be eavesdropping on my parent's private conversations and intimate moments. Pasha facilitates *locasa,* reinstating the hijacked past of the DeTornadas into my mother's subconscious and conscious thoughts. Brokenness floods my soul while images reenact my mother's choices to withdraw me from my childhood, and enter me into the adult world of battle plans, scientific experiments and the engineering of a subterranean team. A child could not be trusted to keep their secrets, so they isolated the child. I view their interaction as leaders, Carles and Quinn, respecting each other's abilities and gifts and blending them to lead the floundering remnants of The 28 United away from the brink of extinction. I love them. I love them both.

I know what is coming. I fear what will next invade every inch of the screen. Pin pricks of terror dot my skin from head to toe. The memories are leading to an ancient stone sanctuary in Catalonia. My father and mother plot with the Catalonia president for the future and protection of *locasa*. Inside my head I'm screaming "STOP!" For her memories do not reveal the subterranean Elite hiding in the vacuum suck at the wall's edge. There, I am waiting to save them, rescue *locasa* and convince the Elite that my parents are both dead. I want to shriek at Pasha *Take this one out! There is no need for a memory of my father's murder. No need.* I close my eyes. I cannot look, but I know Quinn will look. She will remember. Without opening my eyes, I am very aware when that moment comes. When the memory is reloaded and flips into the chamber of her mind, the wail that comes from Quinn's sedated form is one of deep regret and mourning. I have to leave. I cannot watch the rest.

———

Hours later I sit in the new quarters prepared for Raben and me. I am alone, looking at my reflection in a mirror, but all I see is a collage of jumbled images. Somewhere in the center I recognize my mouth, but the rest of my face is a mish mash of Quinn, Carles, Pasha and Raben. There are the eyes of Morris, the nose of Annalynn and the hair of Raghill. And there are bits, pieces and fragments of everyone else I have encountered on this journey out of Reichel. I want to be whole.

Later, a soft knock ripples across my door. I quickly move to open it, hungering for Raben's presence and embrace, but instead Quinn stands, waiting for an invitation to enter, and I extend it. She holds a linen pouch, its top pulled tight with a drawstring. "Come in," I say. Perhaps for some mothers and daughters a long embrace might be the first impulse, especially when a daughter has come so close to death through cage and flames and deadly vials, through biters and brainies. We should crave touch and desperate holding, but instead we dance around the corners of the room, sizing up each other's next move.

"I have your father back," is all she says.

"Right. Now you have the pain of living through his murder again and again, any time you want. Is it worth it?"

"Every moment. *Locasa* not only took my husband but all my memories that the three of us walked through. Now I have all the fine and polished moments, and he's inside each one." She opens the pouch she's is carrying. "Yes, it was worth it."

I pace the room in diagonal lines, afraid if I stop the puzzle pieces of my life will fall from the cardboard frame and lie in a crumpled mess on the floor. I say, "You hardly sound like a commander in The Third."

"And you hardly look like a newlywed ready to lead the world."

"I didn't have the luxury of knowing love before marriage."

"I'm sorry."

"Don't be. I care for Raben. I love being with him."

"Can you see him as the father of your children?"

"Children? In this world?" I stop, finally looking her square in the face. "Here, we already have so many children to provide for. But, yes, in a new world where justice and safety reign. Yes."

"Life doesn't wait for the perfect scenario, Avery."

I soften just a bit. "You saying you want to be a grand-mother? Add another DeTornada to the leadership pool?"

"Maybe in a perfect world." She smiles a small, tired smile, and I return it. Quinn lifts the contents from her bag. She holds it up, allowing it to take the shape of a dress as it swings from the end of her fingertips. The cloth floats as if a breeze had entered the room, and as it moves a subtle glimmer follows its lines, causing the fabric to look at the same time blue and green, simultaneously silk and sparkle. "It's not a wedding dress," she says. "I wore it to a masquerade when you were a child. You probably don't remember."

I walk toward Quinn, stretching my hand out to touch the fabric. "I remember," I say. She holds the dress out to me. "Just after *Jurbay* sliced half of us away, you and I danced. Me in my pajamas and you in this gown, out in the yard, under the moonlight." She takes the dress and holds it up to me. "You said, 'Whatever it takes to keep going—to be normal again—we will do it.' And we danced."

Quinn says, "Try it on."

I slip off my coverall and lift the gown over my head. As it falls onto my frame it is so light I hardly feel it. It cascades half way down my calf, the hem swishing, unable to find a point of stillness. Quinn takes me by the shoulders and turns me to face the mirror, and at last I see me. My mouth—my chin—my eyes and nose and ears. My hair.

"You're beautiful," she says. I can't help it. I turn to her and, at last, we embrace. Soon she will return to be a commander inside The Third, but tonight, she is my mother.

———

Raben and I step out to the edge of the landing dock, our hands intertwined, me in my mother's masquerade dress and him in the only clothes he owns. We are flanked on the right by Quinn and on our left by Old Soul and the other council members: Shaw, Pasha, McGinty and our newest members, Morris and Clef. Over the expanse of the forest below, lanterns glow, illuminating the crowd that celebrates our marriage.

Collections of like-minded travelers are everywhere. Children inventing games with fir cones and sticks; groups of listeners seated on fallen logs, collecting to hear storytellers unfold the terrors and mercies of their escapes; and of course the dancers. They are everywhere. Large groups dancing with total abandonment to the music the minstrels play, without thought or worry about a matched step or a jig in unison; couples who sway to their own music; El and La in a small circle of three with Trellis, weaving in and out through each other's arms. La looks up and sees us. She raises her hand to point in our direction, and like a slow undulating wave on a quiet sea, each group stops their activity, pivoting their bodies in our direction. A cheer erupts, crazing out of control for minutes. I feel uncomfortable to be acknowledged by so many, rejoicing over such a private affair, and yet I understand this is their event as well. The noise is deafening, and I am grateful that we are over twenty miles from the edge of Reichel and that a fire rages on the far side of the city beyond the ear shot of this cheering collection of loyal ones. Tomorrow, maybe we will teach them to fight.

Quinn raises a hand and the cheering dwindles to a lull, diminishes to a whisper and fades to quiet attention. I am amazed at her presence, and her ability to command a crowd. All that power in a single hand.

"We acknowledge the framing of this marriage," she says. Again the crowd erupts and once more my mother lifts her hand. "Does The Third acknowledge marriage?"

The crowd answers back, "No!"

"We tell them, 'You no longer have control over our lives.'" A collective cheer from our united followers explodes. "We say, 'You may never take our families from us again.'" I think briefly about how The Third banned sports events, and how our decibels—right here, right now—mimic a soccer match in volume and excitement. What The Third prohibited we reclaim.

Quinn continues, "We will find a way to get our families back, and when we do we will rule with strength and humanity. We will build an army to protect our people and let the freedom of The 28 United reign." Frantic joy consumes the crowd. She is magnificent. Quinn, my mother. Inside me, there is just enough hope that maybe I am furrowed ground waiting for the seed she has planted to grow into a military leader, honing my skills of common sense and developing my ability to strategize. I think: *time can take care of that.* But this—her poignant words to the multitudes—this I could never do. Where I react out of survival and the protection of others, her passion swells out of faith and a vision for a political force of justice and righteousness. I see now she will do anything to achieve this for *her* people, for *our* people. And in spite of the fact that I felt abandoned for half my life while my mother pursued the salvation of a nation, today—I would follow her anywhere.

Quinn throws her attention to Raben and me, and just as I am about to speak, I turn to Raben and position myself in a palms-up greeting. He places his hand in front of mine and instead of the normal series of seconds where the hands hover inches apart in respect for one another, we intertwine our hands. We connect. For moments our eyes embrace. Then, my focus is drawn to a collective movement in the crowd.

In pairs, as far back as I can see, through the hundreds of followers, they mirror us and are engaged in the palms-up greeting. Then, their hands too intertwine.

From the back of the gathering a bellowing begins, and the crowd parts, allowing a pathway for a hulk of a man to approach the front. The moment I hear the sound, I know it is Shaw, yelling his war cry. I have heard him use it before when he was crazed with the adrenaline of battle. His deep, thundering yell joins forces with unearthly screams from the crowd, cutting through our holy moment. Stumbling through the middle of the gatherers, Shaw pounds forward, blood covering his hands. In one hand he carries his knife with its ten inch blade, dripping scarlet. In the other hand he clutches three ventricles, swaying as he plods to the front. He's a wild man. "Do you know what this means?" He yells. "There is evil among us and you are responsible!" He points directly at Raben. Everyone is frozen, unable to process what he means. "Your sister. Your brother. They were GEBs."

Raben races to the camouflaged door and begins the climb down the tree to the forest floor, and I am right behind him. Leaping down the last twelve feet of tree, Raben races for Shaw, butting against him with every ounce of sinewy muscle he has. Shaw turns his shoulder to fend off Raben, but still holds the ventricles high. McGinty grabs Raben's arms trying to pull him off Shaw. Then I attempt to restrain Raben with Old Soul and several others from the crowd.

Finally, we get him on the ground, but I still need to exert every bit of my energy to hold him down. When he raises his head to hurl accusations at Shaw, the muscles in his neck are taut, and the words he spews are like vengeful arrows directed at a hated mark. "You killed our brother and sister!" Trellis kneels in the dirt, sobbing in Raben's arms. The tension in Raben's body subsides as his anger deflates.

Trellis whispers, "Where are they?" No one speaks. No answer comes. "If they were GEBs where are our real brother and sister?" Quiet fills the forest of Red Grove. Trellis voice seems a desperate prayer. "We could find them." He turns to me. "You got Pasha and Shaw out of the cage. We can go and get El and La."

Pasha releases Herman and Orbit who fly to the branches of a tree and begin a cooing cadence, like the chant of a priest delivering last rites, unwanted but necessary. Pasha nests in the fir needles by Trellis, holding him in her arms, but speaking to Raben.

"Raben," she says. "I worked in the GEB lab for two years." She takes his hand, and now she is connected to both brothers. "I know all the procedures. All the rules. They do not keep the extracted for longer than 24 hours."

"But you and Shaw—"

"Avery rescued us just before termination. I'd been in the cage for less than a day. Shaw was just lucky. No one ever made it past a day before."

Trellis asks, "But how do we know how long the GEBs were here? It could have been recent—not yet a day?"

"No." Old Soul steps forward and speaks. "No. A week ago on the trip from the dump to Red Grove they went missing,

203

you remember? It must have been then." There is a nod in solemn agreement from those of us recalling what seemed to be the simple wandering off of two young children.

Quinn approaches Shaw, examining the bloody ventricles. "There are three, Shaw," she says.

Shaw says, "They were with a man."

"Did you recognize him?"

"I don't recognize any of these people. I found the three of them far beyond the back of the crowd," says Shaw. "I was patrolling, even though we didn't think we needed to. They didn't hear me. They probably knew no one would look for danger. We were all celebrating. The man was plotting how to get back to Reichel to dump their information without us discovering they were gone."

I am struck by the fact that the crowd of hundreds has not moved, has not spoken. Pasha says, "So that means the scientists still are not able to retrieve information from the field. They need to have the GEBs present to dump the collection of information. But they're desperate, The Third. They've never experimented with children before."

I stand. Before I speak the crowd turns to me with expectation. I say, "Immediate council meeting. Quinn, you join us." Quinn nods in agreement. "Before the night is over you may all be headed up to the New Coastline." Murmured conversations begin, but before it becomes a roar, I speak again. "Talk quietly among yourselves tonight. Strengthen one another. And be ready to leave at a moment's notice." The babble starts once more. "Quietly!" I raise my voice enough to be heard by hundreds, and at my voice, they are still.

Raben sits on a log with Trellis by his side. I want to go to Raben, hold him, show comfort and concern for the loss of El and La, but Quinn and the council members move swiftly to the entrance of Red Grove, Shaw carrying the ventricles. I step clear of his path, not wanting to be splattered by the dripping, crimson arteries attached to each ventricle. I already have enough blood on my hands to last a lifetime.

# Chapter 12

# BACK

---

No one sits at the head of a round table. There are eight of us now in the council chamber since Quinn has joined us, and even though I know she will not stay for long, due to the commitment to her subterranean job inside The Third, it is good to have her input. She is seasoned and wise, and with Old Soul and Clef sitting with us as well, I feel the decades of experience from them filtering onto us five novices who might know how to run a lab, fly a reconnaissance mission, build a brainy or lead 50 pickers through a forest, but have no clue what to do at a table in a council meeting.

In this room, tension pumps with a wild and crazy rhythm. I have to focus on being right here in the moment, or my mind will race back to the horrific finale of what should have been a celebration, but ended up with hearts carved from the chests of three GEBs seeking to destroy us. Raben and Trellis lost what they thought to be a brother and a sister. How do we know who is loyal and who is not?

For a moment our round table has been silent then McGinty says, "We have to get those loyal to The 28 United out of here tonight."

"Agreed," I say. "You and Shaw can lead them up to the New Coastline. Appoint those you need to serve as a military escort."

McGinty responds, "For weapons, we'll take half the brainies and anti-brainies and leave you the rest here at Red Grove."

Shaw adds, "We'll ask for fifty or so volunteers to form a protection squad for you and Pasha and those who stay."

"Yeah, I know we can find fifty," says McGinty. "There are enough of them that know how to use a weapon, and they can train the rest."

One of Pasha's pigeons coos, nuzzling her shoulder while she strikes the mechanics on her chipster. "Pasha," I say. "Are you listening?"

"Leave Annalynn with me," she answers.

"I don't know if she'll stay without Morris and the other boys."

"Then leave them all."

"They're children, Pasha."

"They're kids that fly float cars, Avery." Now she looks at me.

"It's best to get them out of here with the rest of the group."

"At least give them a choice."

"Okay, a choice then," I say. "They might not want to stay when up north there's open territory and a chance for rebuilding."

She rubs her head in short bursts of energy, and Morris, who has been following the conversation by staring at my face then Pasha's then back and forth again, says, "Our choice, Avery."

"How about you, Old Soul?" I ask. "Where will you be best used?"

Old Soul rolls a cigarette, and without hesitation says, "I'll go to the New Coastline too. I'm good at mediation, and I'm guessing there might be some squabbles on the way up there."

This all seems very simple. Get these chipsters out of the forest and headed north, but I notice Quinn has been remarkably quiet. "Quinn?"

Her eyes turn up at me from the table, slow and sure. She stares, and eventually says. "Good plans—all of you." A long silence. The intensity of her look sends a foreboding feeling up my spine, and settles like talons clutching at my backbone. "But—what if there's more?" she asks.

"More GEBs?" asks McGinty.

"Yes, GEBs." Pushing the button in the niche in her alcove Quinn sends the table retreating to its smaller size, allowing her to stand, to pace.

"She's right," says Old Soul, inhaling smoke from his cigarette. "We don't know these people. We're just assuming they're loyal because they aren't in Reichel."

McGinty stands, he paces too. "We've got to check every-one before they go north—make sure they all have a chipster."

Shaw places himself directly in McGinty's path, stopping both him and Quinn from pacing. "I agree. We need to con-firm. We know The Third hasn't had time to figure out that we even have the chipsters. So it's the only guarantee we have of loyalty."

"Not really," I say. Those that weren't in Reichel when the inoculations took place—when *locasa* took the memories—they have no chipsters and no #14 tattoo on their wrists."

"And what about those that we gave artificial tats of the #14?" asks Pasha. "We used the same ink as The Third did for their inoculations. There's no way to tell the difference." She holds up her arm and Orbit swoops down from the ceiling of the room to perch. "I need to find a way to scan each person to see if they're a GEB."

"Do you have that kind of technology?" Clef asks.

"Almost."

"Almost?" I ask. "We don't have enough time for 'almost.'"

"And what about kids?" Morris points out. "They don't usually have chipsters, and yesterday we might have assumed they were loyal, but not today. And La had a chipster and she wasn't loyal. Did she get that chipster before they replaced her with a GEB?"

To Pasha that's an insult. I can tell by watching because not one but both of her fists rub erratically on the top of her head, making her normal rats nest even messier.

"Children should be checked out too," says Shaw. "Maybe anyone who's been traveling with children must account for every second they've been with them for the past two months, and if a child has been separated from the group—"

"We what?" I ask. "Rip their ventricles out?"

An uproar erupts from the forest below. We all exchange a look then race for the chamber door. I'm wondering what else could make this scenario any worse.

———

When we arrive outside Red Grove the scene is terrifying. There are about sixty people standing alone, back to back encircled by the rest of the crowd. A woman at the edge of the circle chants: *Take the heart of a GEB. Take the heart of a GEB.* She is stirring up the crowd and draws a knife from her belt. She holds it up for all to see, and the only thing I can think about is getting close enough to stop her. I charge at her with every bit of the strength I have, but McGinty and Shaw both pass me. Before any of us can reach the raging woman she swipes her knife forward and slashes the chest of one of the men inside the ring. She swings her arm back, moving closer for a more lethal jab, and before she can thrust again a hand catches her and holds firmly onto her wrist. It is Raben. "Stop!" he shouts.

"They're GEBs!" she screams. "Like your sister and your brother."

I arrive at the edge of the circle. "You don't know that," I say, realizing we must calm the crowd down and make the one with the knife look foolish. "What grounds do you have to draw a knife on anyone gathered here?

"They don't have chipsters. We checked."

I approach the woman, placing myself inches from her face. "Have you been checked? Do you have a chipster?"

"I don't have a chipster, but I also don't have a #14." She holds up her tattoo-free wrist.

I pronounce my words with power. "You're ready to slit someone's neck to watch them die because they don't have a chipster or a blank wrist?" I jump up on the tree log that Old Soul spoke from earlier and raise my volume to address the crowd. "Everyone step back from the circle." My mouth is dry, palms dripping with sweat, and I sense a tremor rustling up from my knees through my whole body. *What if they don't listen to me?* I imagine my father's statuesque silhouette, standing in the shadows, and I breathe in his courage.

"All those in the circle with a chipster step out." No one moves. "Anyone with a message from a pigeon—display it now." Over half of them fumble through shirt and pants pockets, finding scraps of paper everywhere. One teenager roots through his boot and several more lift their hats, finding the crumpled notes underneath. Together they lift them high in the air. These pigeons' messages look like a salute to The 28 United. "Step out of the circle," I say. "The Third doesn't know about Red Grove yet. Anyone showing up here because of a message on a pigeon's leg is not a GEB." Those carrying the notes cautiously move to the outside of the ring, making sure they don't go near the knife-carrying woman.

211

"Now," I continue, "those of you with an artificial tat of the #14"—I hold my wrist in the air, displaying mine—"hold your right wrist high and step over to where Clef stands." I gesture in his direction. The violent woman springs forward, lunging at the new group, but Shaw moves his forearm toward her, bashing her back and sending her to the ground.

"Clef," I continue to shout the orders that pop in my mind second by second. "In a minute I want you to take your minstrels and those with artificial tats. Go with Pasha and one by one get an account of how they received their #14. Pasha supervised it all and did most of them herself. They'd better have the details because she won't forget a thing."

Only three people are left at the center of the circle: a man of about forty-five who looks terrified and confused, and two women who stand defiant with no apparent fear.

"Who knows these people?" No one moves or comments. "Come forward now if you can verify how long you've traveled with them." Two young men push through the crowd.

"I know the man in the circle," says one of the men. He clutches a rifle that must be over a century old in the crook of his arm. The other man has an SE454 draped over his back. I wonder where he got a weapon issued only to Elite trained soldiers, but then I think about the downed float cars by the library and the battle we had with the Elite at the pool where we lost Prospero. The dead's weapons would have been left behind, and I admire this picker's boldness for finding, picking and brandishing this weapon.

"And I know the women," says the other man. He has one pant leg rolled up, making sure we see the activated chipster in his leg. "They waited in line with me out past the minstrel tree for the doctor to put in chipsters, but right after mine, he had to close up shop. They've been with me since then."

Old Soul asks, "Never knew them before?"

"I didn't know *any* of these people before," the man says. It is then I realize the frailty of having a chipster. Perhaps today a chipster may guarantee one is a loyal citizen to The 28 United, but that guarantee is fleeting. With GEBs infiltrating our group it is only a matter of time—days maybe—before The Third discovers and defines the power of the chipster. Then they will replicate it and distribute it to their own. When that happens these moments of communication, and Pasha's ability to call the chipsters together will never be repeated. From that point on something else will have to determine loyalty.

McGinty turns to me and says quietly, "There's no guarantee. We could put them in the constraint space until we figure it out." I grab his arm and pull him closer.

"Figure what out? Who's a GEB and who isn't? We can't figure that out today, and we can't figure it out in a week. We have to get these people out of here, and trust that we've discovered all the GEBs for the moment." The other council members surround me in a semi-circle, and I speak in hushed tones. "I say we take a chance on them."

Shaw is not in agreement, "No. There could be a hundred more GEBs out there in that crowd."

Pasha pumps her fists in and out like a novice boxer in training. "There aren't 100 GEBs. I haven't been gone that long from the lab inside The Third. They don't have that many ready yet. Trust me." She mutters to herself. "This you know, doctor. This you know."

With every bit of authority I can conjure from my core, I cross directly to the woman who drew her knife. "No one draws a weapon on this group again. If you do," I turn out to address the entire crowd, "or if any of you do, you'll spend a very long time in constraints and probably never see the New Coastline."

"Like Degnan?" the woman with the knife spews sarcasm. I get in her face again and Shaw joins me, yanking back the hair on her head, restraining her. Her body convulses in pain.

"How do you know about Degnan?" asks Shaw.

She is screaming at the whole group now. "You want to know what you got coming from this council? Ask for a little tour up there in their tree." She struggles with Shaw, twisting his arm and breaking away from his hold. Her hands jerk violently out of control. Then her right leg convulses erratically in ballistic bursts. She falls to the ground, her other leg beginning the same movement, and her mouth twists upward into a ghoulish line, forming a crooked arch and finally pitching downward in a lopsided frown.

"Pasha," I yell, "What does this look like to you?" Pasha leaps forward trying to examine the agitated woman, but she rages against Pasha, even though McGinty and Shaw try to hold her down. Her legs flail against Pasha sending her several

feet away, landing on her backside. Pasha rights herself immediately and maneuvers directly back to the woman, positioning above her chest making observations.

"I've seen it once before. Malfunctioning GEB."

"Get her up to the Room of Constraints," I yell.

Pasha stands dusting herself off, saying, "I told
Commander Dorsey and The Third their genetic recipes
weren't ready for activation. This is what happens. You can't
possibly be a spy and a raging lunatic at the same time. He
ought to take a lesson in patience from a pigeon." Herman
lands on her shoulder, and she strokes his neck.

I yell to Shaw, "Constrain her, but don't put her in with
Degnan. Don't let her near him." McGinty and Shaw corral
the woman and get her up the camouflaged ladder. I look for
Quinn for a quick consultation, but she is gone. Of course.
Things are heating up here, and inside The Third they must
be desperate. She'll be needed for recommendations on how
to hunt us down. She'll return with a flourish to play her role
as commander, but I know now her heart stays with me. Such
a brief moment to have a mother.

Jumping onto the log one more time, I raise my voice.
"Dr. Lutnik is working on her technology to discover if GEBs
have infiltrated our 28 United. She's a ways off from succeed-
ing in that pursuit. Maybe someday soon it will be possible,
but for now I depend on you—on all of us to build trust based
not on technology but on our commitment to each other.
Who is loyal to The 28 United?" Without reservation all arms
shoot into the air and a chorus of *Me, I am, Yes* and *Forever*

resounds. "Now look around you." The crowd does so. "This is who we trust."

A young boy, who was originally inside the circle, says, "But the new ones, Commander. How will we know if they are loyal?"

*How can I answer?* I hear my father's voice whisper, *faith.* I beckon the boy to come and stand with me. I take his hand. "I speak to myself as well as to you." I pause, looking into the face of the questioning boy. "We will make mistakes, but in the process we will get stronger at defining trust, practicing faith." I raise my right arm above my head, letting my hand extend to the heavens. "I am loyal," I say. And in my head my father, my mother and a million witnesses of past injustice shout in unison with me. But they are not the only ones who speak. These citizens on the run, this crowd of refugees, this mobile country shouts back at me, "We are loyal."

I spot Raben and Trellis at the front of the crowd. Raben seems stalwart and ready for challenge, but Trellis sits on a decaying log his head down, seemingly unaware of the action around him.

I go to Raben, taking his hand and gently rubbing his thumb with my own. "Change of plans, Raben." While I make decisions for hundreds of people, I long to hold him and tell him El and La were not his fault. They were a part of an ugly conflict that kidnapped goodness and exploited it for evil. But there is no time, so I speak quickly. "McGinty, Shaw, Pasha and I are needed elsewhere." I should be honest with him, and tell him it is now necessary for us to return inside The

Third—tonight—with an army of four. I should tell him that we may not be back, but I can't. Not now.

"Raben," and I reach my arm out to Old Soul and pull him into the conversation, "I'm going to need you and Old Soul to lead The 28 United up to the New Coastline." He looks into my eyes, but they are not as lost or guilty as I imagined. Actually, I see strength and a readiness that make me wonder what facets of this man I have yet to discover. He may be more of a warrior than I ever would have guessed. I like that. Love that.

Old Soul searches Raben's face and asks, "Can you do this? I will need you every step of the journey."

"Yes," says Raben. He reaches forward to embrace me, but it is far too brief as I slip from his arms, running toward the ladder and calling back to him.

"Be ready to go in twenty minutes. I need to talk to Degnan. He knows more than any of us ever expected."

Old Soul joins me on the run saying, "Avery, you should sit with Raben awhile, talk with him."

"Please watch out for him, Old Soul, and for Trellis too. I'm depending on you."

"They're grieving. It's not a quick process."

"Speed up the process. We don't have the luxury of losing two good men."

"You should meet with him—even for a few minutes before we go." I don't answer, so Old Soul quits following me while I keep my pace. I have Degnan on my mind.

Shaw, McGinty, Pasha, Morris and Clef are waiting for me outside the Room of Constraints. I am breathing hard when

I say, "Like we discussed, we'll leave a military team here for protection—trained and untrained. Artists stay in the lab to keep work on Pasha's projects. They'll keep Red Grove going." I am checking my Z-Colt as I talk making sure it is fully loaded. "We'll see if there are a few scientists in the crowd to remain here too. And I'm sending Raben and Old Soul to lead the Chipsters up to the New Coastline."

McGinty and Shaw protest together, McGinty getting the final word. "They have no military background. I thought we decided Shaw and I would lead the group up there?"

"Not anymore," I say. "The four of us are infiltrating tonight."

"Infiltrating where?" Shaw asks.

"The Plethora Plant in Reichel."

Pasha rubs her head with desperation. "You do remember, Avery, that we have a council? We already made the decision about who goes up the coastline," she says.

"We'll we need to change that decision. If we run away from The Third now we don't know enough about their offense. We have to go back in. There's too much about the GEBs that's changing by the day Take a vote," I say and stand my ground staring at the four of them.

"We don't have Old Soul or Quinn here."

"We knew we'd rarely have Quinn when we put her on the council, and Old Soul already said 'yes.' Vote."

Shaw says, "I was trained for infiltration. Better than leading the sheep up to unknown territory. I vote 'yes.'"

McGinty is looking down at his boots, but surprises me with a quick glance up directly at my eyes. "You're the leader," he says. "You know I'll follow you anywhere." Shaw laughs, but I'm not amused by that comment. Besides the fact that I'm not sure what McGinty means by it. And right now, I don't have time to figure it out.

"Your vote, McGinty?"

"Yes."

Clef nods in agreement and Morris says, "As long as we keep us library boys and Annalynn together, I vote yes." I never questioned our wisdom placing a kid on the council, but sometimes I swear he sounds and acts just like a child.

We all look to Pasha. She speaks rapidly, her hands frantic, her arms flailing. "Have to get genetic recipes from the Plethora Plant—all of them. I vote yes. Have to capture *locasa* and get it back."

McGinty asks, "Do you know where to look?"

"There were places I wasn't allowed to go. Hidden storage I never saw."

"Did anyone see those rooms?"

Pasha remains silent for several seconds then says, "Yes." She takes her hands off her head, staring at all of us. She puffs up her petite frame to look as big as possible.

"Who?" I ask.

"Degnan." We groan at her answer. And she motions me to stoop to her level as she adjusts my Z-Colt. "Remember, he was a surgeon inside The Third until he screwed up."

"This, I've heard before," I say. I slam my hand against the button on the constraint space alcove, and the thin-skin reveals the observation window. "Spot me on Degnan. I might need some help." But before I can enter the room we all look in the window, shocked into action. Degnan is slumped, his feet limp behind him, his arms held in the restraints on the track above him. His head hangs lifeless on his chest. We all stampede into the constraint space and Pasha lifts his head to check his breathing. To our horror his lips are covered with green, and the color has seeped into the skin above his mouth.

Pasha yells, "He's taken a last resort pep, but it was created for a body the size of a ten year old in the library. Get him down. I can save him." I am conflicted regarding that statement. I want to let him die and call an end to this, but we need him to get everything out of the Plethora Plant—or at least destroy it.

Shaw presses keys on his chipster, releasing Degnan who crumples to the floor. Pasha loosens his coverall collar, and as she smacks her fist against his chest his eyes open quite deliberately, and he says, "Guess what? I'm alive." The gurgling sound coming from his vocal chords makes me sick, and a fizzy foam rolls out of the corners of his mouth.

I slap his face, grab him by the collar and lift him up several inches, shouting, "Get him back in constraints." McGinty lifts Degnan's hands above his head and Shaw gives the chipster a command. The claw, with its metal bracelets, descends and hooks him up again. Degnan screams like a madman out of control.

I sit on a bench in a niche across the room from him, only air between us. I calm down. "Shut the door," I say. The three of them hesitate, and I can feel their eyes scrutinizing me. They have never seen me like this, and I don't care. The leave and shut the door.

They will watch me outside the window, and will be at my side if they are needed. If Degnan needs them. He has a coughing fit and more of the oozing green foam seeps down his chin. I speak to him, "I can't say I'm sorry that portion of pep wasn't bigger." I hate this man.

"Don't you believe people can change, commander?" he asks, and throws a leer in my direction.

"*People* yes. *You* no."

"Ouch. Play nice."

"Play nice? You murdered one of our children. You let a deadly scald the skin off his back before he died. There is no *play* and there is no *nice*.

"Hey," he raises his voice, "I was under command, and I was under—peps. I don't want to be the bad guy anymore."

"I don't think you get to turn that on and off." He will try to manipulate me. He will not succeed.

"Some do," he says.

I am in complete control. I do not move a muscle, except my mouth, and I stare so hard at him I hope his skin scalds too. "What do you know about the GEBs showing up here among the followers of The 28 United?"

"A GEB made it this far?" he laughs. "Never saw that coming."

"Can a GEB get its collection of information to The Third without leaving the field?"

"No. Not yet." Do I believe him? How can I trust anything he says? "That's all I got for you, commander, unless you've got something for me."

"I can help you if you help me."

Degnan jiggles his wrists that are locked in the constraints connected to the tracks. "I have no choice," he barks.

I unholster my Z-Colt. "You have a choice. I want a yes or no answer. Do you know where the storage rooms are in the Plethora Plant?"

"Storage for what?" he asks, and I send a bullet to the side of the niche he sits in, six inches to the right of his skull. I may have lost my Elite training, but I will never lose my hunting skills taught to me by my father. Until *Jurbay,* our freezer was always full of venison and elk.

Degnan screams, "Okay, okay! Yes. I know where the rooms are." I set the Z-Colt on my lap stroking the trigger. "What are *you* doing for me?" he asks.

"I find that an interesting question, since I have the Z-Colt."

"What do I get? I can't go back to The Third. They'd kill me on sight. So what do I get? You want my help? There's got to be a payoff."

"If we make it out alive, when we get to the New Coastline, you can claim property. Start over." Even I can't tell if I'm lying, or if I'll shoot him the moment the mission is over.

He wipes some of the drool away by dropping his chin and rubbing it back and forth on his coverall collar. "That's not much of a promise. There's only five of us going back in, and we only have a piss-in-a-can chance of getting back out. Maybe no chance."

"It's all I got for you, Degnan. One time offer." He's right. Not much of a chance. We both know it.

"I'll do it." He lifts up the bottoms of his feet, showing me the gaping holes in the soles of his shoes. "I'll do it—if you get me some decent boots." I hate this man.

Just minutes later, Shaw is yanking Degnan down the camouflaged ladder, spitting menacing words in his ear. "I don't want to even think about what cavity you hid that pep in, pocket-watch."

Degnan answers, "You can call me 'doctor,' kid-killer."

"GEBs aren't kids, Degnan. They're expendable experiments."

I worry that Degnan knows about El and La. "How'd you know about those GEBs, Degnan?" I ask as Shaw pushes him to the ground at the bottom of the ladder.

"That crazy woman you just sent up here and put in constraints—that GEB. I could hear her yelling from two rooms over."

"Another failed mission," says Pasha.

"Yeah," says Degnan. "But she has cavities too, and she weighs a lot less than me. More like a ten year old."

Pasha immediately consults her chipster, and finds out quickly from those inside Red Grove what has happened to the raging GEB from the forest crowd. "Dead," she reports. "Green all over her mouth."

Shaw pulls his knife and holds it under Degnan's chin. "Maybe you're a GEB, Degnan. Let's cut your heart out to make sure." McGinty pulls Shaw's arm away from Degnan's neck.

"It's okay, Degnan," says Shaw. "There'll be plenty of GEBs to kill when we get inside the plant."

"No," Pasha yells. "We're not touching those GEBs. We need to get them all back here so we can figure out what they know, find out how they collect information, and how many there are inside and outside The Third."

Shaw stings back, "You mean if we get out of the plant we're headed back here with a band of GEBs?" She nods. "That's worse than dump pickers." I throw him a threatening glare.

We set a quick jog through the thickest part of the forest, and I think about Degnan's new boots. It's going to take him more than restored soles to keep up with us at this pace.

"Wait." I stop our caravan with one word. "Give me just five minutes." McGinty and Shaw throw me a brief nod. Pasha bursts out, "I'm sorry, Avery. I'm sorry, that I ever mentioned the word 'marriage.'"

"I'm not," I say and run back to Red Grove where I see only the backs of the last few 28 United hiking through the forest in the direction opposite us. *Raben will be in the front.* I think. He and Old Soul are leading. I race by the outside edge of the marching refugees, picking my way through the forest.

It takes minutes before I am finally in the right position to see Raben. He is coming toward me. I am relieved that he too felt a need for one last embrace. Our arms encircle each other without a shred of gentleness. This goodbye is bitter, and I feel the power of his muscles, not wanting to let me go. I return his hold without reservation. I try to memorize his hazel eyes, his blonde-brown shoulder length hair, pulled back with a leather lashing. I try to remember the beauty of the night we spent together, but I am horrified to find I can't bring the memories to the front of my mind. For now, there is only goodbye.

"I love you," he says. I try desperately to keep tears from forming, and when I can't, I try to chase them away with the side of his cheek.

"I love you," I say. And then the moment is gone, and we are running in opposite directions. One leading hundreds in search of new territory, and the other sneaking back to the city she hates.

I think of the meaning of escape, and as my boots pound the forest floor the definition hammers in my mind: to flee, run away, evade, save. I hope to save those fleeing for their lives to the New Coastline, and the few of us running in the opposite direction toward a most likely death in Reichel. After I escaped from the cage I said I would never return to that city. Never again invite peril. And yet, in hopes of salvation, I'm going back.

# Chapter 13

# A BOTTLE OF HENNESSEY AND AN OPEN EYE

We crouch behind the justices' station fifty yards from the Plethora Plant. The four story building rises from the enormous, steel roll call area, like an ominous reflection from a metal sea. It is a midnight blue night with a sliver of a moon. Alone, this moon is perched in the atmosphere, wishing us success, but the stars are unwilling to have the courage of spectators. We do not see guards, but we know they are there, watching. Degnan motions us, indicating we must get behind the building, and I know in the back of the plant there is brush and bramble, helpful for the disguise of movement.

Degnan is the frontrunner, crawling on his stomach. Wanting to keep the soles of his feet in view, I start to follow him right away. McGinty reaches for my forearm, keeping me from progress. His eyes lock with mine, and I realize he wants me to wait. I think I understand why. In the dark of this night, if we spread out we will be harder to spot than if we are in a line moving together. McGinty knew to stop me and that was in response to his powerful Elite training, but there was no response from me like there should have been. Not anymore. Nonetheless that connection McGinty and I had through the locking of our eyes came not from training but from time spent together, so much time that every nuance breeds communication; every glance sends a message; and each touch has a code of its own. The two years we lived with Shaw in unit 791, and all that time we spied as subterraneans within The Third knit our connection together. *Locasa* can never steal that.

I whisper to McGinty, "I won't stand a chance against some Elite trained guard."

He says, "We got you covered, Avery." McGinty takes his hand off my arm. "We'll stick to you like glue."

"You've been hanging around Annalynn too long. No one's used glue in three decades."

I begin the crawl on my stomach to the back of the building. How hard it is to travel with elbows and arms operating as legs and feet. I must contend with a slippery metal ground cover that makes moving twice the work. My muscles tire quickly, aching from exertion. What is it about snakes that allows them to glide over anything? Pasha will probably figure that out and pass me from behind.

Even after all five of us are safely around the back of the plant, we cannot stand up for fear of being spotted. We are still on our stomachs at the bottom of a small rise tangled with tall weeds. There are no signs that someone has been here before us, and looking over my shoulder I see Shaw has done his job covering our reptile-like tracks that parted the weeds. I whisper to Degnan, "Are you playing with us or do you really know how to get in there, other than the front door?"

He says nothing, but reaches his arm through the brambles, clearing a space in front of him. A long horizontal window is released. It is wide enough and tall enough for one adult body to squirm through. There is no button alcove, so Degnan turns a simple lever, pushing the framed glass inward and creating an opening for entry. He says, "Even devils weren't devils to begin with." I'm not sure what he means by that, but I'm too terrified to figure it out right now. All I want to do is get inside and regroup, so I follow him through the window.

Pasha is after me, and I help her down into an archaic room that is a large tunnel. She says, "This is not a lab."

"Don't knock the architect when he's in the room, sister," Degnan says.

"Not your sister." Her eyes sweep the area with an initial examination while I give McGinty a hand in the window. "You built this?" Pasha asks.

"Man of many talents."

"How long did it take you?"

"Let's just say I used my free time wisely when I worked my decade as a surgeon for The Third."

Shaw is the last in the window, and we are all a bit in awe of this place. The walls and ceilings are part of the earth, and it looks like Degnan literally carved his way through this. The ceiling is only about six feet high. Neither Shaw nor McGinty clear the height, and it will be necessary for them to duck the entire time they are standing. From side to side the tunnel is only eight feet wide, its length swinging around in a horseshoe shaped corridor. The tunnel might be sixty or seventy feet in length if it were stretched out straight.

"This is my room of secrets," Degnan says, and he wanders the room, visiting each of us for a moment or two, breathing in our faces, making me realize how long it has been since any of us lived on peps and how quick our stale breath has returned without the regulated nutrition. He continues his tour, with his low creepy voice setting me on edge. "My little habitat, my hidden haunt," he stops, looking at us all. "And I've invited you to visit, so play nice."

Shaw asks him, "Why did you build this?" Degnan looks to me as if he has explained himself already.

I say, "Even devils weren't devils to begin with. You were going to get *locasa* away from The Third, weren't you?"

He laughs, strolling the corridor of his structure, saying, "Try a loftier goal, DeTornada. *Locasa*, GEB recipes, GEBs, you name it. I was going to liberate it, all of it."

"What happened to that plan, Degnan?" says Shaw sarcastically. "Lose your way while becoming a deadlies distributor?"

"Watch it," Degnan says. "That's not playing nice, and right now I'm the only one you've got to play with."

"I don't remember you in the lab," Pasha says.

"Oh, I was gone long before your time, Dr. Lutnik. Packed off to be a pocket-watch—a guardian for a vicious group of youngsters belonging to the justices. Trapped in a deserted library that was never a destination for anyone but abandoned children." He sits by the side of the dirt wall, lounging and picking at his nails. "Can't say I'm sorry we lost a few of those little monsters along the way."

I fly across the tunnel at him, landing on his chest and punching at his face. Pasha scurries out of the way, smacking her balled fist into the palm of her other hand chanting, "Odds are two to one—two to one. Avery—odds on you. Two to one, two to one."

"You're right!" I yell at Degnan, smacking him again. "You weren't born a devil to begin with. You were hatched as one." And just as I pull up my arm back to bash him again, Shaw grabs my entire body by the waist and lifts me off Degnan.

"Shut up," Degnan says. "No one knows about this room, but they will if you don't shut up." He wipes the blood off his nose as he struggles to his feet.

"Your plan?" says McGinty.

Degnan responds, checking a time piece on the cuff of his coverall. "The lab will close in two hours. And no one will be there from 2:00 am until 4:00. It will be the same every morning." McGinty hands him a cloth from his pack and Degnan dabs at the dribbling blood from the side of his ear. "Entrance is by palm code, but we'll be entering from a spot that's already in the lab, an unexpected and undetected entrance. We won't need the palm code. The video and audio trails will shoot security pictures in an arc across the room."

Pasha says, "The VATs pick up what is in the pathway in front of them, but not immediately below them."

Degnan holds up a can with some sort of spray mechanism on the top and a few rust spots on the front of its label. He continues his explanation. "So if one of us can get under the VAT and spray it with this freeze-cam—"

Pasha finishes, "It will freeze-frame the VAT image for 90 minutes. The image won't change. It will look like the empty lab it's supposed to be, and we can go in and do whatever we need to for an hour and a half. Brilliant." She shrinks away from Degnan, realizing she just called him brilliant.

"Will it work?" asks Shaw. No one answers.

Finally Pasha asks, "How old is the can?"

"Bought it right when freeze-cam came out, almost twenty years ago," says Degnan.

We all look at Pasha, hoping for an optimistic report. She spreads her fingers wide on both hands and moves like she is a conductor at a symphony. "Maybe. Maybe. Maybe," she says. "Maybe it will work."

Degnan looks again at his time piece. "It's midnight. Two hours and ticking."

I move quickly around the curve in the horseshoe and find a spot to wait. I don't know how long we'll be here but as long as we are, whenever we are in wait-mode, I'll be on the opposite side of this horseshoe where I can't see Degnan. The devil makes me sick. I want him dead. I have never wanted to take a life before. There have been times when it has been necessary for survival, but I have never wanted someone's blood. If I end up being a leader for ten years, twenty years or more will this hate-filled feeling ever go away? I don't like discovering this wretched part of me that hates. Maybe I was hatched from the same brood as Degnan.

When I return to join the group, I find Pasha and McGinty taking an inventory of the tunnel supplies. Four long shelves line the inner side of the tunnel and are filled with medicines, canned food, a can opener, bandages, blankets, notebooks—some that are empty and some with detailed information that pays great attention to the recipe for GEBs and the results of *locasa*. Also on a shelf is a small medical book covering the invention and repair of eye-readers. Then there's the water storage cans. Lots of cans. I wonder how old they are, but Pasha has already tracked the data in her chipster and the date on the sealed water is adequate. A delicate framed photo of a boy about twelve and a rigid woman with braided blonde hair. The wisps around her temples are graying. I hate this picture. It does something to humanize Degnan and that is not right. Also on the shelves there are actual pencils and real paper. Where did he get these scarce items? Other than the pigeon messages and the records of the artificial #14 tats, I have not written on paper for a long time. In some way this seems like a luxury. Stacked on a corner shelf there's a game called checkers and another named chess. I can't imagine having time to play games underneath the threat of The Third. There are candles and matches and a small lantern. Pasha and McGinty inspect flashlights and batteries, things we used to camp with in the forest as a family.

Pasha takes a written count of each item and McGinty records them neatly in a notebook. They find a bottle of something called Hennessey. The bottle is one third empty. We all take turns smelling it, and when I do I shiver and can't imagine why even Degnan would drink it.

Degnan grabs the bottle from me. "Eighty years old. Older than me."

"All the more reason not to drink it," I say.

"On the contrary, cognac gets better with age."

"Doesn't smell like it," says Pasha.

He takes a tin cup from the shelf and pours himself a small amount. He smells it then sips it. "Perfect," he concludes.

The inventory continues. There is a small stack of white coveralls and caps, and each set is sealed in a clear wrapper. I know these are for the doctors and scientists in the plant. I have seen them before when they brought *locasa* to me. I also notice a small pile of cigarette papers like Old Soul's and a pouch of tobacco.

Taunting us—taunting me—Degnan picks up the papers and tobacco and sits, leaning against the wall. He takes elaborate time positioning the paper on his leg, occasionally looking up at me and letting an ugly smirk spread slowly over his mouth. His fingering of the tobacco, removing it from the pouch and placing it on the paper are all accomplished in slow motion. When he has completely encircled the tobacco with a paper, rolling it with expert coordination, he extends his tongue and wets the paper, pressing the moist section against the adjoining end, sealing the cigarette's fate.

"Ridiculous," I say. "You can't light that."

Pasha supports me and says, "They'd smell the smoke."

"Can't light it," he says, "but I can lick it." Once more his tongue comes out, flicking over the cigarette from one end to the other. This he does at a measured speed, staring at me my face, my shoes—everywhere. I stand up and join McGinty at the shelves, pretending to ignore Degnan, helping with the inventory. But I cannot ignore him, even when my back is turned.

McGinty hands the notebook to me, turning over his job, and he takes over Pasha's duties examining the supplies. He says as he offers me a pencil, "Still remember how to write?"

"At least the first part of the alphabet," I say.

"Not sure that's going to work for us." He squats down, and I notice how the ends of his hair have grown out the last couple weeks. The dark color now apparent, no longer a buzz cut revealing only the color of scalp. "Seven rolls of gauze," he counts.

"Well at least we can wrap an injury, even if we starve to death."

He picks up a can of food. "Oh we won't starve." He turns the large can in his hands, reading the label on the front of the blue wrapper. "*Sweet Sue Canned Whole Chicken, Fully Cooked.*"

I laugh. "Is Sue the name of the chicken?"

McGinty smiles. "Not sure," he says. "But Annalynn would love the idea of vintage food. We ought to take her a label back." The thought of bringing something back to anyone surprises me. I expect we may not make it out of here alive. McGinty gives me courage in little ways that I hope someday I can repay. "How about this one?" It is a smaller can and has a red plastic lid, and at the top of the brown wrapper it says *Honeyville*. A cream colored label belts the middle section of the can, and McGinty reads it to me. "*Powdered whole eggs.*"

Shaw asks, "How can it be a whole egg if it's powdered?"

By now we have Pasha's attention and she takes the can away from McGinty to read it on her own. After a long silence she looks at McGinty and asks, "Got any canned cucumber wine?"

McGinty scrutinizes the shelves, "Don't think so." He holds up the canned whole chicken. "But do you recognize Herman and Orbit's family?" Pasha stares at him, snorts and joins Shaw at the entrance window, no comment.

"Hey," Degnan says as he reaches for the canned chicken. "I can get big money for these on the—" He stops himself from finishing the sentence, knowing he's gone too far.

"Where?" I ask, just waiting for him to reveal more of his filthy corrupt self. "Where were you going to get big money for these? You were going to sell them where?" I walk over to him and kick his boot. "Where?"

He takes another lick of his cigarette and says, "Dark Market, honey."

Suddenly, in my mind, it all fits together like a mangled puzzle with disappointing results. I slowly squat beside him, talking steady and low. "You weren't going to get rid of the GEBs and *locasa* for the salvation of the city, were you? You were going to sell them on the Dark Market."

The smell of the tobacco on his breath, now wet with his saliva, is nauseating. "Wasn't going to *sell* it to the market. I was going to *be* the market. I'm sure the New Coastline will be clamoring for entrepreneurs ripe for business opportunities."

His sarcasm sickens me. "You're despicable," I say and walk around the horseshoe one more time, trying to escape his presence. I lean against the wall and slide down to a squatting position, propping my face against my open palms. *Breathe,* I tell myself. *Breathe.* I must gain control. I might be with this monster in a small underground tunnel for days, and I can't let him get to me like this. *Breathe.*

McGinty comes and joins me on the floor. I feel better already. He says in a whisper, "Not much of a honeymoon, is it?" I say nothing. I really don't want to think about Raben right now. "Not what you expected?"

I let myself down the rest of the way until I am seated on the floor and then look into McGinty's face. "I haven't expected anything for a very long time." He nods his head and looks away. "And besides, how do you even know what a honeymoon is?"

"Your mother," he says and fidgets with a cigarette paper from the shelves, staring at it as he talks. "Pasha needed help with the *locasa* reversal. She recruited me. We had to watch the footage," he stops, obviously uncomfortable, "more than once."

My stomach turns at the thought of McGinty, or anyone, watching my mother and father's private moments. "Thank you for being honest." It is all I can think of to say.

"We should try to get some sleep before we sneak into the lab." I think maybe he will get a blanket and lie down by me. I would like that. Instead, he gets two blankets, covers me with one and takes the other around the horseshoe out of sight. Pasha brings her blanket and lies near me. She stares at the ceiling, and I know neither of us will sleep.

Tonight, my first night in the plant, I wonder if I'm trapped in the horseshoe underground or saved within its walls. I imagine I hear the voices of the scientists working in the lab, but I know that's impossible. We are too far away to hear them or for them to hear us. We have blankets to keep us warm and use our packs to rest our heads on. When I hear a chorus of three snoring from the other side of the tunnel, I concentrate on holding very still, so I can sort through this mad plan we have. It will not materialize with four people acting on impulses, or erupting into arguments over the best way to accomplish our goals, the few we have. I practice talking to my muscles, telling each one to relax and be dormant, releasing anticipation. My eyes are alert. My eyelids do not need to resist heaviness. There is none. I unstrap my Z-Colt and clutch it in the firing position, my finger on the trigger, tapping a rhythm ever so gently. Maybe I am letting it know: *Be ready, I am here.* I rest it on my chest so that it rises and falls with the beating of my heart. My heart—I cannot command that muscle to be still. And the Z-Colt? Well, it will forever be along for the ride.

I breathe in the dank air and force an exhale to come slow and controlled. I try to put Annalynn and Morris' faces before me. I am doing this for them, for Carles and Raghill and in hopes that I might once again be with Raben. I try to tell myself that I am capable of all this. My father would have said that to me. *Capable.*

———

Maybe I slept, Maybe I didn't. But it is already time to organize the night. Strategize specifically so the seconds will not be wasted and the 90 minutes will bring us closer to our goal. I move around the horseshoe, Pasha by my side, joining the three men to plan the infiltration. On one side of the tunnel, I stand, notebook in hand keeping track of the ideas. I say, "So we're all agreed that before we leave the plant we must destroy all GEB recipes, find *locasa* and take it with us and somehow get any GEBs that are activated back to Red Grove."

Shaw says, "We're agreed on the goals. But none of us know how to accomplish them."

Pasha stands, "By analyzing."

"She's right," I say. "We go one night at a time. Tonight, Degnan leads us to the information, and we put together the big picture of what we're dealing with. Shaw and McGinty memorize everything about the facility."

"I'll use the chipster when I can," says Pasha. "I'll try to determine what stage of development the GEBs are in."

Shaw picks up the can of freeze-cam for spraying the VAT and says, "I'm the tallest. When we get there, I'll put the cameras on freeze."

"Okay," I conclude. "We're off."

Degnan says, "The first room we enter is storage. No VATs. From there, Shaw will enter the lab first. Then, the rest of us proceed." He whispers as he motions us to follow. "Oh, the power of leadership," he quips. My skin crawls with fear, and I can't imagine not being terrified when this man leads the way.

One end of the tunnel is a dead end, so we head in the other direction, winding around the horseshoe until we come to a three foot high exit with a handle on it. Degnan reaches forward, turns the handle and pulls. With the help of Shaw and McGinty they remove the door and set it aside. Degnan slides his entire body through the hole. He is on his stomach, and I wait until I see his feet move from a prone position to one where he is standing up. Then, I follow.

I crawl on my stomach and have about twenty inches height to maneuver under what appears to be some sort of storage shelves. I must be conscious of remaining flat so as not to be held up and slowed down by the shelves above me. I think this will be an easier job for Pasha, considering her size. It does not take long to realize there are aisles and aisles of these shelves.

Finally, I break through to the open part of the room and stand. I tap my temple for infrared activation and am amazed at the picture I see. In this twenty foot open area at the center of this enormous storage room there are rows and rows of twelve foot high shelves. The ones I just crawled under. The shelves are all loaded with something, but it is too dark to tell what it is.

I hate to admit it, but Degnan's tunnel is genius. With these tall shelves looming no one would ever get down on hands and knees at the last aisle by the wall and look for a camouflaged door leading to a tunnel. He must have really wanted to get his contraband out of the plant.

As my infrared fades and my eyes become adjusted to the dark, I realize what is on the shelves. GEBs. Shelf after shelf, row after row of them. They are neither male nor female and, like Baldy, they have no hair or identifying features. Each is covered in a thin plastic. My great-grandmother might have said they were "shrink-wrapped." They do not breathe. They are in waiting. Waiting for the kind of life that will be given to them by their creators, the scientists. I cringe. This lab is way past recipes. We can find the formulas and destroy them, but we must also get rid of these GEBs lingering in storage.

I feel Pasha take my hand and squeeze it tightly over and over again. Knowing Pasha this is some sort of important communication, but I have no idea what. The peripheral movement of Shaw passing me on the way to the lab sends a chill down my spine. This is it.

No telling how long Shaw is gone. Each second seems like minutes, and I lose track of time. McGinty, Degnan, Pasha and I stand in the center of the storage room, staring at each other, our eyes huge with anxiety. Edginess swims around the room, catching me by the throat and holding on until I see Shaw's hand stick through the door. He motions us to come with a thumbs-up sign Annalynn taught us last year.

As we enter the lab I notice it is small. Much about it reminds me of the salad spinner. While it is not round, the lab has an uncanny feel that at any moment it could become a being and capture us with its power. I chant in my head: *I am capable. I am capable. I am capable.* But do not believe it.

And then I see them. Three GEBs sitting in a line, just like the day I was in the salad spinner. Their heads are limp, hanging at their chests. They do not move. Stone still. Pasha says, "They're in the emotional development stage, waiting for breath."

Shaw stealthily removes his ten inch blade from his waist and whispers in Pasha's ear, "Well, one breath and you and I can do a little ventricle surgery."

"Remember what I said." Her voice is curt and commanding. "These three are coming back with us. We can't get enough of the right information without them."

"We have eighty minutes left," I say. McGinty and Shaw inspect every piece of machinery in the lab, making mental notes to be jotted down later. Pasha filters data into her chipster which she will decipher back in the tunnel. Degnan and I help her record information about each GEB. Not just their body height, but intricate measurements of each finger and toe, the width between their eyes and the slope of their noses. To me they all look exactly the same, and maybe they are, but

241

Pasha wants every minute detail recorded. She wants to make sure. I take stock of the entire room, thinking if I look hard enough a plan will come to me. How do we get three GEBs, which at the moment have not been completely activated, out of here along with us and anything else we need to liberate?

I reach my hand out to touch the scalp of one of the GEBs. Its skin is smooth, cold like the chilled tomatoes we had the summer before *Jurbay* came down, except no color. I recoil and draw my hand away when I see the bluish veins beneath the GEB's skull, running all the way to its neck then down its arms.

———

Pasha says, "Time," and my other four team members immediately move cautiously toward the storage room where we will exit to the tunnel. I take my first step in that direction and freeze. Everything freezes. My lungs do not work, my heart does not pump and prickles race across every surface of my body. Someone is staring at me. I feel it. I force myself to look over my shoulder. The GEB on the end, the one I touched when Pasha and I were measuring, has one eye open, and it's looking at me.

# Chapter 14

# FORGIVENESS IS FOREIGN

From a pile of supplies at one end of the horseshoe tunnel, Pasha and I roll four small barrels to the center of the tunnel where the inventory shelves flank the roughhewn wall. We place three of the barrels in a semi-circle as stools around the fourth barrel, setting a piece of wood across it to serve as a work table. We anxiously await our second raid of the laboratory that holds so many of The Third's secrets. I would call our first entry successful. Our 90 minute expedition allowed us to gain basic information. We've kept busy with the dissemination of the data. Shaw and McGinty have been gone for hours on reconnaissance in Reichel, searching for anything that will help us evaluate exactly where The Third stands regarding their supply inventory and their assets for war.

Earlier today Pasha hung up thin-skin on the tunnel wall. Of course if I hadn't seen her hang it, I wouldn't know it was there. That's the point. She says she's "on the ready," preparing for anything that might need this material, after all she designed Red Grove and covered it with the stuff. All of the Chipsters have thin-skin somewhere on their bodies.

Degnan and I sit opposite each other checking Pasha's measurements of the GEBs. At this point, none of the GEBs on the storage shelves are activated and the three in the lab are in the final stages of activation. They are supposed to be sexless, ageless, hairless, identical molds of human beings, anticipating their breath of life and their individual characteristics that will permit them to blend into The 28 United.

"Pasha, you notice anything unusual about those three GEBs in the lab?" I ask.

"Yeah, they're genetically engineered," Pasha answers.

"Ha," sniggers Degnan.

"Seriously," I say. Pasha says no more, so I prod. "What exactly does 'final stages of activation' mean?"

Degnan says, "Their almost done with their psychological profile."

"Within the week they'll look like someone you know well," says Pasha.

"Can they communicate in this phase?" I ask Pasha.

"Not really, not without final activation."

"What would it mean in terms of GEB experiments if one could communicate?"

Pasha tries to smooth her messy hair, fails and tries again. "Stop asking questions, Avery, and just tell us why you want to know. I saw you touch its creepy head."

"I was curious."

"And..." Pasha rarely looks directly at anyone, but now she has on her interrogation game face, staring at me.

"It was watching me. The GEB on the end was watching me." Pasha and Degnan are silent, eyes locked on me "So what's that mean?"

"It likes the sound of your voice," says Degnan.

"You and I weren't talking," I say.

"Thinks you're sexy."

"Shut up! Pasha, what's it mean?"

"It means the GEBs are making independent decisions," she says. "Decisions not controlled by scientists or time tables." She waits, thinking, then continues, "You shouldn't have touched its head. That was stupid."

"Are you saying me touching it activated it?"

"Maybe. Are you sure you didn't just 'think' it looked at you? I mean there was a lot of tension in there. A lot of pressure."

I cross to the window. "Look, a GEB watched me in the lab. It had control of one eye, and it stared at me. That was not some little coincidence, some knee-jerk reaction or my imagination. It was purposeful, and I caught it the act."

Degnan mocks me, "And you can't get that crawling feeling out from under your skin?"

"No, *that* feeling's from you. Probably won't go away until you do."

The jarring noise of the entry window opening brings us to a standing position. McGinty and Shaw slip in the window followed by a tabby cat, scrawny with patches of its hair missing. It jumps to the storage shelves, facing us with a vicious feral yowl. It flashes its claws, arching its back. Pasha steps forward ready to embrace it.

"Hey," I say, "don't get near that thing. Think about what it might do to your pigeons."

"They're not here. It just needs the right treatment," says Pasha, just as the cat springs back to the ledge of the window ready to pounce and attack.

"It's feral," says Degnan. "Give it up."

"You're feral," she says, "and we can't give you up." She walks stealthily toward the cat in hopes of capturing it, but the feline will have nothing of that and bounds off the window scurrying down one side of the horseshoe out of sight.

I prop the window open a crack. "Ignore it," I say. "It'll find its way out." I look at Shaw and McGinty taking off some of their outer gear. "What'd you find?" I ask.

"Two loyal ones using their chipsters," says McGinty.

"Out in the open?"

"Trying to hide, but if we saw them others might too."

"We sent them north to try to catch up and join the others," says Shaw as he reads labels from the cans on the shelves, looking for dinner. "These Chipsters are doing us more harm than good."

McGinty says, "If their caught, The Third discovers the chipsters, duplicates the technology and then we lose that communication element."

"What about The Third?" I ask. "Find anything?" I'm anxious to record information and get out of here.

McGinty answers, "Not really. Other than their Elite soldiers are out there operating among the ranks of others who are not nearly as trained."

"Might be to our advantage some night," says Shaw, and I notice all his weapons are stacked neatly by the wall except his blade.

Pasha looks at the inventory list and rummages through the storage cans, finding a small tin of peanut butter. This can doesn't need an opener so she pops the tab, peeling back the lid, setting it around the curve of the horseshoe.

"Cats don't eat peanut butter," says Degnan.

Pasha gives him the scientific glare. "Hopelessly ignorant. I studied fifteen cats for a month. They all ate peanut butter."

"Glad you found something useful to do with all that education."

"Shut up."

I'm watching Degnan grope the shelf for the bottle of Hennessey behind the supplies.

"You should be able to smell it out," I say. "It really stinks."

"It's not my fault you don't know aged cognac when you smell it."

"Don't now and won't ever," I say making note of his wrist. "Why don't you have a #14 on your wrist?"

"You're staring at me, Avery. I knew you found me attractive." He pauses a moment, then continues. "I was delivering *locasa*, not receiving it."

"Was there ever really an inoculation for the 14 Deadlies?

Degnan shakes his head and says, "The Third killed off much of the population without even thinking about an inoculation."

"*Locasa* inoculated against families, not the deadlies."

"They didn't have to take a family from me. *Jurbay* did that," Degnan says. I think of the photo on the supply shelf of the woman and the twelve year old child. I notice this picture is now missing. "You'd think they would have developed an inoculation before they eliminated most of the world." He takes a swig of the Hennessey directly from the bottle.

Pasha grabs it from him and puts her nose above it. Taking a deep whiff she examines the amber color through the clear, pint bottle. Then to my surprise, she takes a long pull. Her eyes expand, and her eyebrows rise toward her hairline. At the same time she stands tip-toes and bounces up and down. Taking a deep breath, she whispers in a raspy voice, "Research," and sets the bottle back on the table.

"Research, huh?" I say and retrieve the bottle, lifting it to my lips, sipping more cautiously than Pasha. It burns all the way down my throat, esophagus and into my stomach. It tastes horrible, but the warmth that comes at the end of the burn feels comforting. Degnan checks his timepiece for about the third time in the last half hour. "Got somewhere to go?" I ask.

"In just a few minutes we'll know how the longevity of my scientific excellence plays out and how well that Elite training serves you." Pasha and I exchange a look. He makes me nervous every time he opens his mouth, but this seems like some sort of direct threat. I reach for the bottle, but Degnan blocks my hand, protecting his stash. "Soon we'll know what you're made of."

"Well good luck with that," I say. "If you don't know by now, I'm an ordinary citizen with a powerful name, just trying not to screw this up."

"That may be your self-effacing explanation of what you're doing, but you better get it through your head that they don't care about dump pickers or librarians or minstrels. But you, DeTornada, you they care about. You defied the cage. You collected an army of people outside of Reichel. You married. And that means you flaunted your disregard for their breeding program and their repulsion of commitment. Now they'll be a continual stream of people following your example. Maybe even creating a string of babies—out of *love*." The way he says that word turns my stomach.

"You have no rights here. So shut up. You better not bring peril on us. We have enough of it already. You're directly responsible for welcoming the cruelty of The Third into our world. You worked for them for over a decade."

Degnan's voice croaks back at me while Pasha retrieves the Hennessey, protecting the contents of the bottle we all shared a moment ago. "I'm not responsible for it all. I'm not responsible for brain-swappers. You were supposed to be taking care of those people not me. You bear the responsibility for that and for the library. You brought it on too. I'm not the only one." He looks at me in a moment of awkward silence then says, "You remind me of your mother—sexy when you're mad."

"You don't know my mother. She never gets mad."

"But she does get sexy."

I pin Degnan to the table, face down, with my left hand pushing on his neck and my Z-Colt connecting with the temple of his head. I set the hammer of the Z-Colt in the ready position. "Shut up or I'll blow your brains out."

"And give away our cozy little hideout? I don't think so. Scientists are still working in the lab." I want to blow his head off, regardless of the noise, but can't. So I slam his head to the table again. I release my hand from the back of his neck, keeping my Z-Colt at arm's length, out of his grasp. Pasha pulls his left arm, trying to get him away from me. She's not ready to see me murder our main source of information. But I catch his other arm. We are wrenching him apart. Then, Pasha leaps on my back, trying to pull me off of him, attempting to stop me from eliminating our source, but she is small, and I am huge with hatred. Then her wispy hold is replaced by one of strength, lifting me away from Degnan. Degnan gasps, retreating to the storage shelves, retrieving his Hennessey from where Pasha placed it.

McGinty says, without breaking his hold around me, "Someone might hear you outside the plant. Shut up."

My body goes limp, and he releases his grip. *He should be the leader. I don't want this job.* I say nothing, and walk past

McGinty and Shaw the thirty-two paces around the horseshoe to what I consider my sequestered space. Of course it is in no way private, but around the curve of the horseshoe I can't see Degnan's face. It's true I can hear his taunting, but I can also block it out and bring myself to a point of solitude.

I look at my timepiece, tapping a metal grommet in my coverall that releases a neon number, flashing in the fabric. Eight at night. I sit on the floor with my back to the dirt wall. I know I should be with McGinty and Shaw listening to their reports. My eyes close in exhaustion. I seek just a few moments away from the constant batter of Degnan. I can't imagine that my time here with him might go on a few days more, or even extend to a week.

———

I jump, jerking awake, glancing at my timepiece. I've been out for over an hour. I hear McGinty and Shaw discussing their foray into Reichel, documenting observations about aircraft, ammunition, the use of the web and anything else that will give us clues as to what we are actually up against if we mount an offensive campaign directed toward The Third.

I will my body to get up from the floor, but it doesn't hear. The hard dirt wall pushes at the muscles in my back, and I stare at the ceiling, picking a spot to concentrate on, putting Degnan as far away from my mind as possible. Maybe fatigue makes the wall look blurry, like it's moving, swaying right at the juncture between wall and ceiling. Then I notice that every ten feet or so there's a hole carved in the dirt ceiling. I panic, imagining a camera attached to the inside of those holes.

Movement flicks in each opening, and I know this isn't just me being tired. I inhale a quick breath, horrified. The flicks are tongues connected to triangular reptile heads, and as they slither through the holes I instantly identify them as vipers.

Pasha screams, and before the vipers slink down the wall, I run to the center curve of the horseshoe. Degnan is standing by the window entrance, looking at his timepiece. "9:20," he says.

Shaw and McGinty run from the other side of the horseshoe and stop quickly as they see Pasha staring down a viper. She is maybe six inches from it. She is motionless. The serpent raises its hood-like head unhinging its jaw and opening its mouth 180°. With her eyes never leaving the viper and every part of her body still, she opens her mouth in slow motion, mimicking the serpent's pose. I hear the rustling of the other vipers slinking around the tunnel, but I can't move, if I do the viper bites Pasha. Two of the vipers slither across my boot, and just as I am about to shake them off Shaw swings his ten-inch knife blade at their heads, decapitating them both. The viper facing Pasha strikes and catches her on the shoulder. She stumbles backwards, collapsing on the dirt floor as Shaw slices that viper's head off too, bringing the death toll to three.

I glance at the holes above and don't see any more of the reptiles entering, and I figure there must be about four or five left in the tunnel. One of them winds around the peanut butter can while another curls in strike position on the makeshift table. I reach out to help Pasha and the viper on the table jumps toward me, head unhinged, fangs out. Degnan throws himself over me, collapsing us both on the floor, me on my back and him on top of me. Simultaneously the viper falls, and I hear the patter of animal feet. I think I'm dead from a viper bite or Degnan's weight, until I open my eyes and staring me in the face is the feral cat, holding the dying viper firmly in its teeth, the snake's tail still whipping from side to side.

Shaw yells, "Masks. Gloves." Degnan has wallowed off me, and I see Shaw and McGinty already in protective attire. Pasha reaches in her bag and pulls out her own mask and gloves, putting them on like an expert. Then she takes her second set of gear, grabs the cat and stuffs it in her additional mask while the dead viper falls from the cat's mouth. Writhing in panic, the cat attempts a scream but can only muster a whisper.

"Stay still, Vipe," says Pasha to the feral and stuffs both her gloves in the opening of the mask so the cat cannot escape.

McGinty has carefully pulled out a vial from the back of the supply shelves. Degnan says, "Ah-ha, may I introduce you to Deadly #7."

By this time I've secured my mask and gloves by snapping them in place, leaving no opening for the deadly to seep in. McGinty says, "Avery, get your second set of gear. Give it to Degnan." We all stand still. I am looking at Degnan and everyone else looks at me. *Am I expected to save this man's life?* "Avery," McGinty repeats. I yank out the extra mask and gloves, throw them at Degnan's feet, and he puts them on just as a viper weaves its way from behind the supply shelves. McGinty sprays the Deadly #7 from an atomizer on the vial, covering each of the ceiling holes and the space across the entrance window. The feral cat—Vipe—has finally settled inside the mask that's held in Pasha's arms.

"Keep your gear on for four—better say five hours. Then #7 is gone," says Shaw.

"Quick and deadly. Burns the eyes from the inside then heads for the brain," quips Degnan. "Then it gets around to the whole body, leaving nothing but a pile of ash. Brilliant." I can't stop staring at him. Without thought or restraint he shielded me from death by a viper, yet with malice and intent I came close to withholding protective gear and killing him. Who's the viper here? I don't want to evaluate my hate, but I can't help it. In all the years I watched my mother and father emerging into leadership, I never saw them hate. I may be a DeTornada, but I am not like them.

We all settle on the ground, leaning against the tunnel walls. "Pasha," I ask, "what can we do for your viper bite?"

She pats the mask where the cat resides with the palm of her hand, comforting the frightened animal. "Did you know vipers have a very developed brain?" she asks.

Pasha examines the mouth of the viper that just bit her. "How can you be scientific right now when time might be running out for you?" I ask.

She laughs. "If it had used its venom, I'd be dead by now." She picks up the viper's head with her gloved hands, prying the mouth open and showing us all the fangs. "See. The fangs are curled up in the roof of its mouth, in that little membrane sack. It chose not to release them. Chose not to bite me."

"Yeah?"

Pasha has the viewing window of her mask close to the viper's head, probing. "Not a drop of venom anywhere." I glance at the other snakes sizzling away to ash as the #7 infiltrates their bodies, like the slugs we used to douse with salt before *Jurbay*. Except salt doesn't send a human to ashes like this would have done to us. "This viper never chose to use the venom," Pasha says and shuffles over to Degnan, holding the viper head right up to the window in his mask. "The viper has the ability to make decisions."

"It bit you," says Degnan.

"It bit me, but it chose not to use his venom, and it didn't kill me. It didn't see me as a threat. Maybe it was confused. Maybe it chose mercy. Or, maybe it's 'cause I'm brilliant and it knew it. We'll never know." She throws the serpent head against Degnan's mask and his reflexes send him to the ground.

I look at Degnan, unable to read his eyes through his protective mask. "How could you plan something like this?"

"Wanted to protect my territory." He pushes the viper head away with his toe, watching it disintegrate. "Wanted to make sure no one would take advantage of what I built—no matter who came or when they came. But that was a long time ago that I planned all this."

Shaw says, "Sustainable evil. Good one, Degnan."

I say, "You knew that it could all still be working. You knew at 9:20 those holes might open. You *knew*," I say.

"I wasn't sure."

"You could have warned us."

Shaw twirls his knife in his hand and says, "But you didn't."

"How could they live that long without food? A decade while you were gone?" McGinty asks.

"Oh, they have an access into the world up there." He looks at the holes in the ceiling. "And they've probably already laid their brood. Eggs just waiting to be hatched."

"Not anymore. That #7 seeps up the holes and it'll take care of any eggs left." McGinty says. Then, silence. Nothing left to say. We'll be sitting around for five hours trapped in our securely enclosed gear, protecting us from a deadly, but nothing can protect us from our thoughts.

I push myself to my feet, traveling around the horseshoe to what I have come to call my cloistered world. The others know when I am here they should not approach. McGinty and Shaw never seem to need a world of their own partly because they constantly have eyes on Degnan. And Pasha is always in her own little world no matter where she is. But me? Well, right now I can't stop shaking. There is no way I will ever sleep again. The second the black inside of my closed eyes appears it becomes a backdrop for the triangular heads of the deadly vipers with their unhinged jaws poised to strike. My eyes pop open, and I don't even want to blink. Within my eardrums I have memorized the snake choir hissing as they mark their prey. I plug my ears with the fingers of my gloves, but the sound doesn't fade, rather, it rises in crescendo. I breathe in double-time. Now I force myself to slow my breathing. It takes a while. As I nod off again, the viper's head is replaced by Degnan's face attached to the writhing body of a serpent.

What's happening to me? Until *Jurbay* fell, forgiveness was foreign. My life speeded by, forming the memories all kids deserve. There was nothing to forgive, but as *Jurbay* severed the earth it chiseled away my childhood. The hurts I held were many, guarded in a hidden vault where I would go to inventory year after year. In a matter of weeks my mother has redeemed herself in my eyes. Did I hold the key to setting her free from the score card I've kept religiously at the back of my heart? And now, there's Degnan. God help me. I can never forgive him for the deadly vial and the child's life he took with full intent and no mercy. Never. Yet, today there is a tiny crack in the hate I've harbored against this demon. There is no way for me to ignore, shut out or obliterate Degnan's actions tonight. Without hesitation he fell on me—shielded me from a viper's venom. I hunger to put another tally mark in the column under his name marked "malicious," but I can't. I can only draw a new column and label it "redeemed." And there, for Degnan, the tally mark is small, maybe just half a line, but it is there. Yesterday he asked me, "Don't you believe people can change, Commander?" I thought I had the answer.

# Chapter 15

# THE RACE IN MY STOMACH

Seven weeks into this search and discover mission. Seven weeks too long away from Raben. Our underground habitat brings us daily surprises. Sometimes they come in the form of Vipe leaping in the window with a prize in her mouth: a bird, a lizard or a half-eaten squirrel. Sometimes it's the small acknowledgements of change, like discovering it didn't take long for the effects of a pep-free diet to alter the way life smells. Our stale breath and the residuals of food's foul air from digesting whole canned chicken and powder eggs makes me wish our habitat was not an underground horseshoe tunnel housing five adults. I'm beginning to wonder if I'm sick. My intestines are revolting, playing havoc in my stomach every day, sometimes all day. Each meal chases around my insides, batting chunks of food back and forth. I awake every morning with the palm of my hand tracing an oval shape on my abdomen from my lower stomach to my waist.

"That's normal," says Pasha.

"How do you know?" I challenge her. "You don't know what normal is."

"You're grumpy. Maybe I remember something pre-*locasa*."

"Maybe you don't." I look carefully at her face. I see tears hovering in the corners of her eyes, and I don't remember the last time hints of the gentle, funny Pasha ambushed me. She is comfortable holding those aspects of who she is in a hidden place, out of reach to most. "You haven't tried reversing *locasa* on yourself, have you?" I ask her.

"No." She wipes the corners of her eyes with the heels of her hands. "Once. Maybe just once." She stares off beyond my shoulder, and I am so convinced she sees something, I turn to join her in her gaze, but I see nothing. "*Locasa* worked for your mother. Quinn has her memories back."

I push away from the makeshift table and squat next to Pasha, touching her arm and locking my eyes on hers. "It's too dangerous, Pasha. You don't know enough about reversal yet, and we need you here, fully engaged with us. I don't care what the memories are. We can't afford to lose you. I can't lose you, not a second time."

"You never lost me the first time."

"We almost did." We stay in this position for a while, my hand on her arm, her eyes turning away and avoiding me. "Do you understand? You can't experiment on yourself here. Not now. Do you get it?"

She pushes away from me saying, "Of course, I get it. My IQ is twice yours."

"Yeah, well your social-skill's IQ is non-existent." I rub the top of her head and walk away. I hate it that she is always reminding me of her intelligence. I hate it that she's the one who recognized my condition before I even had time to wonder.

"You're pregnant," she said a week ago.

"Not possible. Peps make sure the creation of human life remains in the breeding banks kept below Reichel in The Third's Artesian Baths."

"You hadn't been eating peps for a while when you married Raben."

I wonder how long I can keep this secret from Degnan, Shaw and McGinty. I don't want to know how they will respond. I imagine Degnan's digs and sarcasm will continue, but over the weeks I've learned to guard my temper, allowing his verbal burrs to roll quickly off my shoulders and seep into the earth. The goal: to limit responses to Degnan, make him an emotional non-factor, beat him at the game he thinks he controls, all the while continuing to extract relevant information from him. I know he meters out the facts he reveals to us. He wants to remain valuable for as long as possible. Will my status as a mother change his nasty mouth or the taunts that have become second nature?

How will Shaw take the news of me carrying another life around on this expedition? Not sure. Ignore it maybe? I'd be happy with that. Coddle me? That would drive me crazy.

Discuss the implications? I'm not discussing anything. And then there's McGinty. It is him I want to tell, and I wish I knew why.

A rustle from our secret entrance to the lab draws my attention to Degnan's return. His bald head pokes through the small hole that we have used nightly to travel back and forth from the tunnel to the storage room. Hundreds of GEBs lie there in a state of readiness, waiting for the moment they are ignited into a life of duplication, a life of surveillance, a life of placing us in constant jeopardy. We've reduced our exploration team to Degnan. No need for the rest of us to go with him as all the scientists' activities and all their progression of adding life-like features to the GEBs have mysteriously stopped. This lab has been the life-line in The Third's strategy, creating GEBs to discover what kind of threats The Third might face outside of Reichel. So what is so urgent that they would throw their most brilliant scientists elsewhere and completely shut down the lab? Where is *elsewhere* and what is going on?

We all look Degnan's way as he dusts off the dirt from the top of his head. He misses the smudges on his face, but we don't use mirrors down here, and it only seems right that the filth on him continues to layer itself into a crusty existence. "Nothing," Degnan says. "No change. Everything's still exactly like it was yesterday and the day before and the day before that. No scientists. VATs disconnected. There's a storage room of GEBs waiting for activation that haven't been touched, and those GEBs close to activation still sit in the lab at the exact same stage of development they were at two weeks ago." I hear the irritation in his voice.

Pasha turns to McGinty, Shaw and me, briefly scanning our eyes then lifting Vipe, talking into her ear like a cat whisperer. Pasha speaks without looking at us. "If the three of you keep scouting Reichel every night, you're going to find the answers." She doesn't rub her head as much anymore, now that she has Vipe to pet.

"Oh, we've found lots of answers," says Shaw. "Fifteen fighter planes in an airplane hangar just waiting for fuel and someone who knows how to fly them. Some sort of giant crematorium that must have worked non-stop for a decade to sanitize this city and the surrounding area, but why the lab shut down and what diverted every commander and scientist from one of their top projects—no answers for that one." And as Shaw reports I remember my own trips to the city this past week.

———

I'd kept my "answer book" zipped tightly in the chest pocket of my gray coverall. How long would Shaw, McGinty and I be able to operate as subterraneans disguised as a night patrol in a city where the unusual brings attention? Anything revealing individuality sent danger signals to the troops that enforce the uniformity of the city. This book I carried, that Degnan created from the pages of unused notebooks stored on the supply shelves of our underground hideaway, had been my own backup system of information. Each time we gathered facts, made observations or discovered stockpiles of arsenals I memorized it all, but also recorded a backup in the answer book. I knew I was capable of memorizing what I saw and making conclusions as to its significance. McGinty and Shaw did it all the time by the nature of their Elite training. I did it with purpose and focus, hoping I could train myself to allow that flawless memorization to once again become automatic. But, also, there was something about holding the answer book, looking at the words that triggered my mind to analyze and brainstorm the makings of a plan. It was like clasping the pieces of a puzzle all jumbled in a bag. If I could just spread out the pieces, get a look at the chaotic mess all in one spot, figure out what fragments should connect to create the border that would eventually frame the picture, then, maybe the answers would start to come and our time inside the tunnel would not be as futile as it had seemed for the last weeks.

One thing I'd figured out on our nightly discoveries in Reichel, as we roamed the alleys clandestinely placing ourselves to avoid contact with the night guard, was that there were two kinds of guards in this city. The Elite guards went through the same training as McGinty, Shaw and me. We knew their skill level well. Always on the ready, they were perceptive, analytical and eerily accurate with their decisions— almost intuitive. The other soldiers in the night guard were trained but were nowhere near as precise or observant as the Elite and occasionally lax in their duties as guards. The Third demanded the allegiance of the citizens of Reichel, complying with every detail commanded. That proved for a docile population, bored guards and an easy mark for the three of us to liberate the uniforms and weapons we needed from the night guards, one piece at a time. These uniforms gave us almost complete mobility to travel anywhere within the city at night, undetected and protected by our anonymity.

Once, three unsuspecting soldiers, two men and a woman, sat on the upturned edges of crates at the end of a deserted alley on the east side of town. They were playing a game. Board games of past decades were nonexistent, holding only a brief mention in the archives of the History Labyrinth. However, boredom was the precursor to creativity. Fashioned by guards unmotivated by the necessity of security, a new board game arose. A piece of light colored leather with an entire city sketched with shades of gray paint provided a backdrop for the simple game. On the leather, between sections of the skyline across the city, stretched pieces of string weighted down by stones. The guards dropped pebbles in a tin cup, shook the cup and spilled the contents on the leather mat. The number of pebbles landing on a building and not on the streets gave the player permission to move the string an equal amount of times from building to building in an attempt to get to the edge of the city. I wasn't sure about all the details of this game, but I named it Pasha Rules. These guards had crafted a game about her zips, and she would be delighted when I told her.

Our key to open travel in this city depended upon our appearance being in perfect unison with each other and with the night guards. We needed one more weapon to make that happen. The DR93 clipped cleanly on the belt of the gray coverall type uniform. It was larger than my Z-Colt but lightweight and deadly. Its electrical charge could stun, maim or kill depending on the vocal command. McGinty and Shaw had secured theirs a week ago. That night I needed to liberate the final element of my disguise.

My eyes scanned the perimeter of the circle where the three guards sat. The circle was lined by a combination of ten gallon and fifty-five gallon drums ablaze with some sort of fuel. This setup looked permanent, not spontaneous. My guess was that the three guards did a major section of their nightly protective duty right here by the fire. It appeared the larger fires in the fifty-five gallon drums provided warmth for the soldiers and the smaller ten gallon ones that were lower to the ground created a barrier of flames, warning rats not to pass beyond the blazing circle. Some of those rats joined me as I lay on my stomach and waited for the right moment to seize a DR93. They nibbled at the soles of my boots. I was sure the smell of canned whole chicken on my breath must have been enticing. I tried to use the humor of it all to quiet the dancing nerves in my stomach.

The abandoned pieces of uniforms scattered casually at the foot of each guard's crate told a story. Only one guard wore his assigned cap. The other two had tossed theirs to the ground where they sat. All three had unsnapped their jackets, but the woman removed hers, setting it below her knees on the ground. Close by lay her belt with the DR93 attached. This was a rare chance, a brief mistake on her part that I must capitalize on now. Even these guards with less training than the Elite were not usually stupid enough to leave a weapon unattended. We planned carefully for each of our thefts, making sure when we liberated a cap from the northern sector it would be several days before we grabbed a vest from a guard in the southern area. We knew that guards felt shame for having equipment and uniforms lost or misplaced. It indicated an inattention to duty, and there was nothing The Third hated more. This enabled our ghost force to go unnoticed, undiscussed and undiscovered. No one wanted to admit his careless ineptitude to a fellow guard.

I heard a single exhale near my head. Then a hand on my arm that reassured me in the stillness. It was McGinty. I glanced at him, and he nodded. Not only did he come from two hundred feet around the corner of the building where he and Shaw were scouting, but he traveled without me detecting a sound. Then in one smooth movement he scooped up two squealing rats and threw them both into the center of the guards' circle. Undetected on the outside of the flames, and in sync with McGinty, I reached between two barrels of flaming fuel, grabbed the belt and the DR93, and squirmed on my stomach to join Shaw beyond the corner of the building. McGinty snaked right behind me, and the guards, screaming like babies, never noticed our presence.

Once around the corner, McGinty and I quickly ended our escape, and I strapped on my new weapon. Now our disguise was complete, and the three of us began our first official guard duty. After weeks in the shadows, now we were about as close to The Third as we could get, posing as members of a night guard that treated their watches with a casual attitude and careless attention. Once again we were subterraneans inside The Third. What were we looking for? Everything and anything that would tell The 28 United what we're up against. How fast was The Third advancing with limited technology due to the loss of satellites from *Jurbay*? Were they prepared to defend their city? Could we expect defensive strategy from them or offensive plans? And why had the lab closed down putting one of their hallmark projects involving hundreds of GEBs on hold? The sooner we discovered the answers the sooner I would return to Raben, and let him know I carried more than a DR93 strapped to my waist.

———

It is just past midnight in the horseshoe, and I adjust my new weapon securely over my hip bone. At the same time I stomp my feet inside my boots before I lace them up, getting the best possible fit on a pair a size too big. A liberator cannot be picky. All these memories of reconnaissance probes over the last weeks rattle around in my brain, and I touch the answer book in my pocket to reassure myself that order will come from facts collected, that I will eventually be able to decipher random notes into vital information that will lead to a plan of action. I hope this happens soon.

I look at McGinty. He leans against the exit window, petting Vipe who is curled in a ball on the window sill, enjoying the attention. I continually catch myself in the middle of an unexpected stare, noting these moments of gentleness in him. This has got to stop. I cannot divert my thoughts from the recon that demands my attention.

Just above my wrist and underneath the cuff of my coverall my timepiece accurately computes the minutes in my day. This inanimate timekeeper is unaware that I don't wear this coverall in allegiance to The Third anymore. This timepiece doesn't know that I glance at it to confirm the beginning of our night patrol. It slices off the seconds of a minute, unconcerned that in a few months I am to become a mother, and I don't know what I'm doing. This timepiece turns minutes into hours without the consciousness that I've fallen into the unlikely job of commanding a stewing rebellion, or that I long for my husband who is hundreds of miles away on the New Coastline. This timepiece is oblivious to the fact that my coverall shrinks by day as I grow overnight. Soon I will need a new coverall, a bigger one, with another accurate timepiece inside the cuff. Soon I will not be able to hide the fact that I must watch the time for two instead of one.

Standing across the room, Shaw zips up the outer vest of his night guard uniform. McGinty and I do the same, our movements in sync with Shaw. My night guard jacket is lying on a crate by the wall. I quickly pull it on in hopes that the changes in my body are not evident to the others.

Something stirs inside me, urging a change of direction regarding our nightly recon missions. For weeks we have suited up in the uniforms of the night guard and traveled a route through the sectors of Reichel in hopes that we might evaluate information about The Third's ability to defend their city and track us down. Yes, we have found clues, recorded our findings, but nothing definitive provided the kind of input we need to build a defense against them or wage an attack upon them.

"Wait," I say. I watch Pasha and Degnan pause, halting their work on notes and research and giving me their full attention. I've interrupted Shaw and McGinty's repetitive preparation. "Listen, every night we search a designated sector," I am pacing the curve of horseshoe tunnel. "We rarely see guards, except the ones playing games around the barrels of fire and—"

"There's an Elite guard by the History Labyrinth," says McGinty.

"Exactly. Why put the Elites there?"

"It's not unusual that the Elite would guard what's left of historical treasures," Degnan says.

Pasha rubs her head, and Shaw hands her Vipe. She immediately transfers her angst to the back of Vipe's neck. She says, "I've been in the labyrinth before. It's what you'd expect from any museum."

"Right," I say. "But what if there's another reason for Elite protection?"

"Like what?" says Shaw as he straps his DR93 to his waist.

"I don't know, but let's go looking for something specific tonight. We need to talk to Quinn, find out if she knows why the lab has shut down and all those GEBs are in limbo. Let's send her a message."

"What kind of a message?" asks Degnan.

McGinty checks his weapon, assuring its perfect function and says, "The chipster in Quinn's finger only validates what's in front of her—true or false. She can't reply to us."

Reaching for the Hennessey, Degnan says, "I want a chipster." We ignore him.

"All we need to do is to put the information in front of her. She'll figure out the rest," I say. After I secure my weapon and lace my gloves through my belt, I look at Pasha for confirmation. "Can you do that? Get a one or two word message to her?"

Now she paces, not looking at us. "Maybe," she whispers. "Maybe, but we have no guarantee she'd see it. She only uses the chipster when she needs it."

"Pasha, she's inside The Third. She uses it all the time to determine "truth or lie." Of course she'll see it." Pasha opens the chipster in her forearm, composing a message. "Give her a meeting place."

"Artesian Baths." Then, Pasha looks at me and says, "Send it?" I hesitate.

"We might only get one chance at getting into that place. You better be sure she's gonna see it, Avery," says Shaw.

I am quiet. Then I say, "Nothing's certain."

"I'll go on recon. I need a bath." Degnan says as he pours his Hennessey. Again, we ignore him.

"Why the baths, Pasha?" I ask

"They're under the History Labyrinth. Completely private. Morris and the boys used to be brought there for baths once a month."

"But the boys are gone now," I finish her thought. "So no one uses the baths anymore. This gives us a chance to check out the labyrinth and meet Quinn at the same time. While we're there, we'll go floor to floor, instead of just a general search of a random sector. More concentrated."

All three of us are suited up now, and Shaw says, "That's assuming we'll get in."

"We've got nothing to lose. We get into the History Labyrinth, search every one of its tunnels and vaults and hope that Quinn will show up at the baths with information," I say.

"And what if we find nothing more than a bunch of constitutional documents and a heap of historical first lady gowns?"

"Then we go back to a sector by sector search tomorrow," says McGinty. Shaw concedes.

"Send the message, Pasha," I say. She does. It's more of a longshot than I openly admit.

"You need to take me," says Degnan. "I know the tunnels, and I know which ones lead to caverns and which one leads to the baths."

Shaw climbs out the exit window and says, "We got this, Degnan. Did part of our Elite training in there." He's whispering now that he's outside the entrance. McGinty follows and I am close behind.

Just as I am about to close the entry window Degnan thrusts his face up to the opening, and with a raspy whisper says, "I want a chipster in my ear."

"And I want a sock in your mouth," I say and close the window. I toss weeds against the exit that is recessed into the small hill, putting an end to his demented face, silencing him, at least for the time we are on night guard.

Several feet beyond the entrance to the horseshoe tunnel we travel together quietly, each of us absorbed in thought. *What prompted my urgent plan to search the Labyrinth? Intuition? Discernment? Maybe.* I remember once, shortly after I had met Pasha, Borden arrived at our door, representing The Third, asking to see my mother and father. Pasha wanted to get away from him, go to the barn, work on her experiments, but there was something that prodded me, urging me to stay. So, I pretended to be working on my studies in a room adjoining the space where the three of them talked. A voice inside me made a quiet impression: *Be present. Be listening.* Now, as I look back at that listening child, I'm sure I learned things. All sorts of things. Like things about Borden that I'm using here today. For example, I recognized back then his nature was charismatic, appealing, but evil was on the rise inside him. Today his sting is merciless, like a predatory scorpion intent on paralyzing its prey. The evil has worked its way from inside him to outside, and now it consumes most everyone.

This gift of intuition, which I believe to be somewhat supernatural, or as Morris would say *Creator-given*, can be honed for good or groomed for evil by anyone who has the wisdom to recognize the gift and the patience to develop it. I am not a patient person, and while recognition of the gift has never been a problem, development has plucked at my nerves. But today I practice. I felt in my gut this change of search tactics was necessary, and I rallied Shaw and McGinty to go with me. But there's something else I've garnered through the years of trying to train this gift. It doesn't always work. This sixth sense is often unruly and can get me into trouble. At fifteen I was convinced my parents Carles and Quinn should not travel to a family reunion in Catalonia and expressed my concerns. They went anyway and ended up developing their powerful connection to the president, who they would eventually assist in trying to protect *locasa,* keeping it where it might accomplish good for humanity. On the other hand, that trip eventually led to my father's death. Sixth sense, you are indeed a paradox.

We are just blocks away from the History Labyrinth. "Let's not have a sense of false security tonight just 'cause we finally look exactly like the enemy," says McGinty.

"You won't find any false security in me," I say. I look up at the night sky and see a small sliver of a waning moon, partially hidden behind a bank of clouds. The zips crisscross the sky from building to building weaving a giant spider web above us. We approach the corner of the History Labyrinth. We push our backs flat against the wall, and Shaw takes off his helmet, easing his head around the corner to scout the entrance to the building. Then, he pulls back quickly and says, "Elite Guard of four. On the ready."

"That's good," I whisper. "There used to be two. They're probably guarding more than outdated memorabilia."

Shaw flips his chipster open, testing for the structural weakness of the building. He looks at us and smiles. "On the roof."

"Of course," I say

"Find the zip ladder on the other side of the building," McGinty spits his words out, and we head around the corner of the labyrinth. We climb. Shaw is first followed by McGinty and me. Above ground the first floor only extends fifteen feet, so the ladder is short. The remaining floors are beneath the ground. Shaw takes a disc-dial from his pack. The ten inch circular tool is flat and looks harmless. He inputs some figures from his chipster and slings the disc toward the center of the roof. It stops and hovers over the precise spot of structural weakness. Then, under Shaw's command through his chipster, the disc-dial settles onto the roof and begins a rapid vibration movement, cutting a hole the size of Shaw's body into the structural materials. When the job is done, McGinty and Shaw lift off the section of the roof and set it to the side, allowing the three of us entrance into the building, and leaving the Elite guard unaware of our breach.

It is dark in the tunnels of the labyrinth, and I am in the front of our line. "Avery," says McGinty, "Help us out here." I tap my temple for infrared activation. With no memories of the Elite training done in this building, this tunnel is new to me, but to Shaw and McGinty, this is familiar, engrained. One of them should be in the front, but I'm the one with the needed chipster.

The tunnels are lined with irregular stones stacked one on top of another to form the walls and ceiling of a narrow hallway. Small trickles of water occasionally swirl from ceiling to floor creating a dank atmosphere. Recessed into the walls are historical artifacts dating back hundreds of years. Some of the protective glass that has sheltered these treasures has been shattered, and some is still intact. Once, these small alcoves were lit so that visitors might view the labeled displays. With my infrared I glance at the display by my shoulder. *Bow and Arrow from a Sioux Warrior.* I note the skill it must have taken to carve and craft this kind of rudimentary weapon. *Rudimentary?* I question myself. Who am I to judge the value of a weapon that probably fed a warrior's family and protected their land from The Third of the day? Lying in my path are pieces of stones that have broken off from the wall. I kick them aside and struggle to regain focus. I want to let my glance linger on the beadwork labeled *Cherokee Princess Ceremonial Jewelry*, but I press on.

"Let's go to the baths first," I say. "Quinn might be waiting." And even as I say these words it comes again. That intuitive sixth sense creeps up my back and holds my shoulders tight assuring me that practicing this gift pays off. Only this time, as I listen, this urging, this impression, this stirring is not a sense of wisdom or clarification. This time it is a sense of *danger.*

# Chapter 16
# DIVE 'N FIND

I have killed six people. Shot some. Knifed one. The Third took my memories of Elite training, but they never extracted the haunt of killing. Why the memory of each of those deaths circle in a continuous thread inside my brain, I don't know, but with each step further into the labyrinth the cycle runs, ticking off the lives I held in my hands and purposely chose to end. A nameless recruit in the Elite guard. He walked in on Shaw and me as we plotted the rescue of the *locasa* device in Catalonia where my father lost his life. I'd like to say he was an innocent victim, but no one who works for The Third is innocent, even if they are a victim themselves. I knifed a woman, an unfortunate necessity to save McGinty's life in a rouge training exercise. Then, there was the Elite soldier who tried to bash Pasha's brains out and almost succeeded. I shot him in the throat, shattering his trachea and killing him instantly, saving Pasha's life. There should be no guilt for that one. But there is. For killings four and five I count the two float car pilots trying to get word back to Reichel headquarters that the library and its boys were burning. I shot their planes and not them, but the results were the same. They died. And the sixth death, well, it has the potential of doing more harm to me than just haunting. It is fresh, it is brutal. I took a loved one's father. And I hate myself for what I had to do.

———

I tap the infrared on my temple. Rats, previously invisible in the darkness of the labyrinth hallways, stare in the gray-toned images of night vision, their eyes red with heat, their teeth waiting to gnaw. With the tip of my DR93 I ease around the entrance of each stone archway branching off from the main hallway. When I know it is clear I nod my head, enter through the opening and sense that Shaw and McGinty follow. Nothing on the other side of the entrance is the same as the room before. Sometimes the entry leads to massive caverns, extending several stories below the ground, filled with nothing but emptiness. A few have intricate mazes built on the floor with balconies providing a viewing platform for an audience wanting an aerial perspective. *What games took place here?* I wonder, but am not sure I really want to know.

Other openings lead to small storage areas with stone shelves built into the walls. This one we enter now has chains hooked firmly to the floor, iron ankle shackles attached. And from the ceiling these ancient man-made chains hang in wait for a prisoner's wrist or maybe even a neck. Nonetheless, all rooms are devoid of people. This macabre series of surprises behind each opening contrasts dramatically with the artistically displayed historical museum items. I'm not sure which I am more fascinated by, the macabre or the historical.

The next arched opening we clear leads to a side hallway with letters painted on the stone walls, not in character with the age of this fortress. Shaw joins me, and runs his fingers over the letters that read "Breeding Program" and says, "Let's visit this one first." I move his hand away, placing my fingers on the words that say *Artesian Baths*. They follow me.

We enter the baths through an archway, our weapons still on the ready. I marvel how this enormous cavern exists within the History Labyrinth. Ceilings thirty feet high, covered with the art of unknown masters, decorating every inch of available stonework in primary hues that have faded gracefully through the centuries. The stunning beauty of the ceiling is matched by the marble columns that line the interior of the pools, crafted by the skilled sculptors who chose to intricately etch the stories of their civilization. This cavern-like room displays three long pools arranged end to end. The giant columns stand mid-pool six feet out from the edges, a clever way to provide privacy for the bathers. Did an ancient Aztec explorer venture north and take up residency here, bringing sculptors and painters to carve this breathtaking room? Or did the native indians anoint some of their warriors as artisans and craftsmen? Were the stories on these ceilings telling tales from two hundred years pre-*Jurbay* or five hundred years before the asteroid fell? I have missed the luxury of deep thinking, of pondering. I have lost the time to let beauty perform its work on my spirit.

All three of us wander the baths for a moment, in awe, reluctant to continue the mission, wondering if Quinn will be able to slip away and meet us here. Maybe she knows why the GEB lab is in the process of being dismantled.

"We don't know that she'll even be here tonight," says McGinty.

"And we don't know she'll be able to get here undetected," says Shaw.

"She'll be here. She'll find a way," I say and run my hand along the button alcove and the modern installation of the vacuum suck. What would the ancient artisans have thought of this intrusive invention that sucks the water off bodies and the moisture out of clothing, should you choose to bathe all dressed up for your daily activities.

"Rudely out of place," says McGinty, examining the tiled section where the bathers stand to be dried.

"Why don't both of you do a sweep of the surrounding tunnels, make sure this place is empty, and we don't have any surprises hiding underneath an archway or behind a column," I say. "I'll wait here for Quinn."

Shaw is quick to take up that command, but McGinty whispers in my direction before he follows, "Might want to take advantage of the baths. That vacuum suck dries everything within seconds." There's a smile in his eyes, and I turn away before he can see the smile in mine.

Waiting, I pace around the pools. I am vigilant in my duty, attentive to any changes in the sounds surrounding the baths. After twenty-five laps and over an hour of patrolling, I take off my boots and set them at the far end of one pool, out of sight from anyone entering the baths. I release my heavy belt and weapon from around my waist and stack it next to my shoes. I ease myself into the water, clothes and all. Anything that is parched absorbs moisture like a life line. That is how I feel, an arid, dehydrated sack of bones whose skin is begging for a drink. The scent of basil and rosemary from a childhood memory pokes at my senses. My job was to water the herbs each morning when I was five or six and the moisture mixed with earth begged the fragrances to rise and greet me. I want to go back to that simple moment in time and replicate my life as a child, reproduce the memories of family. Other thoughts lap at my brain.

———

My father and I played the dive game from the time I turned seven and learned how to swim. Dive 'n Find. He'd throw the rock to the bottom of the lake, and I would dive to find it. When you don't have siblings, if you're lucky, your parents like to play. They can be brilliant strategists, militarily savvy and compassionate, discerning leaders, but they can still have the spark of a child within them. Carles was like that. Quinn was not. Looking back now, I am quite sure he developed this game to increase my abilities in the water and to strengthen my arms so that I might pull my body to the bottom of a pool or a section of a lake. My father wanted me to build my lung capacity to hold my breath longer each time he would throw the rock deeper. And every day we played my curiosity to find the rock, drove me to dive again and again, searching for its hiding place. He would toss the rock for me to retrieve, and if I successfully returned carrying the round gray trophy, my reward was to make him dive for it twice. Our whole family loved the water, and even Quinn, on occasion would dive with us. She always returned with whatever we sent her to fetch. Maybe my father pretended not to find the rock sometimes to make it more of a game for his little girl. But Quinn? She never came back from a dive empty handed.

———

The dull clap of boots descending the stairway at the entrance to the pools warns me that someone approaches, and I swim behind the closest column. All of these round stone creations are three feet in diameter, making hiding convenient. I place my hand on the smooth, cool marble of the pillar's side. The lighting in here is dim, lit by enormous gas lamps along the walls. In the flicker I see the boots first. Her feet, large and just like mine, are considerably more graceful and always wearing impeccably shined gray patent leather boots. Quinn. I knew she'd show up.

I breathe in, readying myself to call her name and my voice sticks firmly in my throat. I'm not sure why. She appears, her silver ringlets shining in the flicker of the lamp flames. She carries a crumpled gray garment in her hand. Laying it out of the way on the far side of the baths, she turns to face the staircase. I am surprised she is not looking for me, calling my name.

Seconds after she enters a man descends the staircase. Shocked by his appearance, I take another breath. He is stunning. I hear Quinn whisper, "Dorsey." And she runs to him and he to her, unable to contain their passionate embrace, I have to look away. This is my mother and she has a husband—had a husband. This is not right. I push the thought aside, chanting silently in my head: *Subterranean. This is her job.* Then it hits me. This is him. She called him "Dorsey." This is *Commander* Dorsey, the ruler of the entire Third. I have never seen him before, and there have been no published pictures of him anywhere for security reasons. And now I know why. The Commander would be mid-60s. A man I imagined as stately, mature, aging. But somewhere hidden from the eyes of the media, the son replaced the father, and this Commander Dorsey is athletic, powerful, and virile, and *he* is in my mother's arms.

Quinn says to Dorsey, "Officer Borden's obsessed with the pursuit of a small band of subterraneans."

Dorsey replies, "I'm obsessed with you." *I can't handle this. He's got to be a decade younger than Quinn.*

Quinn walks away from him. "He's put all the revenue we have and some we don't have into a search for a few people. We don't even know if they exist or if they pose a threat to us."

"And…?"

"And he's useless to me like this. I need to have him planning for a new city. A place to go before that 240 acre monster of a sinkhole that showed up last month swallows us whole." *Sinkhole? News to me.*

Dorsey is back by her side, running his fingers along the back of her neck. I'd been told he was frightening, a pilot trained in combat that had run point on exit ops in Catalonia, instrumental in getting *locasa* out of the country. Right now he poses only passion, no threat. She paces again, breaking away from his arms. He says, "You don't have to have my permission to do what's necessary. Borden can be replaced." *He trusts her.* I think *That's strategic. What she's had to give to get that trust is something I don't want to think about.*

Borden comes busting down the stairs, interrupting the plot of his demise. There is an uncomfortable moment. I wonder if he notices. He is the one who breaks the silence. He is out of breath and says, "Security in the north sector is certain they saw an extra patrol last night." Quinn and Dorsey do not respond. "Avery and her renegades." Still silence. "We can double the troops tonight and finally lock this down. Put her out of commission."

Dorsey turns to Quinn asking, "Avery? Avery DeTornada?" I see the trust he has in her crack, just a bit.

She says, "Doesn't matter who it is. If it were a real threat we would handle it. It's an imagined threat, and we don't need to manage it."

*She is protecting us.* I wonder if her protection is for The 28 United, for us as subterraneans or for me.

283

Dorsey approaches Borden passing so close to his shoulder they almost touch. He begins to climb the stairs, then stops and faces Borden. "Why don't you double the troops for three nights? Give it everything you've got. If you don't find your band of traitors by then, give it up. Put it to rest." The fact that Dorsey gave Borden more time to hunt us down must feel like a loss to Quinn. She wanted an end to the search. How big of a crack in the façade of her relationship with Dorsey is this? I hope not big at all, for her sake and ours. Dorsey continues, his eyes drifting away from Borden, igniting a connection with Quinn. "And you. Make sure the details in the dismantling of that GEB lab in the plant are handled within the next 48 hours. Final shut down. We have other priorities."

"Like stopping the sinkhole that's biting at Reichel's heels?" asks Borden.

Dorsey shows little emotion as he responds to Borden's comment with flawless control and an unshakeable command. "That statement is miscalculated and ignorant." I see Borden swallow hard, even from my hiding place behind the column in the pool. "The sinkhole is important. It is not a priority." *What could be more of a priority than an advancing sinkhole?*

Quinn won't be shut down or be put off by Dorsey and presses him on the details of the lab. "There are three GEBs in the lab already in the process of activation. If we shut the lab down they won't exist by the time the lab is reinstated. Their systems will disintegrate and all that time and funding will be wasted."

Dorsey smiles, an amused look on his face. "Then send one scientist to finish the work on those three."

"And the storage room?" asks Quinn. I can tell she is feeding me details. I think she's sure I am somewhere in this room.

Dorsey laughs. An arrogant laugh. Maybe attempting to put Quinn in her place, but she won't be placed anywhere. "There're hundreds of GEBS waiting to do their job. They'll still be there when our priority is handled. Then, they can be activated and distributed where they will be used best—The 28 United."

"You've given them a name now?" she flips a barb of sarcasm his way, but Dorsey is undaunted, maybe he even enjoys her tone. I suspect he has heard it before, and I am unnerved by the fact that he seems comfortable with Quinn.

"They named themselves," he says. "Maybe they thought a name might give them a chance."

I feel the Goosebumps prickling my skin under my coverall. The water is warm but the eerie reality that somehow The Third's commander knows our name, knows our existence—*that* gives me chills. I take shallow breaths, quiet and measured.

Dorsey exits, and I can't help but watch his fit body climb the stairs with ease.

Borden and Quinn do not speak for a while. A smirk wraps around his attitude. "We'll find and apprehend the renegades. Finishing it in three days is not even a challenge."

Quinn climbs the stairs quickly, and I hear her with the last word before she leaves. "Wasted troops, wasted time." Then, she is gone.

Borden's demeanor changes. He stands straighter, more confident. There is bravado about him, a sneer on his face. This persona of evil begins an ominous slow-motion dance around the pool, heading in my direction. He twirls in deliberate circles, humming a military victory march. He stops at the precise moment he reaches the vacuum suck and removes his shoes and the belt around his waist that holds his weapon, a Shaw-like knife. Then without warning he leaps in the pool. My body stiffens. No way for me to get out of the pool undetected. I don't carry a knife and my DR93 sits ineffective in a pile hidden at the back of the baths.

Breaking the surface of the water, Borden comes up laughing, giddy at winning Dorsey's approval, and I'm sure he is imagining the capture of McGinty, Shaw, Pasha and me. He swims in circles then straightens his path out, moving in my direction, and even with his uniform on his strokes are long and efficient. My pulse races.

I force myself to focus. *Create a plan. Choices are limited.* Either he discovers me and kills me or drags me out of the water as a captured subterranean. Neither of those choices can happen no matter what the circumstances. It would give away the last seven weeks of our discoveries in Reichel under the Plethora Plant. My capture or death would confirm that The 28 United has a plan—is working on a plan. Borden's discovery of me threatens not just my life, but the lives of McGinty, Shaw, Pasha, Degnan and ultimately the entire 28 United who need the information we've retrieved. My hand silently slides through the water, finding my abdomen, placing a protective touch on my unborn child. This man, gliding closer by the moment, gave the command to burn his own son. I saved that son, and I will now save my child too. I reject the choice of my death or capture, and choose the alternative.

My heart rate triples. Five feet from the column now. He is unsuspecting. One choice. Right now. *This* is the alternative.

I submerse my head, silently, beneath the turquoise water. He passes by me. I take my arms circling them around his neck and yank them tight, but his will to live is equally as strong as my will to protect, and he breaks my hold, swinging his head around to face me and slamming his fist into my jaw. The sting of his knuckles against my bones sends pain like a seismic wave through my body. I curl myself into a ball and reach for his mid-section, clasping his clothing, dragging him under the water again. His hands join together like a sledge hammer and chip away in slow motion at the back of my neck. I slam my foot into his lower extremities and know my punch hit its target as he writhes for a split second before he grabs my hair and pulls my neck back with a cruel force. I have no air left. I must breathe. I break away and propel myself upward, kicking against the force of the water, just out of his reach I break the surface in time to grab a breath.

Borden is right behind me sucking in his own air, and I hear the water, slapping at us both and the dissonance of our guttural gasps for life. His kick to my stomach is brutal, but slowed by the power of the water, turning the kick from lethal to painful, not as bad as it could be. He will not kick me there again. I dig what is left of my nails in his face. His arms encircle my chest, his hands reaching upward, crushing my esophagus, with the kind of pressure that can send a soul spiraling down to the depths of any pool for eternity. *This can't happen.* I bludgeon him with my feet and gasp one more time for the breath of life above the surface. Then again we descend, our bodies locked in combat, for what I fear are the final moments of life—his or mine.

I thrash my arms in a desperate battle to catch the back of his garment and gain control. The pressure on my windpipe increases. My vision turns blurry. Fluorescent spots dot my field of vision. One by one the spots turn to black. The only thought consuming me now as my arms turn limp is: *This baby must live.* I command my body to fight back, but my body isn't listening.

Suddenly our funnel of churning water is interrupted by the splash of a third body. Now I'm beyond hope, and I'm sure it is one of Borden's minions who will guarantee the final victory over me. He almost had me in the library fire. He used Degnan to help track me in the forest with a vial of the Deadly #12. And now one of his faithful will help him shut me down. I long for Shaw or McGinty's help as Borden increases the pressure on my neck. Then, I feel a force smash Borden's body. His arms flail, and I am released. Streaming to the surface, I find air quickly, but around my ankle the pressure of Borden's hand, pulls me under. I descend. Some of the bubbles from the third person's entry have dispersed, and I see a form. Then, that form is clear, and I see the white-blue eyes. Quinn. This dive n' find is not a game. Borden recoils with incredible power to fight for life, but we are twice him and we magnify each other.

Quinn's hands are tight around Borden's neck, and I yank my ankle away from his hand, swinging my legs up around his torso, holding him under the water. I feel the desperate pulse of his entire body, willing it to survive, to find the surface, but he does not. Evil is drowning. Quinn takes the knife from her belt, thrusting it into his chest. Drowning was not enough for her.

The three of us make a quick ascent. Quinn and I fill our lungs. Sweet air.

The pool water is red. Borden floats face down. I look directly into Quinn's eyes, trying to communicate my thanks, but I cannot speak. I can only breathe. We float Borden to the side of the pool. Quinn lifts herself from the water and sits on the edge, then quickly stands, placing her hands under his arms and yanking him upward, while I push him from below in the water.

After he's lying on the marble tiles, we drag him to the vacuum suck. Without speaking we know what we must do. She pushes the button in the alcove. Quinn drags the upper part of his body, and I follow, carrying his legs. Just as we have his head positioned in front of the open maw she says, "This isn't just on you."

"So what?" I ask. "We share the murder?" I lose it, dropping my end of Borden's body on the cracked marble floor of the baths. "Does that mean my baby is a party to this too? Do we all *share* in this event? I don't want to share. I don't want any part of this. But I have no choice." My hands are shaking, and I fight to control the convulsions my body sends spiraling out from my core. My eyes rage. Her eyes show a hint of moisture. What a horrible way to announce that she is to be a grandmother. I place my hand on the spot of my stomach where a bump is beginning to show. I thought I hid it well. "You knew, didn't you?" I ask her.

Without a movement, other than her lips, she says, "Of course I did. Pasha experimented with one word messages to my chipster long before today." I am horrified that Pasha chose to give out this intimate information without my permission, and I wonder if she has found a way to let Raben know as well.

"Your baby shares none of this, Avery. Only the destiny of The 28 United."

That thought's enough to yank me out of anger and turn my rage toward our task. I grab the calves of Borden's legs again. Quinn places his body into the large orifice in the wall. I think of the blades inside and what they are capable of. Together we push his body in.

I sit in a curled position by the side of the pool, listening to the halting grind of the blades as they hesitate on bone then glide through tissue and muscle. Holding my legs close to my chest and burying my head on the top of my knees, I cry. Hardly commander-like. I try to shake it all from my mind, but the body-count on my watch is now at six.

In a quiet, comforting voice Quinn says, "Don't cry for Borden."

I lift my face to confront her and say, "I'm not. I cry for me, for you and for this baby."

Quinn takes a step toward me, smoothing the wet hair around my face and placing her hand on my stomach. "Names?" She says. If this is a question, I don't have an answer. Of course, it's Quinn, so she has an answer of her own. "Chapman was a DeTornada. Your father's great-great grandmother. An artist, a general's wife and his closest military advisor." Then she runs toward the staircase. I hear her calling over her shoulder "It's a name for a boy *or* a girl." Just before she climbs the stairs and once again deserts my life, she turns to smile at me, and I catch a glimpse of my mother. Briefly. Then she says, "Can you clean up the blood on the tile by the pool?" And she is gone.

I clean up the splotches, drops and puddles of blood on the tiles. When I am done, I stare at the water in the artesian baths. The blood has already dissipated.

I approach the exit and a clump of rumpled gray fabric catches my eye. I pick it up and instantly recognize it as a coverall from the Plethora Plant, left by Quinn. It is bigger than the one I am wearing. Big enough for two.

## Chapter 17
# A GEB LIKE ME

I join Shaw and McGinty in the maze of hallways in the Labyrinth. "We need to go now," I say.

"Quinn?" Shaw asks.

"I told you she'd show up."

"Did she know why the GEB lab's on hold?" McGinty contributes to the questions.

We return to the hole in the roof and exit there. By the time we're back on the street we are still unseen by the Elite guarding the building, and at this point they suspect nothing. It is only Borden who is concerned about our trio. *Was* concerned about our trio. "I may have lost my Elite training, but I'm the best eavesdropper you've got," I say. "There's a 240 acre sinkhole in the North Sector that's eating the city. They need to relocate Reichel." I say.

"Let me guess," quips Shaw. "Relocate on the New Coastline?"

"Of course. But there's more. Commander Dorsey's on site."

"Dorsey? It's got to take more than a sinkhole to get him here."

"Exactly." I say, and we pass a roving guard of four. I note their casual patrol attitude and realize they are not Elite trained. I smile to myself, running my hand over the stolen DR93 and vow that when we train The 28 United fighting force, we will out match these guards in every way. Our force will mirror Elite standards without Elite cruelty, and I'll have McGinty and Shaw to thank for that.

McGinty asks, "How'd you even know it was Dorsey? His identity's been guarded since he assumed command."

"Quinn called him by name." They both stop and look at me. "They thought they were alone."

McGinty eyes land on his boots and Shaw's laugh emerges from his sneer. "Subterranean at her best," he says. I throw him a wicked look. "What about Borden?"

I say nothing. McGinty presses. "Avery, what about Borden?"

"No need to worry about him anymore," I say.

Shaw responds without hesitation, "Hope it was neat and clean."

"It wasn't clean."

"Knife?"

"Quinn had one. I thought drowning was enough."

"Then what?"

"Vacuum suck."

"Perfect," says Shaw.

I confront him. "What's perfect about murder?"

"It's war. Suck it up. Oh—I guess you did." He laughs. He's over the line with me. I give him a shove, and McGinty steps between Shaw and me.

"Hey, she took care of it," says McGinty to Shaw.

"We're not that far from the North Sector," I say. "Let's get to the sinkhole and take our own measurements before dawn. Then we'll go back to the tunnel and make sure they don't send those three GEBs out into our world."

We use the zips to travel to the North Sector. Hooking up, I am off. Close behind, McGinty and Shaw follow. I hear the subtle hum of our hook-ups propelling us along like a bee headed for the pollen. From the air, with the stars shining and the moon lighting the way, spotting the sinkhole will require no help from my infrared chipster. Before *Jurbay,* sinkholes were classified either as natural or human-created. The natural hole is still unexplainable, but the human created ones were usually due to mining or overdevelopment. But this sinkhole, I'm sure, is just one more of *Jurbay's* buddies that it brought along to the party. Soon after *Jurbay's* amputation of our nation the firestorms began. I'd heard stories of those unexpected rocks the size of baseballs, glowing hot red, hailing down on families just when some thought it was safe to settle. Then there were the roiling embers. I'd seen them myself when I watched settlers attempting to plant new crops, digging into the earth only to find it boiling with burning coals, even after a decade. *Jurbay* left more than a new coastline, sticking the burr of its memory into us in more ways than the severing of our planet. Now, the sinkholes have come.

It's necessary to change zips two or three times to reach the North Sector. We arrive at the edge of the sinkhole, and even on the outskirts of its mouth the magnitude of this devouring hole overwhelms me with my smallness. It is like nothing I have ever seen before and the aerial scope is frightening. I slow on the zip, asking Shaw, "Can you get measurements from the air?"

Shaw reduces his speed too. "Yeah, I can do it from here." He opens the chipster in his leg and within seconds he has it. "Just under 640 acres." I am keenly aware of the figure I overheard Quinn quote: 240 acres. The Third has either grossly miscalculated the size of this sinkhole or it is growing faster than their best calculations. In either scenario they need an exit strategy.

We're only five stories above the hole which is encroaching on a row of buildings three stories high. Churning slowly in the sludge of the sinkhole, I see the concrete from other buildings built to last. They tried to take a final stand against the mouth of this hungry beast and failed.

We are hanging on the zip near the edge of the sinkhole. We came for a measurement, not exploration. The GEB lab demands our attention. I hear McGinty's voice from just feet behind me on the zip. "What's that? Out there to your left about a hundred feet from the edge. Just under the surface." I see it too. "There's three of them." The round shapes, barely covered by the mucky sea undulate like floating jellyfish. One of these moving circles surfaces and it takes only a second for me to recognize the horror of what I'm seeing.

"Biters!" I scream. In unison we reverse direction on the zips. Shaw and I follow McGinty's actions as he taps the back of his coverall belt releasing a tent shield that expands like a blowup mattress of past decades, protecting every part of his body and leaving a sealed viewing window in the front. Now all three of us are covered. I hope we can out zip them and escape before the biters notice us. Too late.

How ironic, I think, that The Third kept up the technology on these protective tent covers, but can't get its fighter jets in the air. The first biter hits my cover. The bump from its connection is barely noticeable, but the noise it makes grinding its teeth is unnerving. I feel a second and third one hit and see in front of me several attached to McGinty's cover as well. I am sure Shaw readies his knife.

A biter slams against the viewing plate of the hood section on my tent cover. Its catlike eyes glow with a malicious purpose, and its teeth come out instinctively, gnawing viciously against the plate, intent on breaking through my protection and eating my skin and bones, leaving nothing for the buzzards.

Just ahead of me, the biters surround the lower part of McGinty's tent, and in a hoard they swarm with a group effort to reach their victim.

Shaw zips far ahead of us and reaches the end of the zip on the rooftop of a building. He unhooks and yanks off his tent, opening his gear bag. In a heartbeat all the biters on McGinty and me disengage their dozens of teeth and focus straight ahead directly toward Shaw who is now fresh bait without his cover. He's slung his SE454 out of the gear bag and toward the biters. He fires. I've never seen a SE454 release from the victim's angle. Glad I'm not a biter. The microwaves bury themselves into the biters, disintegrating them to dust, but not before their screeches cut through the night like coyotes on the hunt. And not before a solo biter eats through Shaw's boot. He slices at it with his knife, and it falls to the ground, but Shaw's face erupts in a painful contortion as he collapses on the roof.

McGinty lands hard on the top of the building beside Shaw. He turns and breaks my fall by catching me before my zip slams me onto the flattened roofline. We kneel by Shaw. McGinty quickly uses Shaw's knife to cut apart the material of one of the protective tents and wrap the strip tightly around Shaw's foot, covering the bleeding section where two of Shaw's toes used to reside.

"That bugger ate my boot," he says through clenched teeth.

"That bugger ate your toes. You're lucky it wasn't your whole foot," McGinty answers.

I reach in my pack and find the aid kit, pulling out a syringe, drawing a dose of pain killer and injecting it into Shaw's foot. "Looks like Pasha's going to have an unscheduled surgery to attend to," I say. We get him on his feet.

"I can walk," he says as he shakes away our help, but he wavers and McGinty and I are there to catch him.

We prop him against the pole that holds the zip hook for this area, and McGinty and I collapse our protective tenting. In a matter of seconds the gear is repacked at the back of our coveralls. We adjust the packs for one another as Shaw loads his SE454 in his gear bag. I say, "And here we thought you were carrying steak knives."

"I have a set of those too," he responds.

"Thanks for not leaving the 454 at the tunnel with Degnan like I did," I say.

"I'm sure you'll get another chance to face off with a biter if this hole continues to grow."

"No thanks. Already had two chances, and I don't want another one."

———

The first thing I notice when I slip through the entrance to the horseshoe tunnel is Pasha stringing the thin-skin all over the walls, like Quinn strung garlands on the Christmas tree when I was a kid. That means Pasha has a plan. Normally I would be consumed with figuring out what that plan is, but the second thing I notice is that they have taken one of the GEBs from the lab and it is sitting at our makeshift table with Degnan who is teaching this GEB to play rummy. The GEB wears part of a blanket crafted into a poncho and the remaining part has been fashioned into a diaper.

"I never cease to be amazed at what you can do with a four hour period of time," I say. Vipe's back is curved in strike mode and a low growling resides in her throat. I'm not sure if she growls at us for surprising her or at the GEB for its intrusion.

"What's going on here?" I press.

Pasha holds up the thin-skin. "It's our experiment."

"Really."

"There's been no activity for three weeks in the lab. Bored," she says without looking at me.

Degnan slams his cards on the table, leaving one card in his hand and yells, "Gin."

The GEB mimics Degnan's actions, throwing down all its cards and says, "Gin rummy. Technically you should say 'gin rummy' not 'gin.'"

Degnan squeezes the wrists of the GEB and says, "Technically you can't throw down all those cards. You have to have one in your hand to discard, and I threw down first."

"You are cheating, Degnan," says the GEB.

"You're an idiot, GEB." Degnan pushes the GEB toward the window. "Let's go for a walk." He guides the GEB out the window and glances at Shaw's foot before he leaves. "You're bleeding," he says. "Blood disrupts our sanitation." His sneer continually taunts and his sarcasm is getting monotonous.

Limping over to the makeshift table, Shaw accepts McGinty's help, easing up and lying on his back on the piece of wood.

"What's wrong with your foot?" asks Pasha as she unwraps the bandage and stares at his toes. "There's only three left."

"I know," says Shaw. "Get me the Hennessey."

After rooting through the shelves of supplies, McGinty is successful and opens the bottle, looking for a cup, but Shaw grabs the entire bottle and takes a long pull, then says, "You got to get that GEB back in the lab, Pasha."

"Just a few more hours," Pasha says. "We have one more trial to run on it."

"Times up," I say. "They're sending a scientist within the next day to do the final commission on the three GEBs and then put them out in our world to do their jobs. After that, they're going to disconnect everything and shut down the lab."

"So go put the GEB back," says McGinty.

She rubs her head, using the part of her arm just above her surgical gloves, looking nervously at the exit window where Degnan took the GEB for a walk. "Can't put it back."

I lean in so my mouth is right by her ear. "Can."

"We made a few adjustments, and it's further along than the other two. The scientist will know right away." Her hands leave her head, and she busies herself with prepping Shaw's foot for surgery.

"What do you mean 'a few adjustments'?"

On this very rare occasion Pasha looks at me over the sterile mask and says, "It's asking for a name." Shaw and McGinty groan.

"What?" I ask. McGinty takes a cup from the shelf and pours a drink and Pasha jerks her head toward the bottle.

"One for me," she says, like a begging street urchin.

McGinty puts the bottle away after his pour. "No Hennessey for surgeons."

"Don't you get it?" asks Pasha. "The GEB can't go back now. They'll know." A shiver runs through her body, but she steadies herself, injecting Shaw with something that makes his eyelids flutter and close. He breathes deeply. Pasha lifts her scalpel looking at Shaw's foot like the discoverer of Venus di Milo, staring at her missing arms. I wonder if Shaw can still hear what we say.

I try to reason with her, but I know reasoning with Pasha usually ends up at a dead end or a new trail through the forest. "Listen," I plead, "Just decommission the one you took and go get a GEB from the storage room shelves and bring it up to speed as a replacement. There has to be three GEBs in the lab when the scientist gets there. So if you can't use this one, get another. Do you understand?"

The final sutures consume her focus, and there is a strange look on her face. She says, "I understand." She takes off her surgical gloves and stuffs them in an empty powdered egg container currently serving as a garbage can. No vacuum sucks here.

Degnan listens to our conversation at the entrance window. He returns without the GEB. "We can't decommission a GEB," he says. "Neither one of us ever got that far with our research when we worked here."

"So get one from the storage," McGinty says.

"There's too much work to do on the GEBs in storage. We can't activate one that fast."

301

"Then put that one," McGinty says as he points toward the outside window, "back the way it was."

"Can't do that," says Degnan.

McGinty and I exchange a frustrated glance. "Why?" I ask.

"One of those biters followed you home."

Pasha races to the exit window.

"You're not going to find it out there. Those biters evolved from piranhas, and they got a couple other hungry relatives in their gene mix too."

Pasha flexes her hands open, close, open, close. "I was going to name it," she says.

"Too late."

I stop Degnan's hand as he goes for the bottle, trying to pour himself a drink. I ask, "If a biter got it, why didn't it go for you first. You're supposed to be more human than it."

"I've been busy while you were gone. Gave that GEB a second set of organs. More appealing that way. More appealing than me, human or not."

"We're out of time," says McGinty. "We've got to think of something before the scientist arrives to finish commissioning."

"Let's all finish our drinks, compliments from me," quips Degnan as he pours, "and then we'll discuss it further."

"There isn't any further," I say. Pasha returns to her thin-skin project. At first I think she is ignoring me, but something about the way her hands tuck and mold the thin-skin plucks at the chords of my memory.

---

We didn't celebrate much anymore in Reichel. Birthdays were forgotten after families were dissolved by The Third through *locasa*. Christmas was indeed considered pagan, for the God of everything was government, and religion was the loyalty of the citizens to The Third. Why worship the birth of an infant king from centuries ago when you could worship scientists, GEB engineers and the commanders of The Third?

I was fourteen and Pasha almost eighteen. And though holidays were wiped from calendars and silenced in the history books, there was one holiday we refused to give up. Halloween. I can actually understand why someone would prohibit that holiday. It seemed incongruous to ask for treats from strangers while dressed up in terrifying costumes that would threaten small children. Of course that was a perfect fit for Pasha. So she decided to put her experiments with thin-skin to work for a noble cause.

Halloween gave her a reason to consider the cultural value of mythology and folklore under the guise of developing her thin-skin. She examined a vampire's tales from the crypt and probed the possible existence of zombies. She considered every trial of her wonder product a valid step for science, for research and for her brand of fun. After stripping down to my bathing suit and allowing her to artistically apply thin-skin to the right places on my body, I began to emerge as the crazed creature she'd intended. So adept was Pasha at molding the product that my fangs looked organic and my face desperate for blood. My artistic application of the thin-skin to her body was not near as successful, leaving her a zombie that was a laughable mass of lumped together tumors. Needless to say Pasha's disappointment in my creation was flung at me in various forms of abuse through the entire night we played "trick or treat." Our Halloween was memorable but definitely enacted in the secrecy of our own home, forcing Quinn and Carles to play a variety of Halloween residents. The Third could never know.

———

"So," says Degnan, looking at me with an eerie, knowing smile, "I think Morris would call you the 'sacrificial lamb.' I however, prefer to call you a 'substitute for science.'"

For only a moment I wonder what he's talking about, but when I turn to find them all staring at me, raising their glasses in salute, and Pasha stroking a piece of thin skin in her hand, I know by morning I'll be saying "Trick or Treat."

———

What I see as Chapman's two month old bump on my abdomen Pasha says isn't visible to others. By the time she nips and tucks the thin-skin to camouflage my shape into a hairless, sexless GEB, I am sweating. "Stop sweating," she says.

"Okay. I'll just say 'stop sweating' and that should work."

"Can't you just calm yourself down? Deep breathe or something."

"You're not the one pretending to be a GEB."

"You only have to look legit for a minute or two," Degnan says. "The scientist comes in, and the guard locks the door from the outside. The guard will leave, and we should be good to go."

"You mean *good* to murder a scientist that's just following directions?"

Shaw wakes up from the anesthetic, groggy, but not missing a beat, and Pasha says, "Avery became a GEB while you were out."

"Life ambition?" Shaw asks. I have no answer to his question.

"The guard's got to be convinced these GEBs are finishing activation and integrating tonight," adds Degnan. "He can't hear anything inside the lab that would indicate otherwise."

I'm not buying any of this. I say, "What if the scientist can't be taken quietly? What if she gets to me and—"

Degnan interrupts. "That's not going to happen. Over the last decade, when I was here, they shut the lab down three times. The guard is done with his duties as soon as he locks the door. He's not going to hang around. Simple."

"Just look like the real thing for a few seconds," says Shaw, "and we'll do the rest. Soon as her back is turned—"

"I'm sweating," I say.

"Stop," says Pasha.

"It's time," says McGinty.

Shaw leads the way, crawling on his hands and knees into the passageway leading to the GEB storage and the lab. He shows no signs of residual anesthetic. Pasha knows what drugs to choose for minimum recovery time. His knife is between his teeth. McGinty motions for me to go next, but I stay put and insist he goes.

"Even though I'm a sexless GEB, I feel a bit exposed right now. I'll go last." I'm sure he thinks I don't see his smile before he enters the passage, but I do. I don't find this funny. I find it terrifying to be GEB #3 in a line of GEBs waiting for the details of life. What if the scientist gets to me, and finds I already have as many details as I need. I think of Shaw's knife, but even that offers little comfort. He can't be close enough. I try to put my mind on the task without imagining the worst, so I concentrate on details and hope I don't snag the knees of my thin-skin disguise, crawling on the rough passage floor before my debut.

We repeat the entry steps to the lab as we have for weeks. The passage, the storage facility, the arched door. This time there is no VAT to worry about, but other worries have taken its place.

When I am in position, sitting third in a line of GEBs, McGinty and Shaw select a hiding spot inside a closet opposite the GEBs. They close the door, hidden just steps away for quick access to the scientist who will carry a razor sharp scalpel in her chest pocket, easily turned into a weapon for her defense or my demise.

I feel incredibly alone until GEB #2—the one in the middle says, "I got my breath today." It waits for me to speak. I do not. "I have language now."

"Me too," I answer trying to think like a GEB, but not able to think at all. The sweat rolls off my hands, trapped in the thin-skin at the tips of my fingers.

Speaking French he says, "J'ai deux langues. I have two languages."

Speaking Tibetan I answer, "So do I."

"Boy or girl?"

"Girl," I say. "You?"

"Maybe tomorrow I will know."

Its head swings briefly in my direction, and then returns to its forward position. "Your eyes are brown?"

"Yes. And yours are?"

"Yellow. Perhaps tomorrow they will be blue." I am aware that this GEB is breathing in and out. I am breathing in and out. It continues. "I received listening a month ago."

"Who have you listened to?"

"Scientists," It says. The sweat from my forehead has travelled to the end of my nose and I hear a slight sucking noise every time I breathe in. Will this noise get louder the longer I stay? The more I sweat? The GEB asks, "Are we having a conversation?"

"Yes," I say.

"Do you have a name?"

"Avery DeTornada." I answer, and realize immediately I should not have given my name. Does it still think I'm a GEB?

"What do you call us, Avery DeTornada?"

Okay, he knows I'm not a GEB 'cause there's an "us" and a "them," but I don't know what to say, so I answer honestly. "We call you GEBs."

Its thin lips make an ever so slight curve upward. *A smile? How can that be?* Then he says, "Genetically engineered beings, I presume?"

If I could scream I would. If I could run away I would. If I could fly to the New Coastline and live in a tree with my husband and the minstrels, I would. But I am trapped in the skin of a genetic freak. This GEB *can't* smile at me. It's not human. I look closely at its profile, and its eyes staring straight ahead. Completely unexpected, its head turns abruptly towards me with a jerky movement, its eyes peering into mine. "Now," he says, "Avery DeTornada, *you* are a GEB like me." All I can think about is Baldy.

It places its hand, with its bluish veins, a partial map of its life, on my arm and says, "Avery DeTornada, have you named things before?" I think of the graves in the children's garden. I think of giving Carles my father's name.

"Yes," I say.

"Please name me."

I just want him to shut up, so I say, "Ulysses."

"That is my name? Ulysses?"

"Yes, that is your name." This time I am not honest. I want to be. I'd like to just say it was the first name that popped into my head, but I don't want to offend it. When did I start believing a GEB has feelings? "Ulysses was a great general. He helped free oppressed people and save a nation from slavery."

"But he could not stop *Jurbay*?"

"No. He could not." I look across the room, and McGinty's face is barely visible through a crack in the closet door. He studies me, or maybe he studies Ulysses and me. I return his gaze, but it apparently does not bother him to be caught in the midst of spying on a teammate. Spying on a friend.

"Could Ulysses have stopped The Third?" asks the GEB.

"Where do you come up with these questions?" I ask him.

"I am curious. I am a quick study."

"Apparently. I think you've listened to more than scientists."

The mechanical sound of the opening lab door interrupts our conversation. "Please, no more talk," I say. Ulysses is silent. GEB #1 has not spoken.

There is only one scientist, just as Dorsey ordered, and I hear her joking with a male guard just before she enters the lab. "Hey," he says. "VATs are still off. How about I come in, and we'll do some creating of our own before you send those GEBs out into the cold, cruel world." *No!* I scream inside my head as the sweat pools under my eyes and rolls down from my armpits to the bend in my elbow. *Not now—don't come in. Meet her later. Not here. Not now.*

"There'll be plenty of time later," she says. "Meet me at unit 543 when I'm done here. It won't take me long." He groans and shuts the door. I hear it lock. The light is dim. I can tell she is in a hurry to get her job done and begins to check figures on a hologram that she activates through the palm of her hand. The weeks we spent extracting data from hard copies and keeping written notes seems senseless now. I hope when she gets to my end of the line she will glance quickly and not discover the color of my eyes. Even thin-skin can't make yellow eyes.

I know Shaw and McGinty wait for her to turn her back to them so they can eliminate her with complete surprise and total silence. We do not know if the guard is still present outside, and even though Degnan seems to believe the guard has left by now, we can't risk discovery due to her screams. *Please turn your back to Shaw. Now.* But she does not. She places her fingers on the wrist of GEB #1, checking its pulse. The basic monitoring of the heart rate is recorded on the hologram and then she imprints her fingers on its neck. *I try desperately not to hold my breath. She really cannot touch me.* I try to breath slow. *I will not give in to the rapid beat. I will force a steady pace. I will.* She finishes with GEB #1, and puts her hand on Ulysses wrist. She says, "Fifty-five. Hmm, very calm and collected, GEB #2."

"My name is Ulysses," he says. *Ulysses! Shut up!*

The scientist jumps back, then recovers. "You can be silent now."

"Now that I have language I have no reason to be quiet."

"Your reason is that I said to shut up."

"I will be silent, scientist." She puts her fingers on Ulysses neck. "But I don't *want* to be silent."

"Learn to curb your wants or you'll be back in storage."

"Everyone knows you cannot deactivate."

"Everyone knows there are other ways to get rid of a GEB." *She moves to me! The scalpel is in her pocket.* She takes my wrist, and I feel the sweat swim back and forth under her fingers as she feels for my pulse. "Ah, things are really loose in there. There may be too many adjustments to finish you." *I don't care. Just move on, forget me. Shaw, please strike now. Please!*

"Do not offend Avery DeTornada, scientist," says Ulysses.

It is at that moment her eyes connect with mine. She sees their color. She sees my fear. She reaches for the scalpel in her lab coat pocket just as my elbow connects with force to her nose. At the same time Ulysses stands and puts his hand over her mouth to stifle a cry for help. In two seconds, Shaw has his arm around her neck and the snap is final.

"Did she offend you, Avery DeTornada?" asks Ulysses.

"You could say that," and I grab its hand, leading it through the lab and then through the storage room toward the tunnel. When we reach the tunnel I realize that just as I hold Ulysses hand, it holds GEB #1's hand.

I see Shaw coming from behind McGinty, his knife unsheathed. *He better not be ventricle happy,* I think, squeezing Ulysses hand even tighter. I push GEB #1 in the passage first watching as it kneels. Ulysses positions itself the same way, following GEB #1. In the process, Ulysses' hand breaks away from mine. It thrusts its hand back up at me, jerking it forward and backward, desperate for me to grab hold. McGinty starts to go next in line, but I step in his way, entering the passage on my knees behind Ulysses. This time I'm not so concerned about my meager thin-skin covering. I am concerned about the life of these GEBs, for they are the vulnerable ones. I hold Ulysses hand. I will not let go.

# Chapter 18
# EXPANDED LIST

---

The sinkhole is hungry. Always. Biting its way through the city buildings, forcing a scout party from The Third, with hundreds of refugees in tow, to head to the New Coastline. We discovered that *Voracious*, which is what we named it, has an appetite that is indiscriminate and carnivorous. Not that there have been many that have been swallowed, but there are always a few thrill seekers, exploring too close the edge. *Voracious'* steady progress, one to five feet daily, allows for no other choice but the eventual evacuation of Reichel. Shaw and McGinty have all the growth stats. Shaw's chipster estimates D-vac (desperate evacuation) at over two years away. Worry edges around my exterior, chipping away at the cool demeanor of objective leadership in an attempt to penetrate my emotions. I'm in urgent mode, needing reassurance from Raben that The 28 United will be prepared if The Third's scout party comes upon our settlement up the New Coastline. The Third is not looking for us up there. That is to our advantage. *Big picture: Do not let the worry whittle through to Chapman.* I must be efficient in decisions for this team, and I need to be strategic for the benefit of my child.

———

Ulysses turned six months old today. Six months since he received his name and came with GEB #1 to the horseshoe tunnel with all of us. That means Chapman is eight months old, yearning and churning within my womb to bust out and explore life. What didn't look to anyone else like a baby bump on my stomach at the two month mark is now a well-developed basketball. *Do I have maternal instincts?* How would I know? All I have to compare myself to is Quinn. Pasha says all mothers have second nature feelings relating to their children. If that means a protective instinct, I suppose I do feel that, but the rest of it is quite confusing.

Unfortunately, I have had way too much time to think about this. I was banned from the night patrols about a month ago when it became way too obvious that I should have been in the breeding rooms on the fourth floor of the labyrinth. It was my call to leave the patrol and no one else's. We all refer to my baby as Chapman now. I didn't want my child called Baby #1 the way GEB #1 is singled out. So Chapman it is. It seems a sensible name to give, honoring the heritage of my family, and since Raben isn't here to give input, I am comfortable choosing the name. The term *single* parent coined a century ago seems appropriate. It is not a label I chose, but rather one stamped on me by circumstances.

None of us expected to be here for seven months, and now Pasha insists that we must leave within the week even if we don't find out why the lab closed and what is consuming the attention of The Third besides the ever-growing sinkhole. Dr. Pasha Lutnik seems to think Red Grove would be a much better delivery sight for a birth than a dirty, dim horseshoe tunnel. Imagine that.

I now wear the larger sized coverall that Quinn left me at the pools and my hand-me-downs went to GEB #1, who we are naming today. Ulysses insists.

"We can no longer continue to call her 'GEB #1,'" says Ulysses. This GEB is a *she* now. Degnan made sure of that. When he and Pasha started handing out GEB specifics, sex was the first, Ulysses a boy and GEB #1 a girl.

The miracle of human creation marches around the interior of my body. My mind processes what I imagine to be an elbow traversing my huge abdomen from north to south. The little pokes and jabs from the inside that I see on the outside, might be Chapman's way of letting me know his arrival is imminent. I determine I will give equal time in my thoughts to the possibility of Chapman being a boy *or* a girl. "You're going to meet me face to face," *she* seems to say. "Get ready for life to change," *he* taps in Morse Code from the inside of my stomach. The tapping gets louder every day. The girth of my body prods me, moment by moment, to return to Red Grove. No way to ever be comfortable sitting on a crate, standing by a window or turning from side to side in an attempt to sleep on the hard ground. McGinty tried to build me a nest out of stored bandages and rags, but the size of it compared to me was not a comfortable match. Pasha says pregnant women have a mystique about them. I'm sure I have none. Dark circles under my eyes from no sleep and poor nutrition, and the normally dull, nondescript coverall even uglier, considering the shape that's inside it. I think it is past time to have this baby, but apparently it takes nine months. And besides that, I have no idea what to do once he/she is born. Pasha says she will help me. I'm depending on that. But mostly I'm hoping I will soon see Raben and together we will explore this new territory and discover the how-to of parenthood as a unit. We are both courageous people. Pasha says we will figure it out.

I do ponder the prospect of motherhood way too much. Yet, with equal intensity I dissect the daily strategy of our stay here, processing the information gathered from nightly patrols that I am now excluded from.

Pasha records data on the chipster in her leg regarding the progress of Ulysses and GEB #1. When Ulysses first came to stay with us we liberated a few clothing items from the History Labyrinth. It's easy to do by popping the glass covering on the recessed shelves of the displays, removing one item from the historical collection and readjusting the remaining treasures so no one passing by would notice the deletion. For example, Ulysses is now decked out in Lycra biking pants extracted from a large section on the third floor of the labyrinth depicting the history of professional cycling. His pants were formerly worn by a cyclist who took a fall from grace, and whose name I can't remember. Maybe it started with an "A." However we never liberated a shirt for Ulysses.

Shaw throws one of his skin-fitting long sleeved shirts that he wears under his coverall at Ulysses whose eyes don't flinch off the salt container he is examining by the storage shelves. "Put something over that scrawny torso, and you'll look more like a general," says Shaw.

Without looking at Shaw, Ulysses continues to inspect the iodized salt and says, "Are all generals 'buff.'"

"Annalynn must be here," I say, "other-wise where did you learn that word?"

"Do not know Annalynn, but know Degnan. Know Mother Pasha. They use that word."

"Mother Pasha?" I look skeptically at Pasha who pets Vipe with one hand, enters chipster records with the other, averting her eyes from my gaze at all costs. I speak to Ulysses. "I notice you have a new growth of grass above your elbow and part of a fork on the side of your right ankle."

"Not a growth. A decoration. A gift from Degnan. Just like the bow in GEB #1's hair is a gift from Pasha."

"She doesn't have hair."

"She wants hair."

"Listen, Degnan has both an amusement and a perversion for playing games with genetics and Pasha seems to be consumed with playing dolls."

Pasha sneers at me, "I hate dolls. This is science."

"No, science does not include hair bows. I'm sure of that."

GEB #1 picks up the shirt that Shaw threw and helps Ulysses put it on. She does not talk, but manages to nod her head in approval, and that is enough to make Ulysses smile. Watching these GEBs from the beginning of their development gives me the creeps. These genetically engineered beings are smiling from pleasure, expressing hopes to have hair and dreaming about being buff.

Pasha observes Ulysses, making notes in her chipster. Focused. Intentional. Unbreakable. Perfect." Ulysses rolls the salt container in his hands then, without warning tosses it in GEB #1's direction. She drops it. Apparently Pasha and Degnan need to add the detail of fine motor skills to her DNA. The salt lands with a thud and the blue cardboard cylinder splits right down the center of the word "Morton" and the picture of the little girl's yellow dress and opened umbrella.

Ulysses squats down, running his fingers through the salt, then, after a moment of concentration, looks at me. He practices exercising the muscles in his face. A smile, trembling with its upward movement. One eyebrow, arching in the direction of his forehead. A forehead, furrowing slightly. "What's May without June," says Ulysses. I have no idea what he's talking about.

Apparently Degnan understands and chuckles. His laugh always causes prickles to dance up my spine. He says, "What's sun without moon?"

Pasha stands taking four or five quick jumps in the air, saying, "What's fork without spoon?"

Shaw glances up, adding, "What's knife without blood?"

We ignore him, watching Ulysses try to finalize his thought process, crossing slowly to GEB #1, touching her arm, saying, "What's salt without pepper? I am like salt, you are Like—"

"Pepper," says GEB #1. I realize these GEBs can now compose similes. Unnerving. In my mind I curse them both. *Go back to the petri dish.* But in my heart I know I don't mean it.

"I have a name," Pepper says. *Okay,* I relent. *Now that she thinks she's got a name, I feel really guilty about the petri dish thought.*

Unfortunately, this banter and game playing has become our new norm. Our seven month norm. I take my answer book and pencil from my coverall pocket and ask McGinty, "What's the measurement tonight?"

He's shining his boots, a ridiculous habit from Elite training, especially since there's no one inspecting the quality of shine down here. He says, "Our mouth *Voracious* hasn't missed a day of devouring ground since we found it. It's up to six zip lengths wide tonight. Won't be long and it'll be chomping at eight."

Shaw wipes his blade so clean its sheen reflects his face. He points that blade at me and says, "And you can add to your little answer book that in the halls and outside the doors of every unit waits a government issued pack. They are identical, small and all of them on the ready."

"Ready for emigration at any moment," says McGinty.

"And you know where all those people leaving Reichel will head?" asks Shaw

"The New Coastline. I know," I say and turn to Pasha. "Have you had any word—any notification from up there?"

"You mean Raben? No."

"And you're trying to let them know that The Third will eventually come?" She ignores me, adjusting Pepper's bow. "Pasha," I raise my voice, trying to get her attention.

She rubs the top of Pepper's head and without looking at me responds, "That is the twenty-third time you've asked me that. I've given you twenty-two answers, all the same."

"And?"

She looks at me, "Don't make me say it again."

"So that means, 'no.' You haven't gotten word to them."

"I think we ought to give her a tan," says Degnan, examining Pepper. "Like the Hollywood babes in the wax museum on the fifth floor of the labyrinth." McGinty, Shaw, Pasha and I freeze. We lock eyes. *There is no fifth floor to the labyrinth.* At least not one we've found. We've searched the labyrinth countless times, every square inch. There is a first floor and three underneath. The fourth floor, the one on the bottom, houses the pools. *There is no fifth floor.*

Degnan is very aware we have all turned our glares at him. He says, "Oh, did I say the fifth floor? I must have meant fourth." I want to tear him apart, but there isn't time.

McGinty catches my wrist as I lift the pack to my back. "You can't go."

I continue to strap it on. "I'll wear a rain poncho."

"Then we'll all wear ponchos." McGinty looks out the entrance window. "There's a drizzle out tonight. Maybe we'll get away with it. I know I can't stop you."

"No, you can't. Maybe the answer as to why the GEB lab shut down is on this fifth floor of the labyrinth." I spit my words, staccato. "How do we get access to the fifth floor? There are no doors, no entrances. Degnan, tell us."

"You're the one that likes to swim, Avery. Figure it out," he says.

I thought I'd kept the secret of Borden's death in the pool from Degnan, but he's an expert at hearing what's hidden. I know what he's hinting at. There must be an entrance to the fifth floor from the pools, and the thought of getting in that water again is horrifying, fifth floor or not.

Pasha helps with the poncho, and we move away from the others, gaining more space to maneuver. I whisper to her, "You need to give me *locasa*." She looks at me, eye to eye, inches from my face. "And Pasha, you need to show me quickly how to use it with reverse effect."

"I can't do that," Pasha says. "You said yourself, it's dangerous. It's in the first stages. I don't know enough. Just 'cause it worked on Quinn doesn't mean it will work again. I need to do tests—studies. There could be permanent damage—damage so prolific we might not be able to correct it."

My words press her. "Listen, you and I both know I won't be able to keep up. McGinty and Shaw are going to have to go ahead to get started on finding the fifth floor."

"You'll only be fifteen minutes or so behind them."

I pull her by the collar close to me, not threatening, pleading, "I'll be on my own for fifteen minutes and there're patrols out there. Consider it a weapon."

"It *is* a weapon."

"Get it for me now."

She manages to go around the curve in the horseshoe where she can't be seen and where *locasa* is hidden. She and I have agreed to change its position every day, so Degnan will never figure out its hiding place. I know today it is stored in her pack. When she returns, I feel her reach under the poncho and slip *locasa* in the front pocket of my coverall.

Pasha whispers, "It's been programed to a four-tap on the green button."

"A four-tap, green. Got it," I say, and I step up on the crate below the window exit and maneuver my stomach through a window that seems to be decreasing in size every day. I feel McGinty's hands lightly on my back, like he is spotting a toddler in the midst of her first steps.

The three of us are not even a hundred feet away from the entrance when I send them on ahead. There is no time to waste, and I can't keep up. Without any interruption in his gait, Shaw continues toward the labyrinth, but McGinty pauses. I feel his hesitation before he stops. I know what he's thinking. He wants to stay with me, but he says nothing.

"It's only a mile walk. I'll be right behind you." I try to smile, but it's a pathetic effort. He nods at me, and then he's off, the night engulfing him in seconds. The cold and wind ripple up my legs causing the poncho to flutter away from my body. Catching the edge of the fabric, I press it down, making sure it covers Chapman's habitat, all the while picking up my walking pace to its maximum level. If they reach the History Labyrinth without any diversions it should take them just over ten minutes. I'm guessing it will take me twice that. My walking pace is quick for my condition, and my stride unencumbered.

I'm seven or eight minutes out from my destination when the sound of my footsteps seems magnified. From behind I hear a very slight, almost imperceptible sound, and I am sure my combat boots are shadowed by someone trailing me. I am tempted to face my tracker, marking his forehead with the laser and releasing the power of the Z-Colt into his skull, ending his pursuit. But to face a trained combatant and draw down on him in an instant, when I know he has the advantage of seeing me turn toward him? He'd be ready for me. The worst thing I can do is pivot around and confront whoever stalks me. He's obviously smart enough to walk in perfect sync with my stride, so confronting him eye to eye is not an option. Better to string him along until there's decent cover, then run for it. In slow motion, I unholster my Z-Colt from my shoulder, desperate for the cover of a building or a vehicle.

I accelerate my pace, and the force behind me shows accuracy and perfection mimicking my steps. My eyes race around the foreground of my route. Ahead there is a pod of slim, three story buildings. If I can reach the interior of the pod, I can slip behind the corner of one of the structures. With the extra weight I carry breathing is labored, fear intensifies. *Do not run.* I tell myself. *Continue steady steps. You are feet from the center of the pod.*

Just as I hit the midway point in the square surrounded by the pod of buildings, I dash to the left and am instantly covered with the protection of the steel building. I support my Z-Colt in front of my body with rigid arms and swing out from the building, marking the forehead of my pursuer. Pepper.

"Hello, Avery DeTornada," she says.

I yank her behind the building. "Pepper!" I lower my weapon. "You were just about dead before you even got your hair."

"Came to protect."

"I don't need protection."

"Not you." Pepper stares at my stomach. "Protect Chapman."

"Yeah, well that's going to be a little bit hard. We're still connected."

"I will make it work."

"You're not exactly camouflaged with that bald head."

"I have a bow," she says.

"Shut up. Did you see anyone else out there?" She is silent. "You're not protecting me or Chapman if you won't even answer a basic strategy question."

"You said 'shut up.'"

"Talk. Talk now. Anyone else out there?"

"Dump pickers."

"How do you know what a dump picker is?"

"Pasha said they look like Degnan. Dirty."

"How many?"

"Four. Maybe five." Looking around the corner one more time, I see them. They are not moving as a group, but separately, keeping low and sneaking from bush to tree to building. One of the dump pickers sprints from behind a street alcove toward a zip at the corner of the pod. One shot cracks the quiet early morning. My lips split open ready to gasp, but Pepper's fingers quickly seal any sound I might make with a hand over my mouth, and I wonder which of her creators made sure she had those lightening quick impulses. Most probably Pasha.

Emerging from across the street jogs an Elite guard with his weapon, a DR93, held firmly in front of his body. He rounds up the other four dump pickers, all teenage children. After he has rooted them out of the bushes, he collects them around the broken body of the dead picker. He kicks at the limp heap, making sure there is no life left. Just as his foot nudges the back of the fallen one, a squeak comes from one of the pickers, a kid of about fourteen. With instant speed the Elite points his weapon, marking the heart of the one who dared to care.

The Elite's back is to the pod. He cannot see us. "Pickers! To the center of the street," he yells. This motley group is so spindly with hunger that the edges of their bones seem ready to jump out of their skin for a final fight. No sniveling from this group. Not a wet eye present. They face their death with chins held high as if to taunt their enemy. Their lips raise no defense. They know they have met their executioner, but they do not acknowledge fear. Intrepid.

I feel Pepper place her arms around my waist from behind, and I sense her gluing her feet to the spot, unyielding and unwilling to release me. I know I can't shoot him. We're in a public square and can't arouse suspicion. My fingers search for *locasa* in the pocket of my coverall. I wrap the pads of my fingers around its cylindrical shape and allow one finger to travel the length of the device until the button is found on the disc at the bottom of the canister. My fingers remember the words Pasha spoke. A four-tap. I tap three times, shaking the arms of Pepper away.

I know the dump pickers' eyes see me approaching, but they have picked all their lives, knowing how to act in the middle of danger, and do not reveal my presence to the Elite. A patch of his skin peeks out from under his helmet, above his uniform jacket. One chance. I plunge forward, tapping the button one last time and placing the disc on the target of his exposed neck. Effect, immediate.

I can only hope the man he was before *locasa* might be a gentler version of what I just saw. He looks at the pickers, his gaze falling on his weapon then wandering to the ground and fixing on the dead picker. He drops his weapon and backs away from the body. "What did I do?" he asks.

"You killed a—" says Pepper, but I stop her before she goes further. I realize this version of *locasa* has returned what The Third took from this soldier: family. His loyalty to The Third is now unfounded, Elite training gone. I expect he will now become homebound, searching for that which was stolen from him years ago. He will try to find those that will fill the hole in his heart, the gap in his soul.

I place my hand on the guard's arm. "It's okay. The Third has required this of you." I notice a definite twitch at the right corner of his mouth. "What's your name?"

"Fredrick." He can't take his eyes off the dead body. "I would never do this." He starts to panic.

"No you wouldn't, and we know that. Right now we're all in danger, and we need you to help us." Tears well in his eyes. "Can you do that, Fredrick?" I pick up the DR93 and hand it to Pepper. "Can you help us?"

"Yes," he says, and to his credit he tries to pull himself together. "What do you want me to do?"

"Gather up these kids and keep them together and quiet. You're going to follow us." I look at the group. "Give him your names as we travel. Fredrick, I'm Avery. This is Pepper."

He nods and asks Pepper, "You from the lab?"

"I have a bow," she says, and I grab her arm and pull her after me. We are back on course, and I try to estimate the length of time we have been delayed—ten minutes? Twelve? How long will McGinty and Shaw wait for me once they have found the entrance to the fifth floor? Our steps begin to take on the sound of a unit, and I hear whispered voices from behind me: *Hunk, Junior, Garland* and *Desmond*.

I glance over my shoulder and see the eyes of the youngest boy, Desmond, shining through the layers of grimy muck on his face. I see the steel cold of his gray existence, but also a spark of hope now flickering, ignited by the fact that he dodged one more Elite soldier's capture and one more brush with death. I acknowledge the value in both.

We reach the labyrinth and gather our group together for final instructions. They are to wait with Frederick until I return with Shaw and McGinty. Once again I lead tag-a-long soldiers who are younger than me, without a childhood, without a #14 on their wrists and without a fear of what's to come. They all stare unflinchingly at me. Four scraggly dump pickers whose existence depends on honing the craft of survival. I can work with that, for in an all-out war for the salvation of this country survival may be the most valuable skill of all. Then there's an Elite trained soldier in the midst of an identity crisis, with questions and confusion that cannot be answered or solved until later. These five, not much of a fighting force, but when I add their names—Fredrick, Hunk, Junior, Garland, and Desmond—to the list of The 28 United, I realize the roll call of the faithful is expanding and that each single recruit, whether through necessity or passion, builds our company of loyal ones. Somewhere deep inside me I pledge to never see this roll call as a *list*, but rather as a citizenship brought together by destiny and as individuals who, united, create our new family through great personal sacrifice. Once aligned with us, they will be hunted until death or victory. Family will rise up through the muck of the dump, the missing fingers of minstrels, the burned books and bodies of the library boys, the loss of family from *locasa* and the death sentence of the deadlies. I'm incredibly captured by these five sets of eyes.

And in spite of the fact that Shaw and McGinty are not by my side, and that I long for Raben and the words "I love you"—in spite of the fact that my swollen body is way past uncomfortable, and that I hate and mistrust Degnan and that the mouth of the sinkhole is chomping at the heels of a city—in spite of all these things, standing here in the past-midnight hour with only the stars as my witness I can say: *This is where I belong.*

# Chapter 19

# UNSATIATED MAW

I tell Pepper she must stay with the new group of five. She isn't very old and isn't programmed to understand the chain of command yet, so she says "no." There isn't time to argue. I point at the five waiting for instructions. Frederick continues to look confused. Nonetheless, he stands in front of the four kids in an attempt to protect them with his weapon, holding it like a child with a water pistol. *It's a paradox*, I think. *I want him to remember weaponry to defend these kids. Yet, I want him to find a family, have a Christmas tree and go to sleep at night without one eye open.*

"They need you, Pepper," I say, showing her the time piece imbedded on the cuff of Frederick's patrol uniform. "In twenty minutes, if I'm not back, you guide these five to the horseshoe. Got it?"

"I will do it for you, Avery. But I don't 'got it.' 'Got it' means I agree. I do not agree."

"You sound like Pasha."

"That is a compliment, Avery."

"Not meant to be, Pepper." But I'm sure Pepper doesn't hear me. My back is to her, and I am performing my version of running to the labyrinth. My belly is taut and hard and heavy. Chapman pushes me onward from the inside.

When I arrive at the History Labyrinth there are no guards. I don't know why, and I don't have time to find out. My DR93 is on the ready and right in front of me, more or less supported by a bulging abdomen. Inside me is a consuming drive to lay out a strategy to defeat The Third. That obsession pings back and forth in my brain intent on the discovery of The Third's newest priority. Is it a way to harness the energy of a sinkhole? Or maybe milking the venom of a viper to develop a Deadly #15? Or is it a quicker way to activate a GEB so that their influx into our world might be more efficient? Who knows, perhaps they're creating a genetically engineered being to replace Quinn. I shiver. She's not the type of subterranean who is blindsided. She'd see it coming. *No. This is for later.* I tell myself. *Shut it down, Avery. You will blow this all if you jump ahead. Here and now. Get this done. Then move on.* I try to stop the barrage of these confusing rabbit holes and focus on my search, focus on what I might find hidden on the fifth floor. I feel abandoned by my sixth sense and speculate if it was always a creation of my imagination.

I head straight down to the pools on the fourth level. I step through the archway, and except for the pounding of my heart, it's like a tomb down here. My breathing is labored and, no matter how hard I try to pick up my pace, my feet seem heavy, weighted with my equipment, my weapon and my baby.

McGinty and Shaw are not here, which means only one thing. They found the fifth level, and they didn't wait for me to join them. The walk past the pools takes a slow-motion minute, and my mind fills with images of our take-down of Borden. I relive the horror of Borden's death in the pool. Borden's *murder* in the pool. I try shaking the prickles of fear out of my limbs, like stomping a boot loaded with dirt, but they hang on. I make it to the final pool and stand on the edge. Puddles of liquid indicate someone has been here recently, and my boots displace the water interrupting the wet, circular formations. I hear Borden's voice so loud inside my mind, it seems to resound off the mosaic walls and art draped ceilings, taunting me to dive in, knowing I must face more memories if I do. The fifth level entrance must be below the surface of the water. We searched this place night after night and didn't find anything unusual. I must submerse and risk the memories of Borden choking me.

I reach to unhook my pack from my shoulders, and a rumbling blusters through the structure, shaking it violently like when *Jurbay* shook us and severed our United in two. Like giant hands, this unknown power rents the History Labyrinth and peels it apart right down the center, shredding open its walls around me and separating the building into two distinct parts.

A column that stood majestically within the peaceful pool is wrenched out of the solid tiles where it stood for several centuries and is thrust upward by the buckling building, entrenching itself against the staircase. The force catapults me through the air too, following the column and landing squarely atop the twelve foot pillar. The column is now at rest and is, for the moment, stationary.

I watch the pool crack and split down the center, sending gallons of water gushing to the crumbling floor below, spilling onto the now exposed fifth level and draining right out the open section of building into a sinkhole.

From my perch on the column I now see a cross section of the other half of the building staring back at me. The water missed the forty or so people that had been working in some sort of lab on the fifth level. They are in chaos, grabbing anything within their reach to hold onto. The people in this lab below are divided, their room sliced in half. Some are on the left side and the rest on the right half, my half. As seconds tick, the people on my side scramble for what is left of the stairs, and in the front of that group, clawing to safety, are McGinty and Shaw.

Our side of the building shivers in waves of violent tremors, rolling up the building, seeming to say: *guess what's coming for you Avery DeTornada, for you and your baby.* I grab the edge of the column, trying to stabilize myself, determined that I will not be yanked and splintered. This will not be the end for me and Chapman.

With horror, glaring into the cavern below, I see the left side of the building beginning a collapse, the sinkhole gobbling it floor by floor. This unsatiated maw bites the left building, gorging itself, starting with the fifth floor below and moving in slow motion through each floor as they collapse on themselves, including the ground level floor, leaving only a swirling quagmire of sludge and arms and shattered walls. This cannot be the same sinkhole we investigated earlier in the week. The first one that we measured was far away and advancing slowly. This is sinkhole number two, and we did not expect a second carnivorous pit to be eating away at Reichel.

My column shifts, sending me swinging off the side, but my fingers cling to the ridges on its edge, my feet dangling mid-air while the pillar tilts. It is no longer leaning against the stairs that supported it, but now it has shifted upright, settling in the debris within ten feet of the crumbling staircase, leaving a small chasm between me and the potential safety of the stairs. I regain my footing and climb once again to the top of the column. The smell of debris comes at me from all sides, its dust twirling around my head, coating my face. I want to leap to the staircase, but it's too far.

I glance at the cavern below. On the fifth level there are still scientists who have not left their half of the lab, but are poised to run for the staircase. They are following orders from a man determined to make them stay. Some try to make it past him, to escape, but he pushes each one back, commanding them to salvage what they can from the destruction. I am close enough to see their desperate need to survive and their blind obedience to please the man. I notice the back of his hair is not covered with dust like the front. Perhaps his cap protected it for a time. I see his hair is silver. I see his body is fit. I see that this is Dorsey.

My heart beats out of control, but in an instant it is still. For a moment or two I do not breathe. Dorsey reaches forward to open a closet still intact. Men emerge from the closet, examined quickly by a scientist. This scientist opens a device in the forearm of the first man, checks it and sends him on his way. The scientist examines a device in the quad of the next man. Then he is released to head for the staircase. The third closet member's eye is tested before he leaves for escape, and the final one from the closet extends his hand to the scientist who examines the inside of his middle finger. *Oh my God!* I say aloud to no one but myself. *They've made a chipster. They've made more than one. This is why the GEB lab has taken a back seat. We can no longer attempt to rally The 28 United through our chipsters. We will never have a roll call again like we had eight months ago. And though we desperately need to continue to find those loyal ones to The 28 United, chipsters have been compromised. The thought of trying to use Pasha's homing pigeons again seems more ridiculous and more antiquated than before.*

Climbing upwards McGinty and Shaw cling to anything stable. There's a rhythm to their climbing, a tentative tap of the boot, a two second test of stability, then they hunker their feet in and allow their right hands to test the next potential handhold. When satisfied that it will support the body, their fists wrap around mangled pieces of metal and they pull themselves higher. They arrive at what's left of the staircase long before the others.

Now that the Chipsters from below are trying to advance up the staircase, they are followed by the remaining scientists from the lab. The scientist that checked out the chipsters reaches the deteriorating staircase, but comes too close to the edge and plunges back down to the fifth level, picking up momentum as he rolls head first, joining the entire left side of the building in a sea of muck. The churning sludge stirs him into its pot. I look away. I cannot bear the fact that three minutes ago these scientists were working for The Third, and their biggest worry was their inability to meet Dorsey's standards, never thinking their night would end by sinking into an unexpected grave. I can hear his desperate screams, and then the muffled suck as his lungs fill with the sinkhole's mire.

I see Shaw has climbed to the first floor, and he leaps to a zip, hooking up and setting loose a second and third zip so that one end of each zip is still connected, but the loose ends sling toward McGinty who has spotted me. McGinty misses the zips on Shaw's first throw, but catches them firmly on the second. McGinty attaches himself to the end of one zip, should he fall he will still be linked to the end by Shaw. Then he gets as close as he can get to the column I am on. It is only ten feet from his spot on the staircase, but there is no way I can jump it.

"I'm gonna get this zip to you Avery," he yells.

"You know I'm a lousy catch," I shout back.

"Show that baby of yours what it's like to be a New York Yankee." And I remember Annalynn and McGinty playing games where they guessed the long forgotten sport teams' and athlete names.

McGinty flings the second zip my way. I catch it and wince in pain at the force of the hard cable banging into the palm of my hand, but I don't let go.

"Hold onto that zip," says McGinty. "Now I want you to ease off the column and when you're free—"

"You mean when I'm dangling in space?"

"I'm gonna pull you up."

"Yeah?"

"Yeah. Now go."

I let one hand move over my protruding abdomen, saying to Chapman, "McGinty's got us." And off the edge of the column I go. I wouldn't exactly call it "easing" over. Gravity knows I'm carrying a child and takes advantage of it, but I don't fall far. In the first few seconds my arms are aching, feeling like they are being jerked out of the sockets. I hear the zip scraping the crumbling staircase as McGinty yanks me up, a couple feet each time he pulls. I picture him on the other end, his foot braced against some seemingly solid piece of rubble, his muscles straining from the weight of me and Chapman.

I reach the staircase and feel the stones at the edge tearing my poncho. McGinty and I are face to face. "What took you so long?" I ask him as he wraps his arms around my body, pulling me the final inches to a momentary safety.

"This might have been a whole lot easier a month from now," he says. I have nothing to hold onto but him. It's not a graceful position, my stomach pressing against his body, introducing him to Chapman. I'm sure McGinty feels my child kicking from inside, making his presence known even before he can speak a word.

Then I feel a yank from the heavens and we're being hauled upward. I look to see Shaw holding the zip with both hands, reeling us in, like the catch of the day, enabling us to escape from the collapsing cavern. It is not a smooth ride. The zip twirls and swings in expanding circles the longer we are in the air. My entire body begins to shake from exhaustion, from fear. I can't tell if this is the mother instinct Pasha insists is real, or if this is simply the instinct of survival. I cannot let go of McGinty, but I know if I do—*he* will not let go of me. The dust from the debris swirls around us as we sail through an atmosphere altered by bits of wreckage.

Shaw offers me his hand. "Glad you were on this side of the building," I say, clasping his arm.

"Yes, sir, Commander," he says and with one motion McGinty releases me, and Shaw pulls me to the top of the staircase. He lifts the poncho over my head, letting it fall and hooking the back of my coverall to the section of zip he is attached to. I catch a glimpse of my poncho floating downward and as it does it passes Dorsey. He looks up at us, even as he climbs the crumbling staircase. There's a moment when all three of us stare down at him, and I know he realizes now the three of us were never a figment of Borden's imagination.

There will be no more subterranean night guards in Reichel—if there is a Reichel. Dorsey will no longer wonder if we are here. We *are* here. We are a threat, and he will hunt us with intensity far greater than the jaws of a sinkhole.

———

When we reach the zip transfer platform the sound of the History Labyrinth's death is behind us, but imprinted on me forever. Pepper climbs the side of the building leading to the platform, followed by Frederick and the others. They arrive and for a moment we all stand, recovering, breathing, and stunned that we are still here to breathe. In silence she loads two of the smallest dump pickers, Desmond and Hunk, on Shaw and McGinty's backs "Load the little one on me, Pepper," I say.

"No. You have Chapman." She answers.

"On a zip I won't feel hardly any weight with one of them on my back." Pepper doesn't move. I order her, "Load Garland on my back." She does and we zip away. I look over my shoulder to see Pepper and Fredrick making sure everyone has access to a zip.

It takes only a couple minutes to get as far as we can on the zips. Shaw unhooks first, sliding his passenger off his back. He then stops my momentum as I reach the roof and lifts Garland off my back before releasing my zip. Shaw leads, picking his way down the ladder to the ground while Pepper and Frederick gather the children together. I come last, assisted by McGinty who eases my final step from the ladder to the ground. We race for the horseshoe, everyone faster than me except McGinty who supports me with his arm around my waist. I set aside my pride and let him help me. I want safety for us all, but I know there is much to be done before we can flee to Red Grove.

Between labored breaths, McGinty says, "The people on the fifth level were scientists."

"It was a chipster lab," I say. "They figured it out. Chipsters aren't just ours anymore." I feel physically ill. Now there will be no communications with the New Coastline. No subterranean messages to Quinn. There will be no future roll calls through the Chipsters who receive our messages. My stomach churns. "Good possibility they know about Red Grove," I say.

"Yeah. Good possibility," McGinty fights to allow his breathing to return to normal.

We reach the entrance to the horseshoe in a few minutes. Pasha's face appears at the window and she opens it, but I don't even enter. "Get out what you need," I command, "What you can carry."

"Right now?" she asks, and I see Degnan and Ulysses' heads appear in the entrance too.

"Right now."

Degnan says, "We'll come back for the rest later."

"No, we're not coming back," I say. "We're burning this place to the ground and every one of those GEBs in storage goes down with it." I've been taught GEBs can replicate emotion, but do not have any of their own. The look on Ulysses face proves otherwise. Is he scared or heartbroken about the burning of hundreds of inactivated GEBs?

The first two items handed out the window and up to McGinty are Pasha's cat Vipe and Degnan's bottle of Hennessey. Glad we got the important stuff.

Everyone but me loads a pack and straps it on. Shaw and McGinty hold bottles of fuel in their hands and run the perimeter of the Plethora Plant, pouring a creek of combustible liquid around the base of the building. Just before Shaw ignites the building where we worked as subterraneans for two years, Pasha grabs his wrist to stop him. She turns to me and says, "Quinn could be in there. I'll send a final message. Maybe she can get out."

"No," I say, and I am shaking as my discernment wins over my parental attachment. "She's smart. Got a sixth sense. Trust her. We can't risk another message. This fire must be a complete surprise. We'll catch as many as we can unaware." My hand touches my coverall pocket where *locasa* still rests. We have liberated it from The Third. Maybe now it will be put to the work of justice and its intended goal. My father Carles would like that. The Catalonian people would like that. We have also freed two GEBs who are now fighting for our side, and we've recorded reams of information in the last seven months that will help us in a battle against The Third.

Shaw sets flame to fuel, and part of Reichel burns. Now our caravan to Red Grove begins again like it did months ago. This is way too familiar. My voice leads the way, but my body takes the position at the end of the line, McGinty by my side. We turn away from the city and feel the heat of the fire's pulse at our backs.

# Chapter 20
# CAMOUFLAGE SUITS ME

"I will climb it by myself," I yell at Shaw when he offers me a ride up the Red Grove ladder to safety. Maybe eight months of serving as Chapman's home slows me down on the run from Reichel, but no one carries me up a ladder on his back. McGinty offers to spot me from behind, but I reject his proposal too. Climbing poses balance challenges that running does not, and I know it will take me a while to reach the top. "I'll go last," I say.

I time the pinches that traverse my abdomen by counting how many steps up the ladder are in between the beginning of the pain and the end. Pasha calls these irritating nips that march across my belly contractions. They are not regular, not intervals announcing arrival, but warnings that there is no way to escape my meeting this youngest warrior that has been catching a ride with me for quite some time now.

Even as I climb to the entrance of Red Grove a small voice at the back of my head prods me. *Don't tell Morris about his father. He's a child. He doesn't need to know about Borden.* There are other voices too—voices about truth—but before I can sort them out the entry above us pops open, and we are each swept off the ladder, landing inside Red Grove. The ladder is sucked in after us to the thin-skin domain created by Pasha. There to greet me is Morris.

I hurry to embrace him because I've missed him, and because I hope his future will not be as chaotic as mine. I embrace him because I've killed his father and the mourning inside me is eating at my soul. If I do not tell him of his father's death, am I hiding a truth he needs to know, or protecting him from information a child should never have to deal with? It's in this moment I realize how much camouflage suits me. Camouflaged as a subterranean in Elite training, using that guise in Catalonia to rescue my mother and *locasa* at the expense of my father's life. Camouflaged as a worker in the Plethora Plant, watching my mother's own cover entrench her into the depths of The Third, wanting her to be a mother, but knowing her allegiance to The 28 United would always come first. Then recently, once again back in Reichel hidden in a horseshoe tunnel, camouflaged in the night patrol. And for so long I camouflaged my child, perhaps wanting to protect Chapman, but my belly is long past disguise, and I am tired of pretending. No more camouflage. I want to be around to guide my child to opportunities that allow her to stand boldly in the middle of The 28 United as a peacemaker instead of raising weapons in defense. I hope Chapman will make policy instead of destruction and friendships instead of alliances. Maybe this child will have a chance to rebuild the world instead of trying to save it from annihilation. I am ripping off the camouflage, starting with Morris, and it is scary as hell.

———

Later on I find Morris sitting on the landing dock in the presence of the galaxy. I join him, placing myself three feet away, staring, not at him, but at the night sky. He says, "You were in Reichel for seven months, Avery."

"We found what we were after."

"Good." There is hesitation in his voice. I'm afraid of the question he will ask me. "I was wondering about my father?" I do not answer. "Wondering—not really caring—just wondering."

I have decided on the truth, but the words don't form on my lips. "Is he dead?" He reads my face. I know he does, and interprets my silence. "Did you kill him?"

I turn my body in his direction, facing him. And even though he does not look at me, my eyes are locked on him. "Yes."

Then, he glances up. His moon shaped eyes peer at me from behind his thick glasses that declare his love for reading. "Tell me how it happened," he says.

343

"No," I say. My answer is final, and he knows it.

As we face one another, sitting cross-legged, close enough to hear each other breathe, I am very glad for breath itself. His eyes return to his lap, but mine remain fixed on him. He has no tears. Mine fall silently. Finally, his gaze returns to mine. He says, "This is war, Avery. I understand." I think, *What an odd response from a child who has just lost his father.* Then I remember. This is Morris. His father tried to kill him. Of course he understands. But as for me, I don't understand a thing.

Morris points at my stomach, and I catch his hand, placing it on the top of the bump. He and I feel the baby push, what I think to be a knee, across the crest of my stomach. Morris pulls his hand away, and with a slight giggle in his voice he says, "What am I? An uncle? A nanny? A teacher?"

I laugh too and say, "A brother."

He jumps to his feet, extending his hand to me, helping me get up, even though I don't need the help. "Then that'll make Annalynn his sister, and that means trouble."

The laughter continues. "Morris. What word have you had from the New Coastline?" I pause, considering how much more to ask.

"Not much. They made it up there in about three months. They're living in a camp. They're building a town." I wait for more. He knows it. "They have a jail."

"First structure?" I ask. He nods. "That figures." His eyes dart over my shoulder like he has somewhere to go. "What about Raben?" He's giving me nothing. "Heard anything at all?"

"Some."

"Well what?" Again a furtive glance beyond me, maybe at the entrance.

"He's—traveling."

"Where? Alone?"

"I don't think he's alone." And now I have to look in the direction Morris' eyes travel. I turn around to find Raben standing in front of me. I wrap my arms around him without a second thought, hardly behavior for a commander.

"Avery," he whispers in between the kisses, and we are consumed in our embrace. He gently pulls me away from him, looking at my stomach. "All they ever told me was that you were safe."

I think, to Raben, this is an enormous surprise that juts between us. I say, "Chapman."

Raben's eyes find mine. "It's a good name, for a boy."

"Or a girl." We embrace again, and I feel a lump-like ridge running along the top of his chest, heart level. I pull the open neck of his shirt down to reveal a four inch scar.

"Battle?" I ask.

"More or less. Even The 28 United with all its hunger for justice—with all its passion for a home—we're not perfect." He turns away, uncomfortable.

"What happened?" I touch his shoulder, tender, yet urgent for the answer. He looks down.

"After El and La there were a few anxious to accuse. Guilt by association."

I stop him, turn his head toward me with more force than I intend. "Where's Trellis?" The shame I read on Raben's face tells me he doesn't want me to know what some of our Chipsters have become. He doesn't want to reveal to me that some of our own have indeed become The Third's secret weapon, not by genetic design or strategy but by human nature.

Raben looks into my eyes with remorse. "They had a surgeon's scalpel ready when they trapped us on patrol one night. An angry group of nine men and women, accusing Trellis and me of being GEBs like our brother and sister. They went after Trellis' ventricle. He didn't make it past the first cut, and as they began to do the same to me our defenders from the camp intervened. Too late for Trellis, but not for me." Raben leans against the alcove door, sickened by his memories. "While one brave mother held a rag tight to my wound, the other rescuers rounded up the attackers and placed them in what would become the first of our prisons on the New Coastline."

"Trellis?"

"Dead."

"His right ventricle?"

"Normal." Once again, I move close to Raben and feel his arms around me, and I wonder what it will take for The 28 United to trust one another and build a place called home.

And in that moment, maybe because the thoughts of trust are painful, I think of Degnan. It hits me hard that he is not with us. He went his own way on our return. He could have dropped off the caravan anywhere. We were too busy with survival to notice, and I haven't even given it a thought until now. I've been so consumed with climbing the ladder, telling truth to Morris and holding the man I love that I haven't had time to realize there is no Degnan. He is gone. I'm not worried about him. I lived with this ratty man for seven months. Hated his biting cynicism. Plotted ways to get rid of him. And rejected those plots to attain valuable information. Overall, I do not trust Degnan. He will never be a friend. But between us there emerged a crack where a small amount of truth oozed through. I know we will meet again. Not on friendly terms, but with no love-lost for The Third and a mutual agreement that we won't kill each other. Maybe even one day, we'll drink a glass of Hennessey together.

"Zoom!" I hear the grating but endearing voice of a kid I hate to love. "What's with all the mush on the landing dock?"

Annalynn grabs me from behind, and I turn in her arms to hug her. "Can't you ever just talk like you live in 2083?" I kiss the top of her head. "Zoom, I missed you."

She runs from me to Raben and throws her arms around his waist. He hardly knows her and frees himself by moving her arms away just as a gush of water falls down my legs, marking the landing dock with Chapman's salutations.

Raben and Annalynn stare at the puddle, frozen for half a second. Then Raben says, "I'll get Pasha." He runs for the exit.

Quick thinker that she is, Annalynn gets a mechanic's dolly, wheeling it over to me and loading me on it, balancing the biggest part of me in the center. "Feet up, Avery, we're goin' crusin'."

"Slow down."

"No time. It's all hands on deck. Got to find Pasha. She's our ace in the hole."

"Spare me the clichés." We round the corner into the corridor headed for the lab and see Raben, McGinty and Shaw rushing toward us. Raben lifts me from the dolly into his arms. My body shivers, trying to reconstruct the moments with Raben in the minstrel tree. Moments that have been completely smothered in the midst of the night patrol on the streets of Reichel, by the biting vipers, the gobbling sinkholes and the naming of GEBs.

I groan as the pain, no longer a pinch, stabs long and sharp at the small of my back. This agony doesn't ease off but surges, gathering momentum, determined to turn my groans into a desperate yell. It wins.

Shaw slams his hand on the alcove button and the door slides upwards to reveal Pasha on the ready at a makeshift delivery table. By her side, as an able assistant, stands Quinn. "Sixth sense?" I whisper my question as the pain subsides. So thankful she is here.

"When you were born you were early too. Just like this," Quinn says. "Besides, it's hard to stay when a building's burning around you, and a sinkhole's biting at your heels."

Raben lays me on the table, and Quinn wipes away the sweat on my forehead with a wet cloth, keeping the drips from my falling into my eyes. The pain is back and smacks into the entire lower part of my body, galloping at a full out run. Faster, faster.

"Breathe," says Pasha, trying to remove my Z-Colt from its holster. I stop her hand.

"Leave my Z-Colt!" I yell.

"Everyone out," Pasha screeches at my audience. Shaw and Annalynn are through the door in a heartbeat, but McGinty hesitates, looking at Raben, then turns to go. Raben is about to follow the others out the door when Quinn grabs his arm.

"You stay," she says. He nods and takes her place, his hands supporting my shoulders.

My yell turns into a scream and Pasha positions herself at the foot of the table between my legs which are now draped with a dull gray blanket from our former quarters in unit 791. "Push," she says, and I hear Raben parrot each word coming from Pasha's mouth. *Push, push.* Quinn joins the chant, and I wonder why I need three people telling me what to do.

"Push," Pasha once again commands.

"Shut up," I say, but my teeth are clenched and I sound pathetic. I feel the mammoth stab recede a bit.

Pasha rushes to my side and, in her typical bedside manner, gets two inches from my face, doing her own brand of yelling. Her intense eyes have not changed since she first appeared in our bathtub a decade ago, pruning her pigeons and twirling her Rubik's Cube. "You're not the commander here, DeTornada," she spits her words. "Do you get it, Avery?"

The torture is back with its troops all pounding on my pelvic bones. "I get it!" I yell.

"Then push!" I push.

The alcove door slides up and there stands McGinty, "The Third is approaching Red Grove."

"How close?" I gasp and I'm not really sure if I'm speaking or silent.

"Minutes."

"Then arm everyone."

"The children?"

"Arm *everyone* and get them into the planes. Fly them up to the New Coastline. And keep Shaw here to fly us out."

"You know that leaves only Morris and Raghill as pilots?"

I tighten my grasp on Raben's hand. "They got us into Red Grove, and they'll get us out."

"Push," says Raben as he sees my body writhe in another contraction. I feel his protection, strong on my shoulders.

Engaged in a yell, I say no more to McGinty, but I do see Quinn run to his side, and in the distance I hear her tell him, "Get the plane ready. We'll be there soon."

My scream pierces Red Grove, and simultaneously I feel our command center quake. We are smashed by some exterior force. I almost slide off the table and expect to see the side of Red Grove ripped away like the walls of the History Labyrinth just hours before. I anticipate the sucking sound of the maw, swallowing all life around me, but instead I hear the piercing screech of Chapman's first objection to the horrors of our world. He is here, and he is crying.

Pasha holds Chapman in the air, this babe all dripping with what's left of his race through the corridor to life.

"Chapman! He's a boy," she says. Quinn swaddles him in a blanket that's been cut to his size. I reach for Raben's hand, but he is gone. The alcove door is open, and from just feet beyond its entrance I hear a retching noise.

"He'll be used to it by your second one," Quinn laughs, and she lays Chapman on my chest.

He is so small, so wonderfully alive. Of course I've known him all his life, but now he is in my arms, looking at me. "Welcome to the world, Chapman," I say. "It's gonna get better. I promise." I kiss his forehead, wishing he would open his eyes to see his mother.

Another bash from outside jerks Pasha and Quinn to the side, and I hold Chapman tight, fighting to stay on the table. The Third's knocking on our door and they won't stop until they get in.

Raben is back. I hand Chapman to Quinn as Raben lifts me from the table, running toward the landing dock. "I got you, Avery," he says. Now they're smashing on walls of Red Grove—a double hit instead of one big slam. A ram with unbelievable force and then a second blow follows. Looking over Raben's shoulder, I see metal piercing through the wall. It's shape, like an oversized sledge hammer. The hole it punches expands as it jack-hammers its way through the exterior of our command center. Even Pasha's thin-skin can't save us now.

We enter the launch pad and a small aircraft stands ready to go with Shaw in the pilot's seat, and McGinty waiting by the cabin door. Through the opening I see a gurney consuming most of the cabin space. Pasha sits next to it, my IV already strung. McGinty lifts me from Raben's arms and settles me on the gurney while Pasha hooks my left arm to the life-line.

"Hold on, Avery," McGinty says. "We're almost home." I hope he's right.

"Let's get this thing in the air," I say.

I struggle to prop myself up, and see Quinn approaching the plane door, carrying Chapman. She turns to hand Raben our baby, and for a split second he flinches, then turns away. "Raben," Quinn yells, "we have to lift off now. Take Chapman while I get in."

Raben turns back to us. "I don't know anything about babies—I don't know..." *Sixth sense. Instinct. Discernment. A split second flashback review in my mind.* I remember the conversation McGinty and I had about GEBs not having a childhood. Trader Bob shunned Annalynn—wouldn't look at her or talk to her or honor her palms-up gesture toward him. Raben—I saw him embrace Trellis as a brother many times, but there wasn't a moment I could remember him embrace El or La. Raben—operating on Pasha in the underground hovel at the dump, chasing the children away with a single voice command. Raben—never a tear or a grieving word for Lear as the brain-swapper gobbled the child to his death. Raben—reciprocal of my affections an hour ago when we were reunited on the launch pad, but never expressing joy about Chapman in the moments we had before the attack. Raben—commanded by Quinn to remain for the birth, but retching just outside the delivery room when the moment finally arrived.

Raben—turning away from his newborn baby in our moment of escape. I look Raben in the eyes. I know he is a GEB, and he knows I know.

In a split second Quinn hands Chapman off to McGinty who lays him in Pasha's arms. Quinn faces Raben. He draws his weapon, and together she and I draw our Z-Colts in lightening unity. I hesitate, but she takes the shot, Raben's forehead the mark. She hits it dead center.

Quinn leaps in the door of the plane and McGinty slams his hand against the alcove button. The door slides shut, and through its six foot square Plexiglas window I see Shaw slip out the pilot's cabin, knife drawn, crouching in front of Raben. I do not see Shaw's violent skills at work, but I do see the bloody ventricle clutched in his hand as he returns to the plane. I shut my eyes, not wanting a carved chest to be my last image of Raben.

I feel a burning in my heart, like a single ember slowly singeing its way to my core. I suppress a scream. The only sound escaping my lips is a solo sob. With every shred of focus I can muster I push my travail on the back burner for a day to come.

I pass my Z-Colt to Pasha in exchange for Chapman. It is a switch I do not expect to last for long. But for a moment, I am a mother.

# REMEMBERING
# ROLL CALL

*Jurbay:* In 2067 an asteroid fell, severing 22 states, plunging them into the Pacific Ocean and drowning half the population in the course of a day.

This is what happens next.

**THE 28 UNITED**—Originally loyal to The United before *Jurbay* fell, they are now scattered and in hiding, hoping to find a leader who will raise an army against The Third.

**The Subterraneans**—A few loyal ones of The 28 United chose to go undercover and work inside The Third, professing allegiance. They are trying to forge a plan to eliminate The Third.

*Carles DeTornada—Avery's father. First commander of The 28 United in its infant stages.

*Avery DeTornada—Reluctant and unofficial commander of The 28 United.

*Quinn DeTornada—Second in command inside The Third. Carles wife and Avery's mother.

*McGinty—Trained with Avery, Shaw and Pasha in the Elite Special Forces of The Third.

*Shaw—Trained with Avery, McGinty and Pasha in the Elite Special Forces of The Third.

*Dr. Pasha Lutnik—Trained with Avery, McGinty and Shaw in the Elite Special Forces. Hand-picked by Quinn as a medical student to work for The 28 United.

**The Library Boys**—Sons of The Third's commanders and officers who live in an abandoned library outside Reichel and are taken care of by guardians.

*   Morris (Borden's son)
*   Raghill (Dorsey's son)
*   Prospero
*   Lear
*   The Littlest Librarian (Carles)

**The Dump Pickers**

*   Old Soul
*   Raben
*   Trellis
*   El
*   La
*   Hunk
*   Desmond

* Junior
* Garland

**Chipsters**—Those loyal to The 28 United who had access to Pasha's chipster technology. All of them have an implant that is covered by thin-skin.

**Annalynn**—Eight year old neighbor of McGinty, Shaw and Avery in unit 791.

**Herman and Orbit**—Pasha's favorite homing pigeons.

**Minstrels**—Musicians in The Third who escaped and live in the trees near Red Grove.

* Clef
* Allegra

**Weapons**
* Shaw's knife
* Z-Colt
* Snake Eye 454
* Brainy
* Anti-brainy

**THE THIRD**—After *Jurbay* fell, while people were in mourning, a tyrannical group assumed command of the government. At first they were appreciated until they tightened control again and again.

**Authority in The Third**
* Commander Dorsey
* Commander Quinn DeTornada (Subterranean for The 28 United)

* Officer Borden
* The Justices

**The Elite Special Forces**

**Guardians**—Hired by The Third to provide the physical care for all the orphans created by *locasa*. Only assigned to provide essential non-emotional attachment services. (food/housing) Known by The 28 United as pocket-watches.

**Pocket-watches**—Synonymous with "guardians." They reside in pockets of housing units only to emerge to watch over the basic needs of orphans.

*Guardian Degnan—Hired by The Third as a pocket-watch for the library boys whose parents are in positions of authority in The Third..

**GEBs**

* Baldy
* Trader Bob

**Weapons**

* Float cars
* Star blades
* DR93

# PLACES

**Catalonia**—Autonomous territory in Spain.
**Reichel**—City controlled by The Third where citizens live under the tyrannical rule of the government.
**Plethora Plant**—A factory in Reichel making peps, the capsules that feed, hydrate and regulate the citizens.

**Cage**—A round, gridded jail cell below the Plethora Plant.

**GEB Lab** —An underground experimental lab working on the perfection of GEBs, genetically engineered beings.

**Horseshoe Tunnel**—A secret tunnel under the Plethora Plant, with access to the GEB lab, built by Degnan.

**History Labyrinth**—The building where past decades of history and artifacts of culture are kept. The Artesian pools and baths are located on the fourth floor underground.

**Unit 791**—The housing unit where McGinty, Shaw and Avery live after completing their Elite training.

**Pigeon Roost**—The outside area of Pasha's living unit where she keeps and trains her homing pigeons.

**Pigeon Square**—A hidden section in the roost where Pasha inks the artificial #14 tattoo on the wrists of those loyal to the 28 United.

**Children's Garden**—The only garden left that grows food. Outside Reichel and tended by the library boys. It is located on the edge of Foxglove Library.

**Foxglove Library**—An aging library converted to housing for the male children of the officers and justices of The Third.

**Dump**—An enormous refuse area. Home to the dump-pickers who are not part of Reichel's rules and regulations.

**Red Grove**—The command center of The 28 United. Camouflaged by thin-skin, Pasha's creation.

**Minstrel Trees**—Trees near Red Grove where minstrels who escaped from The Third reside.

**The New Coastline**—The western section of the severed coastline.

**Dark market**—A small illegal market that Degnan plans to develop on the New Coastline.

## THE UNUSUAL & BIZARRE

**Locasa**—A device The Third stole from the Catalonian government. The Catalans' scientists developed *locasa* to remove very specific memories from the brain with the intent of providing healing for those victims of heinous crimes or those with PTSD. The Third stole the device and used it on their residents, deleting memories of family and home.

**DeTornada**—Catalonian word for homeward.

**Homebound**—A term referring to those who have had family and home removed by *locasa*, but who know there is something missing. They just don't know what it is.

**Biters**—Beasts that evolved from living in the grudge of the dump. Very dangerous.

**Brain-swappers**—Genetically altered beasts whose brains were merged between two animals.

**Chipster**—Pasha developed and implanted chipsters in as many of those loyal to The 28 United to assist them with ways to defeat The Third. Her goal was to eventually communicate from one chipster to all of others simultaneously. Others who were loyal to The 28 United learned how to create and implant chipsters.

**Thin-skin**—An organic product developed by Pasha. Has incredible strength and can be painted to camouflage anything.

**14 Deadlies**—Diseases created by The Third and sent worldwide to diminish the population, making it simpler to invade and control countries. The diseases also destroyed much of the population left after *Jurbay* divided the nation.

# ACKNOWLEDGEMENTS

First and always, thanks to the Giver of the gift. It is for You I turn my passion into words. It is for You I tell the story.

Thank you...

To my young adult editors: I was your teacher—then you became mine. Colleen McInnis, Joseph Morris and Katie Shaw.

To my warriors: Those from my family—Philip, Ellie, Natalie, Mother, Daddy, Les, Gail and Sara. And those on their knees, too many to name, who fought when I was tired and because they did, I finished.

To those who read: Your faithfulness made a difference. Evan, Paige, Brian, Debbie, Terri, Kathy, Daniel, Phil and Denise.

To my friend: Valerie Veatch, a divine appointment in my life.

To Sherri Miller: Glory. You have all the talents I don't.

To Debbie Hamilton and Jodi Brown: For scarves and coats and all things creative on the stage and under the canopy of a forest full of actors.

To My 2013 Creative Writing Class: Andi Avery, DJ Degnan, Joseph Morris, Katie Raben, John Reichel and Katie Shaw—you read and said, "Do it." I did, and I thank you.

To the actors: Who painted the pictures from *Roll Call* in the form of book readings—Hannah Reuther, Ellie Loney, Kyle Addy, Mason Erfinger, Daniel Melin, Ian Wisbey, Ben Lacey, Emma Rose Brown, Darin Brown, Ken Ebersole, Russell Melin, Lauren Walter, Carly Walter, Ashlyn Hanson, Anna Flood, and Marshall Hainer. And to the audiences who came to listen.

To Restoration Ranch: You let us take flight.

# ABOUT THE AUTHOR

Gwen Mansfield loves words, and the thought of a good story sends ideas capering through her mind until they settle down into characters, settings and plot. This is her first novel in the young adult genre. The surprises she found on the pages of book #1 in this post-apocalyptic trilogy made it impossible to say goodbye to Avery DeTornada and her comrades. Book #2, *Inside the Third* (available December 2015) and #3, *Reluctant Warriors* bring the characters back to war against The Third with determination that The 28 United will stand. Gwen completed her BA in theatre from Seattle Pacific University, her MA in theatre from Central Washington University and her MFA in Creative Writing from University of New Orleans. She lives in the Northwest with her husband and children. She is the author of the historical fiction *Experiment Station Road*, the musical *Resistance* and the stage plays: *Grace Diner*, *Experiment Station Road*, and *You've Got 90 Seconds*.

Gwen Mansfield's book *Experiment Station Road,* a historical fiction, may be purchased through the Amazon Kindle catalogue.

In 1962 Ellen Merrill finds herself in the midst of a revelation: the townsfolk of Hayford, Oregon have two sets of standards—one for the Anglos and one for the Mexicans. Ellen says, "It was the only time I ever heard from God. He said, 'Prejudice demands an age of accountability—how old are you'?" Through the next decade of her life Ellen chases equality, and in spite of her parents and the heritage of a town's racism, she catches glimpses of justice. *Experiment Station Road,* a quirky but poignant coming-of-age story, invites the reader through a decade of discovery with Ellen Merrill as she slams into community prejudice, advocates for Cesar Chavez and conceals a clandestine but sweet romance. Ellen's revelation is clear: the value of a solo voice lifted in a community of clatter shakes up the world and allows the experiment to continue.

18572459R00223

Made in the USA
Middletown, DE
12 March 2015